A RISE TO POWER

A RISE TO POWER

Chronicles of a King

RUTH DURANT

VMI Publishers • Sisters, Oregon

Published by VMI Fiction
a division of
VMI Publishers
Sisters, Oregon
www.vmipublishers.com

ISBN: 1933204540
ISBN 13: 9781933204543
Library of Congress Control Number: 2007943403

Cover design by Juanita Dix

Printed in the United States of America

Dedication

To the Men of Valor,
who showed courage when the battle became fierce...

Deliver me from my enemies, O my God...;
...And save me from bloodthirsty men.
For look, they lie in wait for my life; the mighty gather against me,
Not for my transgression nor for my sin, O Lord.
They run and prepare themselves through no fault of mine.
Awake to help me...

Psalm of David 59, Excerpt-NKJV

ACKNOWLEDGMENTS

Heartfelt thanks to Wilma Wharton, a woman of conviction, who said, 'Let us press on'; and to my husband who provided the inspiration and showed patience worthy of a king.

Thank you to Bishop Vibert Lowe who teaches that there is no book more compelling than the Word of the Living God.

Contents

"Now the acts of King David, first and last, indeed they are written in the book of Samuel the seer, in the book of Nathan the prophet, and in the book of Gad the seer, with all his reign and might, and the events that happened to him, to Israel, and to all the kingdoms of the lands."

1 Chronicles 29:29-30, NKJV

PART 1
THE MAKING OF A KING

CHAPTER ONE

Deportation

Jerusalem (Circa 605 B.C.)

O God, be merciful to me:
For my soul trusteth in Thee…
…In the shadow of Thy wings I will make my refuge,
Until these calamities be over-past.

PSALM OF DAVID 57, EXCERPT

uard these with your life," Seraiah hissed urgently. "With your life, do you understand?" The priest's young apprentice received the sack of scrolls with trepidation. His hands shook as he clasped the mouth of the bag closed. Seraiah nervously scanned the west-facing courtyard for soldiers, but there was no sign of movement toward the rear of the Temple. It was a miracle that he had remained undetected for so long, for on several occasions the battle came within a spear's breadth of his hiding place. "Go now! Quickly!" he urged the boy. It bode ill that the enclave of priests should now be forced to entrust the safety of their life's work to a boy of less than twenty summers, but it was an act born of desperation.

The youth sprinted away just as the first smoky tendrils licked the entrance portal of the Temple and flared hungrily along the heavily oiled wood. The fire poured eagerly across the massive beams to engulf the foremost pillars. Feeling the press of its hot breath upon his neck, the trembling priest retrieved a bundle of his own and hurried down the darkened slope as harsh, foreign voices sundered the night. He scurried away to the embracing gloom of the east wall. Moments later the crackling heat surged through the interior of the sanctuary, igniting the altar and consuming the intricately embroidered curtains in a gush of flame.

Seraiah looked back one last time, and tears welled in his eyes. The House of the Lord was destroyed along with the city. *What will become of my people…and the priesthood?* The cleric hung his head and forged on through the shadows. He feared the carnage had only now begun.

$$\approx\ \approx\ \approx$$

Guttural shouts, uttered in a strange language, crisscrossed the vast compound. The hungry fire radiated swiftly through the east quarter of the city as though fanned by an immense hand; it chewed voraciously through palace and stable alike. None were exempt from its savagery.

Thick smoke clawed at Abdon's nose and lungs, yet his mind raced ahead of his frantic steps. He dragged his panicked thoughts away from the anguish of the suffocating fumes and mentally rehearsed the route that would take him through the blood-stained streets and back to the appointed meeting place. "Your charge is priceless!" the priest had confided. "You will need YHWH's divine protection to avoid being captured or impaled on a spear." The young man squelched the terror that bubbled in his gut and prayed for safe passage to his uncle's shop, which lay pressed tight against the other side of the main boundary wall. He resolved to show himself worthy of the faith that Seraiah had placed in him.

Abdon reached the outer edge of the wall and frantically searched the rough surface for the frayed end of a knotted rope that had been hastily hung and secured with a peg to aid his escape. He could barely make out the jagged crenel overhead where his uncle had dislodged a large stone to mark his location. Abdon pulled the stout rope taut and tested his purchase on the dew-slicked stones at the base of the wall. He readjusted the sack and with a grunt heaved himself upward. Barefoot and burdened by the heavy load, he grimaced as the stiff fibers bit into his reddening palms. He used all the skill and agility he possessed to scale the sheer face. Midway through the arduous ascent, he was startled by dim shapes moving furtively below, and his grip momentarily faltered. Fearing discovery, he froze with his cheek pressed against the cold stone. He prayed that no twitch of the rope would betray his vulnerable position. Abdon noticed the telltale warp of shadows below and to his left. He focused anxiously on the blurred movements of the group as it slunk through the well of darkness beneath his awkward perch. The clink of weapons sounded the soldiers' location as they manhandled a stumbling figure pinioned brutally between them.

The captive's voice rose from amidst the mismatched trio. His warbling plea for mercy echoed plaintively in the air. It was Zephaniah! The familiar animation of his tone was now blunted by misery. A dull thump silenced his cries. The youth stifled a wail of alarm and struggled to prevent the cumbersome sack from falling from his grip. Muted speech rebounded off the stone for several minutes then slowly shrank away toward the north corner of the wall. The boy continued his frenetic ascent and at last noticed the decreasing sway on the taut line, which signaled that the end of the climb was mere hand spans above. Clambering over the top of the wall, he gave several sharp tugs to dislodge the peg then hauled in the rope. He pitched his load onto the flat roof below the high parapet. Even as the sack was airborne, the youth started his descent using rough handholds in the rock face—convenient pits worn by years of weathering. There was no time to dawdle. He clambered down a rough ladder to the interior of the shop. His uncle Uliel waited in the doorway.

"Abdon! Thank heavens, boy. Did Seraiah give them to you? Is he well?" his uncle pressed.

Shoulders slumped, Abdon shook his head. "He was already taken by then. Zephaniah met me at the door. I prayed for his escape, but from the wall I saw him taken into captivity. May God have mercy on him!"

Zephaniah was not their only concern. Abdon wondered also how his friend Mishael fared. They had agreed to flee together if the wall indeed fell, but the alarm had been raised unexpectedly at daybreak to signal that the breach by the invaders was imminent. Several days earlier than expected! Abdon had decided not to tarry at their scheduled meeting place. His commitment to Seraiah overshadowed all else. So instead he had hurried on to meet his uncle and the aged priest, knowing that all their worst fears were being realized. Now two of their number were already missing.

In the bleary light of the shop, Uncle Uliel rested his big, work-worn hand on Abdon's shoulder. The young man was still quivering from the ordeal. "All is not lost, Abdon," he comforted. "With your aid we have retrieved many of the scrolls. It is more important that these be saved. Zoreb is still nowhere to be found and we dare not wait. Are you willing to help me further?"

So much had gone wrong that fateful morning! Despite their planning and meticulous preparations, they were required to improvise as the incursion had progressed faster than any of them could have thought possible.

Despite the danger, Abdon was determined to try.

꙰ ꙰ ꙰

Seven years prior to the siege, nightmares had plagued Uliel's friend, Seraiah. He had called upon Uliel in desperation. Though of different standings, the two men had been friends since childhood. Seraiah had entered the priesthood at an early age, leaving Uliel to continue his father's business, which gradually prospered and expanded from small fields into a thriving vineyard and winepress. Uliel wanted to become a scribe but his father forbade it.

"There is a greater purpose for your life. I feel it deep in my bones. Your trust is all I ask!"

He had never been able to tell Uliel exactly what that 'feeling' was, but Uliel obeyed faithfully. Then, six and a half decades after joining the priesthood, Seraiah created another mystery.

"Uliel," he said, "Something will occur at the Temple—some calamity. I know not what, or when, but I fear for the Texts. Your nephew is an apprentice to a scribe, is he not? I need him to copy some manuscripts. I would have done it myself if my fingers hadn't grown stiff with age," Seraiah bemoaned, staring at his gnarled, wizened knuckles. He attempted to flex his hand, but the fingers stubbornly resisted his effort. The high priest sighed remorsefully and returned his hawkish gaze to Uliel. "He will be paid of course—a small sum, but it will be fair. It is tedious work, but invaluable nonetheless."

Uliel had agreed to allow Abdon to journey to the Temple court each second and third day of the week for three years to transcribe the works.

"They make compelling reading," Abdon would say to his uncle, "especially the annals of Jasher—the poems commemorating Israel's heroes are beyond compare!" But he never elaborated—probably on Seraiah's insistence—for some of the Texts were holy writings.

Seraiah himself apologized for his stringent confidentiality. "Some of the priests do not understand why it would be necessary for me to have this done. Still, with or without their sanction I believe it to be a critical matter so I will press on, though I cannot fully explain myself. 'Seraiah, what can threaten the Temple of the Lord?' they often inquire of me. 'Jerusalem is a mighty city. Who can overthrow it!' they say with abundant skepticism." Seraiah snorted, recalling their derision. "I do not know what disaster will befall us, but it is better to be thought a fool than to be complacent I say! Especially where it concerns the sacred scrolls. Jehoiakim is not half the king that Josiah was, and I fear that our sovereign may cause the wrath of God to fall upon us. The people follow him blindly. Even his older brother Jehoahaz, during his short reign of three months, ruled no wiser than his sibling now does; Jehoiakim perpetrates evil openly. Of Josiah's line neither the boy Mattaniah, nor the grandson Johiachin have shown themselves worthy to be king. And we will be saddled with them for a while yet I fear. The prophet Jeremiah, son of Hilkiah, has been forewarning us for many seasons. We should take his counsel to heart, Uliel."

Uliel had listened, though he had not fully understood the magnitude of the danger. Now, with the Temple looted and burnt to cinders, the two seemingly disparate mysteries converged in one fateful event; the utter devastation of their home city by the Babylonian Empire, a conquering force of unbelievable power. Uliel finally grasped the depth of the vision which his friend had tried to express but could not, owing to the horror of its extremity. The massacre and desolation of the city and its people knew no bounds. Those who had not been murdered—the skilled and the elite—were being transplanted to Babylon to serve the reputedly harsh king. And nothing could be done to halt the deracination.

Uliel's pivotal role had crystallized when it became clear that the sacred buildings throughout the city were not to be excluded from the intended ruin; they would be despoiled along with the royal palaces and imperial houses. The sacrilege had been heartbreaking.

Uliel could not say how his father had known of the trial to come, or that he, a simple merchant, would be required to safeguard a precious part of his people's heritage, but that did not matter now. He was willing to give his life toward its preservation.

The cart was already loaded with pitchers of freshly pressed *asis,* emptied from the wine cellar. Rack upon rack was stacked carefully in the rear carriage. Uliel tied the sack of scrolls onto the mule along with a bag of dried rations and two waterskins. He did not seek to disguise the contents of the sack. There was no alternative decoy. He must depend on the mundane appearance of the load to quell suspicion. Hidden in plain sight, he had told his nephew. He aimed to use the elemental distraction of the free jugs of *asis* to avert unwanted curiosity regarding his passage through the streets.

"I am sorry that I cannot carry you boy. They will seize or kill one of your age. Remember! Find Remah in the guard and flee through the gate with the others. But do not—*do not*—follow their route. The soldiers will be sure to pursue any they see. The vineyards are your best hope. Travel by whatever means you can until you reach the Engedi. Beyond the desert, I believe you will be safe. Go in peace!" He clasped the boy tightly for a brief moment then pushed him away. "Go, *go!*"

Abdon left without turning, and Uliel started the mule forward, beseeching God to safeguard their quest that night. Six hours, that was all they would need. Six divinely sheltered hours....

⤙ ⤙ ⤙

The watchful heavens recorded Uliel's desperate prayer. The pall of soldiers' sweat mingled with the dust churned by the chaos of war. Uliel sensed the prowling fear that yet pervaded the narrow streets, but he resis-

ted its gnawing presence and drove the cart slowly between the low buildings, waiting for the shout that he knew would come. The fighting had
ceased, and he made it halfway to the outer edge of the city before he
heard the arresting cry. He veered in the direction of the patrol that had
hailed him. He did not seek to escape.

"Greetings," he said, and bowed. "Your commander has issued a gift.
One crate only for each company," Uliel instructed with feigned severity.
"And not until second watch!" He wagged his finger in pretense of a
warning.

The senior officer inspected the cart. Still he searched the old man's
eyes for signs of subterfuge, but years of ferrying cargo across the wilderness and facing raiders and roving tribes, both eager for gain, had taught
him the art of remaining calm under scrutiny. His routes across the wilds
had frequently exposed him to threats and outright antagonism. Over the
years he had surrendered countless loads of cargo to unscrupulous ban-
dits, yet the profits of his merchandising had been more than worthwhile.
It was his lack of defiance and willingness to surrender his goods that oft
saved his life. His face remained placid and devoid of guile, and he did not
avoid the man's inspection.

"Who did you say sent you?" the officer asked doubtfully, his accent
slurred and his syllables clipped.

"Marsden," Uliel answered innocently. He had guarded the name of
the Chaldean commander close to his breast. He thanked Abdon's sharp
ears and insight for recognizing the value of that tidbit of information and
storing it away.

The soldier's eyes widened with a mixture of concern and alarm.
Marsden was a firm commander not given to the vagaries of men. At half
light that day, he had ordered the beheading of four of his soldiers who,
he discovered, had disobeyed a direct command pertaining to the taking
of spoil. None would gainsay his orders, at least not on this day.

Uliel was certain the soldier would have impounded the cart or killed
him otherwise. Instead he dislodged a crate and with a grunt, handed it
to one of his companions. He turned and waved the cart onward. Uliel
drove the cart in the direction of a second company approaching from the

direction of the gate, which was his primary destination. He knew instinctively that the senior officer still watched his departure for signs of trickery.

As he completed his service of three companies, Uliel garnered other information, which he used to good effect. He strode through the mayhem as though untouched by the chaos of the siege. He raised his chin with an air of power and saluted random soldiers with a flick of his hand. His voice assumed an official tone as he relayed his spurious orders.

"Marsden's eighth and fifteenth deployments have received their allotments. One crate only, mind!" Uliel made his tone as terse and authoritative as he could. Though his heart pounded with fear, his voice did not waver as he delivered his charge amidst the marching companies.

There were eleven crates remaining by the time he reached the encampment outside the gate. He had also acquired a Chaldean garment, which he donned in a darkened shop entrance. He concealed his own clothing in one of the ration sacks.

Grateful to have at last exited the main city, he followed a path beside an abandoned siege tower and passed the outermost rank of the guard, distributing crates on his way. Four crates now remained. He stayed on the road for he knew the soldiers were hunting for fugitives. They would scour the fields first. The open road was being used heavily by military deployments and general traffic supplying the army with food reserves and weapons. Any persons seeking escape were more liable to avoid the main travel route just as prey wary of a stalking predator sought the shelter of thick brush. Four crates remained. He hoped these would be enough.

Uliel encountered two additional groups of soldiers retiring from duty, and he checked his dwindling supply anxiously. He was almost to the wilderness. Almost!

The final assignment of soldiers patrolling the road questioned his distance from the city. Their commander, a bearded man with eyes sunken into shadowed recesses, appeared less inclined to be deceived by specious explanations. The flagellation of prisoners was a common occurrence, and those trailing this company bore gashes along their arms and on sunblistered backs that spoke to the leader's delight in administering punishments. Thinking quickly, Uliel revised his former greeting, hoping to dispel the man's ingrained distrust. "For the wounded," he said simply, gesturing to the cart.

"Half a mile back," the commander directed, pointing in the opposite direction. "Chatrah will show you," he rumbled. He snapped his fingers to a burly man on the rear flank of his troop.

His present position untenable, Uliel nodded in resolve. He abhorred the use of violence, yet for the success of this crucial task, he could not suffer himself to be faint of heart. He was an old man but neither weak nor infirm. As the mule plodded along the roadway, Uliel bent and collected two medium-sized stones. These will suffice, he thought, satisfied by their weight. He flexed his shoulder to loosen tired muscles. Chatrah moved ahead as he neared the site where his disabled companion lay. The soldier dismounted and removed his uncomfortable helmet to dispel the trapped heat. *Perfect! It is now or never,* Uliel decided. If he failed, his death would be assured. He deftly whipped the two stones from his palm. One clipped the man beside his ear and the other thudded dully off his skull.

Uliel rolled Chatrah's motionless form off the road and collected the soldier's mount. The warhorse became restless as it recognized an unfamiliar touch upon the reins. It took Uliel several anxious moments to soothe the agitated beast, which resisted his initial efforts. He eventually succeeded in placating the wary animal. Taking measured steps, he hooked the horse's bridle in the tangle of a copse situated a good distance from the roadside, then backed away in relief. Uliel raised his eyes to heaven in silent gratitude. A spooked warhorse was nigh impossible to control, even by its master.

Uliel traveled a further four miles before unhitching his mule. He removed the sacks then rolled the cart into a sheltered declivity before setting out across the wilderness expanse. He planned to dwell in strongholds until he reached the Engedi, where he would abide until Jerusalem could be liberated. He also knew it would be a long time before the city would be regained and restored to its former glory. He must trust that his preparations with Abdon would be enough to surmount this calamity, which eclipsed the many disasters confronted by his people since their flight across Egyptian borders so many decades past.

Uliel's own son had been taken unexpectedly in the first deportation of captives. Abdon then had been the only remaining hope. And so he had allowed his nephew to take Zoreb's place in retrieving the scrolls from Seraiah. He fervently prayed that the boy had escaped.

≈ ≈ ≈

Uliel would spend the first three weeks in the Engedi, watching daily for his nephew's approach and waiting for the passing of the new moon. If by that time Abdon did not come, he would know the boy was lost to him. He would then secrete the scrolls as prearranged. He must depend on Abdon, if the boy survived, and providence if he did not, to ensure that the texts detailing the royal lineage of his people were uncovered and returned, for many had labored in blood to preserve them. They could not be lost—the sacrifice had been too great.

≈ ≈ ≈

Careening through a narrow lane, Abdon turned right to follow a convenient shortcut and collided heavily with a Hebrew soldier who raised his guard instinctively as if anticipating an attack. Abdon broke stride, but his momentum pitched him precipitously forward. Arms flailing, Abdon thudded soundly into the broad, leathered face of a battle shield. Stumbling, he fell, striking his head on the crumbling cornerstone of a shop that bordered a now deserted sheep market. Abdon groaned and slumped to the street, blinking against the encroaching darkness.

The young soldier spun in distress as he saw his compatriot buckle to the ground. Already a Chaldean patrol was rounding the far corner of the street. There was nothing he could do, so he hastened away, leaving Abdon to the mercy of their enemy.

≈ ≈ ≈

"Don't kill him, he is a scribe, he can write!" a voice shouted in panic. The import of the words razed the dull fog smothering Abdon's awareness. The wash of darkness covering his eyes shrank back reluctantly from a liminal haze of light. The stench of urine and dung assailed his nostrils, rousing him with a mixture of puzzlement and disgust. His pushed himself shakily to his knees. now recognizing the sodden mulch pressed beneath his palms—*the market stockade,* he concluded, raising his head groggily. His senses wavered, defying his will to regain his footing. Muddled sounds unraveled into broken strings of words.

"But he is young…can recover."

"No….weak…not taken."

"But…can write!"

"…Be done!"

"He can write, *he can write,*" a voice repeated in desperation. The familiarity of the accent drew Abdon further from the miring haze, and he opened his eyes to the terrifying sight of an upraised sword that had been halted prematurely in its murderous course. Several yards away, Mishael's outstretched hands pleaded for his friend's life. The soldier paused, as though considering; then he sheathed his sword. He dragged Abdon to his feet and shoved him into the midst of the milling captives.

"But for your talent, he would have struck you dead," Mishael whispered. "These men… They show no mercy! They are taking only those with a craft or a precise skill. Everyone else…" Mishael's voice trailed away as he shook his head bleakly.

Abdon's legs crumpled weakly at each faltering step, and Mishael took his arm firmly, helping to steady him. His spirit grew more despondent as he saw the hundreds of men in streaming columns being plucked maliciously from their homeland. Many had also been injured in the battles that raged across the city. Seeing their defeat paraded before the world, Abdon knew his strength would have failed were it not for Mishael's bolstering aid. His head swam with visions of fire and swords, and he shook it to regain focus. Immediately a concussive force slammed into his senses, and his thoughts fled into the recesses of a black, blanketing core once again.

He awoke hours later within a formidable cordon of soldiers along with other glaze-eyed young men, shattered people whom he might never encounter again after their journey's end. Scanning the desolation about him and the faces twisted with the pain of immeasurable loss, Abdon was firm in the knowledge that, even if he should be favored to live, he would never see Uliel, and perhaps Jerusalem, again.

It was as a result of this seemingly hopeless circumstance, imprisoned for service to an enemy and destined on a boundless journey to a land foreign to all he knew, that Abdon realized the time for secrecy had passed. He must salvage what vestiges of hope remained. He studied the eyes of his countrymen who had been huddled into groups of three score; some fidgeted angrily whilst others stood, plaintive and hollow. *These men, he determined, though they were broken and desolate, could be his only recourse to victory. Theirs would not be a fate spoken of in the Jasher entries, but neither these nor the other chronicles would perish with him,* Abdon vowed.

In the days ahead he would mount an offensive—not with force of arms, for the time for such valiant acts had passed—but with words born of a courage that that had propelled his people to greatness. To preserve for the future the royal legacy of his people, their ancestry, and a prophecy of incomparable magnitude, Abdon would follow the only path a trapped and beleaguered man could envision—as his forefathers before him, he sought to relay the account he had painstakingly transcribed under the patient eye of Seraiah two summers before—the story of his nation's greatest king....

CHAPTER TWO

Shades of Sheol

Wilt thou show wonders to the dead?
Shall the dead [Rephaim] arise and praise thee?
Shall thy loving-kindness be declared in the grave?
Or thy faithfulness in destruction?

PSALM OF DAVID-88, EXCERPT

The man-mountain, Gol-jath, coursed down the side of the steep ravine with agility unusual in one of such imposing girth. His sure-footed gait across this jagged terrain bespoke his utter self-assurance as he pressed on oblivious to the avalanche of rubble created by his passage across the loose stones. The rugged ground had grown familiar to him after more than a month of this seemingly ceaseless trekking. He had been here many times before—perhaps not this particular hill, but another that bore similar markings of death. They were one and the same to him, for this day would end no differently from any other in this land of the Hebrews.

He could sense the subdued rage that emanated from these rock walls. His was not the first battle to be brought to this place. The spilt blood of men had left a stained, enduring presence that still sullied the valley, belying the veneer of calm that rested on the shallow wind. A warrior always knew. He was intimate with death and with absolutes. Each day a warrior would either live, or he would die. The world about them was shaped in violence. What did they know of peace? The word sat uncomfortably on his tongue—peace. Some who had sojourned among these Hebrews had spoken riddles of a balm to come, but the prospect was as elusive as the bitterns of the plain that took wing at the sway of a stalk. No. He could speak more easily of blood. Neither would this be the last conflict to stain the air and mar the memory of the stones beneath his broad sandals.

The first week that he had ventured his challenge, he had expected that his profane railing would arouse enough ire in their king to provoke a confrontation, but after the passing of one cycle of the moon, their recalcitrance had left him disgruntled and edgy. His offer had been fair, had it not—two men, one victor? He grinned at the vision of dismay that always etched the brow of an opposing champion after descending to the meeting ground. The reality of a tower of muscle arrayed for war often loosened the bowels of the staunchest of soldiers. Most would break into a sweat before approaching within twenty cubits of his range, often choosing the humiliation of retreat over an honorable battle. Their fleeing backs were nevertheless hunted down by the true flight of his massive spear. Others overcame their initial paralysis only moments before his sword closed in, descending with alarming speed through armor and flesh alike. The effect of a cloven champion always ripped through the enemy camp, weakening once stout hearts and making the business of war akin to sweeping chaff off the summer threshingfloors. They were all alike to him; fearful men praying to their gods to withstand his infatigable arm.

But now he tired of these pendulous jaunts back and forth across these Baal-forsaken hills, for today was the fortieth day that he would advance the king's time-proven strategy. Would the men of this soil take the bait as had so many hapless foes prior, unknowingly welcoming destruction to their camp? Why had their king not come down? The man was renowned for his prowess in war, was he not? Such a wait was unusual. He had never before needed to taunt an army past the tenth day. Even his slurs vilifying the name of the God they revered had not goaded them to react. Were they that cowardly in the face of an overwhelming force? Reports of their valor and fierceness in taking lands negated this consideration; nevertheless no champion had come forth to defend the valor for which they were commended? Did they hold any options, these men of Israel? They might be stalling in anticipation of some distant aid— from another king perhaps? The battle was pressing upon their doorpost, and men beset by doubt would clutch at a proffered feather in the hope of forestalling the shedding of their life's blood. Although he reveled in their obvious temerity, he was fast growing weary of this daily dance down to the field of combat with no one to play his partner in the contest. He was convinced, though, that it must end soon, for he could almost taste the bite of sharpened iron as it pierced his opponent's guard to meet bone. This uncanny but intoxicating sensation, he realized, always heralded the beginning. Today would be no different, he was sure.

It was regrettable that King Achish was abed with a scourge, for he would have relished this coveted victory over an enemy who had been a thorn in the side to countless invading armies. Achish was a patient, calculating man and despite the delay had issued no directive to allay their strategy, and so he had persisted for nearly three fortnights to accost the ears of these Hebrews with inflammatory curses.

He paused at the edge of the challenge ground and drew breath slowly. The wait always appeared to be suffocating on the cusp of a battle. His childhood had been steeped in violence, and childish brawls had given birth to a shrewd fighter with an unerring passion for brutality. From his early seasons in Philistia he had proven his worth. At over six cubits in height he yet was not the greatest in stature amongst his brethren, but his dexterity with weapons was unparalleled. His standing within the brotherhood of the men of Rapha was of no consequence here, where he overshadowed the majority of warriors by more than a few spans. His talents had been burnished in the cauldron of war, and he had conquered its scouring fire to claim its prize. The marvel he had earned from men who beheld his matchless exploits hung about him like a heady scent. His exquisitely crafted armor attested to his rank. Highly polished weaponry threw glancing reflections that served to dazzle both the heart and the eye. In the blazing sun of a battlefield, an enemy momentarily blinded fell easy victim to a sword thrust. He had studied all the vagaries of battle-hardened men and learned to counter the cleverest of attacks.

In these western wastelands he had grown in renown, and he was aware of the heralds that preceded his kind. A repertoire of primeval legends boasted of their lineage. The oral tradition of widespread peoples had elevated their collective status to that of the god-like sons of El, with his forefathers purported to have sat in the council of the heavens, whilst others viewed his race to be the shades of kings that inhabited Sheol.

His father had claimed that his inexplicably acute reflexes and physical abilities were indeed supernatural, ensuring that he constantly aimed beyond excellence—"Your dominance in battle will be a reminder to all that we are descendents of the *Gbrym* in the assembly of Mighty Ones." Gol-jath nodded assertively. Even now he could feel a power exuding from his bones and strengthening his confident posture. *The heavens have surely favored me.*

He was not certain which of the accounts he preferred, whether sons begotten of gods, or mythic specters from the underworld, but each served his sole purpose in war, to rend the hearts of men. He knew he was no phantom, for through his flesh pumped a warrior's blood, and his heart brimmed with visionary achievements and the pride of glory. He lived for days such as this. His was the stride of a conqueror whom none could gainsay. And today his god would assuredly lead him to another conquest. A smile cracked his leathery lips, and he looked down at hands that had weathered the tests of innumerous killing grounds. It was of no matter who came to meet the challenge, for whether Assyrian, Amalekite, Moabite, or Hebrew he had never been denied a victory. He was no young pup to be daunted by the rage of open confrontation, and the prospect of combat with the tall king fuelled the mounting heat in his blood. Who else could these Hebrews send? Their king was known to be one of the mightiest of their soldiers. He pondered the success of this king who had all but eradicated the Amalekite nation. Perhaps he had the blood of the Anakim in his veins, though weakened through breeding—unlikely, however. These people were stringent about keeping to their own. Miscegenation was not practiced amongst them. It was told that their God forbade it. He had personally believed it to be a scheme designed to exclude spies and cloaked antagonists from their ranks. Intruders could hence be easily distinguished by their unfamiliar visage, habits, or tongues. *A sly people indeed,* he considered.

In years past his father had cautioned him of their ways. "Son, what our people possess now is but a pittance compared to our forefathers," he had declared. "We had nigh upon sixty cities once, with walls to the heavens. Our herds eclipsed the grass and the oaks stretched their mighty boughs as the hands of gods, cleaving the sky. Our seed was *incomparable* amongst the nations. It was in my thirteenth year that this Hebrew tribe wandered up from the lands of the Egyptians and spread before our gates like a prodigious blight. They crossed the brook Zered and sent spies throughout our borders, even to the lands of our cousins. At first we knew not from whence they came, fast and thick as the pestilential summer flies of Ashdod."

The distress in his father's voice had disturbed him at the time, for he had seldom seen the older man so agitated. Gol-jath could still recollect the shuddering sensation that he had felt as his father had continued his recount of the conquering tribe.

"Some said they had breached the waters of the Great Sea, but who could accept such a weaver's tale? Yet they set about to extinguish our clans from the earth. Before, they were as nothing to us, mere insects, and we scoffed at their forays against our defenses; but then their true assaults came, and it was like nothing our people had known. From Edrei to Ashtaroth, our walls were overrun like papyrus reeds. We fought fiercely but some power aided their cause, and at the last our gods did not answer us. Our bulwarks crumpled like dust and we were overtaken. Sure they extended a token of peace, but who could accept such an obvious ruse meant to disarm us on the eve of a battle...but their onslaught...! Never had our people known such dread, and our spirit left us. We suffered a devastating upheaval. A number of our people fled north away from their advance, scattering to the winds like chaff. After this we became divided and grew weakened. A piteous few of us journeyed to the Anakim in the mountains to the west. Our legacy was destroyed within a generation. Take this as a lesson for you. Make no mistake son, the God of these

Hebrews answers their call. If you must ever battle these men you too must be granted favor with our masters."

The intensity of his father's tone rang across the dividing years.

"You have both brawn and wit, Gol-jath. But you will need more than this. I have agreed for you to sojourn in Gath of Philistia after two more seasons in my training. Observe the ways of the commoner and the king alike. These men are not as we are; they understand their disadvantage on the field, and so they are wily in their dealings. There you will be titled Gol-yath until your pact of service is ended. You will be paid well and their battlefields will glow with your triumphs. They will praise your exploits as they reap their rewards in blood. Meanwhile you must learn. Never be complacent nor underestimate their cunning. Watch. Be vigilant. You are sure to be at the nexus of every battle. Think. Be smart! Do not be lured into traps where you are alone and outnumbered more than twenty to one. Grow wise from the failures of others. We will need your expertise when the new city is commissioned. If all goes as we have planned you shall serve in the commanding ranks of our garrison." His father had gripped his shoulder tightly with a strange show of emotion. "I am proud of you, Gol-jath. You have done well."

The unease that he remembered experiencing during his father's unsettled account of the Hebrew conquest he now attributed to the insecurity of boyhood. Since then he had matured in battle— surely his triumphs thus far had proved his high standing in the eyes of the gods, and his father's. There was no longer any man that he feared.

I will tarry until eventide for this mongrel to show. A few more hours, and then....

≈ ≈ ≈

The grim task was, after much dissent, ceded to the young man whose fair countenance had not yet claimed a full growth of beard. Mustering every vestige of his deep resolve, he defied the stinging disbelief and callous jibes which coursed his back on his descent into the valley.

"He shall not last a moment, this son of Jesse," someone murmured from the rocky outcrop to his left.

"'Tis a pity, such a handsome lad," agreed another despondently. "He is sure to balk when he reaches the lower valley. Who can prevail if the king himself is struck with fear?"

And to the boy's chagrin it was true. Within the king's tent, Saul had been despondent as he tried unsuccessfully to fit his own cumbersome armor onto the slender frame of this youth who showed more courage than he. The king had, in a brief moment, appraised the unlikely savior of their nation. The stripling possessed nothing apparent that would commend him to a task of such magnitude, save undaunted bravado and an unparalleled confidence in the God whom none had heard from for many a month now. Such dire circumstances....

"How could a mighty nation come to this?" Saul had muttered repeatedly to no one in particular.

"A solitary boy defends our honor—and our God?" None of his aides had answered, for the tenor of the camp was befouled by a pungent brew of lost pride and trodden courage.

The boy had thrown off the proffered armor, for it was a folly and surely would have been his death rather than his salvation. In any event the mail could scarcely survive one thrust from the huge broadsword that he saw brandished by the giant in the valley of Ephesdammim below. Its reflection seemed to shine as brightly as the side of Saul's chariot, so large was the blade. After weeks of seeing it unsheathed, the men had all lost heart and their innards had sunk within them.

Still, he cared not for the sword, nor the air of marvel commanded by this defiant blasphemer. He heard only the torrent of insults flooding through the valley to scald their ears and sear their spirits. Were the armies of the Living God to scurry like rats in fear of this heathen? Or to be intimidated by his fetid oaths? He could have endured the sneering words had they not sought to besmirch the name of YHWH. He gritted his teeth in disgust. The insidious fear that was creeping through the camp would never claim him as long as he recalled the might of his God whom no power, earthly or otherworldly, could challenge.

As he began his descent from the promontory he measured the range to his opponent with a practiced eye and clutched the small leather scrip at his side decisively. To the few who were charged with safeguarding the cotes that were the livelihood of their families and tribes, the stones of the cliffs were as precious as the jewels of palaces. The weight of each now nestled within his pouch was perfect. *With YHWH they will be enough,* he assured himself. He was going out to this behemoth, and he would return its carcass to the king.

≈ ≈ ≈

Across the ravine, Gol-jath paused mid-stride as an indistinct noise disturbed his reverie. Ceasing his contemplations, he crested a knoll closer to the enemy encampment, but separated from it by the broad valley. Looking into the distance, he discerned a slight shift against the stillness of the baked terrain. The imperceptible movement originated beyond a rambling tangle of shrubs that bisected the valley. He squinted against the harsh glare. Not a man arrayed for war and certainly not the king he was expecting. The vague shape was not large enough to be a warrior. Neither was there any glint of armor on the diminutive figure. His lone burden appeared to be…what was it? The way that it was carried did not suggest a spear. It was…a staff! A loud guffaw escaped his throat. Certainly not! Still the form drew nearer to the meeting ground, shuttling progressively downslope in an unswerving path toward his position. A coincidental wild animal perhaps, taking advantage of the calm to make a desperate foray for food amidst the rambling brush….

He peered more intently, willing his keen eyesight to an even sharper edge. No. It was indeed a man, but one too miniscule to purport to be a challenger. A frown rumpled his thick brow. He could have avowed that the individual approaching was a herdsman of some kind. Did the fool not know that he was traversing a battlefield? Maybe the heat had robbed him of his wits. Would the Hebrews truly capitulate without even a semblance of a fight? Could it be a messenger then—an emissary? If he should slay this one mistakenly, King Achish would be wroth.

Nevertheless he raised his guard, for experience warned of impending danger. It might yet be a ploy to distract him from the true source of an intended attack. He scanned the rim of the gorge in suspicion but detected no indication of an ambush. Nothing moved beyond the back of the peculiar visitor.

His questions would be answered soon enough for the figure came on, purposefully, even aggressively. The demeanor was suggestive of a man who had come to fight, but surely not! Suddenly his lips pursed in incredulity as he apprehended the scope of the brazen tactic. Indeed they had sent him a mutt to battle! What greater affront could be given a warrior than to instigate a battle wherein there was no honour in the victory? His amusement immediately eroded into ashes as the barb sank deep beneath his skin, riling him to fury.

As the man drew near, Gol-jath assessed the brash arrival with intensifying umbrage. Not a man, but an unarmed boy! They did intend insult then, for neither an opponent nor an emissary would be one so young or inexperienced.

"Am I a dog, that you come to me with staves?" he called out disdainfully to the boy, but there came no reply. Gol-jath gauged his quarry's every movement, absorbing the dismissive silence without outward reaction. Given the distance remaining between them, he thought it possible the youngster would turn upon his heels and dash away at the last instant; however, as the boy broke into a measured trot then swiftly veered to his right, it was clear that the battle had begun, and boy or no, he would receive no quarter. His victories would not be marred by even this. His vehemence held no pretense now as he swore at the lad, and at the hills beyond where his proper enemy was secreted. He berated their God and the cowardice that ushered a boy to a certain death. *Cowards!* His eyes refocused on the unfortunate lad. *So be it.* He would make it quick, though not painless.

"Come to me, and I will give your flesh to the fowls of the air and the beasts of the field!" he invited with a derisive laugh.

Visibly impervious to the threat, the boy sniffed contemptuously and framed a retort. His voice carried on the air, its threat unmistakable. "You come to me with a sword, and with a spear, and a shield: but I come to you in the name of the Lord of Hosts, the God of the armies of Israel, whom thou hast defied! This day will the Lord deliver you into my hand;

and I will smite you, and take your head from you; and I will give the carcasses of the host of the Philistines this day unto the fowls of the air, and to the wild beasts of the earth; that all the earth may know that there is a God in Israel!"

As the sling received its captive prize, the Philistine champion relived a flash of glory from his own youth. Why the recollection intruded just then he could not precisely say, but the sight of the boy standing tall in the face of death—a chord in the youth's audacious tone resonated within the warrior's soul. *To be outmatched, yet as bold as a lion!* This he had not seen since—he strained to invoke the memory that lay long-buried within him. It was his own initiation into war. Warfare was meant for men, but sometimes boys were called to fill a breach. He was again with his father in battle, holding aloft the crushed body of a larger opponent. His father, though typically undemonstrative, had clapped his back proudly. "Your great-grandfather served in the company of the king when the Hebrew Wars came to Bashan," he had confided.

"Our family learned well that failure carries a heavy price. Judge each opponent cautiously. Never let a lesser man shame you, Son, nor should you underestimate his courage," his father had said in warning.

The words summoned from the recesses of his mind faded in a haze as the rapid whirr of a sling straining to be discharged interrupted the ill-timed reminiscence. He re-centered his gaze on the boy-warrior.

"And all this assembly," the lad finished, gesturing to the hills around which were filled with eyes that sought to apprehend the remote exchange, "shall know that the Lord saves, not with sword and spear; for the battle is the Lord's and he will give you into our hands!"

The stark impertinence of the boy's words finally infuriated him past his slim tolerance. He surged forward menacingly just as the taut sling sped its final arc, releasing a small nugget from its sheltering pouch. Goljath bristled in irritation. He would not be as easily dispatched with stinging pebbles as a simple jackal stalking a sheepfold. The wind was low, and his spear would find an easy mark. He raised its tip, baring his teeth in anger, but the flurry of indignation was cut short by a sharp *crack* above the bridge of his nose and a throbbing ache that spread like a fiery fissure across his skull. At first he could not fathom its origin. He grappled for the lost moment in time as already the stripling was reloading the sling and carving a keen arc over his head. Its wraithlike whisper pervaded his senses as the words of his father's caution retuned again, broken by the pain razing through his body. A violent shiver shook his gargantuan frame.

"Never...man...underestimate...courage." Eerie images swam in his mind, eclipsing his blurring vision of the boy. Wherein was his mistake? He could smell the acrid scent of the weeds of the valley mixed with the musk of soil. He could feel nothing now and he knew. He would not see the new city that his father had spoken of so animatedly. Neither would he be there to help reclaim their lost heritage. He would join his forefathers and another champion would rise in his place. He too had failed against these Hebrews, and it would cost him his life. He called, but like the Bashan of old, his gods did not answer to usher him into the life beyond. The battlefield was unforgiving and failure knew no reward. He had been shamed by a boy...a lesser....

As darkness overtook him and the scent of his blood on the dusty ground pervaded his senses, a gradual understanding filled him. No, not a boy now, but a man—a man of courage!

CHAPTER THREE

Ephesdammim

Now I know that the LORD saveth His anointed;
He will hear him from His holy heaven
With the saving strength of His right hand.
Some trust in chariots, and some in horses;
But we will remember the name of the LORD our God.
They are brought down and fallen;
But we have risen, and stand upright.
Save, LORD!
Let the King hear us when we call.

PSALM OF DAVID 20, EXCERPT

The corpse, its corded muscles still tensed in readiness of combat, top-pled heavily into the unyielding dirt.

"A cur indeed you were, Philistine. And now, a dead cur!"

The bulbous lips that had moments before cursed the young sheep-herder and spat foul imprecations against the God of Israel framed no reply. The projectile was still lodged between the furunculous forehead and the dented edge of the highly decorated helmet that had catastrophi-cally failed its wearer.

The loud thud of impact carried to the ears of all within the lower reaches of the mountain, but the shockwave that rippled into the hills was one that tore unbidden from the throats of men. The deadly conflict had lasted only a few heartbeats, and then the shackles of fear that had bound the cowed warriors ripped asunder. The clamor swelled to thunder as men incited to wrath poured over the mountainside and into the ravine, their voices merging into a riotous crescendo. Their vicious bellows promised a brutal end to any caught in their wake.

Ahead of the approaching melee, the thwack of the giant's own sword, honed razor sharp for battle, sheared through the thick cords of sinew and bone. The sword stood more than half the young man's height, but his determination outweighed the unwieldy weapon. Already flies had begun to swarm busily around the thick blood pulsing from the severed neck, oblivious to the import of the confrontation that culminated with a death in the barren valley. He was no soldier, this one, but he took no more thought for the carcass than for the beasts he had slain in attacks upon his roving flocks.

A heightened roar erupted triumphantly from the bowels of the mountain the instant the massive head was slung from the shoulders of the giant. The sound barreled into the opposing encampment, announcing the advent of a new aggressor. It reverberated even beyond the furthermost tent, which now lay empty of hope. By now the accursed enemies had turned in fear, their flight heedless of the perilous terrain they must traverse in order to reach the mountain on the farthest side of the declivity. Terrified cries mingled with the tumult of the chase as the pursuing army, made confident by the miraculous rout of the Philistine champion, broke to spread across their flanks. An unearthly wail of despair arose from the emasculated enemy soldiers who trampled fallen comrades in an effort to evade the oncoming attack. The onslaught crashed mercilessly into the chaos of their retreating ranks as the battle was irrevocably joined. The slaughter of the invader, now turned prey, continued to the gates of Ekron in the north and the stronghold of Gath on the eastern border of Philistia. Defeat was inevitable, and prayers for mercy fell on the deaf ears of their pagan gods, wood and stone effigies standing uselessly in the temples of idols where the towering carvings of Astaroth and Dagon stood forever silent, awaiting a victory that would not come on this day. The imperiled conquest now sounded a mournful dirge, beckoning its victims to a sullen grave.

CHAPTER FOUR

A Dowry to Draw Blood

I will behave myself wisely in a perfect way...
...I will walk within my house with a perfect heart.

PSALM OF DAVID 101, EXCERPT

aul had fought a strange mixture of emotions as he watched the top-pling form of the gargantuan warrior from the safety of distant perch. Now his mouth tightened as the implications of the deed bore down upon his back, almost as heavy as the burden he had carried for a length of days before, when the one the enemy called Gol-yath had persisted in his disdainful parade before their army. The odious name had come on the wind of travelers and traders many times. The king had also heard many shadowy utterances revering this one's mastery at slaughter. Saul's own spies had carved into his imagination images of carnage wrought on lone opponents answering the call of the one his people knew simply as Goliath. But the name mattered little, for it was the monster's gruesome deeds that had so preceded him. *How could I have gone down to answer the challenge? My people have need of me. What would it have profited us—to risk my life for such a cheap entrapment? No!* It had been an unnecessary gambit. One more disposable than he would be better suited to sacrifice his life to the Philistine fanatic. He had expected one of his commanders to volunteer in anticipation of glory, but none had ventured forward. And for that their salvation had been secured by a mere boy who had made the slaying seems like child's play! It was a venerable triumph and solemn embarrassment bundled into one muddled lot.

Saul clenched his fists in self-recrimination. The telling of the tale throughout the cities would be both a blessing and a bane. The trepidation that had overtaken both him and his men was evident to all, he realized. Saul closed his eyes and then exhaled deliberately. He would invite the boy to his house in a hope that the victory might be accorded to the House of Saul. Perhaps, though, he could blunt the potential shame of the day. He turned to Abner his captain.

"Whose son is he, this youth?" he asked. Saul suddenly wondered whether the boy, whom he had blithely considered a simple musician, was in fact of a warrior's lineage or possibly of some bearing. The young man had also served as his armor-bearer prior to being accorded leave from the impending war in order that he might return to his father's sheepcotes. However, during that short season of service, Saul had never cared to investigate his parentage.

Abner shrugged his shoulders abjectly. "I cannot say, my lord."

"Seek his father's name, and then bring the boy to me."

"As you wish, my lord."

～ ～ ～

Saul stood quietly surveying his men's pursuit of their enemies through the brush on the far crest. That day Saul alone heard the death knell that sounded a low and ominous moan amidst the jaunting trumpets that heralded their imminent victory over the Philistine host. An intangible unease coalesced within his soul, and he shivered violently. It was no comfort that the prophet Samuel had warned some years past that he, Saul, had lost favor with God and would ultimately lose his kingship. The day's events were perilously prophetic. Saul brooded on the double-edged victory and what he had discerned in the precocious youth. He resolved to watch the boy and hopefully see an end to the matter. He returned balefully to his encampment to await the return of his captain.

In Saul's tent, David disentangled his fingers from the thick dark hair massed atop the detached head and bowed before his sovereign. His stance displayed the brashness of a youth fresh from a triumph. He had no regard for the undercurrents that would have warned a wiser and more experienced man that all was not as it seemed.

"Tell me. Whose son are you, boy?" The nuance tingeing King Saul's tone did not betray the disquiet that raged within the man.

"I am the son of your servant Jesse," David answered easily.

Saul pondered the disclosure but could not trace the family name within the dusty annals of his memory.

"Well, lad! You are to enter my service fully from this hour. You may send tidings to your father. My son Jonathan shall instruct you on your placement and shall direct you to new lodgings." The king gestured to a youngster standing attentively at the rear of the shadowed tent.

"Go now." Saul turned away in an abrupt dismissal, leaving the two young men to put his order into effect.

≈ ≈ ≈

David bowed and exited the tent, his dismay barely concealed. The king had said nothing of Goliath, and nothing of the major victory he had just won for Israel. He frowned ruefully.

The king had not even cast a glance at the giant's head he had brought to the tent as tribute and vindication of their God. The macabre trophy still lay unheralded just inside the tent flap where he had been ordered by the guard to deposit it. David flung an unsettled look at Jonathan, who had now joined his side.

"Is your father well? He did not appear to be overly joyous at our victory. Is he always so melancholy?"

Jonathan stopped briefly and considered the question.

"Sometimes he is. But perhaps it is the strain of the last month and the wound you dealt to his pride."

"Me?" David blurted out, incredulous at the inference that he might have intentionally slighted his sovereign. Jonathan's brow furrowed theatrically.

"Did you not consider the import of a young sheepherder's battling the greatest Philistine menace ever to walk the lands of our fathers whilst our mighty men cowered in the hills?" Jonathan mused.

David winced at the recollection.

Jonathan continued, "Never doubt that my father is glad to be rid of these relentless hounds—for a time at least, until their wrath builds again. He would have done anything to save his people dominion by Philistia. But the giant…he was fearsome indeed."

"Why did you not go? You are arrayed as a soldier. You know the might of our God, that none can withstand Him."

"But could I withstand my father? He would have had my head." Jonathan laughed disarmingly.

"Mine also, had he known," David rejoined. "My brothers surely had the astonishment of the heart; their pest of a brother overcoming a man of such tremendous stature. My older brother Eliab purpled in anger at seeing me. He would see me tending sheep all my days were it his choice," David noted in annoyance.

Jonathan stopped him suddenly with a hand on his shoulder.

"What spirit possessed you this day; were you not afraid?"

"I tell you truly, YHWH was with me that very hour!"

Jonathan clasped his shoulder tightly in understanding. "To our compound then! A new life awaits you. And a better one, I hope!" he added optimistically. "Your lodgings shall not be too distant, and we shall talk more of this triumph, yes?"

David nodded in acquiescence as strode beside the prince, considering mischievously whether Eliab would be made to tend the sheep that eve.

✑ ✑ ✑

A continuous furrow of weeks churned by, each producing greater wonder and exhilaration for David than he had previously envisioned. There was much to learn, yet after a seemingly insignificant number of months in service to the king, Saul had appointed him over the king's bodyguard. His ascension in ranks had been swift, and for this reason alone he knew he must be careful to hold regular counsel with the seasoned captains; his sudden rise in the king's favor was certain to be regarded sorely by the established men of war. After he had proven the wisdom of his judgment time and time again, Abner conceded the authority of David's impeccable command.

"You are truly blessed of YHWH," he had affirmed during a tour of the armed companies. "The men have taken to you. And the maidens!" He broke off with an amused grin, for all knew that David had captured the hearts of the women across Israel.

David shuddered as he recalled his first journey through the cities in King Saul's entourage. They had passed through exuberant celebrations throughout the major towns. During the procession, the women had heralded him even beyond their regard for Saul.

"Saul slayed thousands, and David, tens of thousands!" they had sung. David noticed then that Saul had blanched visibly, his mouth hardening into a grim line. The king stood erect in stubborn defiance of the chanted rebuff of his supreme rulership. The peoples' jovial taunt harkened back to the first days he had reigned as king, when the people had at first rejected him. He had reportedly shrugged off their disdain then and shown himself to be worthy. But now...David could see that the bite of their merry singsong had drawn blood. Throughout the rest of the travels, Saul had spoken nary a word to David, or to his servants who eyed him gingerly, wary of inflaming his mood further.

David had grown more familiar with the king's violent temper as the days etched scores on the chart of time, for he had played his harp several nights in the king's presence, calming bitter tirades or assuaging his anger or sullenness. But this quiet brooding...It brought an air of ill-foreboding and a vague tremor within the pit of his stomach that David could not quell. The seething disquiet spoke of the eve of a battle, yet he could not read the king's intent. He could do little else than abide until the vehemence he could see roiling beneath the king's skin had subsided. He prayed that it would.

≈ ≈ ≈

The evening following their return, in the midst of David's playing, the scouring of Saul's sandals tinged the twilight with disquiet as the king paced the floor of the banqueting room. Like an entrapped beast, he ranged length of the hall, snarling words that no one present could decipher. His low ramblings poured out uninterrupted, until midway in his unintelligible rendering he halted to grasp a javelin from the rack near the west door. He continued on, using the finely honed shaft to punctuate his disconcerting diatribe. David continued to play, pretending not to hear the strange tirade. He plucked determinedly at the harp strings, hoping that the ephemeral harmony would once again quell his king's unexplained lapse. Words were whispered continually of the king's susceptibility to the torment of evil spirits, but no one, not even Jonathan, had seemed capable of relieving their king in moments like these. The music had been a surprisingly effective balm, and David's playing had been requested more and more frequently of late.

David returned his thoughts to his music; it would not do to stumble over a note at such a moment. He himself felt buoyed by the caressing melody. His reverie was interrupted by a sharp intake of breath and the discordant clang of a serving tray falling to the floor as it escaped the grasp of its terrified porter. Puzzled by the uncharacteristic ineptitude, David raised his gaze amidst the quavering clamor that followed. What occurred within the following moments sundered David's heart for the suddenness of the betrayal. His head jerked reflexively, eyes grown wide in alarm, as an ornamented javelin sang effortlessly through the crook of his arms with an eerie hum of vibrating air. It parted the strings of his harp and clattered across the floor to lie quietly among a pile of discarded wall hangings.

David turned slowly to face his lord, whose glower was burnished with a hatred exceeding even that for his enemies. Saul bared his teeth briefly, whether angry at his missed aim or in future threat David could not ascertain. The king watched, seething, as David bowed and removed himself from the hall. He made no motion to hinder David's exit.

＞ ＞ ＞

Saul stood, his eyes fixed maniacally on the door that shielded David's retreat from view. His chest heaved with emotional exertion. Even as the javelin had coursed through his rough fingers and sailed with barely a whisper toward David's breast, Saul had known that it was his own heart he would ultimately pierce with the cold iron tip. For days he had noticed the degeneration within himself, the festering of his jealousy, and it made him desperate.

He was paving the road away from his throne and sealing his own deposition. Yet, desperation made him more vicious still. Saul could see the anointing of God laid over David like a golden mantle. David's every action was blessed, and the people revered him even above their king; their jubilant songs rang incessantly in his ears.

"Saul his thousands, but David his tens of thousands."

It was a dirge and a song of mourning for a king whose anointing had been surrendered. The day on which his supremacy had turned had come and gone so simply. He had just won a memorable victory, and nothing had seemed amiss until the arrival of the prophet.

"You have been disobedient to God!" Samuel had cried, distressed by the outcome of a war just concluded—a victorious war spoilt by a culmination of foolish deeds...one key prisoner left alive against the instructions of God and spoils of war that were to have been destroyed, instead hoarded for the glory of the people.

Now the only vestiges of that doomsday were the harsh recriminations spoken against the king who had failed in his charge to obey his Lord.

"Curse you and your foul people, Agag!" Saul bellowed into the stillness of the hall. His servants cowered in their places, not understanding the peculiar events that they were witnessing and not recognizing the name of the Amalekite king who had been spared against the inviolable will of his Master. The act had seemed gracious enough to the superficial observer, but the breach of confidence had precipitated an avalanche of calamities that he must now bear.

The thickening mass of silence threatened to suffocate the hall until the king at last turned aside and settled uncomfortably on his gilded seat. The mask of death slowly dissolved, leaving an empty shell to bear the weight of accusation now palpable in the room. Still, he was king, and those who valued life would not speak of what they had witnessed. He met quickly averted looks with a grunt and relocated his long frame to a heavily cushioned couch. For the first time in many years, King Saul felt alone against the world. He covered his face in his hands, and then dismissed the entire court with a dejected flick of his fingers. Saul did not raise his head until the shuffling of feet had receded beyond the doorway. The collective hum of low whispers was soon muffled by the heavy timber doors. Saul pursed his lips in fervent thought, then finally purposed in his heart what he would do. They would not replace him so easily. He still bore the crown and all its power. *May the strongest be left standing!*

"Merab!"

Saul's head servant opened the door, bleary-eyed for the hour was late. He peered in with a questioning look.

"My lord?"

"Fetch Merab!"

"Certainly, my lord!"

The servant closed the door quietly and slipped away to summon Saul's daughter. *No man can be perfect continually,* Saul considered hopefully. *I shall find a fault in him, and it shall be his undoing,* he thought with a wistful quirk of his lips. *He shall fall victim to his own lusts as so many men before him. You stand strong before men, David, but a woman may yet be your downfall.*

He was drawn from his pondering by the soft entrance of his eldest daughter. She was truly radiant. That fact would serve his purposes well.

❧ ❧ ❧

"Come, Merab. Our kingdom has need of your beauty this day! Sit and listen." Her father tapped the seat before him in excitement. Merab obeyed, though perplexed by the intensity wreathing his countenance. She was seldom ever called into his presence save for ceremonial gatherings or celebrations.

As Saul divulged his intent to his daughter, his words became consumed with a passion more virulent than she had ever encountered before. Merab's brows rose quizzically after hearing the fullness of her father's intent. She felt a cloying sadness within her, for her heart had been promised to Adriel, the son of Barzillai, many months prior; but now her love would be cast aside for her father's vengeful gain.

"Has not Adriel delivered his dowry three weeks ago?" she asked pointedly, hoping to find some flaw in the bitter scheme.

Saul frowned suddenly as though he had not fully contemplated this facet of his proposal.

"Do not despair, Merab. Your marriage to Adriel will not be in jeopardy. The offer of your hand is merely bait for the imperfections of a virile young man. Any hot-blooded man David's age would surely risk his life for the hope of your hand. Do not worry, my dear. The bride-price I have set is steep—and he will never withstand repeated attacks on the Philistine army. He has too few men at his disposal." Saul laughed conspiratorially as he leaned forward to pat her arm in reassurance. "I have just ordered his command to be reduced to one thousand alone."

The wily pup David had been careful to avoid contact with Saul over the weeks following the unprovoked attack—perhaps he knew instinctively that to do otherwise would have been suicide. He accepted all commands with which the king charged him, never questioning the paucity of soldiers he had been allotted to carry out the tasks delegated to his company. Many of the errands through the wilds had been dangerous, but nonetheless David's valor and that of his men of war whose loyalty and respect he had garnered exceeded Saul's estimation. David's renown grew the more for the wisdom of his conduct. Neither could his deeds be challenged. Moreover, his personal commitment to his men was unmatched in a land where the battlefield consumed men by the hundreds.

Heaped upon the ignominy of Saul's misjudgments were the concessions required of his errors in calculation. Saul was not only compelled to
honor the marriage contract with Adriel, for he had already accepted the
sizeable dowry without complaint, but to his chagrin his bargain with
David for his daughter's hand would also need to be upheld. His disgrace
continued to mount irrevocably with each step he made, but he had committed himself to this course and to turn aside now....*No! I can not! I will
not!* Something could yet be salvaged of this catastrophic slide. He was certain of it.

᠗ ᠗ ᠗

With his course thus set Saul was much relieved, and encouraged, to be
afforded a door of escape from his latter agreement with David to give his
daughter's hand in marriage. The outstanding debt of honor continued to
gall his senses until the morning his servants reported that Merab's
younger sister Michal had fallen in love with David. Pleased with this fortuitous development and reveling in a renewed assurance of his innocence, Saul concocted an amended scenario to keep his hands free of the
young man's blood and yet succeed in sundering life from the youth's
body.

He hastily prepared an alternate proposition for David to be delivered
by his chief servant. In his missive, Saul again named a startling price for
his younger daughter's hand.

A hundred foreskins of the Philistines.

"A fortunate slingshot will not be his salvation on this occasion," Saul
mused to himself. "This dowry will be paid in David's blood."

Saul informed Michal of his shrewdly devised offer. She would not
object, he was sure.

᠗ ᠗ ᠗

Michal knew it was her father's hope to see David perish at enemy hands
while on a fool's errand to retrieve a hundred foreskins of the Philistines
in lieu of a dowry. David was young, but Michal knew he was no fool and
neither was he weak. The skins were to come by David's hand alone. To

slay twenty Philistines was a recognizable feat in a battle but one hundred...Michal hoped her father had truly underestimated David's dominance on the field. It was also said throughout the city that he was blessed of God, having indeed defeated the giant. Still, if she could dissuade her father from this grudge he held, then perhaps...

"But Father, what shall become of this farce if he survives this 'quest' of yours?" she protested.

"Then you shall marry," he said simply. "That should please you...shouldn't it?" His look grew warningly cold. "I have told you of this, but do not let your hopes extend beyond your loyalties. Either way, one of us will win, though I would rather it be me! If David should emerge the victor...?" Saul broke off ominously then regarded his daughter. "Let us wait and see, shall we?"

～ ～ ～

David accepted the change with equanimity. Michal was even fairer than Merab and possessed less of Saul's temper than her sibling did. The risk was not small. Nevertheless, it was possible, with the right men to safeguard him during the foray. Yes! For Michal's hand I will dare this exploit.

David conveyed his acceptance to the king and eagerly quit his quarters to seek his lieutenants. He would make preparations that very hour. He nodded to himself, reconfiming his acquiescence. This is truly a dowry befitting a man of war.

Saul watched from the loggia of the outer court as David rode out a week subsequent to the sealing of their bond. He took a company of only fifty men, which was an unexpected tactic. Saul pursed his lips and puzzled over David's ploy. He had anticipated that David would have taken his full complement of fifty score men in order to increase his hope of success. A contingent of that size would surely have drawn the Philistine main guard from Gath, but a rank of only fifty men...? Saul mulled over David's options. Though a seemingly inadequate number for the task, the small group would attract less notice, for the threat they posed would be seen as insignificant. Saul was compelled to acknowledge that it was a bold, though some would say foolhardy, strategy that could culminate in his death. How it came was of no consequence, so long as it was final. Yet David's confidence made Saul uneasy. The young man was no coward, and he had recognized a few of the men covering David's flanks: Eleassor and Raphah, beside fifteen others in the following. These were true men of war—men of undisputed skillfulness. They possessed an unusual dexterity with a range of weapons: sword, sling, spear, and bow. Abner had twice repeated that these fifty, who had become a tight-knit company over the seasons, had distinguished themselves in David's service, succoring him in battle where courage would have failed lesser men.

The king pressed his lips into a grim line. *A night attack then,* Saul concluded. The half moon was returning within three days, and David would be able to use it to his full advantage. The full moon thereafter would provide a high degree of illumination that would imperil the group should they encounter a delay or need to make a surreptitious retreat. Two days longer and they would chance detection against the open terrain. Errors in timing were the most deadly sort. But David was unused to making such blunders when combat was involved.

Saul's chest tightened in dismay and he exhaled a slow, tortured breath—it seemed his good fortune had indeed ended. He already felt the loss. No doubt Michal would count herself blessed at the end of it all, for a while at least. *But only a while,* he vowed. *Only a while....*

᠀ ᠀ ᠀

Two hundred foreskins! This was double the price the king had stipulated, and did not come at a small price. In spite of the increased risk and danger to the men, David had wanted to demonstrate his commitment to his side of the bargain, and simultaneously make it more difficult for the king to renege. The men had agreed to his plan, opting to fight in bands of ten men. However, as a result of their prolonged attack David had lost five of his squad, one from each band, including Timmah, one of his most admirable lieutenants. Their deaths bore heavily upon him. David fervently hoped that by wedding Michal he would succeed in stanching Saul's desire to see his life's blood spilled to no reasonable gain. It was a dim hope, for to a shrewd man such as Saul, a widow could as easily garner a second dowry.

≈   ≈   ≈

A week after his departure, David presented the bloodied bundle to a sour-faced Saul. This time, unlike their initial encounter in Saul's tent where the head of Israel's most feared enemy had lain discarded at the king's feet, David soon recognized the pastiness in the king's visage and the resentment that distorted his usually stoic manner. He noted also the narrowing in the king's eyes as he beheld him fixedly.

"She is yours," Saul acceded, and turned away abruptly, much as he had on that fateful day in Ephesdammim. David, discomfited by the insult, regarded the king's arrow-straight back then departed without reply. He could think of nothing to say. Indeed, any words he might have uttered right then would have provoked his beheading. Saul's servants, eager to convince David to accept the king's offer of Michal, had spoken convincingly of the king's love for him, but the matter of the errant javelin remained in David's mind as a blatant contradiction of their words. Their protests of their king's ingenuousness made David even more wary. He struggled to determine Saul's motive but could find none save jealousy. But Saul was king, and he hardly seemed the sort to wallow in insecurities. *There must be something more,* he decided. *Something! But what?*

≈   ≈   ≈

In the months following the sealing of the marriage covenant with his youngest daughter, Saul's son-in-law displayed his usual courage and faithfulness in Saul's service as though there were no rift between them. His burgeoning prosperity and renown galled Saul the more. So it was that at the climax of a victorious campaign against the Philistines in the east, in which David's heroic conduct sparked renewed celebrations throughout the cities, that Saul reasoned that he could abide David's vaunted acts no longer. The two hundred foreskins had been an affront; an arrogant display designed to humble him and flaunt David's own prowess. He would remove David for the sake of his crown and the preservation of his line on the throne. His prophesied deposition seemed an entirely capricious pronouncement—*The judgment was unfair.* Hadn't he served well? Did he not tolerate a contrary and stubborn people without complaint?

Well, Saul swore, *I will ensure that Jonathan reigns in my stead, and not some self-aggrandized shepherd!*

≈ ≈ ≈

For a while David had purposed to gauge the measure of the king whom he had come to see as his surrogate father prior to his sudden estrangement from Saul's inner circle. *What was to be done?* he wondered. He would speak of it to Jonathan, for their brotherly affection had grown steadily since their initial meeting, and he was optimistic that some useful conclusion would come of their consultation. Perhaps Jonathan might agree to intercede with his father!

David penned a discrete missive, which he left unsigned. His servant Beriah hurried to deliver it to Jonathan's hand, and it was arranged that they would meet two days hence at the soldiers' command post. Betwixt them they could perchance discern the source of the king's grievance and dispel Saul's resolve against his life.

≈ ≈ ≈

On the morning of the proposed meeting, the glow of dawn ushered in a day of intense heat Jonathan arrived promptly to take his place beside his father. He looked quizzically about the milling group that had gathered in the forecourt. In their haste many had forgotten to don their head wraps and now fidgeted uncomfortably in the broiling rays of the noon sun that served to increase his father's foul humor. Jonathan craned his neck to see beyond the first ten rows of men. Where was David? Had he been detained? He scanned the edge of the court, puzzling over David's absence.

Saul raised his hand to signal for silence. The buzz of speculation faded hurriedly. Saul stood erect as he spoke with resolution to the now attentive assemblage.

"From the first day that David, the son of Jesse, came to my guard he has flaunted his victory over the giant before my eyes." Jonathan's brow creased as Saul spat David's name with uncharacteristic vehemence. He looked askance at his father, whose posture remained rigid, as though confined by an invisible wall of tension. "Despite my initial reserve," Saul continued forcefully, "I will no longer indulge his flagrant mocking and outright conceit. From this hour his life is forfeit. I order that anyone who next comes upon him slay him—immediately—regardless of the circumstance in which he is found. By tomorrow's eve I expect to be told that he has gone the way of the earth!"

Stunned and fearful looks were cast among the servants, who nodded dumbly. Who in Saul's household was mightier than David? Furthermore, who would deign to slay one upon whom the anointing of YHWH lay, and risk a wrath more terrible than death? For it was spoken, though of out of the earshot of the king, that David was blessed, and despite his humble origins would serve well as king, if such a thing had been possible. Now this eventuality seemed as improbable as the dissolution of the heavens. Saul was the ordained king, and Jonathan his successor. Each was a highly capable man of war and both stood, seemingly united, in this inconceivable purpose. Some waited expectantly for Jonathan to object, knowing him to be David's closest friend through the past few seasons. However, the young man said nothing, though his eyes stayed fixed upon his father.

In addition, David would be no easy prey. Many of the servants purposed to avoid the halls frequented by the young captain in the hope of avoiding a physical exchange. Death would surely come, if not by David's hand, or Saul's, then by God's. If they spotted David and chose to do nothing, Saul would show them no mercy. Also, none of the servants harbored any illusions of immunity from judgment by David's blade should his life be threatened. David might refuse to lay hands on an anointed king, but the king's minions would not be afforded such a measure of grace, they were sure. The circumstances were untenable. It would take divine mercies to quell the beasts gnawing at the cords that bound Saul's household together.

As the men were dismissed, Jonathan alone held the gaze of his father, who returned an unyielding glare. Seeing the brusque set of his father's jaw, his stiffened back, and flinty expression, Jonathan wisely held his tongue. He lowered his eyes in deference and quit the court.

∽ ∽ ∽

Jonathan's emotions roiled within him as he hastened toward the storehouses, which lay at the northern edge of the compound. On the previous day, he had consented to meeting David within the grain store after breaking their fast. Jonathan was glad now that he had changed the meeting place to storehouses for they would be deserted at this time of day, hence the chance of confrontation with any of Saul's men would be remote. Would David be there? Jonathan's heart pounded erratically within his chest. He remembered that on several occasions, David had mentioned his reservations about King Saul's state of mind, but ever the loyal son, he had not deigned to believe it of his father. How wrong he had been. Saul was either ill or possessed. Jonathan regretted now that his nonchalance may have cost David his life.

"Jonathan!"

The prince started at the sound of his name. Seeing his friend amble out to greet him, Jonathan waved David anxiously back into the shadows of the large storeroom. The look of dread upon Jonathan's face goaded David to move at once. He whirled briskly and hastened from the open court used to pack the grain sacks.

"What is it? What has happened?" David questioned with urgency.

Jonathan shook his head, his face contorted in sorrow as he searched for a way to convey Saul's terrible command.

"My father—" He stopped, biting his lip in distress. "My father has ordered your death," he blurted out finally. "Surely it must be that he is ill. Surely…" He raised his hands in despair.

David sank down to sit on the dusty ground just inside the door to the grain store. He stared off into the distance, not speaking.

Jonathan slumped at his side. Neither spoke for a time. Jonathan searched within himself for courage. His father's decree was an injustice that he could not allow to proceed unchallenged.

"You are my brother. I will do something!" Jonathan swore at last, slapping the hard-packed earth.

"What can you do? Your father is beside himself," David replied, his voice uncharacteristically subdued.

"I will speak to him tomorrow." Jonathan surged to his feet and dusted his robe. "Hide yourself until then. Please trust me," he urged, attempting to reignite the small candle of hope within his friend. "Go. Hide in the lentil field beside the armory until the day turns. I will bring Father there to talk, and afterward, I will bring you tidings of the outcome. He will relent, I am sure." Jonathan spoke boldly and forced a smile, yet doubt filled David's eyes.

"I shall do as you bid," David agreed.

"Tomorrow then," Jonathan confirmed solemnly.

David stayed hidden in the field despite his urge to flee. He had not missed the distress in Jonathan's features, made sallow with suppressed anguish. But he must trust his friend. How else was this conflict to be avoided? One more day and they would know his fate. He spent an uncomfortable night among the rough-barked shrubs bordering the field. In the early morning, he stirred restlessly, having fallen asleep a few short hours before. What was his recent success worth if he was hated and hunted by his own king? Not much, he concluded dejectedly. What joy was there in slinking beneath bushes like a dog?

Low voices broke through the quiet of the morning. One was suddenly raised in protest.

"David has done you no wrong. Nothing, Father, and yet you seek to kill him. All that he has done, he has done to your honor. Did you not rejoice when he slew the Philistine while Abner and the rest of us hid behind rocks? You saw it! He took his life in his hands that day, and you requite him with this? He has done nothing against you!"

"You do not understand, Jonathan; I do this for you, for our family and our future."

"No, Father. I want no part of this sin—this shedding of innocent blood."

"He—is—not—innocent," Saul bit out forcefully. "Do you not see? You must…" Saul's words sank away into a low drone as the pair gradually moved out of the range of David's hearing. Jonathan shook his head in obvious disagreement and gestured animatedly, seemingly urging Saul to rescind his command. The king resisted his son's appeal. He refused to be placated. His height eclipsed Jonathan, yet the youth refused to abandon his petition. The sun broke the horizon and bathed the field in a warm glow as Jonathan's insistent pleas continued to ring across the field.

"Enough!" Saul shouted.

There was an interminable lapse in the verbal exchange until, at long last, Saul raised his hands in apparent capitulation. He spoke for several moments. Jonathan embraced him earnestly then and departed in the direction of his quarters.

For a while Saul continued to stand by the field looking up at the heavens. He uttered something indistinguishable and shook his fist at the sky. He remained there with his face upraised as though expecting an answer. The leaves of a lone fig tree rustled softly as the calm of the dawn once again began to settle like a fine mist across the field. Saul harrumphed loudly, drew his robe tight about him, and plodded away in the direction of the main compound.

꙳ ꙳ ꙳

Jonathan returned to the field shortly thereafter. His excitement was evident from his gait.

"Father assured me he will no longer seek your life. He has even requested that you return to his dinner table," Jonathan revealed in satisfaction.

David smiled with guarded relief. It was not his desire to become a fugitive, especially if Saul proved relentless in his cause. The consequences would be disastrous, for who would side with him against their sovereign? David put the gloomy prospect from his mind and followed Jonathan back to the house he had adopted as his own.

David returned to his duties, determined to keep as low a profile as was deemed prudent. Saul was plagued by no further outbursts.

CHAPTER FIVE

A Bitter Victory

What profit is there in my blood,
When I go down to the pit?
Shall the dust praise Thee?
Shall it declare Thy truth?
Hear, O LORD, and have mercy on me;
LORD, be Thou my helper!

PSALM OF DAVID 30, EXCERPT

A s always, peace within a growing nation was short-lived. War once again intruded on the calm of several seasons.

"I wish we could be rid of this Philistine scourge for good," Saul growled.

War, always war: Moab, Ammon, Edom, Zobah, Philistia, and Amalek, wherein was his downfall. Would he find no rest?

The captains of the hosts bundled into his tent to make final adjustments to their battle strategy against the Philistine garrison, which was many thousand strong.

"Send my armor bearer and let us go up," he declared with finality. He would not delay the day. *Wherein is the profit in waiting? Either God will be on our side, or He would not.* Saul was determined to find out which, one way or another.

≈ ≈ ≈

The field lay thick with corpses. Saul, lowering his spear, signaled the sounding of the victory trumpet. The day had gone gloriously and the slaughter was great. He returned to the camp to find it abuzz with excitement.

"David was like a lord this day!" someone cried enthusiastically.

"Eight score men!" shouted another.

"He was ever in the forefront! Nine score it was," corrected a third.

Saul ducked into his tent where Abner waited, his eyes alight.

"Today was of the Lord, was it not?" Abner greeted the king. "Did you hear of David? God's hand was surely with him and . . ."

Abner's voice trailed away at the mold that descended over Saul's countenance. His eyes bulged and his mouth worked angrily. "Get out!" Saul bellowed.

"Wha—"

"Leave me. Now!" the king repeated threateningly.

"My lord!" Abner bowed and backed out of the tent, features contorted in puzzlement.

As the tent flap slapped shut, Saul fell prostrate on the ground and wept. The glory of his kingship was being pried unrelentingly from his grasp. For the people the day was won, but he, King Saul, had assuredly lost all.

≈ ≈ ≈

David attended the triumphal banquet oblivious to Saul's acid demeanor. He was congratulated on every side by his companions who were made boisterous by the day's feats. Saul sat silently for most of the proceedings. The king's reticence made David wary, and he eyed the king surreptitiously throughout the evening. He noticed uneasily that Saul bore his javelin at the table. He wished that Jonathan had been there to relieve his anxiety, but his friend had journeyed to Bethlehem at his father's insistence.

Saul himself sat, outwardly quiet, but the play of emotion on his stony features showed David a glimpse of the anguish his father-in-law was suffering.

"Play us a song to gladden our hearts the more," called one of the older captains, raising his goblet high.

"Yes, play us a tune," chorused Abner.

David obliged, strumming gaily on the harp. He played two songs that brought merry laughter from the group and had commenced a third when he sensed, more than saw, the transformation that overcame the king. He heard a collective intake of breath and turned reflexively to parry the onrushing tip of Saul's javelin, which bore down with lightning speed. David, drawn into a battle for his life, tumbled backward over a bench, scattering platters and cushions aside in his desperation to evade Saul's virulent attack. He scrambled to his feet and circled the heavy banquet table as men tumbled to evade the battle-honed king whose sinister advance continued oblivious to the mayhem unfolding in his wake. Saul jabbed menacingly at David's chest across the timber trestle, then with stunning agility vaulted the table and began a downward blow to pin his quarry against the wall. David narrowly eluded the intended death-stroke and bolted for the door. He heard the javelin clatter off the brass insignia ornamenting the portal. David ran without looking back as he escaped into the enfolding night.

∿ ∿ ∿

"Seek him out," Saul thundered, striking his javelin into the earth-packed wall, which shuddered noticeably. A fine shower of dust rained from the cracked plaster and billowed in small clouds amidst the ensuing silence. The king wrenched the weapon free and glared at Abner. He lowered the tip toward the commander whose full chalice had stopped abruptly on its journey to his lips, its contents spilling unheeded as the javelin had sought its target.

"When you have found David, kill him!"

"But he will be with Michal!" Abner protested. "Are you sure you want to do this? Think of your daughter."

Saul pressed his lips together. "In the morning then," he said flatly. "Send messengers to his house. Have them wait there. If David tries to leave, seize him!" Saul drew a deep breath then exhaled loudly. "He will have this final night of bliss, after which he shall see but one more dawn."

⤬ ⤬ ⤬

David continued his flight out of the central compound. He sped to his house and slammed shut the doors. Barring them with a stout timber, he shouted to his wife, who arrived in alarm. He hurriedly relayed the night's events to Michal.

"You must not stay," she implored him, her eyes wide with fear. "You must not! If you do not save yourself tonight, tomorrow you will certainly be slain!"

David peered through a slitted window and saw flickering torchlight splay across the wall of a nearby building.

"I fear you are right. Fetch my scrip. Quickly!" David blurted out, closing the window in haste.

Michal gathered up David's bag from the post hook near the side entry as he threw open a window on the lee side of the house. The bag contained two shekels of silver that jingled softly inside. *They must suffice for there is no time to tarry,* David surmised. Michal slung the scrip about his neck and clasped her hands about his wrist to help him outside. David braced himself atop a small ledge on a wall below then jumped clear. He fell heavily but muffled his outcry. Michal waved him away with sudden urgency, and he slipped into the blackness moments before equally dark shapes surrounded the house. As he looked back, he saw Michal close the window and blow out her lamp.

⤬ ⤬ ⤬

Morning light erased the long shadows that draped the quiet street. Three hours after daybreak stillness yet wreathed David's house where the windows had remained closed throughout the night. At a signal from his troop leader, one of the cloaked messengers arose from his concealment and traversed the entrance court to the house. He banged violently on the door.

"David! Michal! Open the door! The king commands it!"

Michal called out as bravely as she could muster, "He is sick!"

"Bring him out, Michal," the messenger ordered.

"Depart, he is sick!"

The messenger looked a long while at the closed door before turning away.

⤺ ⤺ ⤺

Michal sighed in relief as fading footsteps crunched in the loose gravel and sand on the road beyond. He would come with others, she knew. Yet it would be profitable if she could purchase her husband another hour. Michal sat in the hall to wait, praying that her efforts would be enough.

Time crept forward. Each added moment was a boon, but inevitably the insistent pounding came again at the door. The grim messenger had returned, this time accompanied by more of Saul's men whose voices rumbled with malignace beyond the portal. Michal stood, then shrunk backward several footsteps, suddenly uncertain. She wrung her hands before bracing herself to act.

Michal called out in defiance, again denying them access, "We cannot attend you. My husband ails. You must depart until the morrow."

However, the men were undeterred by her sustained rebuff.

"Stand back, mistress," the messenger announced an instant before the door erupted inward, careening off its broken hinges. The sinister visitors charged past Michal and rushed toward the bedchamber.

"Arise, in the name of King Saul!" the leader shouted vehemently, prodding the covered form in the bed. However, there was no movement beneath the thick bed-cloth. Grunting in annoyance, the man stripped back the woolen spread, revealing a teraphim and a goat's-hair bolster instead of David's sleeping figure.

"Treacherous witch!" he spat at Michal, who looked away and set her features as stolidly as she could.

The messenger took her arm gruffly and herded her back to the king's court. His men accompanied him all the way lest David intercept them on route. However their passage went without incident.

Saul received them at once. He listened through the description of the scene that they had found at David's house. Throughout, the king's face flushed purple with rising anger, and at the close of the messenger's report he rounded heatedly on Michal, whose air of self-control remained. "You would deceive me? And help my enemy to escape?" he shouted in disbelief.

"But he said to me, 'Why should I kill you? Just let me go.' So I let him go! I could not have stopped him anyway, could I?"

Her father glared at her stonily, and then gestured her dismissal.

೯ ೯ ೯

Saul looked out the window at the lightening field. *Betrayed—by my own daughter, while my son defends this renegade. Even my people praise him in the streets.* Saul shook his head. *I cannot allow it—he will not be allowed to poison my hope. I will pursue this cur,* he vowed. *If my reign is to end, so too will David's life. There will not be one established from the House of David. Not one!*

CHAPTER SIX

Flight

Hear my prayer, O God;
Give ear to the words of my mouth.
For strangers have risen up against me,
And oppressors seek after my soul:
They have not set God before them.
Behold, God is mine helper;
The LORD is with them that uphold my soul.
He will reward evil unto mine enemies.
Cut them off in Thy truth.

PSALM OF DAVID 54, EXCERPT

D avid made haste through the gates of the city and fixed his sights on Ramah. He had been informed that the prophet Samuel had last been there, and he needed greater wisdom than his own right now. Where would he hide? What would Saul do in pursuit of vengence? He was not worried for Michal; he doubted that Saul would hurt his own daughter. But his own parents and brothers were not of Saul's House, and he was certain that no mercy would be extended to the House of Jesse. *Saul's fury will be terrible after my escape,* David mourned. *I must find away to protect them, and the prophet is my only resource.*

To David's relief he found Samuel prophesying near the eastern city gate. Samuel listened quietly and took the younger man's arm. "I knew this day would come. Let us go to Naioth. I have others there who can protect you for a short while, and then we shall see what the Lord has planned for your steps.

～ ～ ～

It was scarcely noon when Abner gave Saul word of David's whereabouts. He brought the news hastily to the king's chamber, where he found Saul pacing the floor in agitation.

"He was seen on the road to Ramah, my Lord."

"Ramah? Doesn't Samuel have a place there? Naioth, I believe!"

"Yes, my lord," Abner confirmed with a nod.

"Send twenty of my officers to bring him back, whether he be alive or dead!"

In the evening of the following day, Abner returned. He was given no opportunity to gauge the king's disposition before being summoned to an audience.

At the news of David's continued evasion of Saul's officers, the king was livid. "Where is he?"

Abner held his arms stiffly at his sides. "The officers tried to follow your command, but Samuel…well…they saw Samuel and each threw down his weapons and inexplicably began to rave in the streets. They have been shouting loudly for hours since, my lord."

"Shouting? Shouting what?"

"Unknown things, my lord.… Prophesies, apparently."

"What folly is this?" breathed Saul in incredulity.

"Truth, my lord! Would that you could see it for yourself. None can go near before they are overtaken with the power of God. The prophet pays them little heed and will do nothing to release them from their rambling exhortations."

"Send twenty more officers then!" Saul railed, his consternation seeming to overwhelm his composure.

"Very well, my lord."

Nevertheless, the result was the same. Abner returned his report bashfully. "The same has occurred, my king."

"What? Send the captains, then," Saul growled. "I will not be dis-suaded by tricks!" he vowed heatedly.

However, it was four days later when Abner returned to the compound, no more successful in his mission than on his preceding quests to Ramah. Again he was to attend an audience with Saul empty-handed, yet he could delay no longer. Abner entered the king's presence in doleful silence.

Saul looked up expectantly from his ministrations.

The king's mood was unpredictable at best, and Abner hesitated momentarily before simply shaking his head.

"It is useless!" the commander protested.

Saul glared for a moment, and then bellowed for his chamberlain, "Bring my mantle. This will end today." Abner pictured the once-mighty king under the prophet's indomitable sway, and he muffled a guffaw of doubt under a grating cough. "I shall ready your escort, my king," he informed Saul.

"Go," Saul allowed, receiving his robes from the bowing servant.

Abner watched as the king departed an hour later with a company of five score men as his guard. Abner was left in command. *Would the king not relent before he brought God's wrath upon his House?* Abner sighed in frustration. *Of course not!* There was a spirit of evil about the king, and he was destined to persevere to his own detriment. It had become obvious to most that David had somehow, at some time in his life, been anointed by God. The prospect at first had seemed incomprehensible, yet David's prosperity and fame was not of men. Abner suspected that he himself would be forced to choose between Saul's House and that of David. There would be casualties of the poisonous concoction brewing between these two men, and Abner wished only that the choice would not come too soon. *There is only one sun that rules the skies,* he thought ruefully, *and may it shine upon me.*

＞ ＞ ＞

David trudged the filthy side streets in the town of Ramah. He had spent four days skulking around the city, and at evening watch concealing himself in the stables behind Samuel's lodgings. A glint of the sun off exposed metal made him dart into the shadows, thinking it to be a drawn sword. When he saw that it was merely a copper merchant's wares, he slumped against a grimy wall, the strength draining out of him before he straightened his stance and warily slipped away to a deep alcove. How many more false alarms before Saul's men found him?

For two days now, David had hidden in the dim shadows of an embroiderer's shop off the open court where Samuel prophesied along with other seers from Naioth. He had witnessed the curious debacle involving the second knot of officers commissioned by Saul to find him. The first he had heard of from Samuel. The other he had watched in amazement as one by one, upon entering the court, the men began, with outstretched hands, to proclaim loudly. Their booming voices carried into the shuttered windows of houses bounding the court. Sleep-worn faces poked out, and shutters banged open to investigate the source of the tumult. Men and women strained to untangle the cascade of undecipherable phrases pouring from the lips of the king's officers.

After several hours they had departed exhausted and with reddened faces. These soldiers were men of unimpeachable discipline. Now they were derided openly by passersby. David wished it had not come to this, but neither did he wish himself dead at their hands.

David planned to be more careful than ever, for Saul was certain to send others. He had just begun to approach Samuel when he glimpsed a bulky figure draped in a purple-fringed robe exiting the far lane. He slipped hastily behind a cart piled high with dates that had been set out by an early rising shopkeeper. David recognized Eliel, a gruff captain of the King's Guard. Strangely, as the man neared Samuel, he began a wild cadence that contrasted sharply with the somber soldier whose spoke fleetingly to his men unless he was shouting orders on the battlefield or words to stir their hearts to fight. There were seven captains beside Eliel; for Saul to have dispatched his most worthy fighting men did not bode well for David. Their skill was excelled only by Abner's. David realized then that he would need to leave Ramah. He would—as soon as he had discussed the best recourse with Samuel. That would not be until the following morning, for sometimes Samuel would prophesy throughout the night.

Within the roughly paved square, Samuel was joined by a larger group of true prophets who circumspectly continued their business. They paid little heed to the enquiries of passersby and vendors who remarked idly on the curious scene unfolding under the glowing orb of an unremitting sun. The verbal harangue crisscrossed the courtyard like a tangle of discarded sandal laces.

"You have another student, it seems, Prophet!" cried one tending a cart of scraggly sheepskins.

"The king must favor you, Samuel, to keep sending so many," observed a brawny man tallying beads on a makeshift abacus. "Never a dreary moment in Ramah." His raucous laughter muffled the retorts of his companions.

"A shekel for a prophet these days," lamented a wizened matron. She gave the engrossed soldiers a wide berth and sniffed with displeasure. Samuel, too, ignored the overlapping comments and continued to prophesy as though there were nothing unusual occurring.

David did not understand these events either. Common men prophesying as though unto God? He had never seen anyone other than the prophets, and occasionally an elder, glorifying God in this manner. David suppressed his mirth, for the gravity of the moment did not escape him. YHWH was at work in this, and His reasons were not known to men. It was indeed odd. Yet on reflection, David realized that none of his experience since leaving his father's homestead had been common. His ensuing prosperity and victories had in themselves been extraordinary. He had attributed it all to his anointing several years before. Although, David realized, he had not considered its full meaning nor asked Samuel of its implications for his future. He had merely accepted it as an indication of God's grace, but now he pondered whether his blessing may have some greater import than he had ascribed to it. However, while he was fleeing for his life, he could see small benefit in the token. *I will surely be dead before long....* Pushing the morbid thought from his mind, he hustled on to the stables. He would take each day as it broke upon him and trust his life into the hands of the only Power who could dissuade his executioners; that was YHWH alone.

≈ ≈ ≈

David returned early to the side street purposing to signal to Samuel and depart shortly thereafter. He would ask Samuel's aid in choosing a travel then be on his way. He selected a bustling row where the last trades in popular spices were being made. Finding a position from which he could discretely motion to Samuel, he settled to await an opportune moment. A sudden hush fell over the thinning crowd, and eyes turned simultaneously to behold a man of good stature, lithe and heavily muscled, entering the emptying court. The tall man began to rend his clothes and prophesy loudly before Samuel, who regarded him with a mixture of pity and disdain. David watched in horror as the man tore off his sandals and skirt and prostrated his naked form before Samuel, continuing to prophesy as the others had done. Dust clung to his long hair and puffed away from his lips as they moved unceasing and fervent. Samuel looked up and continued to speak, but David could bear the sight no longer. This was Israel's king—his king—who now lay in the midst of the trodden fruit and discarded leavings of the day's trade, bypassed by peasant and merchant alike. Seeing his sovereign stretched out on the cold earth filled him with a greater dread than he had known previously. The last hope of reconciliation between himself and King Saul would be washed away along with the grime that now covered his belly. When Saul eventually regained his wits, his wrath would be beyond redemption.

If David had not been sure of the depth of Saul's anger before, the certainty of it now lay on him like a pall as he crossed through the gates of Ramah, his fateful flight assured.

≈ ≈ ≈

Saul, Son of Kish the Benjamite, saw his world unravel. In the same manner that he had gained his kingship, he was now losing the authority that he had grown accustom to wielding. He felt it slip away like a bride's closeness at the end of a length embrace. He regretted that he had taken the power for granted. The embrace was another's now, someone younger, more vibrant—and yes, more loyal than he. Power was not a casual trinket, but its familiarity was apt to foster complacence and the expectation that it could be girded on or shrugged off at a whim. But YHWH was not a God given to whimsy, and that had been Saul's downfall. From his first days tasting power, Samuel had cautioned, instructed, and cajoled him to follow the Lord's instructions with diligence. However, as time had passed, Saul had felt his own mastery growing and the intoxication of his own greatness swallowed him up, until today....

Once again, and perhaps for the last time in his life, he would prophesy; but this day would not crown him in magnificence; rather, it would be a jester's coronation. Until this moment, he had retained the full respect of his people and might have still continued as king, but today's spectacle and his uncovered nakedness robbed him of honor. He would be debased in the eyes of the people. He knew that in his disrobing he had been demonstrably stripped of his authority by God.

Another man would rise; a younger, stronger king. He remembered then how Jonathan had robed David in his own princely garments when David had first arrived in his household and how he had been quietly amused by his son's typical generosity of spirit. It had seemed at that time to be David's glorious beginning, but it had in fact been, Saul realized now, his own end.

⤸ ⤸ ⤸

David slipped noiselessly into the armory of Saul's stead shortly after dusk. The peculiar turn of events forced him to retrace his steps in hope of securing a source of aid other than the prophet. He knew he would find Jonathan checking his weapons. The young prince turned as a hand squeezed his shoulder.

"Uh!... David. You startled me! Where have you been? Father has been looking restlessly for you?" Jonathan exclaimed, joyous to see his friend.

"I'm sure he was! Have you not heard?"

Jonathan frowned in bewilderment. "Heard what, David?" A worried look enveloped his face.

"That Saul tried to take my life again, five days ago while you resided in Bethlehem. He attacked me during the feasting hour, again."

"That cannot be so! I would have known! My father keeps nothing from me."

David raised his eyebrows in contradiction. "Do you think I would have deserted Michal on a false pretext?"

"You must be mistaken.... Ah.... Perhaps he was playing a prank or simply trying to scare you. I reasoned with him that last time, and he saw the sense of it, I am certain. There is no reason for him to harm you. It makes no sense."

"I agree, Jonathan, but it is true nevertheless. Your father despises me as if I were a Philistine."

"No! That is unfathomable. He would never..."

"Yes, Jonathan!"

"Why have you returned here then? Are you not fearful that he will find you?" Jonathan asked, his agitation growing.

"He may, but not today. Even now he may still be lying naked in Ramah, prophesying before Samuel. I cast my eyes away and left him there to come find you."

"What are you saying, David? Why would my father be prophesying? And in Ramah furthermore?"

"He went to find me. To kill me; *why else?*" David said incredulously.

"To bring you home, perhaps, to ask forgiveness, even..."

David interrupted him in frustration. "Don't be naive, Jonathan. You love your father, I know. I also wish that it were not so, but I have seen the officers. Eliel was there! Eliel of all people! You know how he loathes petty assignments and loves to shed blood. There is no doubt that they came to seek my life."

"What can I do to help? Ask anything and I shall do it," Jonathan promised with an intensity shared only in a brotherhood that surpassed blood ties.

"At the new moon banquet tomorrow, the king may yet look for me at his table. I will hide again in the lentil field. If he asks, tell him that you gave me leave to go to Bethlehem. You can then see how he responds, but guard yourself. He is likely to be enraged. You will see for yourself."

Jonathan agreed willingly. "David," he said, his voice sounded somewhat melancholy, "make a league with me, that even if we part you shall defend my house as you would me; that it should not be ultimately destroyed.... For who can say what the future holds. Swear it to me."

David made the sincere oath unhesitatingly. Jonathan nodded and embraced him tightly. He stepped back, his face growing dark.

"About this business with Father...Spend three days in the field, and then go to the stone Ezel on the road out. If Father welcomes you back, I will shoot three arrows as though I am practicing, and I will say to the young man with me, 'the arrows are on this side, retrieve them, there is peace.' But if Father indeed desires your life, I will say to the lad, 'the arrows are too far for you, go your way.'"

"All right," David agreed, "I shall wait."

❧ ❧ ❧

On the day and hour appointed, Jonathan approached the far end of the field with his helper. He notched his bow, sighted carefully, and as the lad ran into the field, shot three arrows as though at a mark somewhere beyond the boy. The arrows sang away listlessly in wayward directions. Not at all his usual steady aim, for he took great pride in his dexterity with the bow.

"Haven't the arrows gone too far, boy?" Jonathan shouted to the young man, as he searched the brush. "Make haste, do not tarry."

The boy trotted back immediately, unaware of his contribution to the scheme. Jonathan handed the artillery to him and bade him return to the city. When the boy had departed, David emerged from his hiding place south of the field. He fell on his face and bowed three times before Jonathan. Having to say farewell to David was akin to removing a vital part of himself, and he could see the same struggle on his friend's face. Their bond had grown extremely strong during the years that David had spent in the king's house.

David squared his shoulders. "I feel no vindication at being proven to be right."

The tragedy of the circumstance made Jonathan feel strangely helpless, outmatching any defeat on the battlefield.

"When I told him I had let you go to Bethlehem, my father would have slain me with his javelin. David, he swore at me! He accused me of betraying our family!" Jonathan threw his hands up in disbelief. "The entire situation fills me with shame when I think upon it. It grieves me. I know now that you must go. Father believes that somehow you will prevent me from becoming king one day. Whatever his reasoning, you must go far from here. Do not forget what you have sworn. May God keep us and our families forever."

"Forever!" agreed David. He took up his scrip and bade Jonathan good-bye.

Jonathan stared after him until he was hidden by some distant briars, then turned sadly and retraced his steps to the city, knowing that he was unlikely to be blessed with another friendship as powerful as the one he and David had shared.

CHAPTER SEVEN

The Wrath of a King

Why boasteth thyself in mischief, O mighty man?
The goodness of God endureth continually.
Thy tongue deviseth mischief,
Like a sharp razor, working deceitfully.
Thou lovest evil more than good,
And lying rather than speaking righteousness.
Thou lovest all devouring words,
O thou deceitful tongue.
God shall likewise destroy thee for ever;
He shall take thee away, and pluck thee out of thy dwelling place,
And root the out of the land of the living.

PSALM OF DAVID 52, EXCERPT

A bimelech cast nervously about as if expecting the very shadows to come alive. He wrung his hands for several moments before shuffling toward the young commander who stood at the portal to the sanctuary of Nob. As the priest neared, David willed his features to placidity and leaned casually against the doorpost, hoping to dispel the man's obvious agitation.

"Why are you here alone? Where are your men?" Abimelech demanded, even now glancing over his shoulder.

David was exhausted and hungry. His calamity had made him desperate. He considered telling the priest the truth, but the man was quivering beneath his heavy robes.

"The king has sent me on confidential business." He gestured with a confidence he did not feel as though to say, "Let that be the end of the matter."

Abimelech scrutinized David as though he hoped to read the young man's thoughts clearly scripted across his forehead. Soon David's hunger overcame his patience. "What is it that you have? Give me five loaves of bread or whatever there is to spare."

"There isn't any common bread, only hallowed shewbread reserved for young men who have kept themselves pure."

"We haven't been with women for three days now," David offered disingenuously. "Plus, this is the bread you are removing to replace with fresh hallowed bread, so in a way, it is now common," David reasoned, willing the priest to relent. He had begun to feel faint from hunger. "What about weapons? Do you have anything to hand; a sword, a spear? Anything? I set out on the king's errand in such haste that I neglected to bring my weapons."

Abimelech pursed his lips. "There is only Goliath's sword there behind the ephod. You can have it. There is nothing else here." The sword of Israel's enemy had been stored as a trophy to display to all their supremacy over the Philistines.

"I'll take it," David said quickly. "There is none like it. Bring it to me."

Abimelech hastened to retrieve the sword. David knew the man would not breathe easily until he had departed. Nob was not a town that kept secrets, and David's presence alone heralded trouble. As a precaution he swathed the sword in a coarse cloth and hurried out.

While traversing the forecourt, he felt his hackles rise and glanced back. A shuffling form in dark gray robes moved discreetly at the edge of his vision. The bulky figure hesitated to pull the cowl of his hood close before slipping behind a broad timber column. David squinted in recognition. Doeg! Skulking cur! He was likely to go barking to Saul. David cursed Doeg's name and gritted his teeth in indecision. He did not wish to kill the man in cold blood. He clenched his fists and moved on swiftly. He would pray that Saul's reverence for the priesthood would stay his anger should he discover the source of David's aid. David could neither protect them nor himself should he be caught. He decided to leave it be and left the town in haste. He was eager to put some distance between himself and his betrayer.

Stopping for a rest far outside the city, David devoured the bread. He took sips from the waterskin he had obtained from an itinerant peddler with his last coin. He had scoured the man's cart for any potentially useful items and to his satisfaction, he had also found a faded but sturdy woolen cloak amongst the jumble of goods. He still possessed a signet ring from his father's house and would gladly have traded that for a mule, but he had reconsidered, knowing instinctively that a lone rider would draw too many curious eyes, whereas the sight of one man journeying by foot would be attributed to either poor means or a bout of ill-fortune. Also the ring was distinctive and would be a clear signpost marking his route.

David rehearsed his alternatives as he had done each day since his farewell to Jonathan. He sorely missed his friend and their shared counsel. As he polled his options, he felt the press of desperation, as that of a man discovering his shimmering oasis to be a mirage. In the span of a cock's crow, his once enviable future had been transfigured into a boulder-pocked wasteland, his dreams emptying like the contents of a burst waterskin to be sucked hungrily by the eager ground. He could not kill the king, for not only was he Jonathan's father, but more importantly the Lord's anointed. By the very deed David would both inflame the people and incur the wrath of God, whose retribution would be swift. Further, the loss of such a powerful sovereign would encourage rebellion and incite their enemies to war. And despite his love for David, Jonathan's heart would be torn, for he esteemed his father and his duty highly. All of his options amounted to defeat. The only recourse was to escape Saul's reach, but where could he go? This was his primary stumbling block. There were no walled cities he knew of where he could seek sanctuary. No leader would risk being besieged on his behalf.

After an hour of debating with himself, he had a thought which initially seemed preposterous even in its contemplation, but its sheer absurdity might prove to be his salvation. It seemed to be his only option. He would go to Gath in Philistia. Saul would never seek him there. And if no one recognized him, he would have the opportunity to regain his strength and make better preparations.

"To Gath," he declared. *To the seat of my enemies!*

✺ ✺ ✺

Doeg stood motionless, shielding himself behind the farthest column of the temple, his ears straining to hear the scuffle of sandals on the gritty earthen floor of the forecourt. Nothing. David's return to the courtyard outside the sanctuary would not go unnoticed by him. He strove to discern the slightest pad of footsteps or the scrape of an unsheathed sword. Though he was a herdsman, he was not unskilled with a blade, for times of war made no distinction between any of the king's servants, the poor or the elite. A mattock or coulter, if wielded in familiar hands, was an equal weapon to a sword or spear. He could remember vividly a call to battle many years before when his people had gone to war at Michmash and Gibeah with their ploughshares. Only Saul and his son had possessed swords, yet the victory had been glorious.

Neither was butchering kine for the king's table an insignificant skill. On the days requiring burnt offerings, one could be called to herd hundreds of sheep or oxen to the Temple. As chief herdsman, his deftness at corralling livestock and shearing sheep had made him ropey and strong. But David was specifically practiced in the slaughter of men, and in that Doeg was no match for his precision. Doeg doubted his own accuracy in confronting moving prey. Though Goliath's sword would be bulky in the young man's hands, David was not a sacrificial lamb waiting patiently, oblivious to impending death. Doeg knew he could see himself hamstrung and gutted in a twinkling should he accost this highly accomplished man of war, and he had no inclination to have his bowels spilled in the hot dirt that day.

Doeg waited until the sun had inched farther behind the corner of the building before emerging from his hiding place. Only two women accompanied by small children moved about the street. Each was carrying a water pitcher to be filled at a small well at the center of the town. One laughed gaily at some shared tidbit of conversation. Doeg laughed also but his tone held no mirth. He anticipated that his service to the king should be well rewarded. This was his most promising opportunity yet to gain the wealth that had eluded him over the years. He collected his horse and set out to find the king. As he rode away, he noticed another temple visitor of interest, an older man on his way to see the high priest. It was Gad the seer; a coincidence, perhaps, and then perhaps not. Doeg made a mental note and rode on. Time was running out, and Doeg swore that he would do whatever was required of him. He would not balk at his perceived task or he might ruin his chances to gain the standing he craved. Whatever the cost, he would not be turned aside from his goal.

David's sojourn in Gath promised to be a wellspring of relief. Traders were flooding up the hill toward the city in anticipation of an upcoming festival, and David welcomed the throng. He passed through the gates at dawn, seeking to remain inconspicuous as he mingled with approaching merchants who drove their livestock and carts piled high with wares. He paused to fill his cruse at the cistern and scarcely had time to savor the cool flow of water before an unyielding grip hauled him from his feet. He struggled to gain his footing and to break the hold, but four additional pairs of obdurate hands held him firm. They lugged him unceremoniously through the streets filled with curious onlookers who eyed the unkempt figure floundering helplessly in the grasp of the burly soldiers.

An hour later, David was dragged like a recalcitrant ram through the wide brass-studded gates that enclosed a bustling compound. The sight of a plethora of uniformed soldiers, their stares eager with malice, filled David with dread. His trepidation increased as he recognized the soldiers' destination—a magnificent building on the northern end of the court. Its solid construction and elaborate ornamentation identified it as the king's house. The interior walls depicted murals that captured images from a number of lands—the largest portrayed the Jordan river, its banks abloom with purple thistles, ghurrah and arbutus; a sprawl of cattle flattened the swaths of wild tamarisk that choked the river edge. They passed through two smaller rooms before coming to a heavily paneled cypress door that swayed lazily open to admit them into a two-story hall. Along the longer side of the expansive room sat eleven men arrayed in court finery.

A broad man at the center of the grouping curtailed his speech upon their entrance and moved to the fore to observe the scuffling procession. As the disheveled prisoner was bullied to the foot of his dais, King Achish leaned forward. He stared inquisitively at David, who watched with his head lowered, hoping to be mistaken for an unfortunate straggler who bore a passing resemblance to the veteran enemy of the Philistine war campaigns. His beard was now fully grown and his hair hung limp with dust. David peered between tangled strands of his hair for a source of escape. He was like a man casting his net into the Salt Sea, fishing for a hope that was unknown to its miry depths. No life could issue forth from this poisoned place. He was inexorably trapped.

"My king," the lead officer spoke.

"Who is this?" the king demanded.

"Isn't this David, king of the land?" the commander said excitedly, yanking David's head up by the hair.

David was startled by the reference to himself as king. The incongruity of his circumstance made the claim that much more preposterous.

"Did not his people sing to one another, 'Saul has slain thousands but David his tens of thousands'?" David grimaced inwardly at the praise, which had twice now opposed his cause rather than bringing the glory it intended. Realizing that he was discovered, he wrestled a surge of panic. His heart hammered like a flurry of battering rams as he fought to quell the impulse to bolt.

In a desperate attempt to deceive his captors, David began to mumble incoherently, flailing his head in an awkward cadence. His eyes rolled uncontrollably in his head, and he used the instant of the soldiers' surprise to tear away from their grasp, but it was not escape he sought; he would be cut down summarily before he reached the outer gate. Instead

David drooled on his beard and scrabbled with a long moan at the base of the door. He groveled and trembled with an exaggerated shudder, his limbs thrashing awkwardly. The king's lips curled, his obvious vexation cowing the soldiers who, moments before, had stood proudly with their captive.

David suffered himself the indignity of the denigrating performance for the sake of his life; of what value to YHWH was a proud corpse?

Two of the guards nearest him recoiled in disgust at the odious display. The others looked about uncertainly, hesitating to touch him now. As spittle continued to flow down David's beard, their triumph was translated into humiliation as the king's discomfiture exploded into fury. "Foolish oxen," he railed, standing upon his dais. "Can't you see the man is insane? Why did you bring him do me? Do I need mad men that you have brought him into my presence? Remove him from my house!" he bellowed, his eyes bulging in anger. The mortified soldiers muscled David back through the door and into the outer court. On entering the vibrant sunlight, David feigned distress, clawing the soldiers arms elaborately, resisting their wrenching tugs as though he desired to return to the shelter of the palace yard. Entering the busy market, the soldiers hauled him more forcefully, striving to remove him swiftly from the city, lest the king should question after the laggard's whereabouts.

"Grab his feet, Pelath," the lead guard growled in annoyance. "We will lug him out." Immediately, braced arms jerked his feet off the ground, pinioning them painfully. A stout hand clamped over his mouth to stanch his loud protests. Nevertheless his muffled remonstrance lasted the length of the market, after which he fell silent, allowing the soldiers an easier jaunt.

David's visit to Gath ended abruptly as he was heaved out of the city gate, jarring his limbs. He received a vicious kick to spur his departure. Two of the king's guards were then posted outside to enforce his expulsion if necessary. "Good riddance," one sniffed. "King indeed," the other grunted sarcastically. He spat and ordered the gate to be closed until double light. When David looked back on his trek east, the gate had started to disappear from the edge of his vision. The guards were still standing vigil atop the wall.

↷ ↷ ↷

A mile from Gath David dispelled his assumed bout of insanity and celebrated his narrow escape with a drink of his precious water. Mercifully, the
cruse had not been wrenched from his side. His supply was quickly
diminishing though as the heat sapped his frame. He forged on and discovered a small brook where he could replenish his store. As David traveled the rock-strewn wilderness he considered Jonathan's parting words,
"My father believes that somehow you will prevent me from becoming
king." Saul knew the kinship David felt for his son, that he could not harm
Jonathan as surely as he could not take his own life. David also revised the
soldier's words in Gath. Was it that Saul truly believed he would be king
in his stead? If he was indeed meant to rule Israel, this was a miserable
installment procession. He certainly had never coveted the role, nor enter-
tained aspirations of attaining kingship. He was confident that Samuel
could confirm the answer but he had squandered his only opportunity to
question the old prophet. He now regretted taking such precipitous leave
of Ramah.

While the sun crested the sky, David shielded himself beneath a wide
ledge of rock. He closed his eyes from the fiery brilliance of the noon sun
and instantaneously they popped open in revelation—Adullam. His father
had shown him the site when he was younger. The area with its dispersed
caves was moderately defensible and would serve for a time. David
mouthed a prayer of thanks to YHWH for the inspiration. Jehovah Jireh—
the Lord will provide. David settled back to wait the lowering of the sun.
His burden felt several times lighter.

↷ ↷ ↷

Saul ordered his chariot to a halt in the shade of a gnarled fig tree that hovered piteously beside the dusty roadway in Ramah. The king's frustration
was rapidly fueling his temper as he charted this wild chase to and fro
across this sun-blighted wilderness. He had educed little in the search
among the small villages along the present route. They would proceed a
half day's journey onward before changing course. David might be wily,

but Saul was as persistent as the scouring winds that prowled the wilderness of Judah.

Several leagues outside the city of Nob, Saul's entourage came upon a man driving his horse recklessly. Saul soon discerned that it was one of his scouts, and the realization sparked a sudden hope. Power surged within him as the man reigned in his horse parallel with to the chariot.

"My lord, he has been seen journeying several days hence. He has angled toward the region of Adullam."

Saul nodded in satisfaction, not needing to ask of whom the man spoke. They had been traveling north with speed, expecting to overtake David within a few days, but the pursuit had been fruitless...until today. The certainty that David was within his ambit spurred the king to a murderous passion. He signaled for his servants to assemble before him and stood on the step of his chariot, regarding each with a look of menace that caused the weakest among them to shrink behind the broad backs of more stolid comrades.

"Hear now, you Benjamites!" he bellowed angrily. "Will the son of Jesse give every one of you fields and vineyards, and make you captains of thousands and captains of hundreds that all of you have conspired against me? That not one of you told me that my son made a pact with David and not one of you is sorry for me or would even tell me that Jonathan encouraged David to oppose me and to lie in wait for me? What is David to you that you would protect him in favor of your king?"

Saul's challenge hung like an axe above bared necks, and his wrath sent each man retreating into silence.

Doeg pushed forward through the gathering and stood triumphantly before the king. "I just came from Nob where I saw the son of Jesse petition Ahimelech, son of Ahitub. Ahimelech readily gave him food and fetched Goliath's sword and placed it in his hand." He revealed his news with the air of a man offering a cache of stolen treasure.

Saul seethed in anger. "Fetch me this traitorous priest and his entire house," he exploded. "I will be rid of this treacherous lot today." His fist tightened around his spear, which quivered almost imperceptibly in his grip. The gathered men waited edgily while a company of officers was dispatched to carry out Saul's order.

⌒ ⌒ ⌒

When the captive group stumbled into camp, Ahimelech fumbled toward the forefront, cognizant of the pervading fear seeping through the downcast gathering. He wavered unsteadily under the king's gaze.

"Hear me, son of Ahitub," Saul began in a low whisper.

Ahimelech answered nervously, "Here I am, my lord."

"Why have you conspired against me?" Saul spoke slowly and still softly at first, stabbing his spear into the ground at each syllable. He towered over the small priest, who huddled miserably in his shadow. The king's malignant stare disturbed the priest immeasurably.

"Conspired, my lord?"

"Conspired! You, and the son of Jesse…you conspired against me. You gave him bread and a sword, and prayed on his behalf"—Saul's voice rose to a roar—"that he should rise up against me and ambush me today, even."

"But who is more faithful to you than David, your son-in-law? He goes wherever you send him and behaves honorably in your house! You accuse me of seeking God's face on his behalf? Don't blame me for something I had no part in and furthermore, know nothing of!" Ahimelech's voice grew stronger in defense against the accusation of disloyalty, for he took pride in his service to both his God and his king. But at the priest's recriminatory ire and public reproach, the king's expression hardened into a deadly promise.

"You shall surely die, Ahimelech, along with all your father's house," Saul said coldly. He signaled to his guard, "Slay them! They knew David was fleeing and concealed it in their treachery."

After a stifling pause, Saul turned with a scowl, for all was quiet and not a man was moving within his guard.

"Didn't you hear me?" he growled through clenched teeth. His spear trembled as though he fought not to belay them with it. "I said kill them!"

Still none of the soldiers had set his hand to his weapon for they feared to lay their hands on priests of the Lord more than they feared the king. Saul spun and took a few shocked steps in either direction.

"Am I surrounded by traitors?" he ranted. "You sons of Belial...."

Then his eyes rested on Doeg. He pointed dangerously in the direction of the herdsman. "You! Kill these priests."

At the command, Doeg knew that his moment to exalt himself had at last arrived, and he committed in deed the grievous assault that he had sworn in his heart that he would do if called upon. He drew his sword and attacked the priests who, eyes wide in fear, were too horrified to summon weak legs to carry them out of reach of Doeg's slashing blade which mercilessly cut off their screams. That day, without weapons or the simple knowledge of defense, the priests were as sheep before Doeg.

Seeing his mother fall in a rumpled heap by the well, Abiathar felt his mouth go dry with fear. He hastened through the door of the small Temple, then delayed briefly to bundle his father's ephod under his cloak; the High Priest's robes of office were all he could retrieve of his father's legacy for he had but moments to spare. He hastened to the southern edge of the town. His father had been taken along with the other priests to speak to the king hours earlier, but none had returned. The reappearance of Doeg in the company of thirty soldiers could mean only that his family's deaths had been assured. His mother was beyond his aid and the ensuing slaughter that he had witnessed was beyond his ability to stop.

Abiathar sprinted past his cousin's house and saw his two small children lying facedown in the dirt, long gashes rent in their backs. The ground ran red beside them. Abiathar turned away, retching in horror. In a sheepcote opposite, pitiful cries were bleated out by a ewe in the throes of death. The remains of a small flock littered the floor of the stockade. He had hoped to recover his father's mule from the paddock post, but it too lay with its eyes wide and glazed in death.

Abiathar hurried away, his robe fouled with sour vomit. He clutched his sacred bundle to his breast and melted into the darkness.

A safe distance from the town, Abiathar gasped for breath and slid weakly to the hard earth. The young priest placed his father's ephod beside him. The purple, gold, blue, and scarlet tones of the finely woven garment were muffled by the gloom. The vestments were badly rumpled, a sacrilege that would never have been allowed within the Temple precinct. The onyx stones about the shoulder held the engraved names of the children of Israel; they glinted like innocent eyes in the weak glow of the quarter moon. The names were a symbolic memorial, an apt tribute in the wake of the slaughter visited upon his house.

Abiathar stared unseeing into the night. He recalled a bedtime tale his father had shared with him on several occasions of his family history. "Many, many years back," he would always start, "there was a priest named Eli who served in the Temple of the Lord at Shiloh. He had two sons, Hophni and Phineas, who also served as priests. Unfortunately, they abused their privileges within the Temple—took sacrificial offerings, sometimes by force, and lay with the women congregated outside the tabernacle door. God was angered at their sin and placed a curse on Eli's family, that none would prosper or live to see a ripe old age. God vowed that Eli's line would be cast off from his service. Eli was your great-great-grandfather," he would finish somberly. Then he would chuckle and punch Abiathar's arm good-naturedly, saying, "Let us hope it is really just a story, eh, Abi?"

Abiathar placed his face in his hands and wept bitterly, for his family and for the sin that had brought such a plague upon his line. "Show me mercy, Lord," he whispered. His prayer wafted soundlessly into the endless night to be absorbed by the vast wilderness.

≈ ≈ ≈

Gad the seer unfolded cramped, bloodless fingers from the shaft of his writing quill and squinted into the fading light of the tallow candle. Despite the urgency of his immediate task, he would need to linger to prepare another wick. He laid aside the delicate papyrus scrolls and unfolded his aching limbs. He stood with a groan and massaged his hand gingerly. Rearranging his robes, he exited the warmth of his tent, thinking to relieve his bladder before continuing on.

The night air was crisp and held a strange odor of wood smoke. He was too far out in the wilderness for the scent to be so strong unless… His brow knotted as he gauged the direction of the light breeze that wafted up the rock outcrop. It was almost half night. Gad moved instinctively to the edge of the nearest boulders and peered into the darkness. A faint glow emanated from the opposing ridge more than a league distant. Gad felt the hair rise on his skin. *Nob!* He had departed that town as the sun was at its zenith, his search there having been fruitless—leaving Samuel at Naioth, he had traced David to Nob, but found he was too late; the young man was already gone. It was during his devotions that day that he had received divine instruction regarding David's location. Having worshiped and communed with the priests, he had conducted his trade then started out again. Hours after his departure he had noticed dust rising to mark the passage of a fast-moving party of men, but the direction led them away from his path of travel so he had seen no threat in it. Now he knew that something terrible was amiss.

He scrambled toward his tent and neatly rolled the chronicles, then returned them to their elongated pouch. He uttered a prayer of thanks to YHWH that he had feasted on biscuits instead of building a fire for cooking; so intent had he been on completing the first scroll. It contained several Jasher entries. Others would follow who could update the record, but it was his given responsibility to secure entries regarding the young man.

The ground where he made camp was dusted with loose pebbles. It would make erasing the traces of the campsite much easier. He disassembled the tent within moments for he had grown accustomed to moving in haste. He gathered his provision sack and hoisted the three bundles onto his mount, which shied restlessly. Its nostrils sniffed the air to appraise the danger announced by the smoky air. The smell grew stronger. Gad the seer was no fool. He knew that to continue on his present course would see him apprehended and his throat slit within days of his narrow escape. He praised the mercies of YHWH once again that he had been urged by a wandering trader to exchange his stolid mule for an ugly but reliable mount. He seldom bartered while traversing the desert reaches, but that day the merchant had been unusually persuasive. For that he would be eternally grateful.

He walked the horse down the dry gorge, willing himself not to be impatient with the animal and ruin his chances of evasion through reck-lessness. No. It would not do to be careless now. A lame horse would mean imminent death for both beast and man alike.

He soon broke through the mouth of the solitary ravine and took a retreating course to the city. This would put him back several days but it was necessary given the inopportune turn of events. He was at least two weeks away from the cave of Adullam and prayed that YHWH would con-tinue to shelter the young man until he could deliver his warning. Hopefully he could spare this quarry's life long enough to ensure his des-tined rise to power.

So much had already come to pass. Samuel had succeeded in anoint-ing the boy in secret, but Saul's suspicious nature had discerned some part of the truth. As a result, events had culminated precipitately during the week past to the endangerment of the boy. Saul's jealousy now raged unchecked. Samuel had been sure that Saul would have killed him pre-maturely had the king known that the prophet was planning to anoint a successor to the throne while Saul was yet alive. He had read Saul's heart correctly for the ensuing portents could spell only bloodshed.

Gad sighed wearily. His immediate task was to get the young man out of Adullam and to ensure that a blade did not find his throat aforetime. Gad could not decide whether Samuel's earlier prophecy concerning a king related to this young fellow or to someone else to come. He turned his thoughts back to the journey ahead and settled into his makeshift saddle. Time would tell if David would survive long enough to be crowned. He must press on regardless of the dangers. He kicked the horse into a canter and set his mind on the road, determined not to slack his vigilance until he saw the boy safely to Judah. YHWH would provide somehow for their safety and deliver a way of escape for them all. Gad was prepared to leave it in His hands, for there was naught to do but to continue and to trust.

꙳ ꙳ ꙳

The pursuit, Doeg among them, entered the empty campsite seven hours later. The somber company was led by Eliel, their captain.

"Is it the priest, or another?" Eliel called into the darkness surrounding them.

"No, not the priest. This one had a mount," announced the tracker.

"The prophet then! Which direction is he headed?"

A brawny man with rugged features had emerged at the edge of the torch lit ravine. He was draped in dark robes that hid ample blood stains and the smudges of soot along the hem.

"It is still too dark to say. There are no distinctive tracks."

Eliel hissed in dissatisfaction, and Doeg gripped the hilt of his weapon, aching to sink its blade into their elusive prey. When Saul was told of the presence of the seer in Nob, the king had ordered him found. 'I doubt it is a coincidence that he and David were in the same place. Find him and bring him to me.' The man was long gone though. "We have come this far to no avail!" Eliel said angrily.

"Well, we have but to wait until the break of dawn. We can track him then."

"No. He will be too far afield by that hour." The captain went quiet. "Our lord will be sore displeased," he said finally. "Still, he has others watching along the way. David cannot elude him forever." He wheeled his mount back toward the east. "Come, Doeg. No more can be accomplished this night." His authoritative tone signaled an end to the search, and the band relinquished its quest.

Doeg parted in reluctance. He had hoped to gain the king's favor that night. He was disappointed not to have continued after their quarry, but he would proceed with his own designs. He heeled his mount into a trot then sped to catch up with the company. *There are several ways to pluck a partridge,* Doeg consoled himself.

≈ ≈ ≈

David rounded the hills in Adullam and inspected the depths of the wilderness stronghold with satisfaction. It would suffice. He pressed doggedly through a morass of thorn bushes to gather firewood, surveying the territory as he went and detailing escape routes at need. He was not far from Bethlehem, which lay to the northeast. He decided to go in the evening to find out how his family fared. The thought lifted his spirits, and he was relieved when he saw the sun dip toward its rest. It was harvest time and his brothers would be busy, though there should be a chance yet for a proper greeting, perhaps even supper—David's eyes widened as a terrible understanding intruded upon his joy. At the vision of a banquet in his home, images of King Saul's ill-fated feast resurfaced, drawing gloom about him. He had bargained on having a good headstart to prepare his family for the somber tidings, but he realized abruptly that Saul would not have been sitting idly in his chambers these many days. The king would have dispatched a runner immediately to the nearest garrison. Even now officers could be within a stone's throw of Bethlehem, watching in the hope that David would return home for succor. The cavernous maw of death would expand to envelop those he cherished beyond life as his sanctuary became transformed into a battlefield. His heart thundered with the doom of descending evil. *I shall not endanger my family further!*

Distraught at the prospect of harm coming to his homestead, David devised an alternate strategy. Instead of going into the city, he found a boy in the fields and sent him to his father's house with a short message and a necessary caution. He then returned to Adullam to wait.

Exhaustion overcame him as the stars winked into existence, decorating the night sky with celestial gems. He awoke at daybreak to a clatter of stones outside the hold.

"David!" called a rich, earthy baritone. "David!" came the voice again, a little hesitant. David leaped to his feet in joyous anticipation. He ran to embrace his father and brothers, whose ascent of the slope raised clouds of dust. He peered around them expectantly, worry creasing his brow.

"Don't be alarmed, boy, all is well. Your mother has come also. She would not be kept away. We took extra care in leaving as you requested. The mule was a little slow today, and we took a meandering route through the fields—But come, come! Tell us of these strange happenings. What is this about the king?"

While David recounted his plummet from the king's favor and his harrowing flight across the expanse of wilderness, his mother entered, adjusting her eyes to the darkened interior. She greeted him with a warm smile.

"Raddai and Ozem are on their way ahead of the others. Your older brothers will be along in turn when the light has faded. Your sisters have remained at home until we bid them come. They send their love and your favorite raisin cakes with honey." At his delighted grin, she smiled again. Depositing a basket of freshly baked bread, his mother hugged him tenderly.

"The waterskins are on the mule. I will send a servant with additional rations tomorrow," she promised, squeezing his hands in her own. She set him away at arm's length and inspected him closely.

"Your beard suits you well," she concluded. "Some bread and a little of my home-pressed *asis,* and you shall be hale again."

David nodded, and as his mother busied herself unpacking the basket he motioned for Jesse to come aside with him. He spoke urgently and low. "Father, I am but a step away from death, and you also, if you remain in Bethlehem. Saul is wroth, and his temper flares like the sun. He will surely seek your lives if he cannot have mine."

"But David, we have nowhere to go!"

"I know it will cause Mother torment to leave her home, but you must leave. I have made valuable alliances during my service under Saul. If you shall agree, I will petition Mizpeh of Moab to allow you to come to him until I know what God will do for me. The king is generous, and I believe he will accede. You can all lodge here until then. Please, Father," David implored.

Jesse grew pensive and then agreed. "I will prepare at once."

"Good!" David smiled genuinely. "That is good."

Later that eve, David joined his family in prayer. His spirit was strengthened by their presence.

Before supper, Jesse cleared his throat and addressed them solemnly. "Come, let us fellowship and eat well. There is evil afoot, and we must be strong and ready."

His brothers all nodded in agreement. As the night wore on, David joined in their raucous joviality, revisiting cherished family memories. That night his booming laugh echoed freely off the rocky den, his predicament forgotten amidst the companionship of his brethren. Would that he had his harp, for he would rejoice this hour that overflowed with the mercy of God.

∽ ∽ ∽

David was relieved as news returned of his family's safe journey away from Bethlehem and their warm welcome by the Moabite king. On his way back to the hold, David spent several days scouting the terrain of Adullam. Its rocky glens were harsh but not utterly inhospitable. Closer to the cave, David noticed the displacement of a litter of reddish pebbles he had scattered at the round of a boulder that had rolled off the bluff to settle adjacent to the narrow entrance track. He hesitated briefly. His heart pounded as though to crush the fear that welled within it. Wary of an ambush, he scrambled into a nearby thicket. He forced a calming breath and waited, his ears keen upon the path, seeking signs of movement there or disturbance from above. There was no sound save that of the chatter of a desert bird.

It was an hour before he was in motion again, hugging the ground between the sparse layers of cover surrounding the newfound camp. Over two hundred paces away from his hold, he secreted himself in a cluster of brambles. The berries were dry but evidently edible, for the ground showed signs of quail-pecked remains of the pithy fruit.

Through a wavering mirage, David fixed his eyes intently on the cave opening and noticed the corner of a lapped sandal projecting beyond the cavity in the rock. The seated figure arose, complaining loudly of the heat to an unseen companion. The man's garb resembled the garments worn by the Eznites, but it was the annular pattern of the shield that leaned upright on the wall beside him that held David's gaze; three brass rings broken by large studs were visible clearly even at that distance.

David arose from his hiding place with sudden ebullience. Years embroiled in the chaos of war had taught him the distinctive markings of the tribes, both enemy and friend alike. As a battle raged, the close quarters of conflict could mean the demise of a brother or oneself should you misread the emblems on an upraised shield. There were slim moments in which to distinguish a pattern before a death blow descended.

"Adino," he called out, "Show yourself." A man's towering form enveloped the entrance. He was not a giant but stood several spans above his bretheren. Not a giant—but close in bulk.

"David, you lowly sheepherder! We thought we would never cease your cowardly skulking and come out from behind that bush!"

David ignored the friendly insult. "Confound that eagle eye of yours!" David laughed. Adino's vision was a reputed fact amongst the men who fought on his side. Peculiarly, his keen sight was only in one eye, his right. He was therefore apt to squeeze the other shut to pick out an object on the horizon. Seldom did he make an error when it came to enemy movements and scouting.

"You said 'we'?" David enquired as he closed the distance to the hold.

"I came to find Eleazar already here." Adino said. Eleazar gestured sourly with his spear from the rear of the cave. David looked questioningly at Adino, pondering Eleazar's reticence, for the man was known to be continually full of speech.

Adino shrugged. "His tooth pains. I offered to loosen it with the hilt of my sword, but he refused," the big man joked. "I'll bash it when he is asleep," he whispered conspiratorially to David.

David jabbed his side playfully, "You should be the last to jest. We nursed you a whole season with that ox tooth you broke in a brawl at Zuph during Passover."

"The wretch almost choked me to death. I had to bite him to gain my release. It was my neck on the line, not yours."

David laughed again at the recall of Adino's misery. He turned to see a third man now coming into the light. "Who is this?" he asked.

"Shammah, son of Agee the Harite. He was there at Shochoh. Before your time, lad." Adino slapped David's back. "He's a good man."

"The best!" added Eleazar, his speech slurred with pain.

"He owes a debt in Gibeah of Benjamin. Too much wine and too little work, eh, Shammah?" Adino jibed.

"I plan to honor it." Shammah swore.

"Sure you do. That's why you are here instead of in Gibeah." He crooked an eyebrow at Shammah.

"They were going to have his head a fortnight back when I found him turning tail. On the road out, we met up with an old prophet. Said you would be here. He thought you might be able to use our help, or more so, our muscle. It was not until we passed King Saul pushing north with the speed of a demon that we gave the request any merit. We were glad to be heading in the opposite direction. So, what's your story? Not on the king's business anymore? What? Has the king lost his fancy for the giant-slayer?"

"He thinks that I want his place as king," David complained.

"Well, do you?" Adino inquired.

"No!" David shouted emphatically. "But everyone else seems to want it for me."

"Were you anointed by a prophet or something; given a vision perhaps?"

David raised a protest. "The anointing occurred years ago when I was a boy. The prophet Samuel visited my house with a horn of oil. We had a simple feast of blessing. Surely that couldn't . . ."

"There you go then!" Adino slapped his shoulder as though that settled it. He turned to the others. "Who's with the king?" A chorus of ayes rang out from Adino's companions. Adino's face turned serious as he faced David and made a dramatic bow. "Your servants, my lord."

David threw up his hands in despair. "Which prophet was it?" he asked in retrospect.

"Pardon me?" Adino asked, momentarily perplexed.

"Which prophet did you meet on the road?" David repeated.

"Oh, I don't know," Adino shrugged.

"You don't know? How did you know he was prophet then?"

"He looked like a prophet, and, well, here you are, aren't you?"

David sighed in mild exasperation. "So, what do we do now?"

"We eat, we sleep, we make war. Isn't that how it has always been?"

"Make war with whom?"

"I hear a battle is brewing in Keilah over the raiding of their threshing floors."

"The Philistines again?"

"Of course! Who else would be so vile?"

"Who will make war? Just the four of us?" David mused.

"Why not?" piped in Shammah. "We four are more than enough for those dogs." He spread his hands wide and looked to the others for agree-ment. They nodded with him.

"We shall wait....Scout their numbers. Adino and Eleazar, you will set up a rallying point. Shammah, you will be in charge of securing sup-plies. There are traders plying the route to Bethlehem daily. We shall need a few more weapons also. I shall need a ready sword and buckler myself," David proposed without realizing that he had already assumed the com-mand which he had been granted.

With the aid of his companions, David continued to develop a strat-egy for attack long after the day's crimson light had been erased.

The makings of a king, Adino thought with a knowing smile.

CHAPTER EIGHT

Hunted

My soul is among lions:
And I lie even among them that are set on fire,
Even the sons of men whose teeth are spears and arrows,
And their tongue a sharp sword.
Be Thou exalted, O God, above the heavens;
Let Thy glory be above all the earth.
They have prepared a net for my steps;
My soul is bowed down;
They have digged a pit before me,
Into the midst whereof they are fallen themselves.

PSALM OF DAVID 57, EXCERPT

Over the following days, an influx of men beset by all manner of adversity flocked to Adullam. Their problems varied from general discontentment to the abuses perpetrated by harsh masters, unfair levies, and even harping wives. Many were deep in debt, like Shammah, and in danger of imprisonment or execution. The bond of shared adversity created a union of brotherhood, and hundreds of men rallied to David's side as word spread of the haven for the dispossessed under the leadership of a new king. It was this, amongst other salacious rumors that flew to Saul's ears, that kindled his wrath and impelled him along his murderous course. The stripling would never rule.

≈ ≈ ≈

Gad the seer set his jaw grimly. Mounts were of little aid across the scarred and craggy terrain of Israel, but he had needed the initial speed of the beast to outdistance his pursuit. Still, two weeks on he remained encompassed by the unforgiving wilds. His horse had grown lame as the result of an inopportune fall during a precipitous decent from the rocky plateau five leagues away from his destination. Though his feet were severely blistered, he could not risk delay. He pressed his lips together and resumed his determined plod toward Adullam.

≈ ≈ ≈

The scout still kept his eyes trained on the hazy expanse, yet no rider had passed the narrow road for the day. He had seen neither prophet nor priest in his long vigil. He would wait for the king and rejoin the escort on its way back in. He stood from a crouch to stretch his stiff limbs. Perhaps he would be granted leave to go to his family in Jerusalem at the end of this tedious search. "Well, until then...." He sighed in resignation and squatted to dutifully continue his watch as the lowering sky took on tones of iridescent pink.

≈ ≈ ≈

"You have another visitor," Adino announced to David, squinting into the shimmering mirage that blanketed the parched plain. His hand shielded his eyes against the harsh glare. "This poor fellow is either lame, aged, or both," he qualified after a hard look.

David broke off the discussion he had been conducting with his new officers, checking tallies and supplies. As the number of men seeking refuge had swelled beyond ten score, David had appointed leaders to maintain order and delegate work. Adino, the most experienced and skilled of the lot, served as his captain. With war pending, it was essential that David establish an order through which he could assign roles to each of the men and thereby maximize their talents. Some were thieves and brigands. Even they would prove useful as spoilers if war was launched. Already, their rations were depleted. They had only three ephah of parched corn and one homer of quail to serve the band of men, though figs and raisins were plentiful.

David stood at Adino's side. He could not make out the shape for several minutes. The man's path did not deviate but arrowed directly toward them.

"Izri! Matthiah!" David called to the men and jerked his head in the direction of the wanderer. "Take some water and ashishah. He'll need it."

The pair moved immediately to retrieve a mule from the makeshift corral. They departed to greet the stranger and render aid. David tracked the men's slow return to the hold. Their progress was halting for their guest lurched in the saddle with each step of the mule, and finally he slumped about the animal's neck. Izri then held him steady while his companion guided the beast.

As the trio drew nearer, David recognized the slumped figure as that of a prophet who had spoken with Samuel at Ramah. Samuel had mentioned the meeting only briefly and had noted the old man's name—Gad the seer.

Moments later, David stooped beside Gad as he rested on a mat within the hold. He was not heartened by this newest arrival, knowing that it would mean an added twist to his fateful flight. He was discovering daily that his life was not directed by chance. YHWH was guiding his footsteps and he would be remiss not to follow. The sun sank low below the brow of the hill and cast an orange glow over the landscape. David examined the large, scurfy blisters on the seer's feet. *Severe times require severe measures,* he thought.

"Let him rest," David ordered. "Summon me when he awakens."

David knelt alone in the fading light. He felt moved toward the plight of Keilah, but did the Lord will it? He could no longer waver in indecision. He bowed his face to the ground in prayer. "Shall I go and smite these Philistines?" he inquired. "The men fear it will go hard on us and warn against inciting the wrath of our enemies beyond Judah. Knowing this, shall I go down?"

The answer returned as a whisper: *Go, and there will be victory.*

"Your servant will go," David asserted, pushing upright. His doubt was now erased. "I will go."

He returned to the hold to make final preparations for the war. A victory might be promised, but it still must be won. A complacent man in war was a fool, and a fool on the battlefield would meet ready destruction.

᠀ ᠀ ᠀

When Gad at last awoke he called out, and David hastened to his bedside. The seer quietly issued the warning he had been given.

"Leave Adullam," David mused. "Now?"

"Yes. By the evening watch," Gad insisted calmly, his voice even and assured.

David rubbed this temples. "So soon. Where to then? You see how many men I have here."

Gad glanced in the direction of the grouping who observed the exchange in grave silence.

"The forest of Hareth," Gad suggested.

David mapped out the course mentally and made a decision. "The forest it shall be, then," he acquiesced, pleased with the suggestion. "The concealment of the glade will be a welcome alternative to this blistering sun." He was glad to know that his family was already safely ensconced in Moab.

"We will leave immediately. Shammah, your men gather the supplies. Eleazar, take your unit on. We have a long march ahead of us."

᠀ ᠀ ᠀

Despite their disruptive relocation, David pursued his plans for the war against Keilah and made his attack shortly after the men had resettled. The Philistine garrison was routed within the premier stages of the battle. David was relieved not to have required an extended siege against the fortified town. Servants within the city rendered aid to David's company when they saw the assault on their enemies begin. Entrance was gained and David's tight-knit units marshaled to assail the outer perimeter where enemy soldiers defended the gate, seeking to shore up the breach. The Philistines' efforts went unrewarded, for they were pinned against the fortifications and could neither retreat nor advance. David's well-trained band gained the upper hand as a result of relentless sorties against the heavily armed men whose ranks dwindled steadily. David's men, however, suffered few casualties and continued to erode the strength of their nemesis.

The victory was almost bought at an invaluable blood price when, amidst the fraying cordons of battle ranks, David found himself cornered in a side street as he hastened to deliver orders to his last deployment. He shouted urgently to a group of his soldiers fighting in a mobile attack. Two such groups of men had been dispatched to support flagging comrades wherever they were to be found, and to David's great relief he had drawn the attention of Adino's troop and no better aid could be found in the ravages of war.

Adino slashed his way through the attacking soldiers who harried David's flank. "Not much longer," he grunted with the effort of cleaving a clear path. He reached his liege's side within moments, clubbing the closest of the combatants with his studded arm bracelets.

David relinquished his command to Adino and fought through the widening gap to rally the other companies and to detailed assignments to his other captains. Spoilers were dispatched to herd the Philistine cattle and plunder their supplies. Hours into the night, the spoils continued to be gathered and distributed.

David washed the blood and grime from his face and hands. Sweat stung the cuts on his face and arms. The scars would be negligible compared to this victory. He oversaw the waning scenes of resistance and settled into the task of delegating men to search the houses for hidden enemy soldiers.

The war had gone as God promised.

꿈 꿈 꿈

As the moon ascended to rival the pulsing torchlight that flushed the streets, Abiathar dragged limply through the main gate at Keilah, sickened by the ravages of the recent war and the corpses piled high outside the fortifications. News of the war had spread quickly, and Abiathar had diverted his course from Adullam hoping to reach Keilah before David set out again. He understood that King Saul would be hoping to pin his quarry within the city, just as David had done with the Philistine garrison.

Clutching the ephod protectively, he headed toward the town square, knowing that the troops would congregate there before moving out.

≈ ≈ ≈

David was numbering his men when he noticed the arrival of the forlorn priest. He broke off, leaving Shammah to complete the head count.

"Abiathar," he greeted the man. "What news? What are you doing away from the Temple?" David recognized the garment that was folded reverentially under Abiathar's arm, and his blood ran cold. "What of your father?" he asked in trepidation, though he knew in his heart what he would hear, for Gad had mentioned the flames that lit the night sky weeks past, precipitating the seer's anxious flight.

"King Saul. He murdered everyone in Nob, even our livestock. My father was taken away along with all the priests to see the king. None returned. A man saw you talking to my father. It was—"

"Doeg!" David finished. "I knew the day that Edomite was there that he would surely inform Saul. I have caused the deaths of all the persons of your father's house," he mourned. "Remain with me and do not fear. The man who seeks your life seeks mine also. I will protect you."

Abiathar nodded.

With a heavy heart, David left him in the care of Eleazar and spent the night completing his rounds.

≈ ≈ ≈

David had planned to stay in Keilah for a few weeks while his men regrouped, but if Abiathar had learned of David's whereabouts, so too had Saul. The priest had reasoned the same. The king would be plotting mischief against him, and he could not risk being cornered in Keilah. He sent for Abiathar.

"Bring the ephod," he instructed. Morning was breaking and he would need to move swiftly if his suspicions were accurate.

While Abiathar rubbed the vestiges of a brief sleep from his eyes and girded himself in the ephod. David knelt on the cold earth, praying softly. "God of Israel, your servant has heard that Saul may seek me in Keilah to destroy the city for my sake. Will the men of Keilah surrender me and my men into Saul's hands? Will Saul come down as I have heard?"

The answer came clearly, and without delay.

They will deliver you to him.

David was sorely grieved by the prospect of this betrayal by men he had risked himself to deliver, though he knew that fear often drove men to commit heinous acts to secure their own salvation. But of what use was it to mourn the fickleness of the people. If he was called to lead, that he would do. He would disband until they could find safer territory.

David arose and called to his captains.

"Get your men. Permit them to take whatsoever they have earned of the spoil and depart. Saul is on his way here and each must go his own way. They stay at their own peril."

~ ~ ~

Saul learned of David's departure from Keilah the same afternoon and cancelled his plans for assaulting the city. It would be a useless endeavor, and he wanted to be assured of David's capture. There were already mumblings of admiration for the upstart's propensity for eluding his noose. In addition, his victory on behalf of Keilah was garnering further support for his rebellious cause. The young man's poison was continuing to seep through the life blood of his servants.

I must find a way to halt its course—I will put a stop to his menace. You may run, but I will find you again, boy. I will find you anywhere.

~ ~ ~

For weeks David tacked back and forth between strongholds until he arrived at the mountain of Ziph. There, Jonathan met him. He had learned of David's presence through a servant who was returning from the city, which lay far south in Judah, and set out to find David under the pretext of journeying to Hebron. At his camp in a wood in the wilderness, David greeted his friend with unsuppressed elation.

"Do not worry," Jonathan confided. "My father shall not find you." He sealed his bond with David and said solemnly, "You shall be king over Israel, and I shall be at your side. My father knows it."

David clasped his hand tightly. "Thank you, Jonathan." He could say no more. "Thank you."

※　※　※

Saul was in Gibeah when an audience was requested by two men arriving from Ziph. They were brought to Saul's chamber.

"Speak your purpose."

"If you wish to find David, he is presently in Ziph, lodging in strong-holds in the wood on the hill of Hachilah."

"Where is this?" Saul demanded, leaning forward from his chair eagerly.

"South of Jeshimon. If it is your desire to capture him, we will deliver him to you as our part."

"Blessings on you," Saul said in gratitude. "You have compassion on me. What I need you to do first is to watch him. Find out where it is exactly that he goes, for he is a subtle man. I will find him even if I have to search the thousands of people throughout Judah!"

※　※　※

David's fortuitous escape to the mountains of Judah had proved no deter-rent to King Saul. David learned of this betrayal by the Ziphites and his imminent capture just in time to flee the woods. He fled to Maon on the rocky plain south of Jeshimon couched in bleak pasturelands. Neither did this dissuade Saul, who had made preparations to snare him.

David was reeling from the intensity of the frenzied chase. His men had regrouped and now stood by him, but the strength of the king's malice seemed redoubled, and the band was hard-pressed to stay out of his range.

David's desperation compelled him to demand a reckless pace of the men, making it possible for the fleeing company to outdistance Saul, who,

David's scouts told him, foundered momentarily in his pursuit across the perilous terrain.

Unable to sustain his momentum, the king calculatingly split his troops to create a human vice propelled by the two arms of his force. David could feel the trap closing inexorably around them, and as the men trammeled incautiously across the rocky ground, he prayed for divine aid. They were lost otherwise.

∽ ∽ ∽

Saul was hell-bent on encircling David's position that very day. And so he was incensed to find a messenger waiting outside his tent flap. What news could be so grave as to command his attention now, hours from victory? The messenger at first shuffled uncomfortably at the heat of his king's unspoken displeasure but quickly collected himself and delivered his report.

"My lord—the Philistines; they have taken advantage of your departure to mount an invasion. Abner requests your assistance as soon as you can return."

Saul gritted his teeth—*I am so close!* He balled his fists, chagrinned by the ill-timed diversion. *But to stay will be to jeopardize my entire kingdom,* Saul lamented. The Philistines cared nothing for his personal desire to crush a renegade.

It is not worth the price, he determined in frustration. *I must withdraw.*

∽ ∽ ∽

The near capture and increasing ferocity of Saul's pursuit mortified David. Yet again he must find another refuge. After considerable deliberation, he settled on the Engedi that lay on the west shore of the Salt Sea. The plain, though not vast, was rich and fertile. It was watered by a spring flowing from a high ravine which lay a Sabbath Day's journey landward. The plain sloped gently up to the base of mountains where the men could retreat at need.

Discouraged by the ever-present pall hanging over his waking moments, David consulted Adino to elicit an alternative point of view.

"Why this merry chase across this sun-baked wilderness—running the length and breadth of Israel? Will there be no surcease? No mercy? I was certain he would have given up by this juncture. What could this all be for?" he asked in a rush of questions.

Adino's lips twitched as he considered the dilemma. "Perhaps you are to learn how to be king. Must a king not know his people intimately—the truth of their nature, the disposition of his lands? Are these not the lands for which you will go to war? Will these men you encounter, these Ziphites, these men of Keilah—will they not be your servants? Those who aid you and those who betray you? Take courage as you have before. We will prevail. Maybe it will go better for you if you imagine this rigorous chase to be a royal introductory expedition with a hectic schedule," he suggested with a rough chortle.

"Cheer up, David. We are free men. And we are in God's hands, are we not? Besides, I found you something. We shall not be able to lug the confounded thing about with us, but tonight—*tonight*—we will sing a festive song, yes!" Adino disappeared into his tent and returned with a large bundle. He rested it gently at David's feet. The shape betrayed its identity, and David's heart leaped in joyous thanks. He tenderly unwrapped the harp and lightly strummed the strings. Soft music cascaded from the taut cords. A few men congregated at the sound of the vibrant melody and by midnight the camp was filled with clamorous singing. *Our joy is of the Lord,* David reminded himself. He would persevere and win his deliverance.

꙰ ꙰ ꙰

David's opportunity for retribution against Saul arose with such simplicity that David was convinced that the gift of Saul's life had been presented to him as a test of his faithfulness to the tenets of YHWH. Three thousand men followed Saul into the wilderness of Engedi, aiming to search the splattering of caves strewn across the landscape like flies on a moldy loaf of bread.

They approached a cluster of smaller caves to the south of the massive rock formation. The king dismissed them as unlikely strongholds for David's men since the entrances were low and cumbersome to access. But it was for precisely this advantage of defense that David had chosen these recesses. Deep in the interior they had found interlinking tunnels which honeycombed to provide connections to alternate caves. Some also exited on the rear face of the hill, thereby providing a series of viable escape routes.

At morning watch Saul ordered a halt, and his men set down their weapons and packs to find waterskins or shake grit from their sandals. David and his men receded into the seclusion of the inner cavities. They muffled their weapons against their skirts lest the tiniest clink reveal their presence. David, Adino, and Eleazar watched along the scope of a long tunnel of a side-cave as a tall silhouette crouched low to bypass a protruding overhang and search for a private cranny away from the cave mouth to relieve his bowels. David almost cried out when he felt the tight pressure of simultaneous grips of both his arms; his companions on either side of him released their holds and inhaled sharply as they beheld the stooped figure of Saul, alone in the vault, his back to a side-hole on the right of the tunnel.

Adino tugged his arm excitedly and motioned to the cave nearest Saul's position; its passage wound in a curving arc to another access behind them.

David grasped Adino's intent, but he was certain, as sure as he drew breath, that to kill Saul would contradict the will of YHWH. Samuel had been fervent, even heated in conveying to David the import of an anointing sanctioned by God.

"Don't be fooled," the prophet stressed with an urgency that had startled the innocent boy fresh from the sheepcote and now to be anointed by a prophet of the Lord. He had been excited, overwhelmed to be sure, at being the only one of his brothers to be selected.

"Do not become your own judge, David. God is the final judge of all men, and what He has chosen as His own, one can oppose at one's peril."

David had taken Samuel's warning seriously then, and its gravity struck him still. He quietly circled the cavern to the dark recess adjacent to Saul and stealthily sliced a piece from Saul's skirt. The garment parted noiselessly under the razor-sharp blade. David slunk back into the shadows and moments later, Saul fixed his garments and exited the cave.

Adino was incensed. He vented his anger when the soldiers had moved on.

"Why didn't you kill him?" he railed. "You could have ended it right then. What possessed you to leave your enemy to go free, free to spill your blood, our blood?"

David waited until his tirade subsided. "The Lord forbids that I should do this! He is still my master and the Lord's anointed," he added emphatically. "I cannot—I will not hurt him, for he is anointed by God. No one is to hurt him!" he said with a finality which swept away any remaining vestige of opposition.

David turned abruptly and traced the cavern run back to the exit through which Saul had departed. He was still haunted by the abruptness of the transformations: a surrogate father turned nemesis, his plummet from meteoric fame to beggarly dereliction and an existence hounded by turmoil. Nevertheless, he regretted even having cut Saul's robe—it was an unnecessary slight meant to humiliate the man, but it was also akin to touching the king himself. David's mere presence in the proximity of the cave would have borne the same message—that he had no intention of harming his king.

∽ ∽ ∽

Silent as an apparition, he emerged from the darkness and called after Saul.

"My lord the king."

Saul whipped around in astonishment, and David bowed to the earth.

"Saul," he shouted again. "Where did you hear that I was seeking to hurt you? Today, you see with your own eyes that I could have killed you in the cave. Some bid me to kill you—but I spared your life. I will not raise my hand against my lord, who is anointed by God. Furthermore, look at the piece of your robe am holding. Yet I did not kill you. It should be obvious that I have no evil intent against you. Yet you hunt me to take my life. God will judge between us and avenge me, but I will never harm you. Who are you pursuing Saul, king of Israel? I am but a flea! The lord will plead my case and be my judge."

"Is it truly you, David," Saul cried, weeping. "You are a better man than I. You have recompensed my evil with good. Today I know that you have not borne me ill will, or you would have killed me as any man would his enemy. Now I know that you will truly be king of Israel. Only, swear that to me that you will not wipe out my house."

"I swear it," David declared gravely.

Saul dipped his head in acknowledgement. "Turn about," he commanded his men.

David watched as they redeployed northward, then he returned to the hold.

⤢ ⤢ ⤢

The following year, David received word of Samuel's death. The ignominy of his continuing exile along with his grief angered him. He would be unable to journey to Ramah to participate in the prophet's burial. David had listened to Saul's words of grace, but he had also recognized the hollow look of resignation about the king. Saul's recent repentance was also destined to be short-lived. The king had committed himself irrevocably to a course which he would not relent from though it would precipitate his own destruction.

David's conclusion was borne out when he received news that Saul had given the hand of Michal, David's wife, to another. His sister, Zeruiah, had dispatched her son, Abishai with the unwelcome news.

"When did this happen?" David asked his nephew.

"It was several weeks ago. My mother thought you should know. She said you would not take it well!"

"She was right. I should have expected this. The daughter of a king is too valuable to be kept sitting around. The dowry alone would be a tempting incentive." David exhaled slowly. "This could only mean that Saul counts me dead already. The silver lining is that I know now that he will be returning to seek my life, despite his false show of penitence. He has hardened his heart. So be it!"

David had no option but to remain in the south. It was a decision that resulted in a situation tragic and just. Having occupied wilderness strongholds throughout the region, David's company had grown familiar with the merchants and husbandmen regularly traversing the plains. Unlike the typical bands that roved the wilderness and resorted to marauding or extortion, David's men, under his direction, conducted themselves honestly.

"We should behave as though we were guests," he said to the assembled men, now six hundred strong. "If our hosts become displeased at our presence, where shall we go? Let us not abuse their hospitality."

And as such, they abided peaceably with their neighbors. At times they would defend the land within which they dwelt, and as a result of this regard for their neighbors, David's men received tokens of gratitude from the farmers and tradesmen. Most often, they received provisions in exchange for their considerate stewardship. Owing to this short but amiable history, on a day of feasting, where the informal custom was to share with the needy, David requested a gift from the master of a particular group of husbandmen that operated in Carmel.

He asked ten of his young men to greet Nabal on his behalf and request any token that he would grant, however small.

"Let Nabal know how well we have treated his men and have safeguarded his possessions." he told them. "Ask him to give whatever comes to his hand."

The ten young men left camp at twilight and returned shortly thereafter, empty-handed. Their faces showed both disappointment and anger. David met them outside the hold.

"What happened? Was he away from home?" he asked in bewilderment.

"No." responded Sacar, the eldest of the group. "He was not."

"He insulted us!" exclaimed Sacar's brother.

"What did he say?" David could feel his face darkening.

"He railed at us. He said he did not know you and that he was not about to take provisions that he had for his men and give them to people he did not know;" said Sacar, incredulously.

"After all we have done—that a man could be so selfish," another piped in.

"And on feast day, at that," continued Sacar.

"He lost nothing of his," David growled, "And he returns our favor with ill will? I swear, not one thing belonging to Nabal will be left by morning. Adino! Eleazar! Rally your men! It seems we have protected this ingrate's possessions in vain. Every man retrieve his sword!" David shouted. "Shammah, stay here with your company."

The four hundred men made ready with their usual deftness and began there descent to Nabal's house.

❦ ❦ ❦

Abigail entered from the bustle of the rear kitchens. She noticed Nabal's foul mood but said nothing. Her husband's temper fired hot most days. Today she preferred not to suffer his loud raging and splenetic outbursts. The meal preparations were almost complete. Still, she returned to the kitchen to avoid sparking an argument.

"Mistress, one of your master's servants is waiting in the pantry to speak with you," indicated the chambermaid.

"Who is it? Is it Jehiel?"

"Yes, Mistress."

Abigail entered the pantry to find the young man pacing.

"Mistress, an hour ago, David sent messengers out of the wilderness to greet our master, and he literally flew upon them. These men have treated us well whenever we are in the fields. They assure that we remain safe. Our master, he is so—so stubborn—that no one can say anything to him. Now all of us are in danger unless you can think of something to change this. David has six hundred men, Mistress. Six hundred! I believe something horrible will happen to our household." Jehiel's forehead drew into a deep pucker, and he clutched his robes.

Abigail's darting eyes told of a frantic search for a remedy. She ran to the storeroom. "Jehiel! *Quickly!* Bring a mule to the door of the storehouse. Dinah, leave the stews and make haste. Horeb, wrap the lamb that we have already dressed. . . ."

"But Mistress, these are for the feast."

"Forget the feast, Horeb, this is for our lives."

Horeb blanched at Abigail's tone but complied without further delay.

"Dinah! Put that bread over there in sacks."

"All of it? But—"

"*Do as I ask, Dinah!*" Abigail reiterated forcefully. "Carry it out to the mule. Jehiel will be waiting."

Abigail dragged a pallet bearing raisin clusters to the door and returned for two of their finest skins of wine. Horeb completed his task of strapping the lamb to the mule and he asked, "Anything else, Mistress?"

"Yes, collect the sack containing the fig cakes. "There, Horeb!" She pointed to the rear of the storehouse. "*Hurry!*"

"Dinah, bring five measures of parched corn from the side selves."

Abigail ran outside to the mule, where Jehiel waited. "Find your brothers and go on ahead of me. Go!"

Jehiel sprinted away, calling for his brothers.

Abigail climbed atop the mule, urging Dinah to settle the seahs of corn and readjust the sacks to make room for her to sit. She set out after the young men, taking a path through the orchard to avoid seeing Nabal. The mule moved slowly, its gait ponderous. Abigail kicked its flanks, hoping to urge a bit more speed from the animal. She prayed that the provisions were ample enough to appease David. She would have offered more but the mule was overburdened as it was. She came down the hillside just as David's men appeared beyond. When Abigail saw him, she alighted and fell prostrate at his feet.

"Let this wrong be on me, my lord. On me alone! Let your servant speak to you; please, hear me. Pay no attention to Nabal. He is in truth a fool, just as he was named, but I, your servant, did not see your messengers. The Lord has allowed you to spare us. Please accept the gift I have brought for your men, and forgive this trespass. Your house will continue to be blessed as you have been thus far; although your life is sought, God will protect you against your enemies. Do not let this be on your conscience when you become king. You need not shed innocent blood. When you have dealt with my husband, remember me, your servant."

When she looked up again, David was listening intently. his countenance softening with each word that she spoke.

He inclined his head at her. "Blessed be the God of Israel who sent you to me today and stopped me from committing murder, for so help me, if you had not come, I would have extinguished everything that pertains to Nabal. Go in peace."

≈ ≈ ≈

Abigail returned home to find her husband feasting like a king. He was drunk, so she said nothing to him until morning. As he put on his robes, she stood looking out the bedchamber window.

"Do you recall those men whom you sent away so ungraciously yesterday?" she asked quietly. "Their leader, David, returned with his men to kill you while you feasted. He said he would have murdered the entire household had I not intervened and brought him a peace offering.

Abigail, not hearing a response from Nabal, turned to regard him. He lay slumped on the bed, one sandal yet unstrung. She came over to his side and prodded him gently, realizing that his chest had ceased to rise and fall. She hurried from the room and sought the chief servant.

"Fetch Abijam, and prepare a bier. Your master is dead." She sighed ruefully, thinking how much she disliked wearing black. She pondered a different future where her husband had fulfilled the potential of his youth, becoming the leader he had promised to be, instead of being blighted by anger and greed. She had supported him in spite of his waywardness. There had been no need for it to come to this. Now, without an heir, Nabal's line was ended. He was ineffective in his household, yet he was its only head, and without him the family legacy would perish. The tragedy of his wasted years made her weep far into the night.

≈ ≈ ≈

"God returned Nabal's wickedness on his own head," David stated grimly when word came of the man's sudden demise. David considered the information then nodded introspectively. The loss of Michal had been a blow, yet he decided to take the initiative and establish his own future and family name.

"Joreb, I have a message to be delivered to the mistress of Nabal's house." David spoke at length to his footman, whose volubility qualified him for the delicate task, then dispatched him, satisfied that he had acted honorably, and in the process had attained a formidable blessing.

"Adino," he shouted happily, "gather the men. I have a banns to call and a wedding banquet to prepare!"

⌒ ⌒ ⌒

David himself possessed little adornment ahead of the proscribed day of the wedding. As it would be his second marriage, as custom allowed, he chose to wait only days before formalizing the bond of marriage. While abiding in Saul's court he had waited in excess of a year for the marriage contract with the king's daughter Michal to be sealed. The first arrangement to wed Merab had been a sham, David had discovered later. Still, he thought he had triumphed over the king's deception at the last. Michal was a prize worth winning, even though he had been denied his bride by his turn of fortune. Now, time was a precious resource given the exigency of his current circumstance. There was so much that could change within moments.

Despite the simplicity of his preparations David expected the day to be one of his finest. He could not supply the traditionally lavish feast; nevertheless he was pleased that the camp supplies were sufficient to toast the day.

Today David wore a new robe that Adino had purchased in a nearby town. He had also returned beaming with a pair of ornamented slippers as a gift for the bride.

"They are very like the ones presented to my mother on her wedding day," Adino explained. "As a boy I came upon them stored safely in a small cupboard in her bedchamber."

"These are perfect! Izri and Matthiah will present the gifts and also escort Abigail here. They are my best footmen." David himself had sourced a bolt of fine linen and a slender silver bracelet as presents for his new bride. The bracelet was decorated with finely turned palm leaves.

His men welcomed the hub of activity generated by the imminent union. With more sentimentality than David could have thought possible for such an avid man of war, Shammah had even woven a crown of myrtle leaves for the bridegroom.

Recognizing their increased joviality, David was forced to impress upon the watchmen the increased need for vigilance since many a feast had ended in bloodshed. Unwary celebrants were wont to be cruelly slaughtered amidst their festivities. Today he intended to be even more fastidious in his defense. David called to Shammah, who had deposited his token on a rock shelf and begun to depart.

"Shammah, find Eleazar. He is in charge of the perimeter today. Have him set a double guard and send out three early scouts. The men will not be pleased to be awarded extra duty; nonetheless someone must safeguard the camp. Have the captain inform them that they shall be given three days reprieve afterward, but today… Today I take no chances."

Abigail reveled in the heady scents emanating from the luxurious bath prepared specially for the extraordinary day. Her handmaid left briefly to retrieve a tiny earthen jar of spikenard from the hall closet where an array of perfumed ointments and rare spices were stored. She returned and placed it on a small table where selected oils awaited her mistress's preparation and veiling.

Abigail cast her eye over the treasured assortment. The traders in Carmel stocked some of the finest creams and unguents. While attending sheep-shearing in the city, Jehiel would keep his eye out for traveling merchants carrying the unique blends. He would often run small errands on behalf of his mistress since Nabal had seldom permitted his wife the opportunity to leave their estate. It was indeed a new day. She exited the fragrant water and toweled her skin lightly, appraising the extra smoothness of her skin; the further softness was induced by the suffusing warmth of the bath and an infusion of emoluments selected specially for the occasion. Her handmaid moved to spread the aromatic oils gently across her shoulders. Her varied stock of liniments, garnered over several years, had been costly to attain but there was no circumstance more deserving of their use than the one at hand.

Dinah had made her a chaplet of sweetly scented henna blossoms and leaves. Abigail's heart smoldered with a new fire that had been lost since the second year of her marriage to Nabal, whose violent moods had quenched the flame of her youthful desire. Now it was alight again.

She returned her thoughts to the task at hand as her handmaid brushed her waist-length hair with balsam oil, her artful sweeps rearranging the long tresses into one glistening swoop.

"You are radiant, mistress," her handmaid stated in satisfaction.

Abigail nodded in acknowledgment of the compliment.

"I hope my husband-to-be will be equally impressed," she said. A slight shiver coursed through her body. She was experiencing a sudden bout of nervousness, though it was more so due to excitement than apprehension. She had not even a hint of reluctance. The marriage proposal had been delivered honorably and with as much aplomb as the noblest courtier. No woman could have asked for more. She would be marrying a man of both stature and might, and further, it was clear that he had been blessed by YHWH. He was destined to rule Israel. She knew it deep in her breast. In a few hours her life would be irrevocably changed.

≈ ≈ ≈

Near midmorning, David watched Abigail's arrival, along with her two handmaids. She was not the daughter of a king, but her resplendence that day captivated him. At their initial meeting, she had been unadorned, wearing a brown rough-spun dress. Today, she had donned a lilac linen robe accentuated by a crisp white shawl. A fine silver rope was braided into her hair and reflected glimmers of sunlight. Her beauty called to him like a fig tree in flower on a desert plain.

She walked within four paces of him, her genuflection graceful and poised. David approached and took her hand, gently raising her to her feet. He looked over the wave of men that had gathered at the base of the hill selected as the greeting place. Their faces wore broad smiles to match the rare joy of the day.

"My future wife, Abigail," David announced, raising her hand high in his. The host of men erupted into a boisterous cheer that echoed off the dell. The din of their celebration began as the sun dipped toward the horizon, and lasted for hours into the morning.

≈ ≈ ≈

David was uncertain how much longer he could remain in Hachilah. He had taken another wife since his marriage to Abigail. He began to consider the ramifications of having two wives with child should flight become necessary once again. He could be compelled to hide them within the city while he escaped. Still, he could not trust their safety there if coins were all he could offer to buy their protection. A man with more coin to his name could as easily purchase their deaths. His second wife, Ahinoam of Jezreel, was younger than Abigail but less hardy. Neither would fare well should he be forced to flee, yet there was no other choice. David resolved to place his full trust in YHWH, for no alternatives were at hand.

≈ ≈ ≈

It was shortly thereafter that David's spies confirmed his worst fears. Saul had again been informed by the Ziphites of David's whereabouts and had departed Gibeah with one hundred and fifty score soldiers. He had reportedly justified his motives saying, "Should Jonathan be denied the crown? My son is an equally commendable a man, isn't he?"

David wanted to witness Saul's deceit for himself. He hoped that the scouts had been mistaken, though in his heart he knew otherwise.

"Abishai, are you going with me to investigate Saul's camp?"

"I am!" said Abishai. "I need to see this treachery firsthand." He grabbed his spear and stalked off, following David's lead.

It was pitch black. The large camp lay eerily still in the dim glow of the moon. David slid stealthily to the brow of the ridge above Saul's position. The entire camp lay asleep! David looked questioningly at Abishai, who shrugged. *What insanity is this—everyone sleeping? Is this a fool's parade? Does he discount me as a worthy foe?* David wondered. He could see Saul lying in a trench. His spear was stuck in the ground next to him, and Abner lay at his side. Other guards positioned around him were also dozing.

David was incensed by the lack of vigilance and slack defense of his lord. No soldier who respected his position and treasured his king or his own life for that matter would dare to sleep at his post.

Abishai fidgeted gleefully. "God has delivered your enemy to you. Let me go kill him with his own spear. Rest assured that I won't have to pierce him twice." He started to move down the slope.

"No!" David ground out through clenched teeth. For a moment he regretted soliciting the company of the hot-blooded youth. "You will do no such thing! A man cannot accost the Lord's anointed and escape a free soul. God will either smite Saul or the king will die at war, somewhere, somehow. But it will not be by my hand or by my order. What you can do though is to take his spear and the cruse of water at his side, then let us go."

Abishai frowned in disappointment, but obeyed.

The duo stole away to an incline some distance away, their bounty in hand. David shouted toward the encampment. "Abner, son of Ner, do you hear me, Abner?"

"Who is that?" replied Abner, his voice groggy. He stood and peered in the direction of the voice, but at that distance and in the wan light, David knew he and Abishai would seem as vague outlines.

"Are you a brave man, Abner? There is none like you in Israel. How then is it that you did not protect your lord the king? Someone came in to destroy the king, and you were asleep! It is not good what you did. As God lives, you deserve death for that—leaving God's anointed unprotected, as though he were a commoner. And now, where is the king's spear and where is his cruse of water that was at his bolster?"

The silence in the camp bespoke the commander's uncertainty. David observed calmly as Abner rummaged frantically at the king's side. The officers watched his desperate search. Finally Abner stood limp, comprehending his grave lapse, and a furor descended on the encampment.

≈ ≈ ≈

Saul was startled awake by the racket pervading the camp. He followed the stares of the soldiers to the brow of the hill. He gained his feet as the soldiers parted to allow him to the fore. Saul peered questioningly at Abner, who remained woefully silent. The king's eyes took in the extra long spear that David held, its gilded shaft as distinctive as a handprint. "Is that you, David, my son?"

"It is my voice, yes, my lord king. Why are you pursuing me? What evil have I done? Listen to me, if God has sent you against me let him accept a peace offering. But if it is men who have stirred you up against me, I curse them before God, for they have driven me away from all that was mine through the Lord, forcing me to flee to ungodly places. So do not let it be that you kill me bold-facedly in front of God. I am but a flea! Why are you wasting your time hunting me like a solitary partridge in the mountains? The king has more important things to do, surely!"

Saul's head drooped. That David had pardoned him a second time—it was too much! He knew he could never have done the same. He groaned inwardly. *What have I become?* he thought. *I shame even myself. I have lost everything to a better man than I.*

He steeled himself and forced his voice to speak above a whisper. "Blessed are you, David; not only will you do great things, but you will also succeed at them! You do not need to worry about me anymore."

With that, Saul turned and walked back to the trench, where he sat alone for the remaining hours of the night, his tears falling silently in the darkness.

꿈 꿈 꿈

"Is that it?" Abishai asked. "He is simply going to leave?" He did not entirely hide the dismay in his voice.

David, saddened by his nephew's zeal for war, told him, "No. This will scarcely be the end. His lips are like swords. He is a man with nothing to lose, and that will make him even more dangerous." He turned, feet dragging and shoulders slumped as they made their way back to camp. "We must leave this place."

"Leave where? Do you mean Hachilah?"

"No! We must leave Israel."

CHAPTER NINE

Exile

Be merciful to me, O God, for man would swallow me up;
He, fighting daily, oppresseth me.
Mine enemies would daily swallow me up,
For they be many that fight against me, O Thou Most High.
What time I am afraid, I will trust in Thee.
In God I will praise His word,
In God I have put my trust;
I will not fear what flesh can do unto me.
Every day they wrest my words:
All their thoughts are against me for evil.

PSALM OF DAVID 56, EXCERPT

D avid gathered his six hundred men and their families and sped toward the land of the Philistines. It had not been an easy decision to make but, as well as he had grown to understand Saul and his inconsistent contrition, he knew assuredly it was necessary. Saul's remorse would dissipate by morning.

David would not risk the lives of the women and children. He needed a secure shelter—a place where they could maintain livestock and crops to sustain themselves without the constant fear of reprisal. Philistia was the closest of the neighboring lands, and it held the greatest promise for refuge. If they conducted themselves discretely, the king may be convinced to succor them within his borders. King Achish had no love for Saul, and he would pride himself in harboring the man's enemy. David's presence amongst the Philistines would be a deliberate thorn in Saul's side.

David did not wish to goad King Saul further, but he needed to protect those who had placed their trust in him. The way was open, and he in turn would put his faith in One who was greater than them all.

≤ ≤ ≤

Saul reasoned with himself during the night and squelched his repentant heart, his hatred renewed afresh. David was the charlatan, lulling him deceptively into inactivity while creeping enduringly toward the throne. Saul shrugged off his indolence and renewed his pursuit with a vengeance, but realizing David's intention as the course he set toward Gath became clear, Saul soon gave up his pursuit and ordered his soldiers back to Gibeah.

≤ ≤ ≤

This time, on the journey in, David planned as thoroughly as he could. He rehearsed his intended speech for his audience with the king, and prayed that YHWH would provide a way for his brazen scheme to work.

David left Adino in charge of the men at the border and entered Gath with discomforting memories of his last visit. Achish gave him an audience on the third day of his petition. David approached him boldly. He bowed and pressed his forehead to the ground, awaiting the king's leave to stand. The light dust discarded by the sandals of petitioners irritated his nostrils and he stifled the urge to sneeze. *Another perfomance,* he considered wryly. Yet there were few options open to him.

Achish spoke after a tense interval. "Arise. State your request."

David stood, drawing upon the eloquence that his days in Saul's court had imparted. "Mighty king, I beg the favor and the hospitality of a great warrior and a mighty nation. Your servant has been exiled from his home by your enemy, the king of Israel from whose service your servant had departed many years hence, and has lived as a worm burrowing beneath the earth, rejected by his people who hand him over to your enemy whither he goes. Your servant begs refuge from the clutches of your enemy to sojourn in peace with my family and the family of the few men who also suffered exile to aid your servant in his flight from our enemy. Your servant places himself at the mercy of the king."

Achish conferred with his advisors, whose heads shook emphatically. His former pretense at insanity would likely color their disposition toward him now. At what appeared to be an impasse, the king dismissed their protests with a summary wave.

"My servant will abide in the city until the month of Adar. But know this—the king will be pleased to slay his servant should his servant or any of his charge foment rebellion. Does my servant agree?

David bowed again. "It shall be so." He exited the king's palace counting his blessings.

⤺ ⤺ ⤺

David's relief burst forth as he neared the border of Gath where everyone was gathered.

"Is it well? Adino asked.

"Yes, it is well," he said with a broad grin. "We are to go to the city."

He stood atop a large rock and addressed the assembled people.

"You all know where we are going. This is not Jerusalem. Have care to your words and your actions. You will be your neighbor's keeper. Every man have care to your household. No one, not any one of you, is to digress or we shall all be slain. All of us!" David made the emphatic slash of an imaginary sword. "Take heed. Look at your wives, your husbands, your children, your neighbor's children. Your neighbors put their lives in your hand. Take heed! David sprang light-footedly from atop the boulder. A worried hum emanated from the mass of people. That was good. Without a fear of their lives foremost in their minds, some fool was likely to provoke the deaths of their entire company.

With that they headed city-ward, each man bearing a mixture of simmering hope and simpering trepidation. Endless months passed in the city without incident, but David felt the unease and dissatisfaction within his people swelling like a festering boil. He would need to act decisively to preempt the brew of trouble that he foresaw would ooze out like pus to ruin their sanctuary.

He was granted his second meeting with the king. As he entered the audience hall, Achish sat brooding. He seemed to ignore David, who experienced a fleeting wave of hesitation.

"Your petition?" the king asked suddenly.

David bowed down low.

"If I have now found grace in your eyes, let me be given a place in some town in the country that I may dwell there. For why should your servant dwell in the royal city with you and continue to be a burden?"

Achish looked piercingly at him, but David did not flinch. The scrutiny continued for an uncomfortable duration. At last, the king spoke.

"Ziklag. It is depleted but should serve." Achish continued to peer at David intently. When he said no more, David bowed formally and departed.

$$\approx \quad \approx \quad \approx$$

When the doors had closed completely behind David, the silence broke in a rush within the chamber. Achish motioned for silence from his advisors.

"It has been six months and neither he nor his people have done anything against my authority, spoken any words to discredit themselves, nor committed any act that was remotely suspicious."

One of the advisors raised his voice emphatically. "Nevertheless, you should not trust him. He is our enemy."

"If he has a fault I have not found it. Neither have any of my spies. He is dispossessed and broken. A true enemy of our people would not have the discipline among that many persons to maintain a facade this long without displaying some sign of rebellion against our order, however small. There has been nothing whatsoever to accuse them. All this while you can lay nothing to their charge, Phergon; if you can, let us hear it."

"The history of his actions speaks of treachery He has done nothing to commend himself to us?" Machtath insisted.

"Even their children have spoken honorably." Achish slapped his chair in conviction. "Also, will it not be better that they will now move beyond the city limits, far to the south of the land if they are the evil that you claim, eh, Machtath?" The king's tone was adamant.

Achish looked in the direction of the second outspoken dissident. It was his chief advisor. "We need no longer be concerned to safeguard ourselves from within, and yet they will be within our border and our reach, should it become necessary to crush them. Is this not preferable?"

The advisors relented in their opposition. Machtath deferred reluctantly.

"We shall see, my lord. We shall see."

The large band of skilled men of war descended on the plains approaching Shur like a storm from the desert. The raid was as efficient as it was deadly. The rivalry that had been formed between the inhabitants of the land—descendents of Amalek—and the children of Israel had not been extinguished by the passage of time. The fateful task that Saul, in his disobedience to YHWH, had failed to complete remained as a blot against the name of Israel. The error had precipitated Saul's demise, and still the duty awaited completion. Neither man nor woman remained alive at the end of the battle that raged for two hours. There was none left in Geshur to tell of their plight and none to say from which direction the raiders came. From Geber to Gezer, the men of war obliterated towns and villages. Each time there was no one remaining to lay claim that after moving east toward the border of Judah they abruptly altered course and veered northward to their home in Ziklag.

CHAPTER TEN

Broken

This is the man that made not God his strength;
But trusted in the abundance of his riches,
And strengthened himself in his wickedness.

PSALM OF DAVID 52, EXCERPT

It had been inevitable. War burst like pus from an infected wound to seek fresh victims from Israel and Philistia. David was called to Achish's court for a war council.

"You and your men must know that you can fight at my side." Achish assured David.

"Surely you know what your servant can do," David replied.

"I will entrust myself to you; your men will go to battle at my side," the king stated flatly. "We leave for Aphek on the third day."

"As the king commands." David bowed and exited from the court. He knew how his men would react, yet there was no alternative course open to their fugitive band. When David relayed the king's command, the captains reacted as one, "Never!"

Adino accosted him angrily. "Did you agree to that? Are you mad?"

"Over my dead body!" Shammah growled, ramming the butt of his spear into the ground.

David allowed them to give vent to their displeasure, and then raised his hands for silence. "What could be done? A refusal would be tantamount to suicide," he said pragmatically.

"I don't know!" Adino said. "Make some excuse..."

"What reason could be given for six hundred men to abstain?"

"But to go to war against our brothers?"

"They had no difficulty hunting us, though," Eleazar allowed.

"That was a different circumstance," Shammah countered.

"All in all," David interjected forcefully, "either we go forward and trust our Lord to devise a way out of our predicament, or we go back to face Saul and a life on the run until he perishes."

The men grumbled but stayed silent, for none wished to restart their lives as fugitives.

"Are we agreed then? We journey with Achish and trust in our God to deliver us as he has done on countless occasions in the past."

"Agreed," chorused four of the five captains.

"Adino?"

"Okay, but I still think it is madness."

"It is settled then," David said. "Prepare the men for first light.

⤳ ⤳ ⤳

The first day of battle dawned and still no way of escape had been made. King Achish rode along with David's men as the rear guard. The king sat casually in his saddle, his light banter describing his anticipated victory. David's soldiers exchanged worried looks but continued on behind the last rank of Philistine soldiers. David was uncertain whether he would call on the men to attack the Philistines from the rear, knowing that his men would be decimated by the huge army, or to desert Achish at the last moment, or to fight along with the king from Gath. Seeing the swarming mass of the Philistine garrison, David feared for the plight of Israel. Never had he seen so many troops. The battle would not go well for his countrymen. This scale of battle belonged only to the Lord.

Abner and Saul viewed the vast size of the Philistine army spread like a plague of locusts across the wilderness below.

"Abner?" Saul croaked. He turned in dismay to his commander.

"I see them, lord. There are four times their previous numbers and they come with archers by the thousands…" His voiced trailed off as he stared at the fearsome hosts and envisioned the carnage that would ensue. A sick feeling settled in his stomach.

Saul shuddered. "We need help, Abner."

"Only the hand of YHWH can make a difference, and we have not sought him for a span of seasons. I'm afraid it is too late." Abner continued to stare out.

"Find me a medium," Saul said, breaking the silence.

"What?" Abner cringed, his breath coming faster.

"You heard me."

Abner's mind raced to find the right answer for his king. "My lord," he said finally, "you had us expel the spirit-readers on pain of death years ago. Any who remain have ceased their practice or hide from our eyes. They will scarcely show themselves and risk death. Besides, it is against God's law."

"Don't you think I know that, Abner? But do you see Him here to help us? I must act now. I cannot stand idly by and have our men massacred if by any means we may gain an advantage. Find me a medium, Abner. If we make it through this, I'd be happy to discuss the appropriateness of my actions, but for this moment, do as I command."

"I will inquire of your servants, my lord." Abner bowed and moved away at a crouch. Saul was making a heinous mistake, he knew, engaging the spirit world in the affairs of men. It was a reproach to all that was holy. With this latest digression of Saul's, God would surely be against them if he had not been before. Saul had gone too far and there would be no coming back this time.

Abner determined that he would not die on the day of battle because of a king's indiscretion. He would not shun the battle, but neither would he die a needless death. Saul's transgression would be on his own head, and may God have mercy on him.

≈ ≈ ≈

Saul disguised himself as ably as he could before setting out to visit the medium. There was time yet to reconsider, but he could not turn back.

"We should proclaim a fast," Jonathan had urged, but his father would not hear his entreaty.

"Father, we cannot win without our God before us. Our numbers and resources are too few. God forbid, this is ill advised. Listen to me, Father."

But Saul would not listen. He was frustrated with the rules, the commands, the holy ordinances, and he was incensed with the Living God who intended to depose him as king. Saul felt the victim of a capricious Higher Power, and so his resentment crystallized. How could YHWH have rejected him? In his jealous anger, Saul had grown to hate the one whom he believed had usurped his position of favor in God's eyes. His indignation offered him no recourse.

Saul donned his robe. His footmen had brought assorted raiment from the city market, some old, some new, and he had selected two pieces typical of traders in the south.

At second watch the king-turned-merchant joined an escort of two men from his guard. They too wore unfamiliar garb.

"Take me to her," the king instructed. The trio hastily embarked upon their clandestine journey.

≈ ≈ ≈

Abner watched the king depart for his illicit mission from the shadows of his quarters. He hoped that at least one of Saul's older sons would survive this ill-fated war. Yet Abner feared the worst. Neither Jonathan nor Abinadab, nor Malchishua despite his keen love of life, would leave their father's side if the battle went sore against Israel. They were faithful and esteemed Saul beyond measure. They would willingly die in his stead.

Saul's youngest son, Ishbosheth, had remained in Gibeah. He would be invaluable if the war claimed the lives of the king and his three older sons. Ishbosheth, though biddable, was young and inexperienced in leadership. Abner would need to guide him.

The commander's primary reservation about the war stemmed from the enormous rank of archers they had seen on the enemy front. Once in close quarters, his soldiers would fight commendably; but where there were archers to combat, both the initial advance and the call for retreat would be orders that sent men to their death. When the battle lines were separate, arrows flew unabated across the gap. The only safety lay in either close proximity to the enemy or at a distance too great for the deadly shafts to find their marks. Abner made a mental note and returned to his bed, knowing the trumpet's call heralding untold death would come too soon—much too soon.

≈ ≈ ≈

The house at Endor where the spirit-reader resided was confined and dank. Since the king's decree had been passed, she had successfully hidden her skills from prying eyes. She had taken nondescript lodgings far from Jerusalem were she had first practiced her craft. Tonight's proposed meeting made her uneasy, though the man's plea on behalf of his master had been convincing in its urgency; however, she was having second thoughts about her visitor. Perhaps it was a trap to ferret out her kind. The prospect of exposure and public beheading rekindled the fear that she had initially subdued upon hearing the request for a reading.

A knock rattled the shaky boards of the decaying door. Once she had lived in luxury, but now she was reduced to dingy hovels and a meager existence amongst slatterns and indigent street dwellers. Still, her bitterness at her fate had long been exhausted. She did not serve any god, and so had no savior to whom she could appeal against her miserable state. She moved cautiously to the door. "Who is it?" she asked tremulously.

"One in grave need," came the reply.

She opened the door and bade them to enter.

To the woman's insightful gaze, Saul seemed anxious as he confronted her directly. "Please, call forth the person whom I shall name."

The woman, disconcerted by his abruptness, cried, "You know what Saul has decreed, banishing spirit-readers and wizards; why are you trying to ensnare me and bring about my death?"

"Nothing will happen to you. I swear it," he promised.

The woman wrung her hands. She placed an array of bowls on the roughly carved table that stood between them. Her arts had long since claimed her spirit, and though on occasion she had resisted the terrible urge to cast spells, the lure of the power sucked at the marrow of her bones, demanding its due. There was always a trade for using the elements that she conjured—the price often being paid in blood. Yet her petitioners knew the risks and would decide if the need was great enough. In spite of the horrifying taint, hers was a need as vital as air itself, for after decades of dedicating her soul to the practice, she was inexorably bound by its damning cords. "Who is it that you want me to bring up?"

"Bring me Samuel."

The woman flinched at the name, yet continued her conjuring. Within her inner vision an apparition rose and coalesced into the figure of an elderly man covered in a mantle. The spirit-reader paused, listening to the old man's stern words. He gestured in warning and she threw herself back with a cry of terror, cowering by the far wall. "Why did you deceive me," she wailed. "You are Saul!"

"Don't be afraid," Saul said holding out his hands in a calming gesture. "Tell me what you saw."

The medium turned about, searching for some escape from this trap. Saul and his guard yet stood between her and the door. He could force her to answer. Her hands trembled as she realized the danger of her predicament. ""I saw—I saw a god—ascending out of the earth."

"What is his form?"

The medium reluctantly described her vision.

"Samuel!" Saul whispered. Stooping, he bowed to the ground.

The medium paled as the prophet brushed her will aside and spoke directly to Saul. She had lost control over this reading and wished only that it would end.

"Why have you disturbed me?" Samuel questioned coldly.

"I am in great distress," Saul answered. "The Philistines are primed for war and God has deserted me. He doesn't answer me using either prophets or dreams, nor by using the ephod; so I have called you to find out what I should do."

"Why would you ask me, if God is gone from you? If He is now your enemy? The Lord has done what I told you He would. He has torn the kingdom from your hands and given it to your neighbor David. You did not obey Him nor execute His judgment on the Amalekites. This is the reason for your fall. Moreover, Israel, along with your host, will be delivered to the Philistines and by tomorrow you and your sons will be with me."

Saul's face slackened, and he fell prostrate on the dusty floor. The woman knelt by him, anxiety making the pitch of her voice high.

"I have obeyed you and done as you asked, now please, let me get you something to eat so that you may regain strength for your journey."

"No!" Saul cried, "I will not eat."

"We must get back," his man urged. "Eat something."

Saul did not respond.

Finally the combined pleas of the medium and the guardsman stirred him to rise.

The woman hurried to prepare a beef broth and unleavened bread. "It is almost half night, please accept the food."

The aroma of the broth and the freshly baked bread encouraged Saul to eat. He soon regained his vigor. "Thank you," he said and promptly left with his escort.

As soon as the door shut, the woman hastily gathered her sparse belongings. She wrapped the remainder of the bread in a coarse cloth and hurried out into the darkness. She unstrung her mule from a post at the rear of the house.

Promises or no, she reasoned with herself, *I shall not wait for death to come knocking.* She would go north to Tyre or Sidon. I should have left Israel a long time ago, she concluded. She had no reason to doubt that the prophet spoke the truth, and the likelihood of Philistines conquering Saul's army made her shiver. War was coming to Israel, and she should have left a long time ago. Whatever the outcome, Israel would be no welcome place for a witch.

≈ ≈ ≈

Camped in Aphek with the heavily armored garrison in array, King Achish assembled the princes for a final confirmation of their war strategy. On the journey in, a few of the lords had expressed concern that the battle might turn unexpectedly as in times past.

"Not this time, eh, Phergon?" Machtath assured the older man. "Your company fared the worst at the last confrontation, but Saul will not best us today. He has underestimated our strength on this occasion, and the archers that you have trained are unmatched!" Machtath rubbed his hands together in gleeful anticipation. "Our scouts report mere thousands pitted against us, whereas we have tens of thousands geared for combat. The day *will* be ours."

"What of those men with you, Achish?" inquired the chief commander.

"What of them?" Achish responded.

"Isn't that David, our enemy?" Phergon said, leaning forward in emphasis. "Wasn't it agreed in council that the Hebrews should not be trusted? Will you send them to battle with us to betray us? Furthermore, you entrust your life to him over your brethren? He could slit your throat at any time and rob us of victory. You should never have brought him here."

Achish's gut tightened. "I have found no fault in him. I have questioned him repeatedly throughout his sojourn here."

Phergon quirked a brow. "And what has he been doing these six months to sustain his band?"

"I am told that they already have flocks and possess—"

"He said he has been raiding along the Egyptian border," the king interjected.

"And you took his word?"

"What? Have you heard otherwise?" Achish countered.

"Well, no! Nevertheless, he is not to be trusted. He should not go with us against the children of Israel. He is sure to rejoin Saul and do us harm. Let him return to the place you have given him."

"Is this how all of you feel?" Achish asked, searching their grim faces.

"Yes! We agree with Phergon."

"Let them all return to Ziklag."

Was his judgment failing him that his advisors held such a negative view of a man he trusted? "That is enough for now," said Achish, silencing their protests. "Let us complete our other tasks and then I shall give my decision."

᭟ ᭟ ᭟

Even as Achish and the princes deliberated within the king's tent, David remained in supplication. He knew his men were in anguish over the pending battle with their countrymen. Ever near, they watched him closely for any signal to quit the encampment, but he gave none. David sat alone, his eyes upon the movement of the troops. He saw the men before him, but his thoughts were racing heavenward. "We need your help, Lord," he said repeatedly. "Deliver us!" The frontlines had already mustered as planned, yet there was still time. The trumpet had not yet sounded for his rearward battalion to advance. *Patience. Patience!*

As the king's tent cleared, David was summoned to join Achish.

"David—as God lives," the king stated sadly, "I have found your conduct among us to be upright since the first day you came, but the lords of the Philistines . . ." He glanced back toward the tent with a shrug. "They do not trust you. I need to ask you to go in peace so that you will not displease them—Phergon especially."

"As you command," David said with a bow, trying to appear downcast as he parted.

As he approached his men, they regarded him with anxious eyes.

"We depart for Ziklag," he said with a wide grin. "Did I not tell you? God has made a way."

The men stirred enthusiastically and quickly quit the encampment. They were looking forward to returning home.

᭟ ᭟ ᭟

As the returning company neared the brow of ridge overlooking their town, a choked cry tore from the throat of the lead scout.

"What is it, Ithai?" David shouted. The man stood affixed, his gaze drawn into the distance. David reached his side at the same time as four of the captains, and they gasped collectively.

Tangled tendrils of gray smoke unwound from the charred husks of buildings and escaped into the noon sky. A flurry of men bundled to the crest, their cries of disbelief alarming those too far back to view the desolate scene below.

"God preserve us," David cried and joined the panicked race down the steep incline toward Ziklag. Stores scattered and men fell, each one oblivious to his compatriots, hoping to be the one exempt from the grief promised by the blackened walls and empty sheepcotes and stockades.

The men whirled through streets and vacant remnants of buildings. Voices carried frantically over the low houses. Men emerged tearing at their hair in dismay. The shock of the loss bereaved the eldest of their strength. Several wandered in a daze while others sat on the ash-strewn ground, rocking in agitation.

The absence of fighting men from the small town had been too tempting as pillage for the wilderness rovers. David noticed a glint in the dust and knelt beside an armored head that had been broken from a wooden spear. He picked up it up and turned it in his hand.

"Amalekites," he said, his voice hollow. "Any dead?" he asked Adino who trundled toward him breathlessly.

"None," Adino replied crestfallen. "All taken—women, children, and all the stock."

Strangled cries continued to pervade the town streets, and an underlying moan grew louder as the might of Ziklag wept out its sorrow.

A young Benjamite accosted David, fanning the living flames of anger that now sprang up to consume living flesh. "Look—what—you—have—done!" he screamed violently. His words cut out in staccato bursts like slingstones pebbling a city stronghold, aiming to penetrate the wall of stolidity that enveloped their leader, who stood with a strange calm. "Taking us to war—along with those—those heathens—to oppose our brothers! *Now look!* We have nothing. *Nothing!* We should have lost our lives rather than see this." He gestured to the smoking embers of a nearby house.

Tears of the hundreds of men spilled to the ground, unable to quench the flames that ate steadily through the kindled wood and fleshly dwellings alike.

Eleazar approached David, walking swiftly. "There is talk of stoning you, master," he whispered urgently. "Should we leave?"

David regarded him.

"Should we leave?" Eleazar repeated urgently, as though he thought David had not quite perceived his words.

"No!" David ground out. "God has not brought me this far to see me abandon my own in time of need!" He knelt in the street and bowed in the midst of the scattered ashes. "Send for Abiathar and the ephod," he said quietly. His men turned pain-dulled eyes to regard him, seeming puzzled by his composure.

David remained kneeling until Eleazar re-emerged from the ruins with the priest in tow. Abiathar was wearing the sacred vestments.

"Jehovah Jireh," David said, his voice raspy. "You are a mighty deliverer. Should I pursue after this band? Will I overtake them?"

Pursue and you shall overtake them and, without fail, recover all.

"Thank you, my Lord."

David wept—not tears of loss as had the others—but tears of encouragement and a gladdened heart. He surged to his feet. "We are going to retake what is ours!" he shouted. "Fill your waterskins. We leave at once!"

⇜ ⇜ ⇜

After two days of pursuit still nothing could be seen ahead. His men struggled against the discouragement that ate again at the core of their bellies. The pace David set was unearthly. Crossing the brook of Besor, he realized that many of them were floundering, too weak from the recent trek from Aphek. A third of his men were compelled to remain behind, despair and fatigue overcoming them. David directed the men to unstrap all except their weapons and essential supplies. They entrusted the items to the care of those who were to stay at the brook.

David pressed on with four hundred of the strongest. He was bent upon finding the Amalekites before nightfall. He was sure they were within reach, for the coals of the conflagration at Ziklag had still burned hot on their departure, indicating that the fire had been ignited recently. So keen was he on his target that he almost overran a man lying outstretched in his path. Adino and David stooped beside him. "He's an Egyptian. Probably a slave," Adino informed David.

"Bring some food and water," David ordered.

They held the waterskin to the man's parched lips. He drank thirstily. David fed him pieces of a fig cake and a handful of raisins. The man at last sat up and spoke words of thanks in stilted Hebrew.

"Who do you belong to and where are you coming from?" David questioned.

"I am a servant to an Amalekite. I fell sick three days ago and he left me here. My masters were invading the south, toward the Cherethites and along the coast of Judah and south of Caleb. Then we raided Ziklag and burned it to the ground."

David inhaled sharply. "Can you show me this company?"

"I will, but you must swear by your God not to kill me or return me to my master."

David agreed without delay and aided the young man as he struggled to his feet. David waved two of his men forward. "Support him," he commanded. "We must travel quickly."

≈ ≈ ≈

It took another day to reach the rovers. The lightening sky revealed a troop of hundreds spread across a shallow ravine, celebrating their successful campaign and the immense volume of spoil they had garnered.

David motioned for his men to spread out and draw their weapons. His men were outnumbered, but the sight of their families, some bound at the wrist and others tied to makeshift posts, enraged each man as a tormented bear protecting its young.

David's company descended on the Amalekites like thunder from the mountains. They rent life mercilessly from the stupefied men, some of whom were drunk from feasting. The battle raged until sunset on the following day. As defeat loomed for the Amalekites, twenty score of the younger men fled to the camels and escaped into the desert.

David's men heaved with exhaustion. They hastened to release their families, who huddled under the security of their protectors.

"Any missing?" David shouted to his captains who were dispersed throughout the valley.

"None."

"None, my lord," came the replies.

David was heartened by their reports. His wives had been found at the south of the camp. He veered toward the small tent where they had been confined.

"Abigail! Ahinoam!" He opened his arms to greet them, and despite the blood drenching his clothes, each embraced him gladly.

"I was sure that you would rescue us," Abigail said with pride.

"It was only by the blessing of YHWH," David replied simply.

"Still," Abigail held with a smile, "you are indeed fit to be king."

⌐ ⌐ ⌐

The trip back to Besor lasted several days longer than the outward journey since the men now traveled with their families and bounteous spoil. The men that were left behind at the brook cheered loudly, re-enlivened by the sight of the victorious party. They ran to salute the company.

"How do you fare now?" David asked in concern, for the men had stayed with meager rations throughout the six days during which they awaited their companions return.

"We have life again," shouted Hashtub, a slim man of middle years. "God be praised!" He rejoiced, capering in an impromptu dance of celebration.

David nodded with a laugh, his heart lightened even more by the man's exuberance. He then turned his attention to the division of the spoil. The livestock they had garnered were numerous, and each family could be rewarded generously. The largest allotments were parted first in order to unburden the makeshift corrals. The silver and gold vessels were weighted and numbered—jeweled bracelets, chains, and rings. These were apportioned according to the size of each family.

As each portion was divested, David noticed a ripple of discord amongst the men. Frowning, he approached two of the troop who grumbled loudly regarding the distribution of the spoil.

"What is it causing this dissent?" David wondered aloud. "Is this not a day of joy? We have been reunited and not a man lost in the effort! Why do you grumble?"

"These who did not go with us to fight, should they be rewarded in equal measure?" the man complained heatedly. "We say they should be given their wives and children and be sent on their way,"

David's tone suddenly became low and as hard as flint. His heart burned with the fire of a rage that made the contentious man recoil.

David was absolute in his command. "You shall not do so, brethren, with what God has given us, who preserved us and delivered our adversaries unto us. The men who remained with the supplies will receive the same as those who go to battle. The same!" he growled. He turned his determined eyes on his warriors in a silent challenge to any who dared contest his authority. None spoke. "So be it!" David announced and spun away, calling for the resumption of the task. David's declaration was never forgotten, for it became the hallmark of his campaign.

Upon their arrival at Ziklag, David dispatched emissaries with goods as tribute to the elders of Judah and to all the places where his men had been sheltered during their flight from Saul.

"A wise man remembers his friends in his day of harvest." This was his father's constant proverb during the days of sheep shearing or the gathering of sheaves, and the son of Jesse took heed to his father's advice. Generosity always bore fruit.

∽ ∽ ∽

War surged through Mount Gilboa. Despite his clever deployment of troops, Saul's army became enveloped on three sides. Harried ruthlessly by archers and beset by an unremitting influx of swordsmen, they struggled to remain united. Several times the lines threatened to break but were held by the valor of the fighting men in the fore, whose immeasurable courage cost many their lives. As evening beckoned, the number of front runners dwindled dangerously.

Saul could see that the battle would be lost within the second day.

"Retreat!" he bellowed. "Jonathan! Retreat! Malchishua—" Saul broke off to impale an onrushing soldier on his spear. He called the retreat again, and his trumpet sounded. He hurled his spear at the chest of a closing swordsman and drew his sword. *Jonathan!* Saul saw the purple and red of his son's cloak disappear amidst a sally of enemies. He roared his grief as he attacked one man, then the next, plunging through the battle toward his son. Jonathan was a superior swordsman, but a vice of close to a dozen Philistines tightened around him. When Saul broke through, he was too late. Though several slain enemy soldiers lay beside the young man, his life's blood mingled with theirs, ebbing out to stain the earth a dusky red. Saul's throat constricted as he wheeled to slash at an incursion of men. He parried the first lunges and swung his sword in a wide arc, cleaving through armor and breast bones.

"Abinadab," he screamed, but his elder son did not answer from the fray. "Abner?" The cry was absorbed by the tumult as Saul mounted his chariot and careened it through his troops. Strength fading, he sounded the retreat just as a singing wave of arrows descended from the sky, piercing his arm and upper thigh. A cry of despair blazed through the ranks of Saul's men as their king went down. He fell heavily from his chariot and shouted urgently for his armor bearer, who had been separated from him in the melee.

The youngster sped to his side, shield upraised to deflect another flight of deadly shafts.

"Do not bother, boy," Saul groaned. "Draw your sword and thrust me through before these uncircumcised Philistines come to mock me."

The boy trembled, his sword hand hanging limply at his side.

"Slay me, boy!" Saul ordered forcefully, but the youth knelt, whimpering in fear. Saul cursed and grabbed for his fallen sword. He raised himself on one leg, tilted his breastplate, and dropped his weight fully on the sharp blade.

≈ ≈ ≈

The armor bearer slumped to Saul's, side bereft of strength and will. He had failed to protect his sovereign. The boy wept silently over the still form of his king whose eyes stared unblinking at trodden stubs of grass. Suddenly, with a grunt of resolve he drew his own sword and followed the example of his king. His lips mouthed a passing prayer as a wave of arrows crested the sky and made their deadly decent to disperse the remnant of Saul's army. None could stay to mourn a recusant leader who would have been established in greatness with all his household had he remembered the One who made him king.

≈ ≈ ≈

"I told you we would surpass Saul this day, did I not?" The Philistine lord looked down disdainfully at the body of the Israelite sovereign.

"He took his own life. Better for him I suppose," Phergon concluded, waving to catch the attention of the spoilers.

"Remove his armor and take his head. We will display it before the house of our gods." Phergon moved away as the spoilers set about their gruesome task.

CHAPTER ELEVEN

Miscalculations

He that worketh deceit shall not dwell within my house:
He that telleth lies shall not tarry in my sight.
I will early destroy all the wicked of the land;
That I may cut off all wicked doers from the city of the LORD.

PSALM OF DAVID 101, EXCERPT

For the next two days, the inhabitants of Ziklag labored to remove burnt timbers from the remains of their houses, salvaging what possessions they could. It was nearing double light when David was overseeing the construction of temporary roofing for a neighbor's house. Nearby movement alerted him to the arrival of a sturdy young man out of the wilderness. His clothes were rent and dirt marred his exposed skin. David climbed from the top of a rugged wall that had borne the fire's heat well and went to meet the man, who trundled toward him and bowed.

"Where are you coming from?" asked David.

The man wobbled and grasped the wall for support. "From the war up north." His voice cracked, and his breath wheezed in his throat.

David called for water and waited while the man slaked his thirst in great draughts. "How did it go? Tell me."

"Many of the soldiers are dead or fallen, including the king and his son Jonathan."

Grief welled within David's chest as he continued to question the stranger. His words caught as he struggled to overcome the rising ache that choked his senses and cast his thoughts into disarray. "How—how do you know this?"

"I passed by chance through Mount Gilboa. Saul was pressing the battle with the chariots and horsemen, but it went badly and he was wounded. He saw me and called to me and asked me to slay him because his armor bearer refused, so I slew him because his wound was severe. He would die eventually. I took his crown and bracelet to bring it to you, my lord." The young man produced the bejeweled items from his ripped coat.

A violent cry tore from David's throat, its anguish cresting with racking sobs that brought men running from within the town. Many stumbled in their haste to attend their lord, weapons coming unsheathed with fearsome speed. The first to reach David's side, Eleazar seized the stranger roughly as others flooded from the lace of streets. They crowded around David in concern, each regarding the new arrival with open aggression.

"Has he caused you hurt?" Eleazar questioned, tightening his grip on the wayfarer's arm. David's face contorted with sorrow, and his chin quivered as he sought to speak. He stooped to the ground and covered his face in his hands. Eleazar gestured for the men to fall back a pace that he might have breathing room. David struck his fist to the ground, then after a moment rose with grim decision. "Saul has fallen in battle," he announced in a tight voice, his jaw clenched in spasms. "And Jonathan with him," David added softly. "The people of the Lord and the House of Israel have been slain!"

The men rocked back in shock. Several dropped to their knees in silent disbelief. Hearing of King Saul's end and the loss of Jonathan, who was highly revered by the men of war throughout Israel, sapped their strength. As stricken as his men, David could not bear to work any longer and refused all sustenance that day. Through David's grief, an unsettling suspicion about the young messenger nagged at him. In the late evening David broke his mourning to call the man back.

"Where are you from?" David asked.

"I am an Amalekite," the man replied.

"How is it, I wonder, that you were not afraid to kill the Lord's anointed?" David wondered, his voice deepening with emotion. He called out casually to two of the men who drew near to hear his bidding.

"Kill him," David instructed simply, nodding toward the Amalekite, whose face registered a swirling mixture of disbelief and terror. His confusion left him rooted despite his imminent peril.

David addressed the man again. "Your blood is on your own head, for your mouth testified against you, that you killed YHWH's anointed servant."

The man shrunk back. War-hardened hands grappled him and flung him to the ground. An instant later the warriors' sharp swords descended with killing speed.

David withdrew as the death sentence fell. As he made his way back to his house, Eleazar shuffled to his side and hurried to match his leader's resolute stride. "Did he truly believe you would reward him?" he asked.

"Who? The Amalekite?"

"Yes."

David snorted. "Perhaps he thought me a true enemy of Saul, given our obvious fall from grace, and this being Philistia and not the hallowed halls of Jerusalem." He gestured to the wasteland around and sighed. His banishment from his home still wore heavily on him. "He probably expected an honorable welcome, or perhaps planned to inveigle a generous reward. Many still believe that I coveted Saul's crown." David shook his head, regretting the disharmony that his parting from Saul had engendered. "He may have been hopeful that I would pay handsomely for it. He could hardly pawn it in the marketplace—Opportunists, these Amalekites. They would steal a mite from an orphan's hand."

"Do you think he actually did the deed? Killed Saul, I mean?" Eleazar posed the same question that David had considered.

"Hardly. Saul would rather have taken his own life than have it stolen by one of such low standing. However, to boast of having slain the Lord's anointed? It is an affront equal to committing the deed. How is it that some men have no fear of the Living God?"

"They have never seen His hand at work, I suppose?"

"Well, I have seen it my entire life and I pray I never forget."

ᕙ ᕙ ᕙ

It was the loss of Jonathan that David mourned above all else. "How the mighty have fallen," he said sadly, "And the weapons of war perished."

It took David several days to shut away his grief. His people would need him now to build a future and repel the enemies of his people. *Who is in charge of the land? Where should I start?*

He sent for Abiathar, who stood in the outer room awaiting him.

David entered and knelt reverently. God would show him where he should go next.

"Shall I return to Judah, Lord? Where shall I go?" he prayed.

The answer came and David stood, satisfied.

"We go to Hebron."

ᕙ ᕙ ᕙ

Abiathar sat alone with the ephod in his lap. David had asked for the words of his lament to be taught to the children of Judah, and Abiathar was one of the few among David's band who could write. He prepared his notations. He would send the scroll to the prophet Gad. It could then be recorded in the Book of Jasher in commemoration of Saul and Jonathan. Therein the memory of Israel's emerging dominance would be immortalized in the heroic deeds that brought renown and blossoming freedom to a harried nation.

ᕙ ᕙ ᕙ

Despite Abner's assurances that Saul's servants would answer Ishbosheth's call in his father's stead, the bereaved prince bore no inclination to rule. The youngest of four brothers, he had been last in the line of succession and had never dwelled on the prospect of supreme kingship. But Abner was persuasive.

"Aren't you, after all, the son of the king? And the only remaining heir?" the commander argued. "If David seeks the crown he will surely take your life to secure his reign. You are the son of his enemy and a threat to his future. Your best hope of survival would be in claiming dominance within the kingdom. And if perchance he does not with wish to be king"—Abner gestured expansively—"then the crown will be deservedly yours. What is David other than a renegade servant of your father's? He is popular, but illegitimate. The elders of the tribes will agree."

Ishbosheth had grown accustomed to the quality of life enjoyed by the king's household. He therefore decided to throw his lot in with Abner. The commander devised the means for Ishbosheth's ascension to power, and the younger man acceded blindly. Now, he was king over a nation, and he would be forced to contend with a rival for the crown. He was king over the north, but the son of Jesse had harnessed the power of the southern reaches of Judah. To Ishbosheth's consternation, David held his people's hearts for he was a born leader and had been given command by Saul. Also, David could never be erased from the minds of the people as their savior against the Philistines.

Ishbosheth himself had never trained to be a warrior. He was tall as his father had been but more of a spindling, and his father had never seen the need to impose rigorous training on the second-born. Neither had he been schooled in the chicanery or strictures of command—but what he did know was that the strongest leader would survive, and for that he depended on Abner's fortitude to buttress his deficiencies.

Still, he did not relish the thought of civil war. His servants would be required to challenge David's prowess at battle. David was a tactician and Abner's experience at war was unparalleled. Hadn't the commander been one of the only survivors of the Philistine offensive?

Under Abner's direction, he would establish himself over the tribes and woo any rebels to his service. Abner had embarked upon the first official charge in support of Ishbosheth. His mission would find its foothold in Gibeon, then he aimed to push further south with an envoy of Benjamites.

Ishbosheth was anxious for their return. He felt unprotected without Abner to guide him. The contingent was due to return on the fourth feast day. Until then he would prepare the feast—a feast fit for a king.

⊰ ⊰ ⊰

Joab, the most diligent of David's captains, prepared for the inevitable civil war. He had won his position with the stealth of his blade, and his wits were equally sharp. David had ascended to his place as king over Judah, but the remainder of the kingdom would need to be established under his feet, and that would require the elimination of David's enemies within the land.

Other than the Philistine scourge, Abner's preemptive installation of Ishbosheth had caused instability and contention amongst the people whose loyalties were torn between the two houses. The House of David had waxed stronger, its influence expanding since the seizure of the city of Jerusalem, but the time for feasting had not yet come—complacence was for fools. Joab recognized that Ishbosheth was simply a figurehead of the kingship. Abner, he knew, was the primary antagonist within the House of Saul.

Joab's spies spread through Israel like ash cast into a gale. The harlots became his eyes and ears, for they moved freely throughout every city in Israel. Many were young widows, their men swallowed up in the mill of the country's vicious wars. Others had been discarded by perfidious mates seeking a way out of a matrimonial bond.

Men of war were notoriously fickle in their nuptial loyalties. They were also prone to boast of brave deeds that they had yet to complete, or brag in anticipation of a great conquest. The collection of information did not require Joab to jeopardize his own men to strangers. He paid the wenches moderate coin and was rewarded with a wealth of tidings that none other could provide. Muscled flesh wrapped in soft arms became the more pliable when encouraged with wine.

Joab was thus rewarded with news of Abner's pending journey from Manahaim. Disposing of Abner now would prevent much of the bloodshed that was to come. It would also strengthen his position amongst the captains. He would track Abner to Gibeon and engage the Benjamites before they could move on. His brothers, Abishai and Asahel, were eager to press their advantage.

"Let us make haste before he departs. Victorybeckons," Asahel urged his brothers.

"Death will also beckon if we are overly hasty," Joab chided, girding on his sword belt. "We must go carefully. No heroics on this outing, Asahel. If we can take him, we shall do so. If not, there will be other opportunities."

Asahel hung his head. He gave grunt of agreement and fell a few paces behind his brothers. Joab looked askance at Abishai, whose eyes narrowed, but he said nothing. For the period of one month, Asahel had been given charge as one of David's captains and had relished the opportunity, serving loyally. He was a valiant young man, but hot-blooded, and the taste for war burned upon his tongue, they knew. But some tastes were poisons best avoided.

Joab excelled in war, but he did not thirst for open warfare and where possible sought the quick end to any battle. As many conflicts could be won off the field as on, if a warrior was astute. *I cannot succor him as though he is an inexperienced boy and yet... This skirmish will at least assuage his constant lust for battle.* "We will shoulder each other," Joab muttered through clenched teeth. Abishai nodded his understanding.

Asahel followed his older brothers to the armory, disgruntled by their mothering. They had both earned their renown as men of war at an early age. Sitting at meat and listening to their toasts to victories for his entire youth had whetted his appetite beyond measure. Now that he had claimed his armor and proven himself, he longed to earn a permanent captaincy. He had served commendably thus far, though there were none of the exploits heralded by the campfire. Activities of normal men held no interest for him outside of the occasional contest where he could demonstrate his agility with the bow or the sling. He struck his fist to his palm and glowered at his brothers' backs. Would they deny him a share in their celebrated triumphs? *I am no owlet to be sheltered under their wings. I will show my full worth,* he declared, throwing his shoulders back. *And my name will be made great!*

≈ ≈ ≈

On the outskirts of Gibeon, Joab halted the men at the tree line in order to review his strategy with Abisahi.

"If a challenge is brought, I will send Shushem, Johath, and the half troop of Beshem," Joab proposed to his brother.

"These will represent themselves well, but they are hardly the most proficient amongst us. Why not send Ibishe's troop? They are sure to prevail."

"They would indeed, but what I need is to gauge the strengths and weaknesses of Abner's company while maintaining a strong reserve. He will be traveling with his best warriors to protect his hide, and in his arrogance he will commit these to the fray in order to humble us. Even if our men lose, Abner will have wearied his best warriors, and while he gloats we will have our finest to commit to the ensuing battle."

Abishai smiled conspiratorially. "And it is the battle that we need win, not the challenge."

"Exactly," Joab confirmed.

"Shrewd, Brother."

"I fight to win," Joab stated with a matter-of-fact firmness. He gestured for Asahel to join them.

"Abishai will take two of the scouts and locate Abner. Asahel, carry two dozen of our men to salute the elders at the gate. Greet them in the name of King David and offer the hand of the king against their future need. Receive their reply and then return to us."

As his brothers separated to follow his directives, Joab stood tapping his finger against the sheath of his sword. He was convinced that Abner was a man who would not stand in the face of death. How else could he have survived the Philistine war when so many of his company had fallen? Joab had heard the reports of the rain of arrows, the thundering horsemen trampling the blundering retreat of Saul's men. Abner would have been at Saul's side, faithfully defending the king or his sons; or at least he should have been.

No one from Saul's battalion had left the field, and many other valiant men had been lost on the forefront of the lines. So Abner's return from the war had been a surprise. Some had thought him to be blessed by YHWH. Others had revered his skill as a warrior, which Joab admitted was undeniably beyond compare, but Joab suspected that Abner had quit the field before the retreat was called, and such a man was not worthy to serve the king of a great nation.

If Abner did propose a challenge, Joab was prepared to sacrifice the smallest troop necessary to gain an advantage. Abner might turn heel if he smelled defeat too early, and Joab did not favor a long chase across the barley fields of Gibeon. He would prefer a head-to-head battle to decide the kingship—*and the command of Israel's might.*

≈ ≈ ≈

Abishai returned at a run. "He rests at the pool!"

Joab immediately snapped away from his mulling thoughts. "Ready, men!" he shouted with command. "Johaida, wait here for Asahel and then you may join us." Joab hoped that the confrontation would be ended before Asahel arrived. He had not wished to leave his youngest brother behind, but he would do his utmost to keep him away from the heaviest of the bloodshed. It was not that Asahel was an incapable swordsman, in fact the opposite was true, but he was not experienced enough to defend against tactics which seasoned men like Joab himself had used against cocky young men; and unfortunately, Joab knew his brother lacked the discernment of either himself or Abishai, both of whom had constantly protected him as he gained his knowledge of war. Today he would be safer at the gate.

≈ ≈ ≈

Joab's approach to the pool of Gibeon placed him on the side opposite Abner. The men all sat down watching each other across the expanse, their derisory stares cutting through the illusion of a peaceful meeting.

"Let the young men arise and play before us," Abner said at last.

Joab shrugged his agreement to the challenge he had expected. "Let them arise," he said, feigning nonchalance. He signaled his chosen men with a perfunctory nod.

Twelve men arose from each side and met to battle each other for the honor of their houses. The conflict was decidedly brief as each of the twenty-four caught hold of his opponent's hair, and locked in inescapably close combat, slew the other with his sword. The sudden end to the fight blanched even Abner's face. None of the young men assayed to stand. The contest was ended, and even as Joab vaulted from the ground, his long stride closing the gap to engage his adversary, he savored the outcome.

A chorus of screams rose from the formation that closed briefly around Joab then disintegrated as the lone swordsman hacked it asunder, discarding the hopes of Saul's house like the soil from a night chamber. Mere paces behind his brother, Abishai spearheaded into the right side of Abner's company, which reeled backward, stunned by the ferocity of the assault. Soldiers descended like a storm in the wake of the two commanders' bludgeoning charge. Splitting in twain, the prongs sliced through the deep gouges carved by their leaders and closed like the jaws of a leviathan, trapping the prey in its voracious maw. Rows of swords bit into the flanks of Abner's men, rending the enemy with the ease of the scaled giant. Only nineteen of David's men fell to Abner's three hundred and sixty casualties. Abner, grasping the inevitable, sounded a retreat and raced with his men toward Ammah, a barren place beyond the city.

Joab sniffed in contempt, allowing his opponent to withdraw. He signaled to the men with his sword. "Let him run."

As Abner bulled into a copse of trees in the distance, Joab glimpsed a youthful figure, lithe and fleet of foot, pursue his prey into the grove. A pocket of nauseous dread emptied itself into Joab's gut. The young man's build was unmistakably Asahel's.

Joab broke into a run.

"Asahel!" he bellowed. "No, Asahel!"

At a cleft in a low promontory, Asahel hesitated to look back at Joab.

"Stop, Asahel!" He plowed through the low scrub, but his brother beckoned him onward and set out again, his eyes fixed on Abner's broad back.

Asahel! Joab wept inwardly as the exuberance of youth lashed the young man on to seek vengeance upon his enemy. The distance between them gradually expanded, but the agony of his brother's pending fate urged Joab's burning legs forward.

❧ ❧ ❧

Abner felt the press of the chase hounding his back. He glanced over his shoulder and cursed his fortune. Were it any other young man he would have stopped immediately and slain the upstart where he stood, but Asahel…? He had seen the fellow a few times and was almost certain it was he. He knew how dear the boy was to his eldest brother, and one life spared would be an insignificant allowance in the scope of this deadly conflict. Abner ran on, silently beseeching the youth to relent in this frantic chase, for his life's sake, but his prayers went unanswered.

At the crest of a hillock Abner turned and shouted down. "Are you Asahel?"

"I am!" the young man confirmed, pausing briefly to look up.

"Turn aside, either left or right and take hold of one of the young men and take his spoil!"

Asahel launched into a fresh pursuit.

"Turn aside from following me!" Abner implored. "Why should I need to kill you? How then would I face Joab your brother?"

Still Asahel refused to desist or alter his trajectory. As he assailed Abner's position, the older man, using the advantage of his higher elevation and the reach of his spear, brought the armored shaft down on Asahel's unguarded wrist as he drew his sword. The weapon clanged a death toll against an exposed boulder as Abner smote Asahel in the ribs; the spear penetrated the young man's breast to protrude behind him. He fell at Abner's feet and died within moments.

Abner grimaced, pressing a clenched fist to his forehead.

"Why could you not have turned aside, boy?" At the edge of his vision he saw dark shapes coming toward him. Asahel's brothers would be along in minutes, and there was no reason to tarry. The day had been a tragedy in more ways than one.

～ ～ ～

Joab and Abishai knelt over Asahel, their faces contorted masks of sorrow. *Why could he not have halted?*

"We would have taken Abner eventually! Why, Asahel—*why?*" he shouted at the prone form. Joab pounded the ground with his fist. His men congregated at the base of the incline. Cognizant of Joab's deep grief, they hung back.

"We go on," Joab swore.

Abishai nodded and the chase began anew.

Sunset preceded the thick gloom as night draped a velvety curtain of darkness over the wilderness. Abner waited atop the hill of Ammah, clearly visible against the sky as Joab and his cluster of men approached across the rugged terrain.

"Joab!" Abner called loudly as the milling mass drew within earshot of the hill on which the Benjamite battalion was perched. "Shall the sword devour forever?" His words bounded off the boulder-strewn terrace and echoed to the oncoming men. Joab slowed his men.

"Don't you know that it will be bitterness in the end? How long before you bid your men to cease from following their brothers?" Abner's voice rose in pitch, pleading for reason.

Joab halted and squinted into the dark. He raised his voice to the hill. "As God lives, Abner—unless you had spoken we would have hunted you till dawn."

Joab fingered his trumpet, considering his course. Many more men would in fact die should he press an attack in this light, and it was Abner he wanted. The man could easily slip away, clothed in darkness.

I can wait longer yet, Joab decided. *His end is drawing nigh.*

The dissonant wail of the trumpet shushed the night insects in their dusty domain. There would be no further bloodshed this night. Joab returned his troop to the site of Asahel's body, which he swathed in a cloak. Abishai joined him to carry their brother home.

PART 2
THE FORGING OF A KINGDOM

Chapter Twelve

Civil War

The LORD hear thee in the day of trouble;
The name of the God of Jacob defend thee;
Send thee help from the sanctuary,
And strengthen thee out of Zion;
Remember all thy offerings,
And accept thy burnt sacrifice.
Grant thee according to thine own heart,
And fulfill all thy counsel.
We will rejoice in thy salvation,
And in the name of our God we will set up our banners!

PSALM OF DAVID 20, EXCERPT

The Philistine occupation of the northern cities on both sides of the River Jordan sounded a discordant note throughout the kingdom. Under Abner's leadership, the tribes rallied to dislocate the Philistine host, eroding the resources of the army. The men despaired of ever subduing the Philistine threat. In addition to this persistent sore that festered in their midst, the tribes suffered the wrenching of internal rivalries. The civil war between the House of Saul and the House of David stormed unabated for several years.

The constant hum of disharmony wore on Ishbosheth. His nerves frayed as incessant reports came in of skirmishes and errant battles across the wilderness. He grew edgy and quarrelsome, ever hoping for an end to the feud but finding no means of escape. Although Abner continued to provide valuable counsel, the waning of his house told the story of his flagging leadership.

Abner, too, grew intolerant of Ishbosheth's insecurities and inexhaustible queries. Ishbosheth considered each of Abner's actions to be a test of his mettle or a challenge to his authority as king. Conversely, Abner regarded Ishbosheth as a disappointment to the crown and unworthy of the respect that his father had earned.

≈ ≈ ≈

On a night of unusual serenity, Abner, having deployed his companies and scouts to their duties, took a long-anticipated hiatus from the clamor of command. He relaxed in his quarters, savoring the quietude. He had denied himself the company of women for several months, especially since he had discovered many of the city wenches to be loyal to the House of David, or at least to their purses. Abner's men, officially denied the illicit company of perfumed bosoms and lilting laughter, grew increasingly restless and unruly. Abner could presently find no solution to the dilemma. He had considered putting the women out of the city, but he understood that the implications would be far-ranging; their expulsion would spark animosity and ill-will between the soldiers and the people. Moreover, with Ishbosheth's failing grace in his people's eyes, Abner did not wish to chance the generating of further malice toward his rulership.

He chose to visit Rizpah, who was once a favored concubine in Saul's harem. Her two sons to Saul, Armoni and Mephibosheth, now looked to Abner as their father figure. Ishbosheth should have been their mentor but he had no exciting tales of war to stir the blood of a young boy and so the youths had gravitated toward Abner, swearing him their loyalty. He knew this minor unfaithfulness would rankle Ishbosheth; since the death of his father and brothers, Ishbosheth had treasured his family's closeness above all else.

Rizpah's delicate smile welcomed Abner, and her reminiscence of the days of the dominance of the House of Saul comforted him. During a quiet moment, her downcast eyes made him inquire about her thoughts.

She met his gaze. "I hope you might take my sons' training into your own hands."

"And eventually promote them to a place in the king's guard?"

She nodded, then turned the conversation back to lighter matters. Abner was comforted in her presence, for her ease of conversation placated his thoughts of war and conquest. It allowed him a pleasant surcease form his duties.

This night Abner's elevated mood led to an indiscretion that he would have avoided had his wits not been dulled by a brew of mimsach. The strong blend flooded his senses and his ensuing advances to Rizpah went undeterred.

On the following morning neither said anything regarding their tryst, but as Abner made his slow way back to his quarters, his head still tight with the debilitating aftereffects of the wine, Ishbosheth accosted him in the confines of the narrow hall.

"For what reason did you take it upon yourself to bed my father's concubine?" Ishbosheth demanded with heated displeasure. A king's concubines were not simple bedmates, but an honor granted to him as royalty. Abner had knowingly infringed upon a symbol of the crown, but a man of his position should be allotted a few concessions.

Wrath flooded Abner's frame, now drawn tall over Ishbosheth.

"Do you think so little of me? Am I a nobody who simply happened by to pit himself against Judah as a kindness to the House of Saul your father, and have not delivered you into David's hands? That you come today to accuse me regarding this woman?" Abner's rage made his powerful muscles tense and bulge.

"So do God to me and more if I do not fulfill God's promise to David and turn the kingdom over from the House of Saul and set up the throne of David both over Israel and Judah, from Dan even to Beersheba."

A passing servant cowered, averting his eyes in fear as Abner's anger ignited in the hallway. The concussive force of his bellow rattled the coward Ishbosheth who backed away in terror. Abner bunched his fists;

withholding the brunt of his anger lest he crush his former king's son made his eyes bulge painfully. Ishbosheth retreated down the hallway, his diatribe aborted.

Abner slammed into his room and crashed the door against the wall. The heavy panel splintered from its hinges. He snatched his cloak and went directly to the main courtyard to seek messengers.

"Elam! Reuel!" he called to two of his runners near the gate. They approached with due alacrity and bowed.

"Master?"

"Relay a message to the House of David…"

⤙ ⤙ ⤙

David regarded the messengers robed in the regalia of Saul's house with a mixture of disbelief and exhilaration.

"Who does the land belong to?" the first was saying. "My lord bids you make a league with him and he will support you in conquering Israel."

"I will make a pact with him," David replied, "on the condition that he first brings Michal, my wife, when he comes. Also, tell Ishbosheth to deliver my wife who I espoused with the foreskins of Philistines."

The men acknowledged his requests and David released them, pleased at the outcome of the day. The bloodshed might at last be coming to an end.

⤙ ⤙ ⤙

Ishbosheth's worst fears haunted his waking hours. He was not quite sure what Abner had done, but with the messengers' departure he'd understood his hold on the crown was broken and with it his days of security. He would have commanded the king's guard to slay Abner had he believed they would heed his order, but he bore no illusions as to his position in the eyes of the men. He was helpless to halt the disintegration of his reign, which was incited only by his dispute with Abner. His only hope now was that he would be granted his life if he cooperated with Abner in the transferal of power. The elders of Israel would capitulate if Abner required it. After all, hadn't he been crowned at Abner's bidding? It seemed now that his brothers were more fortunate than he. *I am now alone—abandoned to the whim of my sworn protector, yet obliged to live each day in fear of my life,* Ishbosheth thought in irony.

Ishbosheth was therefore resigned when the messengers returned to speak first with Abner. Their exchange brought a smile to Abner's face.

It is settled then, Ishbosheth realized. *David will be king over Israel. And what will become of me?*

◦ ◦ ◦

One of the messengers approached him and knelt. *A worthless show of obeisance,* mused Ishbosheth bitterly. He motioned for them to rise.

"King David bids you deliver his wife Michal, my lord."

Ishbosheth received the command with equanimity. He knew it was not meant as a request.

"Send to Phlatiel, son of Laish and let him send her out. Take two of the guards."

The messenger bowed his head and set out to tear the king's sister from a union that should never have been.

An hour later, Michal appeared through the gateway. She was escorted by a double guard. Her new husband trailed behind weeping piteously.

Abner came over to the distraught man.

"Go, Phlatiel. Return." The man seemed not to hear.

"Phlatiel! Enough!" Abner spoke firmly into his ear. He placed an unyielding hand on Phlatiel's shoulder, commanding his obedience. "Take a hold of yourself before your father is told of this shameful display. Remember your pride, man. There is nothing for you here."

Phlatiel mumbled an incoherent phrase and moved toward the gate. He raised features contorted with grief to Ishbosheth, imploring a reversal of the order, but the king returned only a dejected expression. What could be changed? Phlatiel squeezed his eyes shut to stifle a sob and shuffled away. Ishbosheth had the uncomfortable sense that his physical stature had somehow diminished. The crown was as easily lost to him as Michal was to Phlatiel. Who would mourn the injustice? There could not be two husbands. Neither could there be two kings.

∽ ∽ ∽

Joab returned at nightfall from a campaign against raiders in the south to news of David's pact with Abner.

"He did what?" Joab's shocked outburst carried throughout the stable yard, rousing the servants in their quarters from a short slumber.

"Tell me this is not true!" he appealed to Abishai.

"I'm afraid that it is,' Abishai confirmed mournfully. "Abner came with twenty men. They spoke of Israel and the House of Benjamin. Apparently he succeeded in swaying the loyalties of the Benjamites. The king prepared a feast and Abner vowed to gather all Israel in under David. Abner went away in peace."

"But how could he do this knowing what Abner did to Asahel?"

Abishai shrugged woodenly. "In the interest of peace, I suppose."

"There shall be no peace as long as Abner lives," Joab ground out, slashing his arm through the air. "Take two score men. Go after Abner. Detain him until I come. Say nothing of this. I will join you after I visit the king.

Joab stomped off to confront David, his thoughts churning angrily. *To make my brother's slayer captain in my stead? And for the sake of an allegiance to secure his crown? No!*

The king sat in his antechamber, savoring his bargain with Abner. More than anything he was anticipating Michal's return.

"Joab!" David greeted cheerily, and then frowned. "Did the campaign not go well?"

Joab waved aside the query. "What have you done? Abner comes here, and you send him away in peace? You let him simply leave?" He threw his hands wide. "You must know that he came to deceive you and to spy on you?" He stared incredulously at the king.

"Joab," David said in a conciliatory tone, "I know that you are aggrieved at the loss of Asahel, but we must think of sparing the people more bloodshed."

"Is that it then?" Joab bit out, incensed by the king's passive response. David offered no further consolation.

"We shall see about that," Joab said fiercely. He spun and shouldered his way past David's chief servant, who had stood wide-eyed at the door.

⟡ ⟡ ⟡

Abishai followed Abner's route to the well of Sirah. It lay less than an hour's journey from Hebron. Abner's eyes narrowed as he witnessed the arrival of the David's men. He spoke a word to his men whose hands had already closed on weapons. Bunched shoulders settled but each man maintained a grip on his sword. Abishai's men hung back as instructed, allowing their commander to proceed alone.

"What do you require, Abishai. Do you come in peace?" Abner asked suspiciously.

"In peace," Abishai said with disarming placidity. "The king bids you return."

"For what reason? He sent me in peace!"

Abishai replied as though disinterested in the matter. "For some issue pertaining to the kingdom, I presume. He alone must say, for I cannot." Abishai did not press. Abner's reluctance was reasonable, for the wounds of war ran deep, and there was yet a rift of blood between them.

Abner frowned but chose to comply. "Very well! I will come."

⟡ ⟡ ⟡

Within an hour Joab joined his brother on the road back to Hebron. As they entered the king's gate Joab hailed Abishai, who slowed his small troop to a walk. The two dismounted and stood aside for a brief exchange.

"For Asahel," Joab said grimly.

Abishai nodded and sidled away to relieve his men of their duty. The soldiers walked their mounts to the stables, their conversation light with the prospect of merriment before half night. Joab watched them round the bend, then turned to Abner with a hearty smile.

"Let us speak of the kingdom before you go in to the king," Joab offered, placing a hand on the commander's shoulder.

"There is much to discuss," Abner conceded. He stepped aside with

Joab, who shuffled his feet to disguise the sound of his weapon exiting its sheath.

"For Asahel!" Joab growled as he slid the razor-sharp blade beneath Abner's breastplate. The commander's life ended in a gurgle of blood. Joab shoved him away from his blade and walked away from the body without a backward glance.

"Take him back to the well and leave him there," Joab instructed Abishai. "Now we can speak of peace."

⟋ ⟋ ⟋

David broke his fast the following morning on goat's milk and bread. The elders of Hebron would be in attendance in the court on the following day. He intended to send messengers to Gibeah and Mahanaim. Abner would be instrumental in securing the allegiances of the remaining tribes. David loathed conflict between brothers; it was contrary to the way of the Living God. Ending the strife would be a victory indeed.

Midway in his meal, the chief servant appeared in the doorway, wringing his hands. David offered a slight nod of invitation, and the man came to his side and bent low. He whispered that Abner had been murdered. The grave tidings soured David's stomach; he pushed away his plate. He hastened to the audience hall where the elders awaited his arrival. As he was entering, one of the chiefs from the tribe of Asher received a small bit of parchment from his messenger. The elder read the missive and exclaimed loudly.

David moved to the front of the hall and spoke in a subdued tone. "You will all know soon enough. Abner, son of Ner, is dead. I and my kingdom are guiltless before the Lord forever from the blood of Abner." He turned to the trestle where Joab stood in attendance with the king's guard. "Let it rest upon the head of Joab, and all his father's house; and let the house forever be cursed," he said softly and vehemently.

Suddenly David injected his voice with thunderous power. "Rend your clothes! We shall don sackcloth and mourn Abner." He turned to Joab. Never had he thought Joab capable of such treachery and he clenched his jaw for many seconds before he felt able to speak to the man.

"Return Abner to Hebron. We shall bury him here." An icy veil fell between him and his captain. Joab's eyes hollowed into pits that read clearly of his understanding—this act he would not be forgiven.

∽ ∽ ∽

King David followed Abner's bier through the streets of the city. At the grave, he knelt and wept. Another part of his past was eroded and he was left forever with hard, cruel men. He vividly remembered Jonathan—his father and brothers all slain—their mutilated corpses pinned to the wall of Bethshan by the Philistines—the heroic recovery of the bodies by the men of Jabesh-Gilead—the cremation—the burial of the bones in Jabesh. The men of Jabesh had never forgotten Saul's call to all Israel on their behalf. His intervention had saved them from the brutality of the Ammonites. It was the mighty battle that had launched Saul's reign.

The memories surged forth with a sudden pain that wrenched David's body. So many mighty men, fallen. David tore at his clothes amidst a flood of anguish. His servants hovered nearby, their whispers and murmurs of scant comfort to him. No one had first believed that the king was not a part of Abner's murder, but his open grief belied their suspicions.

"You fell as a man falls before wicked men," David lamented. His mourning seemed unceasing, and as the day wore on, his servants bustled nervously at the door to his chamber, debating whether to intrude. Near evening Eleab, the chief servant, called softly at the door. David gave no answer. After several moments, the servant cried out for a message to be sent to the kitchens. They brought him food but he refused it.

"So do God to me and more, if I eat before sunset," David swore, glaring at his chief servant. "Don't you realize that there is a prince and a great man fallen this day in Israel?" he shouted to the gathering.

He sat down on the ground, his head drooping. *I might be the anointed king, but today...today I am weak. These men, these sons of Zeruiah, are too cruel for me, but God rewards evildoers accordingly,* David consoled himself. He would not destroy them—for his sister's sake and the sake of unity amongst his men.

God will requite Joab, David thought to himself. *My hands will spill no more blood.*

≈ ≈ ≈

Word of Abner's fate dispersed like a thunderclap across Israel. Ishbosheth paled with foreboding when one of Abner's guardsmen delivered the foul news. Abner had been so certain of himself. "David is a man of peace and of reason," Abner had told him. "I will hand David everything and cease this game of crowns. Then you can go back to your princely play, while we men manage the kingdom."

But now there was no *we* for the son of Ner and perhaps no future for the discarded prince. The House of Saul reeked of treason and death. Nothing was certain save Death's unquenchable thirst. Ishbosheth thought of fleeing, but where in Israel could he escape the reach of the king? He could think of no one who would aid a man who was lost even to himself. He could not forget the years of David's own flight from his father, Saul. There was nowhere that one was safe from the king's influence within his own kingdom. Perhaps David would see him as Abner had—a man, alone, with no innate strength but living only at the behest of the more powerful. With Abner gone, David might allow him his freedom, and his life. He would abide, for he could do little else.

≈ ≈ ≈

David looked down at the severed head borne him as a gift by Baanah and Rechab, sons of Rimmon the Beerothite. Weren't they from Benjamin, from the House of Saul? He struggled to recall their rank.

The older brother knelt and addressed David.

"Look, the head of Ishbosheth, the son of Saul, your enemy, who sought your life. Today the Lord has brought vengeance on Saul and his seed."

David took a deep breath and rolled his head to ease the pulsing wave of tension about his neck.

Ah yes, he remembered now—They were captains of bands. *Was a king always to be plagued by traitors?* He returned a stony gaze to the men who waited proudly, expectantly, with their trophy. They had told him heartily of their entry into Ishbosheth's house, finding that he lay unsuspecting and asleep—And at noontime even! His ignorance astounded them.

Neither man seemed to read David's subtle reaction. *And they have called Ishbosheth a fool?* The king found himself responding as calmly as though he spoke of a drifting cloud.

"When another man told me, 'Behold, Saul is dead,' thinking that he was bringing me good tidings and that I would give him a reward for his news, I killed him in Ziklag." David fixed his eyes on theirs, watching their brows rise in cognition and their pupils widen in fear.

He continued to speak, his tone level. "How much more when wicked men have slain a righteous man in his own house, upon his bed?"

The men fell on their faces before him, beseeching the mercy of the king.

"Shall I not require his blood of your hand and take you away from the earth?" David questioned quietly.

The brothers moaned piteously and prostrated themselves, the younger soiling himself. David, ignoring their imploring cries, signaled the King's Guard to approach.

"Slay them and hang them over the pool in the city," he commanded, not wavered by the escalating wails of penitence. There could be no contrition to equal the magnanimity of their shameless trespass.

So much blood...

As the doors closed to seal the sentence, David sent for a royal bier to convey Ishbosheth's head to Abner's sepulcher where it would be buried. Ishbosheth had not been a warrior nor had he been a threat even without devious men like Abner to guide him. These Berothites, they knew the ways of war and the wages of courting violence.

David closed his eyes and tried to pinch away the throbbing along the bridge of his nose. *What will become of me amongst these sons of Belial! Indecent, dishonorable men with secret machinations. Ishbosheth had always been ignorant of their ways. He was a mild and fearful man who Saul had shielded. Ishbosheth had indeed been naive, but he did* not warrant the death that had been laid upon him. The king sighed. He was exhausted by the day: obsequious servants, cunning enemies, wayward captains....

At times it was difficult to discern the truth of a man's heart, but God's heart he knew; it was merciful and pure, and he knew also that it was toward him, a simple man now cloaked in His Power, and that would be enough. David prayed as he had so many times before that his heart would remain untainted by the treacherous ways of the men he succored—that the simple manner of the sheepherder would not be lost to the boy-become-king.

CHAPTER THIRTEEN

An Old Enemy

How long shall mine enemy be exalted over me?
Consider and hear me, O LORD my God;
Lighten my eyes,
Lest I sleep the sleep of death;
Lest my enemy say, "I have prevailed against him";
And those that trouble me rejoice when I am moved.
But I have trusted in Thy mercy;
My heart shall rejoice in Thy salvation.
I will sing to the LORD,
Because He hath dealt bountifully with me.

PSALM OF DAVID 13, EXCERPT

Thirty years old! It seemed too insignificant an age for a man to be crowned king of all Israel. *How old had Saul been?* he wondered. *Had there been doubt among the people then also?* Today, if they acquiesced to his headship, he would be anointed by the elders of the tribes of Israel who had been gathering consistently for three days in the city of Hebron.

On the fourth day, the multitude crammed resolutely into the open court and spilled into the streets beyond. The leaders came forward from the forefront of the eager congregation. As they drew near, David approached the outer edge of the low, sunlit dais. He was garbed in imposing linen robes, the gold embroidery gleaming in the bright rays. He stood before them, solemn and regal as any sovereign throughout the land.

"We are of your bones and of your flesh," the guiding elder began. "When Saul was king, you were the one who captained the tribes as appointed by God." The truth of this had been challenged before in rebellious corners, but none of the elders would now contradict the validation of David's reign, which had been ceded by the highest Power—that of YHWH himself. Each had witnessed the time of severe declension that had followed Saul after he had countered God's authority.

"We surrender to the will of the King," the Chief Elder intoned. They bowed as one, sealing their united decision.

David knelt and closed his eyes. *It is as was revealed. I will be king!*

The peculiar warmth of oil coursed through his hair and dripped along his cheek and into his thick beard. The sensation cast him back to that lonely night in the plains with only sheep for company. . . .*His brothers were feasting without him. A visitor had come. He would miss the festivities once again. Most of his evenings were spent in grim solitude. The incidents involving the lion and the bear that he had slain in seasons past were unusual occurrences. He had been celebrated enthusiastically then, but there was to be no excitement this night for the youngest son of Jesse. It was his lot, he supposed, to be the least regarded of his brothers. He heard the gaiety of instruments! Was there to be a sacrifice then? The visitor must be a person of some importance—probably one of the Bethlehemite elders—for his father had several friends in the Gate. He jolted as his name was called at the edge of the darkness that engulfed the pasture.*

"David! David, your father needs you to come in. I will take your place." The voice was that of the keeper. "You are free tonight, boy. And a surprise awaits you!" the man whispered mysteriously.

David hurried toward the welcoming glow of his homestead. His curiosity was earnestly piqued. Was father giving them each a blessing? Was one of his brothers to be betrothed? Was a dowry being set?

None of his guesses had matched the wonder of the reality—Samuel, the prophet of God, had chosen to anoint him, a youth of humble lineage. He had not known then that it had been an anointing to rule a nation. This was the wis-

dom of YHWH alone; a mystery as deep as the slow but purposeful rotation of the heavens...

David's vivid memories merged with the feeling of the oily runnels that trickled down the nape of his neck. The slick flow caressed his back, entwining him in a new purpose—a betrothal to his people and to the God of Israel.

Flesh of my flesh...blood of my blood. The covenant was sealed. He was king, and now he had a kingdom to win back.

෴ ෴ ෴

Day after day, thousands of men of war poured into Hebron. The largest contingents came from the House of Zebulun and across the Jordan. These men were expert warriors with the knowledge or varied instruments of war. Their ability to keep rank during battle was renowned.

Food was brought in from the nearby cities on mule-carts, camels and even yoked oxen; meat, meal, raisins, wine, lamb and oil flowed in abundance. The might of Israel in the hundreds of thousands had come to turn Saul's kingdom over to the anointed of God as had been decreed by divine utterance. No one could withstand the word of YHWH, not even the Philistine host whose might was washed away by a people reborn under a new king—a king of power.

෴ ෴ ෴

With the sudden expansion of the ranks of David's military force came a throng of distinguished captains who all eyed the second rung on the ladder of power erected by King David. Who amongst them would lead?

Adino's departure after the torching of Ziklag had cleared the way in David's army for a younger man to earn his armor.

Adino had opted to return, following his own course, perhaps to secure his family's lands—areas in Cabul were rumored to be under attack by rovers from Aram in the north.

"Who will suckle you now, eh?" he had joked to David, clasping him in a bear hug. "Rule well," he told the king, suddenly becoming serious.

"I will miss you, my friend." David's gut constricted, for other than

Jonathan, none had been closer to him than the jovial older man, who had admitted with a chuckle to also having been a sheepherder in his youth. The stolid man had been David's bastion throughout the seasons of tumult. The farewell was decidedly brief.

"Be true to the Lord of Hosts," Adino had cautioned gravely, "and be true to your men."

"My brother…" David's words trailed away and he embraced his comrade fiercely. "May we meet again."

Adino nodded and his broad frame trembled with emotion. "I leave behind me a man who is like a son of my bones; a son that is a king."

◠ ◠ ◠

Joab rued the day his eagerness to claim the position as chief of the captains almost sheared away his life. The call came to take the city of Jerusalem from the Jebusites, who denied David entry access to the city. The Jebusites were notorious for their resistance since the Israelites had crossed the river Jordan; they did not relinquish ground by mere request, and their capability to uphold their stance was known abroad. The refusal was a blatant rejection of the king himself and as the messenger bearing the missive took his leave of their camp, David's face solidified into stone. Among the captains, Joab eagerly awaited the king's pronouncement. "The first of you to go up against Jebus will be made the head of the host!"

Joab bristled with anticipation, so much so that when the first trumpet blast erupted, his company was the first to rush the city, followed closely by that of his brother Abishai.

A hail of sling-stones assaulted the headlong crush of soldiers. The opposition they encountered was ferocious, and Joab's men were unprepared for the Jebusites' well-coordinated attack.

Abner has been here ahead of us, Joab deduced bitterly. The dead commander's past strife with David had seeded many pockets of resistance within the kingdom in order to guard against overthrow by David during the civil war. He would have provided armament and training to unskilled guardsmen, knowing that Jerusalem was a king's true prize. It lay in the heart of the Promised Land, between the northern and southern tribes and therefore had a strategic advantage for military deployments.

The reinforcements displayed were unusually formidable. Some of the men in his vanguard toppled, struck unconscious by the intense volleys. The second and third flights of stones temporarily deterred the trailing sections, leaving Joab and Abishai within the perimeter of aggression. Retreat was not an option. Joab braved the artillery to reach the city's defenders. He cut through their ranks with abandon, the exalted title he sought spurring him onward.

Joab found himself trapped in the midst of six of the elite guard. He parried and slashed in a desperate defense of his life, for these men would have been captains in their own right had they been serving the king. Their proficient thrusts shredded Joab's attack as they rotated their strike in pairs to blunt his impetus. Two of the soldiers dropped with slashes to their legs and Joab drew his knife from his belt. He stepped inside the reach of the third combatant, sinking his blade into the exposed flesh of the man's forearm, forcing him to withdraw to stanch the bleeding. Joab retreated and firmed his grip on the hilt of his knife, now slick with blood, and threw it left-handed to impale a fourth man. He kicked hard at the bare shin of the new attacker. The soldier grunted, stumbling awkwardly. Joab leaned away from the soldier's pitching fall and sliced the man's sword arm; the fighter's weapon clattered ineffectively to the ground, and the last of the six attackers made a determined surge. Joab's sturdy armor deflected several killing strokes but deep gashes sliced his arms. He gritted his teeth against the mounting pain and the burning in his limbs. Joab fought with new vigor as he envisioned the shame that defeat would visit upon his family. He slapped aside a menacing cut and leaned out of his stance to sweep the man's feet with a deft arc of his leg. The soldier's resistance faltered as he caught to regain his balance. Joab neatly reached in to cuff the man's temple with the bronzed haft of his sword and watched his opponent tumble limply at his feet.

Joab's chest heaved from the exertion. The fighting around him had begun to ebb. He braced his hands on his knees and shook off a dizzying rush. Sweat dripped from his nose as he continued to draw ragged breaths in an attempt to recover his composure.

Abishai pelted to his side, concern softening the hard lines etched into the warrior's features.

"Are you well, brother?"

Joab nodded, still winded.

"Well then, chief!" Abishai teased, giving Joab a jesting shove as though to topple him. "Enough of this coddling. You're no newly dropped camel. Let's go sew you up. Beating six men alone and you look like a patched wineskin. Fine way to celebrate your promotion!" Joab glared fondly at his brother's back as it receded down the street, shaking with smothered mirth.

⋍ ⋍ ⋍

Achish was inconsolable. "I was truly deceived, Phergon. King of Israel— and I had him in my hands!" Achish struck his balled fist to his knee in self-repudiation. "What can we do? I thought us to be fairly well positioned with the elimination of Saul and the strongest of his sons. *Now this?*"

"David is cunning," Phergon offered by way of comfort. "It was good that we sent him away from Aphek, was it not?"

"Indeed!" Achish conceded. "He shall look to strike at us while he is heady with the wine of power. We should prepare ourselves. Let us seek him before he seeks us. Do what you must, Phergon."

"I propose we attack Bethlehem. It is poorly defended, and it is also the place of the king's birth. To secure it would be a symbolic victory."

Achish shrugged his shoulders in final agreement. "Bethlehem it is."

⋍ ⋍ ⋍

King David surveyed the parched wilderness landscape from the shade of the cave Adullam.

"Never thought you would be back here so soon, did you?" Eleazar stood with David as they reminisced of their days in the hold.

David wished again for the solace of his father's confidence in his son's ability to defeat the odds against him, his mother's enduring smile, and the sheer peace derived from being home. "Yet here we are again. This time harassed by an enemy instead of by our brothers. Several times I have thought that life to be a peculiar dream!"

"It seems the Philistines have come to celebrate the commencement of your reign."

David's lips curled downward briefly. "Yes, with my head balanced atop the posts of their idols."

"I'm sure that Achish berated himself mightily for letting you go."

"Undoubtedly," David said, stifling the memory of his narrow escape.

"Our spies say that they have blanketed Bethlehem."

David walked a mental map of the town. "How I wish that someone could give me a drink of water from the well that is at the gate; it is so cold and pure!" He paused for several moments, then returned his thoughts to the war at hand. "We shall spend another day in preparation and then we go down."

At half night, three brawny figures moved stealthily across the terrain between the hold and the city of Bethlehem, which lay as quiet as the calm that ushers in a violent storm. Escaping from the hold unnoticed had been a difficult task since David's patrols moved with increasing vigilance. They preferred to make their journey anonymously lest word should return to David and he curtail their effort. No words were spoken by the three who were resolved in their mission, which some may have denigrated as trivial, but they served a master unlike any other, and they would give their lives in his service.

The trio encountered military tents obscuring the entire plain in front of the city gates. The men slowed to a walk and simultaneously pulled their cloaks tight about them to conceal their array of weapons. They traveled at a sedate pace that would not attract curious eyes. Many of the enemy soldiers were sleeping on the ground on reed mats or blankets. The men strode as though they were a part of the vast contingent and were a mere hundred paces from the open gate before their cloaked forms drew the notice of a young captain who eyed with suspicion the gray, rough-spun weave of the intruders' coats.

"You there," he shouted, "Hold!"

The men did not slow their advance toward the gate.

"Stop at once!"

The three men broke into a run, unsheathing weapons as they pelted toward their goal. Their charge carried them through the gates, where they encountered a cordon of soldiers on patrol inside the wall. Their cloaks fell away to reveal full armor, in addition to a curious object clutched protectively in the crooked elbow of one man. He sprinted away from his companions, leaving them to secure him a precious moment to carry out his task.

He returned in what seemed like a heartbeat to join his two companions in a pitched battle. Blood pounded in their ears.

"I have it, let's go!" he shouted and the three pitted their might against a thickening knot of men. With their backs turned inward, the three carved their way toward the tents, each knowing that his back was defended and whoever lay ahead of their blade was no friend. The armor hung heavy on their muscled bodies, but their strength was such that they moved swiftly toward the tented encampment.

Realizing the intention of his quarry to escape into the dense rows of tents, the lead officer gave a cry to alert his men of the infiltration. The existence of three enemies had seemed to be a minor inconvenience on the night rounds so deep within the outer perimeter of guards, but as the men efficiently bludgeoned a path to the outer camp it became more apparent that the men had endangered their lives for some critical purpose unknown to any but themselves. Their skill exceeded that of the Philistine guard, which found itself encumbered by the malaise of off-duty soldiers. It was too late to turn the three men aside, and they reached the dense rows of tents, breaking into a run through the milling soldiers who gave startled cries. Others looked up to discern the source of the disruption.

The three men had appeared to be an insignificant threat, yet along their escape route; hundreds of men lay dead. It was impossible to coordinate an effective counterattack in the confusion of the packed campground as more soldiers were dispatched. The three men of war broke free of the encampment and exploded into a headlong run into the darkness. Their pursuers halted at the edge of the camp, hurling curses into the night, for they could not discern whether the men's goal had been to lure them into an ambush preceding the war or to attack the core of their command. They opted not to follow.

"Juir, what did they want?" a senior officer questioned the commander who had first discovered the intrusion.

"I cannot be sure. One retrieved something at the well. Beyond that, I cannot say."

They may have come to poison our water." The older man's voice betrayed his concern.

"Have five of our slaves and a few animals drink some of it. It may not be poisoned; still, we would be equally disadvantaged if our soldiers were to be struck with a plague of loose bowels during the battle. We will not drink until we are certain. It could mean our deaths either way."

≈ ≈ ≈

In council with his captains, David was missing three of his key men. No one could say where they were to be found.

"My lord," one said quietly.

David broke from his discussion, relieved to see the three absentee faces. They knelt before him. He looked enquiringly at the earthen jar offered in upraised hands. David's eyes widened as he recognized the drinking jar and intuitively knew its contents.

"No!" he cried. The jar remained upraised and he stepped forward to take the gift. He opened the lid and peered in at the crystal clear water. The magnanimity of what the men had done to gain him his request gripped his heart like no other his deed within his memory. His men's loyalty and devotion to him was evidenced by their bloodstained arms.

"Thank you!" he said.

The men grinned to one another and arose, congratulating each other on his prowess. David dismissed them all and went to the rear of the hold. He knelt and closed his eyes, raising his face to an imaginary sky and a real God.

"How can I drink it? I cannot! Oh Lord, be it far from me that I should do this. Isn't this the blood of the men that went in jeopardy of their lives?" His heart felt full to the brim, for their sacrifice was more than he could bear alone.

"I offer this to you, Lord." He poured the water slowly out, an offering to the God who bolstered him and protected his men as they risked their lives on his behalf. He had not drunk, yet he tasted something more powerful and longer lasting than a few cool drops of water on his tongue. He was blessed to have received an outpouring akin to nothing he had experienced before. It infused the very core of his being—trust, faith, and a knowing that even more than what he gave would be offered back in the pace of a heartbeat.

ᕽ ᕽ ᕽ

A sea of soldiers poured into the valley like water tumbling from a breach in a dam. Phergon reeled in surprise, for the strike came even as he was mustering the troops. Having been the aggressor throughout countless incursions, his men had grown accustomed to completing formation whilst the defenders observed and prepared desperate measures to counteract their offensive. He felt now the same panic that emptied men's bellies when they realized that war was descending and their backs were yet bare.

To Phergon's horror, the coordinated rush of David's host found him composing battle lines and readying the soldiers' weapons. Many of his captains were still in the rearguard dispensing orders when the air was sundered with chilling screams that promised retribution to his camp. He shouted for the men to fall back and reform their lines, but the thundering shouts of the onrushing enemy swept away his desperate cries, and his soldiers scattered like debris before a flood.

Without the captains to hold the companies together, the men deserted the ragged lines, scampering to escape the onslaught. Phergon turned in desperation, racing to his command tent for the sword that would be his only defense when the first wave broke upon them. He was amongst the hindmost who fled toward the opposing hill in search of a place to mount their defense. Fear soured the hot wind that razed their retreating flank. Phergon gave hasty orders then braced himself for the impact of the rushing assault. Two captains came to stand with him.

"All will be well," Phergon said to each in encouragement, but the words were like hollow gourds that offered no living water. He looked ahead to the approaching wall of men whose steady advance swept away the makeshift altar bearing the Philistine offering to Dagon. The noise grew louder and Phergon readied his stance. He dared not contemplate the significance of the trampled tributes. "We must stand," he yelled as he dug his sandals into the dirt to brace himself. *We must!*

David's men of war felt the supernatural rush of the Glory of God as the weight of their army bent the enemy back from the valley. The predator had become the hunted. Under David, Saul's armies were reunited in strength, their faith having been restored by their new king. The battlefield was strewn with wounded men, and interspersed in their midst lay miniature statues of lifeless gods, crushed by the stampede of soldiers who were terrified for their lives. As the Philistines were regrouping for the second time, David envisioned the debate within their ranks. Had their gods deserted them? Did the king, David, have a mightier God? Were they destined to be overrun? David knew that the answers would haunt their steps and drain their impetus. Aiming to capitalize on their weakness, he selected two captains and instructed the spoilers who flowed behind the battle lines. "Hasten now. Our men will return at evening light. When you go out, I need you to collect all the idols or images that you find. We shall burn them in the midst of this field. When our enemies return on the morrow, the ash will seed despair in their hearts and weaken their resolve."

David assigned five groups to the task. Night would soon fall and little would be achieved thereafter. He retreated to the shelter of his tent. The strategy for the coming dawn was still to be determined, and the finest battle lines were etched while on his knees.

≈ ≈ ≈

On the second day of the battle in the Rephaim Valley, the Philistines spread themselves out like sentinels. David gathered his captains on the ridge to observe the Philistine deployment. Their movements appeared crisp, but David noticed that their lines were drawn much farther back than on the previous day.

"Already they shrink away." Joab pointed out the terrain markers that had been noted on the previous day's attack.

David squinted into the gloomy light, unperturbed by the withdrawal of the front line. "It will work to our advantage."

"Do we proceed as we did yesterday, then? Their formations have remained unchanged apart from two dozen supplementary companies of archers in the vanguard. They hope to deter an early strike from our side or to reduce our numbers if we do attack."

"We shall be going around them to attack from the rear." David made the pronouncement without taking his eyes off the enemy camp.

The captains reacted as one. "Around?"

"Surely, you *cannot* be serious! That is three hours' march; it will be nearly half light by then and the men will be exhausted by the heat of the day," reasoned Joab. He looked to the others for assistance in dissuading David from the proffered course.

Shammah leaned in. "We could simply overrun them again."

"The Lord has decreed that we should attack from behind." David slapped his hand to his leg with a crack of finality. "We go in faith or we do not go at all. Our victory is in our obedience. Do any here wish defeat?" He was greeted by silence.

"Good! The Lord shall provide me with a signal. At the appointed time the trumpet will be sounded; until then, we do nothing." He looked around firmly. "Is that understood?"

The captains nodded in affirmation.

"We leave at double light."

≈ ≈ ≈

David watched expectantly for the promised signal. The tops of the mulberry trees cresting the ridge began to rustle. Only the wind, he realized after a moment. He was unsure what the sound from God would be, but he would know it when it came. Of this, he was certain. "It will come through the tops of the trees," his Lord had said.

David closed his eyes and drowned out the mélange of external sounds—the faint clinks of men shifting their armor; the whispers of a few, impatient for battle; the soft scrape of sandals on the rough stones beneath their feet. David's heart pummeled within his breast. He forced himself to ignore the throbbing and to remain calm.

The sun had begun its indomitable descent and his men were anxious. David stilled the clamor of his desire and the taste of victory and then he heard it, low and rumbling. The crescendo was so sudden that David's eyes popped open with the shock of its force. The trumpet bearer saw his master stiffen and raised his trumpet to his lips, glancing to David for confirmation.

David mouthed, "Yes," and the trumpet blast followed hard upon the supernatural roar that echoed down the valley.

The men of war responded instantly. Three thousand soldiers united under the banner of the Lord of Hosts, shaking the rim of the gorge as they followed David to victory.

≈ ≈ ≈

The triumph over the Philistine invaders rekindled the fervor of the twelve tribes and loosened the grip of fear which had persisted too long over Israel. The king felt the lift in the spirits of his people, yet his perception was awakened to the absence of the full glory of God amongst them.

We need the continuing presence of the Lord now, more than we ever have, David thought. He recognized an air of complacence about his men of war that was reflected in the faces of the people, and he instinctively knew that their assured demeanor was as dangerous as any physical threat to the kingdom. *The presence of YHWH must be paramount!*

As David lay abed, his thoughts ranged outward from Judah, and he arose with a start. *Where was it now?*

"Elead!" David shouted, excitement quivering in his voice.

The servant entered at a run. "Is something amiss, my lord?"

"Abiathar, send for him!"

"The priest, my lord? At this hour?"

"Yes, Elead. I will be waiting in the Hall of Audiences."

The servant bowed and exited swiftly.

David gathered his cloak and grinned to himself. He would reestablish the order of the kingdom, an order which had died before the days of his predecessor and was long overdue. Saul had never acknowledged its importance, but David vowed not to repeat his error.

≈ ≈ ≈

Abiathar shuffled from his bedchamber, willing his mind to alertness. What could be of such importance? Second watch was already past. He yawned and quickened his step. The king was pacing as he entered the hall.

"My lord?" Abiathar said, bowing.

"Abiathar, the ark of the covenant, where is it now?"

Abiathar shook the last dregs of fogginess from his mind. The ark—where was it? His father had told him. He paused, stroking his chin as he strained to recall. Yes, he remembered now.

"Abinadab tends it, my lord."

"Abinadab? How did this come about?"

"During the priesthood of my great-great-grandfather Eli and the Philistine domination of our land, the ark was captured at the battlefield of Ebenezer and taken to Ashdod. Thousands of men were slain. At that time the people were worshiping Ashtaroth in addition to other false gods and the Lord was wroth. Eli died when he was given the news of the ark's capture."

For a brief moment, Abiathar became pensive; the misery of the curse God had placed upon Eli and his house haunted the young priest daily.

"So," he continued, somewhat forlorn, "the Philistines suffered plagues as a result of the theft. The statute of their idol, Dagon, overturned twice and finally broke into pieces at the threshold of their temple. It is said that their priests haven't trodden the threshold of Dagon for almost a century now." Abiathar laughed bitterly. "We priests believe that we have such power...." He shook himself away from his melancholy thoughts and looked into the king's eyes.

David regarded the priest with sadness, but said nothing. Abiathar wondered if the king rued his part in Saul's vengeful extermination of his family.

"After several months of continuous plagues and destruction, the ark was dispatched from Philistia. It was placed on a cart drawn by a driver-less kine. The animal was guided by a divine hand by Bethshemesh toward the border between Dan and Judah. Unfortunately, the men of Bethshemesh looked into the ark and the Power of God was loosed; over fifty-thousand men were killed. It was therefore sent on to Kirjath Jearim, one of the four cities of the Gibeonites. Some call the place Baale Judah now. There it was entrusted to Abinadab. Actually, it was his son Eleazar who was sanctified in order that he might tend it safely. It was Samuel who convinced the tribes to forsake the false gods so that we might break free of the Philistines; if only we could have held to our faith." Abiathar sighed.

"Samuel's sons were not half the man of God that he was. They were as wayward as my grandfathers were." Abiathar noticed David's puzzled expression. "Hophni and Phineas, Eli's sons; they also took bribes and perverted the way of God. That's why they were killed, you know! That is also why my family was killed in Nob. My family has a curse placed upon it," Abiathar admitted, revealing the cause of the peculiarity of the deaths in his family.

David inhaled sharply. "I'm sorry," he offered sincerely.

Abiathar gestured dismissively. "Nothing can be done." The priest felt somewhat uncomfortable under the king's scrutiny and chose to redirect the discussion to its earlier course. "The ark has remained with Abinadab since that time," he said returning to the heart of David's query. "The elders of the tribe never saw fit to simply put their trust in YHWH. They did not want Samuel's sons Joel and Abiah either, so they asked for a king to judge them, and God obliged. That is how we became saddled with Saul. It worked well for a while, I suppose, but you can see how it turned out at the last. He never even remembered the ark. It was a travesty."

"I intend to change that," David said firmly. "May God go before us."

CHAPTER FOURTEEN

The Return

They shall fear Thee as long as the sun and moon endure,
Throughout all generations.
He shall come down like rain upon the mown grass:
As showers that water the earth.
In His days the righteous shall flourish;
And abundance of peace so long as the moon endureth.

PSALM OF DAVID 72, EXCERPT

The reconveyance of the ark took several weeks to arrange. David commissioned all thirty thousand of the chosen men of Israel to go with him to Baale for the return. The king made enthusiastic plans. He deliberated with the priest and elders over the necessity of removing the instrument of God to Jerusalem. He consulted with captains and leaders throughout the nation and called a gathering of all the congregation of Israel. He thereby gained the consensus to send abroad throughout the cities and villages as far as Egypt for all the priests. He invited the House of Levi, a priestly caste of men specially dedicated to the service of God.

"Let us bring again the ark of our God to us," David declared, "For we did not enquire of it in the days of Saul. It will be a new beginning."

It was agreed that Abinadab's sons, Uzza and Ahio, would drive the new cart from its place in Gibeah to the city of David in Jerusalem.

∽ ∽ ∽

The day of the return dawned in wonder. The ark was transferred safely to a cart, and David was immediately encouraged. Harps, psalteries, and timbrels sang in unison to herald the majesty of God. David motioned Uzza and Ahio to the fore of the procession. Abinadab came forward to join them. He offered a final caution to his sons in transporting the ark.

"I cannot make the passage with you, my sons. If there is a difficulty, call for the priests at once. Do not handle the ark itself. You have watched my care these many years. Do not stray from all I have taught, and you shall arrive safely."

"Yes, Father. We shall be cautious," Ahio reassured him.

"I will walk behind the cart while Ahio directs the kine." Uzza scanned the milling crowd in awe. His home was typically a quite place, and the recent fanfare was exhilarating. "We have a multitude here to aid us. Including the king! So do not fear, Father."

The young men took their designated places. Ahio started off slowly with the cart. His movements were halting but as the day progressed, his pace grew increasingly confident. The musical celebration streamed behind him.

By midmorning they had left Baale Judah far behind. The rejoicing continued unabated as throngs from nearby villages joined the march.

Passing through the threshingfloor of Chidon, the kine encountered a rough patch of terrain and stumbled forward, jerking the cart and its precious cargo, which lurched alarmingly.

Uzza reacted automatically and reached to brace the ark from falling. Sizzling power surged through Uzza's body as the anger of God was released with killing force. Uzza fell dead, his corpse contorted grotesquely.

Gasps of shock overlay distressed shouts.

David stared at Uzza's lifeless form, and Ahio stood beside his brother, shaking his head in disbelief.

That could have been any one of us, David realized despondently. *How will I be able to bring the Ark of God home to me?* He scanned the nearby crowd. Confusion, hesitation, anger, fear, commiseration—he recognized a gamut of emotions emblazoned on their faces. He also saw echoes of his own question, but he had no immediate answer.

The king signaled his chief servant, "Have the priest take the ark to the house of Obed-edom." David turned to Ahio. "I will send my servants to assist you in escorting your brother back to Gibeah."

Ahio nodded silently.

As the ark was diverted toward its new destination, David felt his hopes shatter and he grew suddenly tired. "Come Elead," he called. "Bring my horse. There is little more we can accomplish today."

"Yes, my lord."

For several nights David contemplated the disaster at Chidon. We have done something wrong. He doubted that it could solely be attributed to Uzza's rash attempt to safeguard the ark. It was late when the king summoned Abiathar. This time, Elead did not hesitate and Abiathar arrived promptly.

"What did we do wrong?" David asked plainly.

"I know of three things," said Abiathar, "but there may be others. I will need to consult the archives to be certain. First, the Levites and the House of Aaron are the designated caretakers of the ark and ministers to the Lord. Second, we failed to sanctify each person involved in bearing the ark, and third and most importantly, the ark is to be carried on staves, not on an ox-cart!" Abiathar's raised hands fell to his sides with a slap, showing his inability to conceive why they had not followed the correct protocol initially. But David knew. The excitement of the undertaking had overwhelmed their good reason.

David felt ashamed of his ignorance. He had assumed that it would be mete to utilize the same mode of conveyance as had been previously used. Despite all his preparations, he had allowed some basic errors in his anxiety to reclaim the ark. *Forgive me, Lord,* he prayed. *Forgive me, forgive me. We have dishonored You.*

"Abiathar, assemble the children of Aaron and the Levites. We shall do everything in due order, for I suspect there shall not be a third opportunity."

~ ~ ~

David made exhaustive preparations. "Use whatever funds are needed from the treasury. They shall be recovered ten-fold should we succeed," he told Abiathar.

Every pertinent instruction regarding the ark was carefully examined and followed. David constructed houses within the city and pitched a tent in which the ark would be contained.

"None are to touch it save the Levites. They will also be the only ones allowed to serenade Him," David insisted.

Doorkeepers, porters, singers, musicians, captains, elders—each person was instructed in the rules of his participation. Sanctification, dress, sacrificial offerings, sequencing....The king was rigorous in his attention to detail. He verified the historic records with Abiathar's aid and clarified the most mundane of the requirements. It would be done exactly as was proscribed or not at all.

~ ~ ~

David rose before the twinkle of celestial lights was dimmed by the glow of daybreak. He bathed and purified himself and girded on an ephod of fine linen; its gold and scarlet as fiery as the morning. His hair was washed and finely combed and fixed with a shining cord about his forehead. A smile parted his lips. The joy he was experiencing within himself was indescribable. He could easily have been fifteen again, playing his harp to the pleasure of the wind or climbing the crags outside Bethlehem for no reason other than the sweet lure of freedom. His laughter would canter through the valley, exalting in the boyish strength and vigor. Was anything beyond him? Not on this day. Today, his dreams awaited his touch like a lost lamb eager for his shepherd's jubilant embrace.

Over the preceding three months, his anticipation had slowly ripened like the fruit on the vine ready to be harvested. David strove confidently into the crisp air of the morning. The first part of his journey would seem too long, he knew. Thousands of anxious footsteps with miles yet to journey to be in His presence. A shiver ran the course of David's body, and he laughed in spite of himself. It was as the day of his wedding to Saul's daughter. Michal had been a breathtaking bride, tall like her father and proud—too proud sometimes, he had learned, but lovely to behold. This morning, the wonder of God far surpassed her radiance and made him reflect on His majesty.

"There is none like unto You, Lord," David shouted joyfully to the breaking skies. "None!"

⋽ ⋽ ⋽

The fourteen bearers emerged cautiously from the doorway of Obed-edom's house, balancing the staves expertly on lean shoulders. Their muscles tensed as they crossed the threshold, careful to sense the nudge of their brothers as their cleared the narrow opening. Obed-edom observed the procession happily as the carriage moved away. Having sheltered the ark in reverence for three months, he had experienced divine blessing, yet he was relieved to see the ark depart safely to the home of a greater master. The strictures for maintaining the sacred artifact had frayed the nerves of his household. None of his family had wanted to stir the wrath of the Lord and cause the destruction of their house. The ark belonged to the people and all Israel would now be blessed.

When the ark had been borne six paces, David sacrificed a multitude of his best oxen and fatlings. The congregated host shouted in exultation, rivaling the trumpet blast that announced the initial success of their painstaking labors. The ark came to the city of David, and the jubilant noise of the people radiated through every street. The king leaped with the abandon of a spring lamb. In the midst of the procession, his joy had been too great to contain within measured steps or lowered eyes. His voice rang out along the crowded route and he danced as though he was alone before the Lord, with no one to judge his exuberant display. He was king and servant all at once and wished nothing more than to revel of the glory of his own Lord.

The ark drew increasingly nearer to its resting place, and the people made a grand arc about the tabernacle that David had pitched. The Ark of the Covenant was set delicately in the middle of the large tent behind curtains of twined linen; blue, purple and scarlet, embroidered wondrously with golden cherubim. Ten curtains hung twenty-eight cubits high. On either side of the ark five curtains were coupled to each other and fixed with golden taches.

The ark itself was constructed of shittimwood and laid two and a half cubits long. It was overlaid with pure gold and bore a crown of gold around the top. Four rings were set around the corners for transporting the ark. The staves remained in the loops, never to be removed. The table on which it rested was also of shittim timber and was similarly gilded in gold. The entire assembly glittered like fire in the lamplight.

Once more, burnt offering and peace offerings were made. David blessed the people and to their delight distributed bread, cakes, roasted meats, and flagons to each person in attendance, both men and women. The celebrations wore on and people trickled away to their homes, satisfied in body and in spirit.

≈ ≈ ≈

Michal ambled toward a high window in an upper room of the king's house that lay in the City of David. Her eyes roved the fortifications and traveled far along the new walls that Joab had commissioned to be constructed when her husband had captured Zion so many years ago. An intensifying musical cacophony drew her to watch the fantastic procession now emerging from a distant quarter. The porters with the carriage came into view beyond the square where the tent had been erected. Her husband had made such a fuss over this object, so much so that he had spent little time with her of late. Her father had never mentioned this "ark." Why was it of such importance to David? At least it had arrived and some normality might return to their lives. David's disappointment many months before at the failed recovery of the ark had caused him such distress that at times he had been brooding and distant; but for the entire week he had been joyous and talkative. He spoke mainly of the ark, the priests and their preparations. Still, she preferred this to his mournful silence.

Michal watched intently as the processional approached the open square and smiled at the lilting antics of the celebrants. *They are so enthusiastic—overly so,* she thought. Her gaze lighted on a figure in the forerunning lines. The celebrant wore fine linen and at this distance, bore a striking resemblance to her husband, who she expected would arrive shortly astride his favored mount. Yet as she continued to watch her mouth fell open in surprise. She recognized the cavorting figure with a linen ephod tied about his waist.

Michal cringed in shock. What was David doing? Had he indeed taken leave of his wits? The king prancing like a commoner in the streets—exposed in the eyes of his people—her handmaids—his servants? Did he not respect his office and the honor of his position as king?

Her lips curled in disgust. Was this the man that she had married, who gave this regrettable performance? She slammed the timber-paneled window closed and stalked the long passageway to her chamber. Sitting alone she hung her head, pressing her hands to her face as the scene replayed vividly. *What more should I have expected from a sheepherder?*

≈ ≈ ≈

David, having blessed all the people, returned to his household in exultation, wishing to bless them in turn. He was startled to see Michal come out to meet him. She usually avoided the outdoors and the blistering haze of the sun. She gave him no greeting but accosted him angrily.

"How glorious was the king of Israel today who uncovered himself in the eyes of the handmaids of his servants, as a vain fellow shamelessly uncovers himself." Michal flicked her skirts up, mocking his jaunting display. She turned her back on him and stomped inside.

David's frame stiffened, his joy instantly scoured away by the rage that flooded through him. He followed her to the empty audience hall where she stood with her arms folded, a scowl marring her exquisitely contoured features. David's mind reeled at Michal's rejection but he countered with the one certainty in his life. *God chose me when I was of no standing. He saw value in a young boy tending flocks. Now, everyone else sees power to be exploited. I slew two hundred men to win her, yet that is not enough? Am I to prove that I am fit to be a king? Must I play the part of an imperious ruler? I will not! God has chosen me above princes and that is enough. My love was enough for the Lord, even if it is not enough for my prideful wife. Michal, daughter of Saul, will never bear me a child as long as she lives,* he swore to himself.

David faced Michal, resolute in his decision. "It was before the Lord, who chose me over your father, before all his house, to appoint me ruler over the people of the Lord, over Israel." His voice was frigid. "Therefore I will play before the Lord. And I will be more vile," he ground out. "The maidservants of whom you have spoken, they shall honor me in your stead." Turning aside, he walked past her into the darkness of the house.

CHAPTER FIFTEEN

Supremacy

O God, Thou hast cast us off, Thou hast scattered us,
Thou hast been displeased; Oh, turn Thyself to us again!
Thou hast made the earth to tremble; Thou hast broken it;
Heal its breaches thereof, for it shaketh.
Thou hast shewed Thy people hard things:
Thou hast made us to drink the wine of astonishment…
…God hath spoken in His holiness:
I will rejoice; I will divide Shechem,
And mete out the Valley of Succoth.
Gilead is Mine, and Manasseh is Mine;
Ephraim also is the strength of Mine head;
Judah is My lawgiver; Moab is My washpot;
Over Edom I will cast out My shoe:
Philistia, triumph thou because of Me…
…Through God we shall do valiantly:
For He it is that shall tread down our enemies.

PSALM OF DAVID 60, EXCERPT

The presence of the Ark of the Covenant transformed the life of the
kingdom as a stronghold sheltering against the violence of a sand-
storm. David experienced a calm unlike any he had previously

known. There were none of his usual enemies skulking across his borders, no plagues, famines, or pestilences so prevalent throughout the harsh expanse of lands from Egypt to Syria. His people were no longer captured as slaves to marauders along the coast toward the Great Sea. The fame of the king had spread like a dust on the wind. The surrounding nations feared him and envied his growing supremacy.

And so it seemed a grave injustice that the source of Israel's greatest power should rest within a simple tent while his own prosperity blossomed. David's favor extended north to Hiram, king of Tyre, who gifted David with abundant craftsmen, masons, carpenters, and an ample supply of timber in order to construct a house for the king in Jerusalem.

David was also blessed with nineteen sons, and the strength of his bloodline continued to grow with the passing seasons. No heir, though, came from the lineage of Saul as Michal remained in ward, her scorn for David having burnt away the love that would have returned her to his embrace. He was free of a union with the House of Saul, once great but now tainted by disobedience. The House of David would stand on its own merit.

All this, David thought, and more. He was especially thankful to be granted the presence of a prophet of the lord within his city; Nathan had filled the void left by the death of David's mentor, Samuel. He was privileged to be able to consult the prophet on matters pertaining to the governing of the lord's people.

On a morning of uncharacteristic ambivalence, David felt driven to consult the prophet concerning the recent disquiet within himself; he was troubled by an issue he had been unable to suppress since his journey from the house of Obed-edom. "Look at this," he said, bidding the prophet follow his lead. He indicated the solid walls with fine tapestries. "I dwell in a house built of cedar, but the Ark of the Covenant resides behind curtains. YHWH deserves the finest any man can provide, does He not? Shouldn't the Lord's supremacy truly be evidenced in all things?"

Nathan studiously rubbed his chin. "I cannot fault your reasoning. God has found favor with all of your intentions thus far, and this latest seems a reasonable proposal." He gave an emphatic nod. "Go. Do all that is in your heart, for the Lord is with you."

David was pleased that the prophet had agreed so wholeheartedly with his aim, yet a sense of unease vibrated within him. He felt no peace with respect to this desire; he did not wish to commit any further errors in his handling of the Lord's instrument. How could he be certain? If it were a matter pertaining to the logistics of war, he might have ventured further, but this exercise, though seemingly simple, could risk the posterity of his people.

He stood at a tall, ornamented window overlooking the inner court and beseeched the endless depths of the skies for guidance. *Would YHWH answer?* No inner sensation tinged his thoughts with the warmth that he had grown to know intimately, and he sighed.

Perhaps on another day.

∿ ∿ ∿

The air pulsed with night sounds and the early morning scent of bread baking for the king's table that day. Nathan lay in his quarters, unsleeping. What more could he have said to the king? God had blessed all of David's endeavors until now and this particular objective, to enhance the shelter for his Lord, did not appear to be untoward. The tabernacle tent housing the Ark of the Covenant seemed a mean lodging huddled in the shadow of the splendid edifices within the City of David.

Nathan turned upon his bed and bowed, his prayers mirroring David's request for direction. As he finally lay to resume his rest, the voice of YHWH brimmed within the prophet, and he clasped his hands above him in humble acknowledgment to be again visited by the Word of the Living God.

Tell my servant David that I have said, 'Will you build me a house to dwell in? I have not lived in any other house since I brought the children out of Egypt to this day, but have walked in a tent and in a tabernacle. In all the places that I have gone with the Children of Israel did I say to any of the tribes who I commanded to succor my people, 'Why haven't you built me a house out of cedar'?

Tell David that the Lord of Hosts says, 'I took you from the sheepcote, from following the sheep, to be ruler over my people. And I was with you wherever

you went, and I have destroyed your enemies and made you as famous as the
great men of the earth. Moreover, I will appoint a special place for my people
that they will no longer need to wander or to be afflicted by wicked men as
before. Also I will make you a house. And when you have grown old and pass on
I will establish your son after you. He will build a house for Me, and I will estab-
lish his kingdom in perpetuity. I will be his father and he will be my son. And if
he errs I will chasten him, but I will continue to show him mercy, unlike Saul,
whom I put away. Your house and your kingdom will exist forever.'

Nathan experienced a long period of stillness and understood that the
presence of YHWH had departed. He unfolded his limbs and rose excitedly. He hastened to David's quarters, his ancient limbs managing a shifting trot.

≈ ≈ ≈

David greeted Nathan gladly and dismissed his servant. The prophet hurriedly ushered himself in and, foregoing the customary obeisance in his
haste, he animatedly repeated the words spoken to him by God. David's
body was effused with burning emotion. How could a man as base as
myself be given such honor? To be the father of an eternal nation! The
scope of the promise was incredible.

Nathan had scarcely concluded the delivery of his message before the
king squeezed his hand in wordless thanks and ran through the dark halls
and out into the stillness of the morning. His flight took him to the tabernacle, where the full weight of the revelation suffused him. His tears of joy
mixed with the fine dust of the floor as he sat in the presence of YHWH.

"Who am I, Lord God? Of what value is my house that you have
brought me to this point?" His words poured out as sobs of gratitude. The
tribute that was promised to be bestowed shook the foundations of his
awareness. God's confirmation of his love for his people and his intent to
bless them reverberated within his violently thundering heart. His sur-
roundings seemed aflame with light and life. The posterity of the people
was assured. Assured!

"You have spoken it, O Lord. Let your servant's house be blessed forever."

From that night, David's power swept outward with invincible force, encompassing nations in successive waves of unstoppable might. The first to succumb were the Philistines. David recovered his besieged territory and launched an offensive that rivaled the Philistine conquest under Saul. David sought out key strongholds and strategically placed cities. Rending Metheg-ammah from their hands, he redistributed his armies to capture the royal city of Gath, then quickly moved east in a blistering attack on Moab, who forestalled the slaughter with hastily wrought gifts. Nevertheless, David subsumed their lands under his emergent authority.

Securing Moab, the king blazed his men of war northward, intent on regaining his border at the river Euphrates. As the battle turned against Zobah, its king, Hadarezer, begged support from his neighbors in Syria-Damascus to fend off David's incursion. Reinforcements were sent swiftly but were unable to shift the balance of the war in favor of Hadarezer, and twenty-two thousand of the northern army fell before David's onslaught. David then lodged his own men in the prominent cities of Betah and Berothai, successfully displacing his enemy.

David's dominance in the war prompted King Tou of Hamath, the principal city of Syria, to send his son Joram as an envoy bearing tributes of gold and rich artifacts.

"My father salutes you and bids me to bless you. Hadarezer was a mutual enemy and your cause has benefited our people greatly. Please accept the king's tidings and his gifts."

David received them amiably, dedicating them to the Lord. He preferred allegiances to the bitterness of perpetual war. An alliance won stanched further bloodshed. *There will be an end,* David thought, *but the time to do battle is still upon us!*

The king opted to return south to engage Edom. Abishai led his companies against the Edomites in the Valley of Salt and secured the city. David installed his garrisons to maintain rulership. He made an alliance with Nanash, King of Ammon, whose past defeat at the hands of Saul had made him leery of opposing the children of God when the Power was with them.

David's renown churned like a whirlwind through the nations. His men were feared for their prowess in war and as always their Lord went before them, dispersing his enemies like the chaff of wheat in a tempest. David unerringly dedicated his bounteous spoil and costly tributes to God, who poured out the windows of heaven upon His faithful servant.

"Without God's guidance we will be slaughtered by our enemies as in times past," he reminded his captains before each battle. "Follow my instructions diligently, for they come from the Lord of Hosts, who cannot be defeated. Do not harbor disobedience in your ranks. One man's variance may seal all our deaths."

Though there had seldom been a lapse in discipline, David continued to issue his admonitions. His captains demonstrated a high level of order among the men. They were worthy of the victories and deserving of the rest they would eventually bring to an entire nation.

The king eagerly anticipated this long overdue hiatus from the fighting. He wearied of the brutality of the battlefield, though he would press on wherever the Lord bid.

Still, life's journey continued to claim casualties outside of the present wars. Nanash of Ammon was one such whose death was untimely in a season of conflict.

David sent his servants to Hanun, the son of Nanash, seeking to comfort him and to extend in return the kindness that had been shown by his father.

≈ ≈ ≈

Hanun had seldom ventured into his father's affairs. The old man had been efficient at ordering his kingdom and infrequently invited his son to participate in matters concerning its administration, and the arrangement suited Hanun well. He knew nothing of King Nanash's allies, nor did he care to. It was the king's foes who were the more notorious and well-publicized throughout Ammon. Now, his lack of familiarity with his father's circle of friendship, coupled with his suspicion regarding the princes' views on his ability to rule with comparable sufficiency, sent the newly coronated king to court the advice of the young princes of Ammon.

The princes berated Hanun with questions that contradicted the inclination of his heart.

"Do you believe, truly, that King David honors your father and that he has sent you comforters? Hasn't he sent his servants, rather, to spy on the city to overthrow it? Then, should we not return them in shame? Should we turn a blind eye to their trickery?"

The voices joined in unison to paint a damning picture of Hebrew deception. After considering their persuasive words, Hanun, was convinced of a plot against his nation.

"I will do as you have advised," he avowed. "Send the city-guard to escort the men to my presence."

Hanun paced the forecourt of the palace, strengthening his resolve and devising an appropriate rebuke for the conniving strangers. In several moments he was smiling, buoyed by the originality of his scheme. *In this my authority will be affirmed.*

"Send for Deshor and Melthun," he told his hand servant. "Tell them to come at once and require them to bring their tools."

The guards arrived with the men in their charge moments ahead of the two servants summoned to the court of the king. The messengers were impatient to deliver their message of amity and return home, and so they had come eagerly to the court. The king did not reply to their introductory greeting but regarded them with a severe look.

"We will send a simple message to your king," he stated. "Melthun! Deshor!" he called, gesturing his men to the fore. He whispered to the first. The man returned a conspiratorial grin and spoke in turn to Deshor, who had approached carrying small boxes wrapped in leather. He undid the wrappings to reveal sharp implements, which he removed with care.

The guards prodded the men forward.

"Hold them still," the king commanded as the messengers began to scuffle against their confinement. Melthun further sharpened a blade he had extracted from its case, then gripped the jaw of the shorter two envoys. With skilled flicks of his blade he removed half of the man's thick, exquisitely groomed beard, which hung to his breast. Deshor, who had moved behind the man, seized a handful of his robe and sawed through the rough material. His honed implement easily sheared away the garment from the middle, baring the man's buttocks. Melthun and Deshor repeated their open castigation with each of the messengers who was held fast by a double guard.

"Be still or you may slice yourself," Melthun warned the third, but the man struggled even more violently. He spat and hurled insults at the king, but Hanun preferred ignoring the man to killing him over his provocative words, knowing that the despoiling of their long, oiled beards was a fate no Israelite man would wish to face. Their full beards were a sign of status that was equal to the maturity of the man and extolled the privilege of being free. The prospect of returning to their home doubly disgraced would fill them with mortal trepidation. They could steal clothes to cover their nakedness, but the half-shorn beards would take years to grow to their original length. And now the men would need to suffer the distress of shaving the other half themselves. Hanun chuckled as he watched the squirming messenger finally succumb to Melthun's and Deshor's blades. As intended, the indignity that Hanun had visited upon the unsuspecting messengers would endure far beyond the day.

꙳ ꙳ ꙳

King David bridled in anger. He regarded his heralds, sent out in peace and returned in dire shame. "Tarry at Jericho until your beards are fully grown, then return," he said consolingly, and then bade them leave. As they trudged away, he turned to Joab. "Could you have imagined such an insult? And to ones who come in peace?"

Joab grunted and shook his head. "This is the antic of a fool, but it cannot be ignored." "And it shall not be," David swore. "Assuredly, it shall not! Take Abishai; the entire host is at your disposal. Hanun's jibe will be bought at a dear cost."

꙳ ꙳ ꙳

The price of Hanun's audacity was revealed to him only when Nanash's chief advisor returned from journeying to Syria-Damascus. He bore unsettling news gathered on the road that King David was mustering for war against Ammon. Hanun's heart sank when he was confronted regarding the reasons that could have precipitated such a malevolent attack. The new king told dejectedly of the reprimand he had devised for David's envoy.

"You did what?" the advisor shouted, disbelieving.

"I did not think the reproof could so inflame a man who resorts to using spies. It was a just condemnation."

"King David is—was—an ally of your father!" the advisor bellowed.

Hanun's mouth fell as his eyes roved the room frantically to assess the gravity of his miscalculation. He weighed the extent of the consequences. "What shall we do?"

"Their men of war have already departed, Hanun." the advisor exclaimed, throwing his arms out in exasperation.

"But we haven't the soldiers, skill, or physical resources to start a war!" The king's voice faded to a whisper.

"You should have thought of that from the outset. No insult to a king can be underestimated," the advisor scolded. "We will need to hire men of war. Hadarezer is sure to lend us aid since the humiliation of his defeat at Zobah at David's hands. We will send to Shobach the captain. He can advise us on a war strategy, for we may need to alter our tactics if we are to survive this debacle."

Hanun's shoulders drooped and he slumped against the dais as the advisor continued.

"When a war came to your father's gates, he preferred our companies to launch smaller columns to gauge the size of the attacking force, to retreat within the gates, and to drive the attackers back to wilderness regions where the food supplies are scarce, even during the months of harvest. The army would then be forced to move on."

Hanun rose to his feet. "We can dispel their attack even if we don't defeat them," he noted as hope sparkled to life.

"However,"—the chief advisor raised a cautionary finger—"David's recent campaigns have fared well against this ploy. The Moabites attempted it to their detriment, and you can see the results of their ruined defense. With the support of Hadarezer, we may instead succeed in pinning them between our gates and the men of Zobah. If they are prevented from retreating, Shobach will decimate their ranks. It will go even better for us if we can commission warriors from Bethrebob and Ishtob to expand our numbers. King Maacah also owes your father allegiance for his aid in years past. Our combined might should outmatch David's force. It is the most we can hope for. However, if David's God is with him as is told since the retrieval of the Ark of the Covenant, we may fall. If anything goes wrong, Hadarezer's men can flee north to their homeland and we shall retreat into the city."

Hanun was encouraged by the scheme. "Thank you, I will dispatch messengers to Hadarezer and Maacah at once."

⤳ ⤳ ⤳

To Hanun's delight, his adviser's battle plan had been working exceedingly well against the Israelite men of war. He observed the combatants from the bulwarks as the children of Ammon repulsed the men of war from the gate. Any who retreated from the forefront were caught against the aggregate bastion of mercenaries from the north. He saw the enemy commander wheel through the field seeking a means to shore up the breeches in their lines. Their offense had become a desperate defense of their lives. Waves of soldiers fell in the vanguard and rearguard, which were equally beset. *Perhaps I will recover from my mistake after all. The Children of Ammon will win,* he decided, and cheered inwardly. *Ammon will be the first to depose the mighty David.*

Hanun returned to his throne room to await news of their victory.

It is good to be king, he thought.

⤳ ⤳ ⤳

The crush of mercenary soldiers along the battlefront raised the hairs on Joab's neck. Soldiers for hire were the most dangerous opponents, as his men were discovering. Their archers had wounded many of his reserves, who were fleeced with barbed shafts as they assayed to gain the field. Joab had encountered this type before and knew firsthand of their deadly motivations. As wealth beckoned they set about their task like a legion of devils. His front line stood alone, hacking at the press of men whose visions no doubt glistened with the promise of gold talents or some other reward. Joab's soldiers, bloodied and rent, defended their ground only through their dual skill with sword and spear. The majority of the companies had abandoned the grouped battle formation that had been planned and now used their short swords along with javelins to fend off the attackers. Many had lost their shields and armor bearers in the tide, and the clang of swords on armored bracelets resounded across the battle ground. His men were war hardened, but they could not resist the garrisons pitted against them indefinitely.

Joab moved from the fore and surveyed the battle grimly. It was going against him in front and behind, and they would surely lose if he did not reverse his tactics. He had not expected to oppose two armies since the children of Ammon typically depended on the defense of their massive gates. Neither had he anticipated the influx of reinforcements from Zobah, and least of all, Rehob and Ishtob. Maacah too, was a painful surprise for he had never known the king's men to be for hire. Joab's jaw ticked as he made a final decision. If he could break the Syrians' offensive, his men could at least retreat, whereas they would yet be pummeled against the city walls even should the Ammonites be defeated in the forefront and the Syrians hold strong in the rear. Sobach's men would press their attack, which had been highly effective, owing to the large rotations of men available to the Syrian commander on his front line.

The Syrians must be broken as a priority. He must split his command on two fronts for any hope of victory.

"Abishai!" Joab shouted above the screams of battle. He slashed his way through the bloody fray to reach Abishai whose companies were pitted against the Syrian line. "Abishai! Drop back and pull the finest of our men off the Ammon front. Direct them here to me. All the remaining companies are at your disposal. Array them all against the Ammonites. If the Syrians are too strong for me, then you shall help me, but if the children of Ammon are too strong for you, then I will come to help you. Take courage and let us show ourselves to be men for our people and for the cities of our God. The Lord will do as he sees fit."

The elite of Joab's guard careened through the battlefield, and Joab's heart lifted when he saw the number of them who were still battle ready. He had expected no less of such men, for their skillfulness in war was undisputed. Joab waved them on with a roar. The subsidiary companies were redeployed under Abishai's command. Joab promptly formed a wedge of his chosen men and spearheaded the force into the enemy line. The veteran troop fought without the hesitation of the younger men of war, rending their opponents with a dexterity born of confidence. Each stroke merged courage with an innate power.

The virulent eruption within the Syrian ranks unstabilized their order, which until then had been crisp and efficient. The third rotation of soldiers into the line was interrupted by a surge, which moved left.

Joab's men were experienced enough to recognize the pending arrival of new strength that would brace their flagging compatriots on the opposing line. Denied the expected relief, the belabored Syrians fled the frontline under the press of the champions from Israel whose blades sang a funereal dirge. The precipitous flight of soldiers from the Syrian line seeded fear into the hearts of their companions, who milled in confusion, unsure of the reason for the panicked retreat. Joab's concentrated pulse tore through the unraveling offensive.

A cry went up from the wall as the Ammonites saw the dispersal of their Syrian counterparts. Their ranks shredded raggedly and men retreated to the safety of their gates, propelled by a lashing whip of Abishai's men who spurred them in their frenzy to reach secure home territory. The rout had begun.

∽ ∽ ∽

Hadarezer, posted on a ridge above the siege, saw the disintegration eat along the central battle lines, causing them to splay outward. He raced to the signal post, garments flapping wildly.

"Call them back," he shrieked, waving his arms to gain the trumpeter's attention as he ran. "Call the men back." The blast resounded over the valley, further disrupting the defensive flurry of the Syrian army. The men peeled away like the skin of a crushed fig, skidding backward to the command tent. Hadarezer motioned to two captains of the relief companies.

"Disperse the fleetest of your runners as messengers. Have them summon all the men who battle beyond the Euphrates. This war is no longer worth it to us. If we are slaughtered here, our cities will be laid bare for the vultures. Therefore, let us retreat with haste, before we die here. As soon as Shobach returns, send him to me."

Hadarezer searched the mass of men ascending the hill. Already he could see a bulky figure approaching at a run.

"Your sounding was as timely as the sun," Shobach hollered as he entered the camp. Five short blasts announced the final ingathering of the host that now tumbled raggedly over the crest to evade the combatants uniting in the valley below.

Shobach and Hadarezer led the host out of reach of Joab's men. They intended to regroup at Helam before moving northward. The war was a loss. Ammon would be left to rally alone.

⤙ ⤙ ⤙

Joab strategized with Abishai, whose primary opponents now stood behind the confines of the wall of Ammon that loomed like a mountain before a child.

"We must turn aside," Joab said. "The season is against us, and our men shall starve if we institute a siege here. Send messengers to King David. The men of Israel can hound the Syrians north and possibly gain a mighty victory. If they are dispatched at once, our forces can merge with theirs in a fortnight. Until then we shall plague Hadarezer's rearguard."

Confident that King David would send supporting ranks, Joab proceeded with his proposal. He harried the retreating companies and wearied Hadarezer's men with the constancy of a lion tracking a wounded buck.

The bulk of the men of Israel catapulted north, arriving within Joab's estimation. They attacked Hadarezer's straggling flank, setting the flagging company to renewed flight. The stampede to escape the fresh forces barreled heedlessly across the plains to Syria. Shobach alone valiantly held his defense, hoping to rally his men and allow Hadarezer's escape. His exhausted guardsmen, however, were overwhelmed by the incursion from the south and the commander was slain in a blistering sally that did not relent until the troubled land had drunk its fill of blood.

≈ ≈ ≈

Hanun's hands trembled as he read the scrap of parchment sent by swift messenger across the wastes that separated Ammon from Syria. Hadarezer had offered David a peace offering, and was thus bound in David's service to withhold further assistance from Ammon.

Hanun held his head and stared over the battlements to the barren hill where his salvation had encamped only days before. The ground outstretched beyond his walls was eerily quiet, but the lull, he knew, would not last.

The king retired to his throne room alone and sat there shaking. *No one will aid me, now.* David's men would retire, but only until the winter had past. His people would have mere months until spring when war would see its resurgence against their walls. Without help, they would be vanquished; this was a certainty. He would be known as the king who had single-handedly sealed the destruction of his people for a farce. He cried into his hands. His reign would end before it had truly begun and the disgrace he had meted out would be visited upon his people a thousand fold. His gods would not hear his weeping and neither would the shade of his father. The price of failure would be borne, not by him alone, but by all his people. This was the way of kings.

CHAPTER SIXTEEN

The Unguarded Moment

I acknowledge my transgressions:
And my sin is ever before me.
Against Thee, Thee only, have I sinned,
And done this evil in Thy sight:
That Thou mightest be justified when Thou speakest,
And be clear when Thou judgest.

PSALM OF DAVID 51 EXCERPT

D avid was unprepared when his moment of weakness finally came. The war against Ammon had been waged from the advent of summer after the grain harvest had been completed. The host had marched to besiege the royal city of Rabbah, but David remained in Jerusalem. The outcome was months away and the king needed a respite from war. He sojourned in the city awaiting messengers from the front line.

It was now the time of Siran, and the heat and the dust were already building. Most of the warmer evenings such as this he preferred to spend in uninterrupted solace on the roof of his house. The air was free of the smell of horses in the stables and the clamor of activities in the forecourt. He paced the roof, pondering the state of the battle. Hanun had been granted ample time to prepare for the siege that he must have known would come upon his people. David prayed to be rid of the Ammonites before Tishri, the month of creation, for maintaining the foreign encampment would place a strain on Jerusalem's resources. Nevertheless, he was committed to it, and Joab was willing to lay a long siege if necessary.

The king's eyes aimlessly surveyed the grounds and the adjacent buildings. His gaze ranged to and fro before his vision strayed haplessly upon a figure at a bathing pool within an open courtyard to his left. Dark hair fell like spun onyx to a delicate waist, and David could not close his eyes to the woman's beauty, which surpassed that of any of his wives or concubines. *She is exquisite,* he thought in wonder, leaning over the parapet in an effort to improve his perception. *Whose house is that?* He traced an imaginary map with his finger yet was unable to accurately identify the location.

"Eleab!" David shouted below. The king's servant appeared after several moments. David pointed to the courtyard where the woman had just donned her robes.

"Who is that woman?" David asked.

Eleab followed the line of David's finger, narrowing his eyes to distinguish her features. "Isn't that Bathsheba, Uriah's wife?"

"I did not know he had taken a wife," David replied, never taking his eyes off the court where the woman lounged.

"Dispatch one of the messengers. I wish to speak with her this very evening," David instructed. "We can speak of her husband." *I would simply like to meet her,* he told himself. She is extraordinary, *and talk is so dull....*

≈ ≈ ≈

Bathsheba received the summons reluctantly. She had never met the king, and with her husband away, the meeting seemed even more unusual. She hated to be suspicious. Perhaps Uriah had been killed, but why bring her back to the palace? The messengers could have delivered the news to her house, couldn't they?

Uriah had always spoken highly of his lord. As one of the king's thirty finest men of war, Uriah was privileged to serve with the mightiest of the captains and as such, held a favored position in the court. Her husband would speak dotingly of his king, of his humble beginnings as a keeper of sheep, his dedication to his men, his God, and his people. Uriah spoke admiringly of a day when the king had called Mephibosheth, Saul's grandson and the son of Jonathan, to his house. He had sat the young man at his table and taken him in ward, fulfilling his promise to Jonathan that he would preserve the seed of Saul's house. He restored to Mephibosheth Saul's lands and property and had provided servants and keepers. The king had assigned Ziba and his sons to be Mephibosheth's servants, because the young man was lame.

"Mephibosheth eats at the king's table as though he were David's son," Uriah marveled. "The man is incapacitated and can be of little use to the king, yet he is saluted as a prince. The king is truly honorable, is he not?"

Such was the manner in which Uriah often spoke of his lord, and he considered it his duty to spend his blood if necessary to King David's cause. The war against Ammon would take Uriah away for a while, but she had grown accustomed to his jaunting routine. He served in the vanguard of the hosts, and despite his expertise, she knew it was possible that he might not return at the end of a war campaign. The service was brutal and he bore deep scars from the seemingly endless conflicts. She knew also that Uriah would die before he conceded his commitment to his king.

Someday, there will be one battle too many.

Bathsheba closed her eyes to banish the mournful thought. She dressed herself in a simple yellow robe cinched at the waist with a silver tassel. Her handmaid oiled and brushed her hair thoroughly and tied it with fine silver ropes. She was careful not to go overly adorned, but neither did she wish to trivialize the meeting.

As the time wore on toward the meeting, she grew more unsettled. The messengers returned to escort her to the king's house but spoke nothing of the nature of the engagement. They were cordial and unassuming in their invitation. Bathsheba could deduce nothing from their speech or their manner. She followed and was ushered through the main gate into the king's forecourt.

Some of the servants stared openly, they too questioning the reason behind her presence. Bathsheba maintained an air of aloofness, keeping her focus on the messengers' backs. She passed through several plain rooms before being issued into a grand space with long timber trestles, some packed away on one side of the room. At the far end was a large table with gilt high-backed chairs. Seated at its head was the king. Bathsheba had seen him during the return of the Ark of the Covenant and recognized him instantly, though on this evening he was clothed in resplendent maroon robes. He was dining alone. The table was layered with a diversity of platters bearing sliced meats and preserved fruit. The aromas reminded Bathsheba that she had not eaten since receiving his summons.

The king rose and gestured to a seat beside him. She made a low bow and joined him at the table. David greeted her with a smile and then dismissed the servants and began to eat.

Bathsheba sat silently. Her eyes stayed fixed on her hands, which lay folded in her lap. The king motioned to the goblet at her right hand. She declined, still discomfited by his presence and the mystery of his invitation.

He continued to eat, speaking generally of the kingdom and the new era of peace that was to come. Bathsheba's gaze was then drawn to his hands as he spoke. They moved erratically between his platter, the goblet, and the carved armrest of his chair, where they settled with a slight tremor.

Was he nervous? The revelation caused her even more disquiet, for his intentions were now becoming clear, for they had spoken little of consequence throughout the evening. *How should I respond? It is unlawful, he must know!* She was not ignorant of her beauty, but would the king defile himself in defiance of God's law? *I'm not that beautiful, am I? Can I refuse the king? What would become of my household? My husband? I will be stoned if I accede, but how can I cry out? The stringency of the law will allow me no escape, but will I be murdered if I do not comply? It is possible that he wishes only a moment's diversion after which he may remember me no more. What would Uriah do if I told him? Would he put me away? Would my husband still serve the king? No, he would not. My husband thrives on honor; even knowledge of the king's surreptitious advance would destroy him. My Lord, what should I do?*

The myriad of questions continued to swirl about her like a seething vortex even as the king took her hand and led her beside him to his bedchamber. Should she raise a cry? Who would aid her in any event? The answers did not come that night, and neither did her salvation as she was swept into a world from which she could not return.

≈ ≈ ≈

Months later, Bathsheba lay abed. The cakes of figs she had eaten minutes before roiled within her only to be retched ungraciously into the shallow clay bowl at her bedside. She wrestled with the incessant plague of questions that haunted her waking hours, but could find no rest from their scourge.

Should I send a message to the king? Will he conceal his culpability? Or will he choose to suffer the shame of discovery? The latter seemed unlikely. Still, she would need to do something, for Uriah had been away at war all this time and her trespass would eventually become obvious to all. If she was to bear the blame, she would not bear it alone. *The king will know the results of that night,* she decided.

She struggled to her feet and summoned her handmaid. "Fetch your brother," she instructed gravely. "I have a message for the king."

≈ ≈ ≈

David reeled about his quarters, now infected with the harangue of questions that had surely been afflicting Bathsheba for several weeks. Could she truly be with child? If she was, what was to be done? It cannot be known. What would Uriah do? No, it will not be known. David stopped his pacing as a way of escape blossomed in his mind. It had only been four weeks. If he sent for Uriah now, the man of war would return within days. Uriah would be overjoyed to be reunited with his wife. *A union would absolve me of the deed. It can be claimed that Uriah has sired the child.*

David hurried to the courtyard and dispatched a rider to Joab in Ammon, with the directive to send Uriah home to the king forthwith.

≈ ≈ ≈

David needed wait only three days for Uriah's arrival. Uriah came directly to the king's quarters, his clothes marred with sweat and dirt accumulated over the rough journey. David greeted him warmly with a kiss to the cheek then inquired of Joab, the men and the state of the war.

Uriah described the recent confrontations in detail, and David listened attentively though impatience welled within him.

As Uriah concluded his report, David patted him on the shoulder. "I am pleased," he said smiling. "Go to your house, relax, have a good night's sleep."

When Uriah left, David ordered the kitchen servants to deliver a rich meal to Uriah's house.

The following morning at breakfast, Eleab informed David in puzzlement, "He would not go though I bid him as you asked. He insisted that he would remain here at your door. He is as intractable as an ox!" David exhaled loudly and stalked away to find Uriah, who still resided in the servants' quarters. The king quickly smoothed his composure. "Uriah, haven't you just come from traveling? Why haven't you gone home?" he asked pleasantly.

Uriah straightened from his task of cleaning his armor. "The Ark, and all Israel, and Judah live in tents. My lord, Joab, and your servants are camped in open fields. How then can I go home, eat and drink, and lie with my wife? I will not do it."

David realized that if he pressed the matter, Uriah would become suspicious. "As you wish," he conceded. "But stay here for another day. Tomorrow, I will allow you to leave again."

On the second evening, David prepared a feast and invited Uriah to dine. He plied the man with strong drink and rich food, yet neither could persuade the recalcitrant man to return home. The king ceased his efforts to encourage Uriah's departure to his house. Finding it impossible to foist his desires on the man, David settled on his alternative course.

As Uriah prepared to depart the following dawn, the king brought a letter to be delivered to Joab. Uriah, faithful to his master, unknowingly delivered a missive commissioning his own death.

$$\backsim \quad \backsim \quad \backsim$$

In Ammon, Joab received the parchment and read the surreptitious command:

Set Uriah in the forefront of the hottest battle and leave him that he may be killed.

"Is it not good tidings?" Uriah asked, noticing the intensity of Joab's glower.

Joab folded the paper slowly, and then balled it in his fists. "I'm afraid not." He shook his head and turned away. What had provoked the king to sacrifice a man as loyal as Uriah? *Whatever the reason, it is best that I not know.* Sometimes knowledge was a perilous friend, and death followed in her wake. *I bear my transgression against Abner, and the king will have to bear the stain of this.*

⇌ ⇌ ⇌

As the gate closed for the final time behind the retreating men of Ammon, a swarm of arrows flitted from the high wall driving back the pursuing soldiers, a few of whom were blessed to still possess their shields. Those who did not perished swiftly from the arching volley of piercing shafts.

Uriah, unlike others, did not run. *I will not die like a coward, impaled in the back.* In earlier attacks, he had found a stray shield or a fallen breastplate that he had held to deflect the blizzard of enemy arrows. But today, he was caught in a patch of open ground with no defense.

He heard the collective flitter of quill feathers and knelt in a final prayer. There was no fear in his heart. *May I have found favor in your eyes, Lord.* His lips moved in silent prayer, and the end came swiftly.

⇌ ⇌ ⇌

Joab's succinct report slashed across David's conscience like a whip:

Valuable men lost at king's command.

David moved to the window overlooking Jerusalem's core. His misdeed was like a yawning pit, growing ever wider—and he had spread the weight of the burden on Bathsheba's shoulders. He would resolve this somehow, or his life would ever cower under a shadow.

David's chamberlain responded to his call, and following his precise instructions, made preparations for a discreet wedding. It was the only way David knew to erode the traces of his imprudence. *I hope that*

Bathsheba will find some peace at the end of all this. When her period of mourning was completed, he would inform her of the proposed marriage. But first, there was something she needed to know.…

≈ ≈ ≈

David's messengers hurried word of Uriah's death to Bathsheba's house. She collapsed into uncontrollable sobs. The strain of the lie she concealed; the guilt and her inability to offer sacrifice for absolution; her defilement and the weeks in hiding and now the death of her beloved Uriah all conspired to overwhelm her. When will it end? How was she to survive this? She began her period of mourning for her husband and for herself. She would not be able to receive Uriah's forgiveness now and the world would know her shame. She lay on the floor, shaking. Her handmaid moved to her side, trying to guide her to her feet, but she batted the girl's hands away.

After an hour, a servant brought her a thin soup, but she did not rise to sup. The evening melded into night, and finally she crept into her bed where she stayed, curled into a ball. In the morning she changed her garb and covered her head. The days of her suffering would be long, but she was prepared to stand. The servants flitted about her, offering soothing brews and incense, but what comfort could be given? *Uriah!* His strength—his embrace were lost to her. The coursing fire that had once filled her heart slowly ebbed away. Even after the ashes of her loss had been washed away and the entreaty came from the king with a delicately wrapped token, she felt nothing—except for the life now burgeoning within her.

Her heart was put away, but she would accept David's betrothal. Perhaps a type of love would grow within her for the king, who sought avidly to make things right. She could not reverse Uriah's death nor erase the mountain of hurt that dwelled in her breast, but she could be strong for the child she succored within her womb. Her life had been unraveled only to be restrung with a pattern of changed purpose. She would enter a new life—a life enmeshed in deceit and power.

❧ ❧ ❧

The messengers attending David bowed to Nathan as he entered the king's throne room. David drew his attention away from the reports on the war in Ammon. Since completing nuptial arrangements with Bathsheba, he had been able to confront issues pertaining to the northern campaign.

David waved the prophet in as the two runners did obeisance and departed on their errands, one bearing instructions to Joab regarding the distribution of spoil at the culmination of the war and the other a dispatch for supplies.

David fumbled with his robes, then hastened to offer the seer a cushioned seat. "No word was sent of your coming. I would have—"

"There are matters more pressing than my comforts, David." The prophet stood with his hands folded. "I came to advise you of two men who were found in one of your cities," Nathan said promptly. "One was rich and the other poor."

David's brows pulled together as he sought to glean the direction of the prophet's discourse.

"The rich man had abundant flocks and herds whilst the poor man had nothing save one little ewe—a lamb that he had bought and nourished, and it grew alongside him and his children. It ate and drank of the man's own and lay in his bosom as a daughter. A traveler came to the rich man, and rather than taking from his own herd to provide for the wayfarer, the man took the poor man's lamb and dressed it to feed his guest."

David's anger lit as Nathan related the tale of woeful injustice. He saw that Nathan awaited his response. "As the Lord lives," he vowed, "the man who has done this thing shall assuredly die, and he shall restore the lamb fourfold, for he had no pity!" The king's face grew hot with indignation against the wrongdoing. Such perpetrations were intolerable.

Nathan looked squarely into David's eyes, his voice growing hard in indictment. "You are the man! The Lord God of Israel has said to you, 'I anointed you king over Israel, saved you from Saul, gave you a house, wives, the House of Israel, the House of Judah; and if that had been too little, I would have given you even more. Why then did you despise my command and do this evil? You have killed Uriah in battle and taken his wife to be yours. As a consequence of this, your household will forever be beset by the sword. Your own house will turn against you, and you shall lose your wives publicly to another. You trespassed in secret but all Israel will know your shame.'"

David moaned, "I have sinned against the Lord."

"You will not die for it. However, you have created an opportunity for men to speak evil of God, and because of this, the child that Bathsheba has borne to you will not live."

The sanctimony of David's act contradicted the principles of righteousness he had aforetime espoused, and he would not be granted unbidden redemption at the mercy seat.

David's heart fell. Bathsheba would be twice heartbroken because of him, and he realized that in all his power, he could take life, but there is only One who can return it. The child would soon emerge from the succor of Bathsheba's womb. *I have already doomed her first child to death. If only I might be able to change it!* His only recourse was to seek that single Power that could restore what was destined to be taken away.

David committed himself to his planned intercession. He lay on the ground in fasting and prayer throughout the night hoping to save the boy. After the birthing, the child immediately fell ill. He was desperate to allay the grief that Bathsheba would suffer, but the boy grew worse by the hour. On the seventh day of the severe malady, the whispers of David's servants betrayed their shielded words and David asked bluntly, "Is he dead?"

"He is dead," they replied in timid dread. But David simply rose, washed, and anointed himself and went to the House of the Lord, where he worshiped. He returned home and ate calmly, observant of the consternation of his servants, who could well expect him to bitterly grieve the boy's death.

With uncontained bewilderment at his mild manner in light of the night's tragedy, Eleab asked overtly, "What is it that you are doing? While the boy was alive, you fasted and wept but now that he is dead, you rise and eat?"

David was unperturbed by the inquiry. "While the child lived, I considered that God might yet show me grace and save the child, but now that he is dead, why should I fast? Can I bring him back? I shall go to him, but he shall not return to me."

David spent a long while comforting Bathsheba, whose distress tore his heart. There was no more he could do. He shook his head. It was useless to berate himself. He would turn again and seek the One who had brought him from the sheepcote to the highest seat in all Israel—turn, and honor His gift.

It was therefore a balm when Bathsheba bore another son, whom David named Solomon as decreed by YHWH. David held the child tenderly and recalled God's promise of a son to bring peace. He declared his own blessing upon the boy.

"You shall be great, and there will be none other on the throne like unto you."

Chapter Seventeen

Brothers Apart

For His anger endureth but for a moment;
In His favor is life;
Weeping may endure for a night,
But joy cometh in the morning.
And in my prosperity I said, "I shall never be moved."
LORD, by Thy favor Thou hast made my mountain to stand strong:
Thou didst hide Thy face, and I was troubled.

Psalm of David 30, Excerpt

The curse that David had engendered through his misdeed took root as a black thread that wove maliciously between his sons. Amnon, the firstborn, found his days empty of the power and authority that he had anticipated as the firstborn of a king. He had undergone none of the hardship that his father had endured, yet his life grew emptier year by year. His thoughts filled with lusts of varying kinds and trapped him in a writhing net from which he was not inclined to disentangle himself. Day after day, his eyes discreetly admired his half sister, Tamar; her fair countenance smoldered like embers in his mind. He became restless and distracted, unable to corral his wayward desire or divert his attentions along more enthralling avenues. Some of his brothers had trained at war and practiced daily with the sword or bow, but he was disinterested in such exploits now. Hadn't his father conquered all the surrounding territories and spoken often of the Lord's promised peace? Why then waste his energies fighting unnecessary battles? However, without purpose or direction for his passions, Amnon's obsession with Tamar festered until it became a debilitating malaise.

Tamar is still a virgin. It would be hard for me to do such a thing to her. Still, having no outlet for his youthful lust, he continued to pine feverishly. His friends pondered his failing pallor and assigned his cousin Jonadab to investigate the cause of his progressive sickness.

Jonadab subtly broached the matter with his comrade. "Amnon," he said. "Why would you, being the king's son, grow leaner by the day? Will you not say?"

Amnon was reluctant to divulge his secret, but he was severely discontent, and Jonadab provided his only opportunity to relieve some of the burden he had taken upon himself. "I love Tamar, Absalom's sister," he disclosed mournfully.

Absalom, his younger brother, had been born to Maacah, David's third wife, while David resided in Hebron. His other brothers, Chileab, Adonijah, Shephatiah, and Ithream had also been sired in Hebron. It was a wonder that they were not close despite their father's admonitions of the necessity of brotherhood.

Jonadab considered his friend's dilemma and offered his solution. "Amnon, why don't you do this—lie on your bed and pretend to be sick. When your father comes to see you, ask him to let Tamar tend you and prepare you a meal. In that way you can be alone for a long while and thereby decide what you wish to do."

Amnon listened intently. His heart burned with thoughts of a conspired evening. He followed Jonadab's suggestion and savored the success of the gambit. He prepared a sallow expression and practiced his downcast demeanor.

Tamar arrived as his father had promised and stood kneading flour for cakes. Amnon's excitement grew as he observed her moving about the room. *She is here—in my home!*

As she served him, he asked her to dismiss all the servants, and she complied unwittingly, still oblivious to his feigned illness and fraudulent intentions. Amnon permitted himself a smile. The moment had at last come. *I must remember to thank Jonadab,* he thought. The evening had been perfect thus far, and it promised to be even more than he could have hoped for.

≈ ≈ ≈

The satiation of Amnon's desire ruptured a venomous tumor within him that hitherto had lain unbroken. He had forced himself on Tamar expecting to be released from the torment of not having her, but it was not her body alone that he had wanted, he realized in hindsight. He had hoped for a shared love and admiration that was now denied him by the illicit act and the violence of its consummation. The theft of his sister's innocence brought with it a millstone of irrepressible guilt in addition to an unexplained anger that deformed his previous visions of enfolding bliss. The love that he had professed for his sister slowly contorted into a vicious, all-encompassing hatred. It was her fault that he had succumbed. Had she not enticed him, flaunting her beauty, he would certainly have restrained himself from this vulgar act that had yielded him nothing other than a well of acid reprisal.

"Arise! Get out!" he growled.

"Why?" Tamar asked. "This evil in sending me away is greater than the first that you did to me."

Amnon's heart turned to stone under the weight of his self-condemnation. It was too great for him to abide. He barked for his chief servant. The man entered hesitatingly.

"Put this woman out from me!" he ordered. "And bolt the door after her!"

Outside, Tamar sought the discarded remnants of the coal fire and rubbed ashes into her hair and tore her colorful robe. She placed her hand on her head and wept the length of the journey to Absalom's house. It was the only place Tamar could bear to go. Her entire body shuddered uncontrollably as gouts of shame washed over her slender frame. This indecent betrayal would deny her the true joy of womanhood—to be chosen in purity by a future husband, and cherished thereafter as an unblemished jewel. Instead there would only be bitterness.

Her brother met her in consternation, immediately troubled by her unplanned visit. She knew he was aware she had been summoned to aid Amnon, who lay ill, and had not expected her at this hour. As Absalom's gaze traveled over Tamar's tear-stained cheeks and the ashes of mourning blackening her face, his face hardened.

"Has Amnon been with you?" Absalom asked tenderly in spite of the fury pervading his features. Tamar nodded through a stream of tears.

"Hold your peace, Sister. Do not let your heart dwell on it."

Tamar said nothing as her body shook with grief. There could be no consolation and no pardon given for her ravaged chastity.

❧ ❧ ❧

David could determine no ready salve for the depth of the wounds inflicted. *My children!* To justify one will be to irrevocably condemn the other. *Could I impose such a harsh penalty on my own son?* He was torn and could settle on no satisfactory recourse. What was he to do? He could find no answer to relieve the intense burden with which his family was now stricken. David's servants kept their distance as he paced the halls. Would that Samuel were yet alive. The sage prophet would have offered wisdom to counter the ill, and his judgment would not be challenged.

However, there was no one to turn to in this, and each passing day made redress more difficult to accomplish. His prayers faltered as he feared to know what would be required of him. He was loath to inquire of Joab, whose occasional obstinacy and violent resolutions appalled him. The man was an excellent captain, but he solved every dispute with the sword. *I will bide a day or two more before committing myself to a set course— just a few days.*

❧ ❧ ❧

Absalom spoke nothing of the incident to his half-brother, but in his heart he seethed. Words would be of no effect. They had told their father but to no avail. Weeks had passed without any notable censure of Amnon in

Tamar's defense. The unspoken clemency was unacceptable. There would be justice done, brother or no! Absalom sought occasion but none arose until two years later, on the occasion of Absalom's sheepshearing in Baalhazor. He invited his father to attend the event but David declined, offering his blessing in lieu of his presence. Given his father's polite refusal, Absalom requested that Amnon take David's place, but his father balked. Absalom was nevertheless persistent in his request.

"Let all my brothers come, then we will go together. When last have we done anything together, Father?"

David agreed reluctantly. "You must ward their safety, Absalom, as you would mine. There is peace roundabout, yet the road is a dangerous place."

Absalom smiled reassuringly. "Thank you, Father." He returned to his house and gathered his servants before the hearth. "I have arranged for Amnon to be present with us in Baalhazor. Watch to see when he is drunk with wine, and then kill him! Do not fear. It is by my command that you will be doing this so be courageous and valiant. We travel tomorrow. All my brothers will be there but it is Amnon alone that we want. Do not hurt the others. My brothers are likely to flee rather than fight. They may practice at war but they have no experience in battle. They will surely leave Amnon to his fate."

So, as the journey progressed, Absalom spoke jovially with his brothers.

As unsuspecting as my sister was, so too are you, brother, Absalom thought. *You owe a debt for her stolen innocence, Amnon, and it shall be collected—in full!*

Absalom did not deign to return to Jerusalem. He had already arranged to seek refuge with his grandfather Talmai, king of Geshur. His father would not harm him, he knew, for David loved all of his sons beyond measure, but it would be difficult nonetheless to be amongst his brothers soon after the incident. Absalom preferred to be out of reach of darting glances and sullen whispers. A quiet retreat would be prudent for all.

~ ~ ~

David surged from his writing table, scattering his inkpot and quills as frantic shouts arose from the courtyard. The torches were bright yet he could not distinguish the face of the crier from the others. He hurried from his room to ascertain the truth of the disturbance. A tumult arose from the centre of the crowd of servants, and the bawling escalated so that could discem a man's anguished voice.

"Absalom killed all the king's sons. There is none of them left." David's blood froze within his veins. *It cannot be! But Absalom was so insistent, and he pressed me with a definite urgency. What treachery is this? Absalom! No!* David tore at his clothes and fell to the ground, his strength draining from him. *All of my sons? Dead? This cannot be, Lord! Is this my penance? Let it not be so! It would be too cruel!* Anguish wracked his body with sobs of despair.

Jonadab pushed through the servants and came to David's side, where he knelt with a solemn countenance.

"My Lord, do not assume that all your sons have been killed. Only Amnon is dead. Absalom purposed to slay him from the day that he forced his sister Tamar. Do not mourn, thinking them all dead. Only Amnon is dead. Only Amnon!"

Yet David feared to be consoled lest Jonadab be misinformed and he should hold out false hope. A second cry came from the watchman who announced an incoming party of men.

"It is your sons coming," Jonadab said. "I told you it was so!"

David stood shakily and embraced his sons and they wept together.

~ ~ ~

David missed his son's face at his usual place at the table. *Should I have responded differently,* he wondered. *I will not suffer myself to approach Talmai; neither will I beseech my son to return home. He has set his path and must now walk its course the same as any man.*

David collected his thoughts and departed to his Audience Hall. He was to hear a petition that day. A woman, he noticed. She stood abjectly with eyes lowered beside the attendant guards. David sat and awaited her approach. The guard introduced her as being from Tekoah. She entered in mourning apparel and from her appearance looked to have been grieving for an extended time. She fell on her face in obeisance and said, "Save me, my king!"

"What troubles you?" David asked genuinely.

"I am a widow and I had two sons who fought in the field and one slew the other, and my family wants me to deliver my only son and heir so that they might kill him."

"As the lord lives," David comforted her, "Not one hair on your son's head will fall to the ground."

The woman looked pleased. "Then, I pray, let your handmaid say just one thing to the king."

"Go on," David said, surprised by the woman's sudden change in attitude. She seemed more forceful and intent.

"Why then have you done the same concerning Israel? For your judgment will surely be faulty if you do not similarly forgive the one that you have banished and bring him home. God has spared his life so there must be a way for him to return. I leave it to the king to decide what is right and what is wrong."

David sank back into his chair and regarded the woman who he understood had brought a false petition, much as Nathan had on the night of his chastisement. *Will I always be duped by these subtle exchanges? Once again I have been entrapped. It was all about my son from the outset, yet she is a stranger.* David peered at her acutely. No, she was indeed a stranger. *The only person close enough to me to discern the ache within my heart for the loss of Absalom is Joab! He is also one of the few persons devious enough to have concocted this ruse.*

The king leaned forward suddenly. "Tell me woman, and do not lie. Wasn't it Joab who put you up to this and told you what you should say to me?"

The woman seemed startled. "My king is truly wise. It was indeed Joab who put the words into my mouth."

"Go now," the king said in abrupt dismissal. "I will pursue the matter on my own."

The woman rose and left hastily, happy to be freed of her part in the dance, for she was a wise woman and knew how easily these matters could go awry.

❧ ❧ ❧

David summoned Joab to the hall. He was annoyed that Joab would attempt to manipulate his decisions regarding his own family. *Although, he admitted to himself, Joab is never one to rest on his haunches, idling while a matter stands unattended.* It was this same attribute that made Joab indispensable as chief of the host. The cacophony that swarmed the battlefield demanded the attention of a fearless, well-disciplined, and decisive commander. Time was an elusive resource in the thick of battle. Orders were given instantaneously and could mean the sacrifice of several companies in a maneuver orchestrated to protect the bulk of the host and win the war. Joab was also clever, and that alone made him dangerous. David often wondered what other acts of subterfuge Joab was engaged in, but it was a fruitless pursuit to attempt to spy on the leader of the army. He commanded the most valiant men of war whose allegiance was divided between the king and the man who safeguarded their lives daily.

After Saul's death and during Ishbosheth's two-year reign marked by his incompetence, Abner had proven the value of having a capable commander. He had kept Saul's army intact despite the loss of their king, and Joab's abilities were equally valuable, if not more so.

Joab's entrance forestalled further reflection. "It is done. Fetch Absalom home," David instructed without preamble.

"My lord." Joab bowed, putting his face to the ground. "Thank you, lord! Thank you. Today I know that I have found grace in your sight, in that you have fulfilled my request." He bowed again.

❧ ❧ ❧

To Absalom's disappointment the homecoming was unlike the celebration that he had imagined.

"Let him return to his house," his father decreed. "But I will not see him." Despite David's censure regarding the murder of Amnon, Absalom longed to greet his father.

Two years passed and the king did not relent.

Absalom did not challenge his father's reticence initially, but as the months streamed by he grew impatient and a dark fury simmered in his gut. He sent for Joab, hoping to suborn a visit with his father, but Joab declined to come, even after a second missive had been sent.

Absalom was incensed. *I will not be ignored! I will have my audience with my father one way or another.* Absalom called his servants to the court and issued brief instructions. He discharged them to complete the task and sat down to wait. It would not be long now, he was sure.

❦ ❦ ❦

Joab sprinted to the promontory that looked down upon his barley field. Huge gouts of flame ascended from three different sections of his field. *Arson,* he thought angrily. His crop would be utterly consumed within an hour. *I will lose a fortune!*

Joab squinted through the smoke at the large house that neighbored his ground.

Absalom! Joab thought in rage. He descended the hill at a run and charged directly to Absalom's house, which sat north of the furthermost edge of the field. There was no fire erupting within two hundred paces of the edifice. The mild breeze would carry the flames away from the property, which would therefore be in no danger from the conflagration. Joab barged through the entrance court and into the greeting hall where Absalom rested nonchalantly on plush cushions, his hand propped beneath his rugged cheek. He looked up slowly. No surprise registered on his face at Joab's precipitous entry.

"Why did you have your servants set my field on fire?" Joab bellowed.

"Oh, hello, Joab." Absalom's speech was calm and deliberate. "I sent to you requesting that you come, that I may send you to the king to ask, 'Why did I leave Geshur?' It would have been better if I had stayed. Now," he ground icily, "let me see the king's face, and if he finds wrong in me, then let him kill me!" Absalom's voice rose now as his rage began to seep out.

"Very well," Joab bit out. He restrained his bunching muscles for it would be foolish to instigate a brawl with the king's son, whatever their differences. *It will be wiser if I simply wash my hands of Absalom after this day,* he thought, disenchanted by Absalom's petulance. He would inform the king and be done with it. Absalom truly had been better off in Geshur.

Joab had come to regret his easy involvement in the matter. His duties did not afford him time to play nursemaid to a churlish son. Absalom's fate was now in the hands of the king.

⟋ ⟋ ⟋

The reunion of father and son, though two years overdue, passed favorably. *My rebuke has been long enough,* David decided. Absalom had endured the chastening, and David was weary of hardening his heart. His sons were his life's blood, and he was content to curtail Absalom's estrangement. To have allowed his son free rein in spite of his transgression would have been an open sanction of murder and a reproach to his crown. He would pardon Absalom, for the youth had come willingly to submit himself to the king's judgment. David prayed that it would be the last such confrontation, though in his heart he knew otherwise. He recognized the glint of ambition in the eyes of several of his sons, not all for the crown, but definitely for power. It was a trait that he himself had never cultivated, and as a result of this humility, his Lord had elevated him to the highest stature imaginable.

He would give his utmost for God's people, for whom there was a divine purpose, distant yet real. The future lay in his son, Solomon, whom he had also named Jedediah—Beloved of the Lord. David rued the day that he would need to bypass the older children to bestow his ultimate blessing on Bathsheba's son, but God had chosen the boy, and David would not pervert God's decision by choosing another. The day would eventually come for conferral of the crown, yet David hoped that it was many decades away. His body still pulsed with vigor and the wisdom of God's guidance. If he could, he would rule until his strength was but a glimmer so that he could save Solomon the strain of kingship. The boy was merry and tender. He seemed better suited to be a scribe or Temple aide, shielded from the corruption of the world. It was good that God had promised peace in the boy's time on the throne, for the harshness of war eroded the structure of one's soul and left throbbing scars. His had been a life of bloodshed—too much it seemed for one man.

God had promised that Solomon would build Him a house, a temple to the Lord. It would be glorious. David had already been allowed a glimpse of its wonder. He could describe and pattern it, but he would not be allowed to build and dedicate it to YHWH. *Too much blood on my hands!* The Temple must remain unsoiled from its inception. The task of its construction must therefore be delegated to one without the burden of such a rich stain of blood, and there was no one more qualified to the task than Solomon. He possessed an unencumbered spirit, and his eye for beauty encouraged David mightily. The king had stored the best spoil from the recent wars to supply the rich decorations and fittings of the promised Temple. Solomon, he knew, would ensure that they were used to the glory of YHWH. Another might be tempted to pilfer some of the wondrous riches, but Solomon, he knew, would dedicate them all to the Lord. David could see the finished work in his mind's eye. Although he would not be there to see the finished glory of the House of the Lord, its magnificence already shone in David's vision. He had paved the way for Solomon's reign but the time had not yet come. The boy was too young. God had marked a day in the heavenlies for the ascension of His chosen servant. Until then, David would safeguard the young child.

The years trod softly by, and David became complacent in his vigilance. Solomon was grown and the peaceful equilibrium of the twelve tribes had remained steady. Absalom employed himself at the gate, greeting petitioners, and David was satisfied that he was causing no disturbance, so he left him alone. They spoke occasionally of the trials of rulership. David remained as vague as seemed reasonable, for he did not wish to instill in Absalom a comfortable disposition toward the crown.

In the fourth year, Absalom approached his father with a request, bowing low to the ground.

"Father, please let me go to Hebron to pay a vow I made while I was in Geshur. I swore that if the Lord should return me to Jerusalem, I would serve him."

"Go in peace," David said, seeing no reason not to grant his son's desire. Absalom had sheltered under his wing for a long time. Perhaps a journey to Hebron would help him to establish his own footing. Absalom had been blessed. He now had three sons and a beautiful daughter whom he named after his sister Tamar. David was also pleased to hear of Absalom's pledge and his commitment to serve the Living God. It would be a good departure for a new life. David considered that, had Solomon not been the one favored by God to assume the crown, he would have preferred Absalom to reign. He was strong and presented the bearing and visage of a king. His unblemished stature drew attention wherever he was lodged. His hair fell like a thick mane about him. Each year, the hair polled from Absalom's head weighed about two hundred shekels and was the envy of the younger warriors. His appearance and nature reminded David of the lion he had slain in his youth. Absalom's proud stride and innate aggression charged the very air around him.

How would such a man fare as king in a time of peace? It became more apparent why Solomon was preferred above his other sons.

The Lord knows the heart of each of my sons better that I do. Your will, Lord, David said. *Your will be done.*

⤙ ⤙ ⤙

The truth of the king's assessment struck hard the following month when messengers flooded in throughout the twelve tribes, all bearing the same fateful declarations:

"Absalom reigns in Hebron!"

"Absalom reigns in Hebron?" David sent quickly for Joab, growing more anxious by the second. "What have you heard of this? Does Absalom truly reign in Hebron?"

"I'm afraid he does, my lord. My men report that he left Jerusalem taking two hundred men, I assume to witness his self-appointment. They were unaware of his intent but the effect was essentially the same. He was heralded in Hebron. It seems that the years he spent at the city gate have finally borne fruit."

"What do you mean?" David asked, perplexed.

"Did you actually believe he was there from the break of dawn with chariots, horses, and fifty runners to merely observe and salute those entering? It appeared to be an innocent enough occupation, but Abishai has gleaned that Absalom greeted each petitioner with a kiss as a brother, promising that, were he made judge in the land, he would do justice to everyone who had a grievance. He gained a large and devoted following over the years. As Abishai put it, 'He has seduced the men of Israel and stolen their hearts.' Now his rabble-rousing has incited them to insurrection."

David slumped into his chair. "I have been a fool," he said in a low voice.

"You have been a father," Joab corrected.

"What more has he done? Four years is a long time to have plotted. Absalom would have ensured that he paved a solid road to the throne." David shook his head in bafflement at the scope of his son's duplicity.

"Ahithopel, your counselor from Giloh has joined him, willingly. Absalom has involved many of your servants in his conspiracy. It will not be safe for you here with the tribes following him. You might go to Mahanaim or Jabesh-Gilead, but wherever you decide, it should be beyond the river Jordan. Absalom will not be content to live in peace, and it is not to our advantage to make war without establishing firmer ground."

All these things cascaded through David's thoughts. He made his decision and called his servants to the wide courtyard.

"Collect your belongings. We will be leaving Jerusalem. If you have not already heard, my son Absalom has set claim to the crown. We shall resist him, but until I can make alternate plans, this is the only way we shall escape him. We must depart before he overtakes the city, so make haste!"

His servants bowed to his word. "We will be with you no matter what you decide."

David clasped his hands in thanks. Their support was vital for his household was vast. He assembled his wives and children and outside, selecting ten of his concubines to abide to keep the house. These women, who had travailed more seasons, would be spared the strenuous passage that might claim their lives before its end. If he could put several days' journey between him and his son, Absalom should be appeased.

David thought again of his penance. *Have mercy, Lord.* Whether the curse of disobedience would ever be erased, he did not know, but he was detemined to persevere for the sake of the covenant of Blessing that God had made. *This too will pass,* he encouraged himself, *and the kingdom will be restored in peace.*

Absalom was trying to follow in his footsteps, even in choosing Hebron to launch his reign, but God would not neglect His promise to David, who had seen enough of the Living God to know that Absalom's coup was destined to fail. If it was in his power, he would preserve Absalom's life. *Have mercy on my son, Lord. Have mercy on both of us.*

≈ ≈ ≈

David left Jerusalem with a greater contingent than he had anticipated. The men serving under Benaiah, one of his thirty trusted men of war, met him with a mass of his followers. The Cherethites and Pelethites and in addition the six hundred men who had shared his exile in Gath chose to come to his side. To David's surprise, Zadok, Abiathar, and the Levites appeared bearing the Ark of the Covenant and set it down before him. The king was moved by their show of support, but he also knew that the Ark of God did not need to be protected, and if God willed, he would be blessed with or without the presence of the Ark.

"Carry the Ark of God back into the City. If I find favor in the eyes of the Lord, He will return me once more; but if He finds no delight in me, look, here I am; let Him do to me as seems good to Him. Furthermore, aren't you a seer, a prophet of God? Return to the City in peace, both you and Abiathar, along with your two sons. They can be my ears when Absalom comes."

Ahimaaz and Jonathan each looked to their fathers, who signaled them to join the march back into the city.

"I will sojourn in the plain in the wilderness until you send word," David told the prophet as he departed. "Do not fear. All will be well with the king."

Zadok nodded and motioned for the Levites to raise the Ark. They turned as one and reentered the city gate to await the coming of Absalom.

⁓ ⁓ ⁓

David's passage took him through the ascent of Mount Olivet, where he covered his head and removed his sandals in reverence. The people followed his example, for it was a place sacred to the twelve tribes. At the top, they worshiped God dutifully.

"Lord," David prayed, "Turn Ahithopel's counsel into foolishness." Ahithopel's gift as a counselor was highly revered and likened to visiting an oracle of God. The man would be a dangerous tool in Absalom's hands.

While David prayed, his trusted friend, Hushai, arrived and saluted him. He too mourned over David's self-imposed exile. His clothes were rent and there was earth on his head. However, David sought to dissuade Hushai from leaving Jerusalem. The journey would be hard and its end uncertain.

"If you go with me, I will need to continually be looking out for you, but if you return to the city, you can help me to oppose the counsel of Ahithopel. You must go to Absalom and pledge to be his servant as you were mine. Zadok and Abiathar will also be there. Whatever you hear in the king's house, let them know. Zadok's son is named Ahimaaz. Jonathan is Abiathar's son. Any information will be sent with their aid."

"Very well, my friend. I will do as you have asked. God be with you."

"Thank you, Hushai."

The man waved it off with a small smile. "I will do more if I could."

"Go carefully," David cautioned.

"I will! Until we meet again." Hushai collected his scrip and wove his way back through the multitude.

"Yes…until then!"

≋ ≋ ≋

Late in the day the plains east of the Jordan could be seen stretching in the distance. During the slow descent, Mephibosheth's chief servant, Ziba, met David with two mules laden with loaves of bread, raisins, summer fruits, and wine.

"Why are you here?" David asked.

"I brought the mules for your household to ride on, the food for the young men, and the wine for any who faint in the wilderness," Ziba answered simply.

"But where is Mephibosheth?"

"He stayed in Jerusalem," Ziba said, his tone disparaging. "He said, 'Today the House of Israel will restore my father's kingdom to me.' He still harbors fantastic ideas of ruling Israel, I think."

The spoken betrayal angered David. The love he had shown many was being rejected all around him. "All that was Mephibosheth's is now yours, Ziba."

"May I find grace in your sight." Ziba bowed in acceptance of the gift and turned back on his way to Jerusalem, leaving David to continue his course.

The procession passed over the brook of Kidron and veered toward Bahurim. Their progress was steady despite the heat of the day. David stayed ahead of the main grouping, shouting occasionally to motivate his people to endure. Soon, songs were being raised throughout the march.

As David walked in conference with Joab, a large stone clattered several feet away from him. Three more quickly followed in its wake. Joab and the men of war moved rapidly to surround their king as a man appeared some distance away, cursing as he approached. He continued to launch stones in David's direction. The king's back stiffened and he stopped abruptly. He shielded his eyes with his hand as he scanned the rise that the man traversed.

"Who is that?" David asked angrily.

Joab spat toward the hill, his vehemence mirrored in Abishai's scowl. "Shimei, son of Gera, from the House of Saul."

Shimei continued to swear and hurl insults at the king. "Come out! Show yourself, you bloody man, you son of Belial. The Lord has returned to you all the blood of the House of Saul in whose place you have reigned. The Lord has given Absalom the kingdom. See how you are caught in your own evil because you are a bloody man!"

"Why should this dead dog curse my lord, the king!" snarled Abishai, "Let me go over, I pray you, and take off his head."

"What am I to do with you, you sons of Zeruiah? Let him curse," David said. "The Lord has allowed him to curse me that I may reflect on it." David spoke to Abishai and all his servants. "Look, even my son, who came out of my loins, seeks my life; how much more may this Benjamite do it? Leave him alone and let him curse, for the Lord has bade him. Maybe the Lord will look on my tears and requite me good for the cursing I received today." David started to walk onward again, drawing everyone else along.

Shimei followed on the opposite hillside, still cursing and casting stones at the king. At last he turned back, as weary of his abuse as his victims were of his torment.

David plodded on dismally, looking forward only to the day's end.

≈ ≈ ≈

As darkness swathed the camp, David received word of a messenger. David took the young man aside to a small tent and issued him quickly through the flaps. "What word? Did Absalom arrive? Is there peace?"

"He entered two days ago with soldiers. None have opposed him, my lord."

David nodded in relief. It was good that they had chosen not to tarry. "How does Hushai fare? Has Absalom received him?"

"He has. He was suspicious at first, but Hushai bowed and greeted him as the king. Although Absalom did ask what kindness this was to show a friend. He was curious why Hushai did not go with you."

David groaned. "And how did Hushai answer?"

"He said, 'Whom the Lord, his people, and the men of Israel choose, I will also. Whom should I serve? Should I not serve in the presence of the

son, just as I have served in your father's presence? I will stay with you.'
Absalom was satisfied with this and dismissed him."

"Good. That is very good."

The messenger fidgeted uncomfortably and David felt sudden panic well within him. He grabbed the man's arm, giving a sharp tug.

"What else has happened? Tell me!"

"Ahithopel, my lord—"

"What of him?" David urged, apprehension making his voice waver.

"He advised your son to go in to your concubines whom you left behind so that all Israel would be assured that you despised each other and had parted ways."

"My son would not do such a thing!" David shouted. *"He wouldn't!"*

The king stared at the messenger, who hung his head in distress, unable at first to respond. He gathered himself then spoke.

"Absalom erected a tent on your housetop—"

He broke off as David closed his eyes, raising his palm to silence the scream of pain that echoed through Absalom's transgression. *How could he? Especially after Tamar—*

The word of the Lord to David suddenly resounded within the walls of his mind, which still bore the imprint over the years of the fateful declaration, "Your own house will turn against you and you shall lose your wives publicly to another. You trespass in secret but all Israel will know your shame."

꙾ ꙾ ꙾

Hushai waited in the shadows of Absalom's court where several commanders traded strategies. He listened intently, focusing on the group nearest Absalom. Ahithopel was being given the charge of directing Absalom's hand, and of devising a way to smooth the road of Absalom's rise to power. "I say you choose twelve thousand men, and I will pursue David tonight while he is still weak and weary," Ahithopel proposed. "He will be afraid and all his servants will flee. Only the king will be killed. I will then bring back all the people and there will be peace."

Absalom and the elders gauged the suggestion, the majority finding it suitable. Nevertheless, Absalom hesitated, his keen eyes searching the wide room. "Where is Hushai? Come forward. Let us hear your voice in this."

Hushai moved to the front of the assembly. *He seeks to discern through his counsel whether my heart remains with David.* Hushai put on a pretense of brooding as Absalom posited Ahithopel's proposal. "Shall we follow Ahithopel's plan, and if not, what do you suggest?" Absalom sat back expectantly.

Ahithopel sucked in a sharp breath and Absalom quieted him with a severe look.

Hushai answered immediately, "You know your father and his men are mighty and that they are bitter, as much a bear robbed of her cubs; and your father is a man of war and knows better than to stay with his people. He will be hidden in some pit or another and when some of the people have fallen in your first sally, whoever hears of it will say, 'Absalom slays his followers,' and men will lose courage. I believe you should gather your people like a multitude and go to war against David, so that you may be able to find out where he is hiding with his men and exterminate every one. Furthermore, if he is in a city, you will be able to break it down."

Absalom smiled. Hushai could see by the sparkle in the young prince's eyes that the prospect of full-scale war did not deter him. *He sees only that Ahithopel's proposed exploits will bring him no glory—his pride—No! Not pride alone, but the mercies of God.* How else would Absalom have so easily discounted Ahithopel's insightful plan. David would have been be caught and slaughtered on the plain like a sacrificial calf.

"I will take your advice, Hushai. This is a better plan, I believe." He heard rumbles of assent from Absalom's men. The tide of agreement soon swelled to a consensus.

Hushai felt relief wash over him. A war would take longer to plan, but the possibility of a conflict would appeal to Absalom's blood-lust and desire to dominate. To slay his father on the run and alone—Absalom would see no victory in such a mean feat. He had long yearned for the fame garnered in battle, the rush of victory, and the blazing triumphs of which his father had spoken since their youth.

Hushai waited patiently until further plans had been discussed. At the meeting's conclusion, he forced himself to stroll leisurely from the hall. He went directly to Zadok and Abiathar to relay the plans that had been made.

"Send quickly! Warn David not to stay in the plains tonight but to pass over the river lest he and his people be overrun."

≈ ≈ ≈

"A message from the priest," the woman whispered into the deep recess of a closed shop off the town's main street. Zadok had commissioned one of the wenches whom Joab used regularly to spy within Jerusalem. to deliver a missive to Jonathan and Ahimaaz, who were waiting for instructions in En Rogel; to enter the city and leave again would create suspicion for either of the young men, who were well known to many, including Absalom.

"Hand it to me."

The woman fished beneath layers of cloth and produced a small section of papyrus. Her duty discharged, she slipped away into the bustle of the street. Ahimaaz read carefully, and then ground the delicate parchment beneath his sandal.

"We will take the bread and the supplies we already have. Jonathan, fetch the bag. We will leave by the west gate, as though to the valley, then we shall circle as the sun lowers."

As Ahimaaz exited the city, he shielded his face and hurried past a young man traveling in with a peddler's cart. Fear bubbled within Ahimaaz when he saw the man's furtive glances. He recognized the trader from the market in Jerusalem and occasional business in the king's court. Ahimaaz increased his pace; rounding the wall, they moved beyond the view of the merchant. Jonathan followed behind, concern etching his face.

"What is it? Do you know that man?"

"Just keep walking—hurry!" When the wall angled again Ahimaaz signaled Jonathan and they fled to Bahurim. The two were welcomed at the house of a friend.

"We must leave soon," Ahimaaz warned when the woman offered them a meal. "We have already been seen."

"Take some bread with you then; you should journey at once."

Jonathan accepted a small bundle wrapped in a thick cloth. The bread was still warm from the oven. The woman opened the door to let the young men outside but closed it sharply. She grabbed the bundle of bread from Jonathan's hand and pushed them back toward the court.

Through the doorway, Jonathan had glimpsed a group of men in a far street. One had been pointing in their direction.

"That looked to be Shimei," the woman groused. "That son of perdition! He will reap his reward, someday. Come! Come!" she said urgently, prodding them toward a well in the centre of the yard. She drew up the bucket and directed them to climb in. The woman used the bucket and winch to aid their decent. "There is a ledge halfway down. Stand there, but be careful! It is slippery."

Ahimaaz clambered over the low wall, joining Jonathan, and the two peered at the circle of light high above. It was soon blotted out by a dark cloth, and the men stood silently listening.

After a painful duration, they heard loud voices enter the court.

"They went over the brook of water," the woman said. There were other muffled sounds and the slam of a door before a long period of silence. The two endured a harrowing wait before the covering was drawn back, and a fine shower of ground corn rained down upon them.

Jonathan looked questioningly at Ahimaaz. "To disguise the cloth," Ahimaaz explained.

The woman had indeed spread a fine layer of corn atop the thick cloth in order to distract the searchers from its true purpose. They climbed out and the woman handed them back the bundle. "Go now but go more northward. They will be looking for you on the road."

The young men bowed in gratitude. They hurried to find their king and see him safely over the Jordan.

≈ ≈ ≈

Ahithopel pounded the wall of the stable with his fist. He buckled his lips to suppress a sob. For the first time in his recent memory, his counsel had not been heeded. Absalom had accepted the word of Hushai, a nobody, over his own. He saddled his donkey and departed Jerusalem. Ahithopel sat limp astride the mule, listlessly guiding its slow plod. When he reached Giloh, he set his house in order and gave instructions concerning his affairs. Taking a tightly braided rope used to make bridles for the mounts, he closeted himself in his bedchamber.

At the call for the evening meal, he did not appear. His servants, growing concerned, sought him in his room. He was found hanging from the thick roof beam, his face fixed in a tortured mask.

~ ~ ~

Absalom received the news in irritation. How could a man be so thin skinned? I need strong men about me. He sent for Hushai and relayed the incident. "I have no time to mourn one who did not value his own life; if he did not want it, I will not crave it for him," he told Hushai, whose fleeting smile suggested he approved the sentiment.

They conferred on plans of the war and Absalom summoned Amasa, Joab's cousin whom he had chosen to lead the host. It was agreed that their offensive would be launched from Gilead, by the wood of Ephraim. Word came that David had crossed the river Jordan to Mahanaim, where he was aided by Shobi from Rabbah, Barzillai from Gilead, and Machir, the son of Ammiel. Absalom remembered the latter from the days of Mephibosheth's disfavor. Machir had succored the lame prince in Lodebar until the day David had taken him in. It was said he still had hopes of winning the crown back to the House of Saul. Absalom scoffed at the notion. *A lame man? Leading a war?* The day would not come while he drew breath.

~ ~ ~

David's army numbered in the thousands. It was a small but highly skilled force. He divided the men into three parts under the leadership of Joab, Abishai, and Ithai the Gittite. David announced that he also planned to go to battle, but his people protested.

"You will not go out. If we flee, they will not care, even if half of us die, but you are worth ten thousand of us. It is better if you encourage us from within the city."

David agreed reluctantly. He stood at the city gate and watched the thousands of men muster for war. *My son should be my responsibility.*

"Joab, Abishai, Ithai...Deal gently with Absalom for my sake," he charged the captains, and then returned within the gates. He would give directions or aid if it were required, but no call came from beyond the wall. For the first time in his life the gate closed on the battle, and he held no weapon of defense—not for his body, but for his soul.

≈ ≈ ≈

The lone sounds puncturing the morning air were the ringing of clashing swords and the far off cries of death. The confrontation became increasingly fierce as the cresting sun blistered the backs of the hosts. The battle spread through a network of declivities and spewed into nearby groves. The assault was widely dispersed and Absalom's men were disadvantaged by the unfamiliar territory. The wood of Ephraim became a snare for the men of Israel; many were swallowed by the hazards hidden among the twisted trees; deep pits and sharp stumps that could founder the unwary. Loose rock covered by trailing growth concealed deadly ledges and pitching boulders. Legions of Absalom's men were falling to his father's army in this sinister place.

Absalom himself became separated from his troop as a retreat was called. He escaped into the wood on a mule, but in heeding his pursuit, he was caught unawares as his mule stumbled under the gnarled, ramulose boughs of an oak. His sword flew from his hand. Absalom was suddenly swept from the animal's back by a protruding limb that viciously entangled his thick hair. The recoil of the branches snapped his head back painfully, dragging his tresses taut. Absalom thrashed in an attempt to free himself but without his sword he was unable to release the knotted mass, neither could he break the rigid boughs. He assayed desperately to keep his footing for he was perched unsteadily atop the dew-slicked roots that had made the woodland floor a roiling death trap. Although his need was dire, and despite the knowledge that there were thousands of his men in the woods, he dared not call out lest he hasten his own demise. It was clear to him now that the Lord was with his father, and had always been.

This contest against David had been ill-advised from the outset and he hesitated to further misstep. He feared that any call might bring death rather than deliverance.

Absalom watched in dismay as the face of a Judahite suddenly loomed ahead of him. It disappeared momentarily into the partial concealment of a thicket then reappeared after a brief interval. One of David's men had happened upon his precarious entrapment and was emboldened by the obvious incapacity of his entangled enemy. The man approached with his sword drawn and then he stopped abruptly, eyes widening in recognition. The man cast about for nearby soldiers, his indecision plainly etched across the ruddy features. Absalom read in that darting glance a barrage of emotions—shock that gave way to jumbled expressions of hate and bitterness then fear and finally pity. To the latter Absalom's eyes returned a plea to be given quarter. Absalom's inward hope of clemency was sparked as the man stood for an interminable while before turning to move away. However, the man's deliberate course southwest warned Absalom of impending doom. The retreating form was veering in the direction of the nearest camp, which lay in the command of his dire enemy. Absalom silently sought a means to his deliverance ahead of his looming fate. This foe would show him no mercy....But then there was his father, the king— he would without doubt be paraded before David as a war trophy—theirs a gloating victory, his a shamed defeat. Still, at his father's feet he would surely find grace. He was confident of it. Of course he would be forced into years of subjection, or exiled, but he would recover. Absalom smiled. He would exploit that one weakness of his father, his love for his sons, to secure his life. All was not yet lost!

∽ ∽ ∽

Joab bade Emmiel to enter his tent.

"Speak," Joab said brusquely. The toll of the day's battle and the apparent escape of Absalom left him tense and bilious.

Under Joab's intent glare, Emmiel relayed the circumstances of his peculiar discovery. Joab stared as he listened to the strange report, unbelieving at first, then with emerging anger.

"You saw him? Why didn't you smite him to the ground? I would have given you silver aplenty!" Joab bellowed incredulously at the man's naïveté.

Emmiel flinched but held his ground. "Even if you were to give me one thousand silver shekels, I would never attack the king's son. We heard his charge to you not to touch Absalom; otherwise, I would have acted falsely, and to my own detriment. Nothing is hidden from the king; and you yourself would have been against me."

Joab chafed at the brazen retort. "I cannot waste time here with you," he ground out angrily. Joab gathered ten young men and departed the camp forthwith.

They picked their way decisively toward the location indicated by Emmiel. The going was steady but slower than Joab would have wished. *Let him still be there,* Joab begged the heavens, *and I will end this for all time.*

Absalom's position was easily pinpointed as the search party drew close to the place of Absalom's captivity. At their approach, the insolent pup glanced up unabashedly. Joab parted the brush, and his men surrounded Absalom with a ring of weapons.

"Joab." Absalom greeted him with a wan smile. "I surrender to the king. Take me to my father, Joab. I am at your mercy."

"That you are," Joab snarled. "I aided you once and you bit my hand like the cur that you are. We have no more need of you!"

Awareness congealed over Absalom's features. He cried out and struggled to break free. Joab stepped forward and without delay thrust Absalom through the heart with three darts. Absalom's cry was muffled by the dense wood, and none else was within reach to rescue him. Joab moved back dispassionately to allow the other young men to blood themselves on their prey. Each smote him with murderous intent, but Joab's unforgiving strikes had already initiated Absalom's journey through life's doors. Joab watched until Absalom's body slumped lifelessly, though it was still held erect by the pinioned tresses the man had taken such pride in.

Joab at last blew the trumpet to signal an end to the rest of the pursuit, which still combed the woods far and wide. He took his troop of ten and buried Absalom in a pit in a wood as though he were a commoner.

They covered him with a tremendous heap of stones.

"Let's go," he told the men.

Every man of war knew his fate should he be held by his enemy. Joab discerned the war had been a game to Absalom, but the rules were set by violent, hard men. Men like Joab, who cared nothing for showing favor to the sons of kings or for the tender love of a father.

෧ ෧ ෧

"A runner comes!" the watchman bellowed from the wall. Though expected, the shout jarred David, who was sitting in his position of kingly authority between the two gates of the city of Mahanaim.

"If he is alone, he brings good news," David pronounced eagerly.

"Another runner!" the watchman cried. "I think the foremost is running like Ahimaaz, Zadok's son."

The king was encouraged. "He is a good man, he must bring good tidings," he asserted confidently.

Ahimaaz entered the gate, breathless from his sprint to the city. "Peace be to you," he said, falling to his face before the king.

"Blessed be the Lord who has delivered us your enemies."

"Is Absalom safe?" David asked abruptly.

"When I left, there was a scene of confusion but I do not know the cause." But Ahimaaz would not meet the king's gaze.

"Step aside," David said dismissively to Ahimaaz as the Cushite runner now entered the gate.

"Tidings, my lord, God has avenged you this day of your enemies—"

"Is Absalom safe?" David interrupted.

"He is as your enemies who sought to harm you!"

David's chest heaved as he struggled to control the pain that wracked his senses. His glimmer of hope was snuffed out. He longed to strike out at someone but could see only pitying faces staring back at him. Sheer willpower kept him from ordering Ahimaaz's death on the spot as grief blazed through him. It was a fire that threatened to break forth at the merest provocation and would consume any who stood before it. David's reaction to King Saul's death had been severe. He knew the summary execution of that unwary messenger had been spoken of for many seasons thereafter. And David had not even held favor with Saul. But his son—his emotions swelled, pounding him with brutal force. Ahimaaz shrank away.

David's body jerked with a sudden spasm as he fought to suppress an upsurge of violent reprisal. He stumbled to the gatehouse, where he leaned against the wall, weeping bitterly. "Oh my son, Absalom! My son, my son, Absalom! God knows I would have died for you! Oh Absalom, my son, my son…"

The watchman and runners averted their eyes. The sight of the king's grief was too much for them to bear, and their victory, their day of rejoicing, turned sour as the king mourned their enemy—his son.

❧ ❧ ❧

Joab received the news from Cushi, who returned to give the king's answer.

"He weeps and mourns as though an innocent man were slain."

"He said nothing of the people, the victory…the return?" Joab asked angrily.

The Cushite, who had been nicknamed Cushi by the men, shook his head in lament. His homeland was in Egypt where the rituals after a death were not the same as in Israel. Still, grief and pain respected no borders.

"It was woeful to look upon. The people came back to the city with an air of defeat, as though they were cowards fleeing from a battle rather than the victors. All were dispirited when they saw their king in tears. He shouts his son's name constantly as though he stands beside his bier. What shall we do?" Cushi asked.

Joab stood purposefully. "The triumph of my men shall not be turned to sorrow by his pitiful display. He is wrong to turn their joy into defeat, as though some evil were done. It will not be so. I will not allow it!" He slammed his fist against his thigh and marched off toward the king's house, caring not for the demands of protocol. He found the king weeping still.

"You have shamed all your servants today—everyone who has saved your life and the lives of your sons and your daughters and the lives of your wives and of your concubines—for you love your enemies and hate your friends. Today, you have shown that you do not care for princes or servants. I see now that if Absalom had lived and all of us had died today, that it would have pleased you all the same. Get up!" he growled dangerously. "Go out and speak to your people, for I swear by the Lord, if you do not go out, there will not be one person staying by your side tonight, and it will be worse for you than all the evil that has befallen you from your youth until now."

◅ ◅ ◅

David arose. He fixed his robes slowly and deliberately. He dried his tears and went to the gate. He knew that Joab was a man of his word, and this day his soul and his spirit were weak—too weak to oppose a man such as Joab. He would still the ache and strengthen his heart in the Living God. Though he mourned, he would not forget nor make forfeit the covenant with his Lord.

The people breathed a collective sigh when David reentered the gate with his poise returned. David saluted them as they trooped before him. He relived the trauma of a bloodied nation after Saul had been killed. Would they receive him again? Who else was there to shepherd Israel? At the day's close, he sent for the priest. He would build a new start in his homeland amongst his tribe. Beyond Judah, he would need once more to woo the loyalties of Israel. As the hours progressed, his strength reemerged until he felt equal to the task.

"Zadok, I want you to speak to the elders of Judah and ask why they are the last to usher their king home, seeing that they are my brothers, my bones and my flesh, and seeing that all Israel is coming to greet me." He expected the words to goad them to action. "Abiathar, you will go to my nephew Amasa and let him know I have sworn to make him captain of the host in place of Joab."

David was certain that the tribes who had followed Amasa under Absalom's rule would more easily accept his return if Amasa, their commander, decreed it. Joab would be sore, but David had determined that he would not undergo another lengthy separation from his anointed place as king. For all Joab's prowess, David despised his manner that night. Joab's declining deference toward the king made him unpredictable. *He is mighty, but he is not indispensable; no one is.* It had been a hard lesson for a king of power to learn.

≈ ≈ ≈

David was conducted over the Jordan River under the blessing of Judah. The men of Judah had been moved by his communication and had come to Gilgal to escort the king home.

He was shocked to see Shimei among the welcome party, bowing before him. *Is this the same man who cursed me to death?* David thought in wonder.

Shimei addressed him plaintively. "Let not my lord hold this thing against me, nor remember my perversity that day, for your servant knows that he has sinned. So I have come first with my entire house." He gestured to a group of approximately one thousand men standing beside the river's edge.

Abishai came forward and spoke briskly into the king's ear, "Shouldn't he be put to death for cursing the Lord's anointed?" David shrugged him away.

"What am I to do with you and your brother, Abishai? That you cause me such trouble and would bring about my demise? Are we going to put a man to death in Israel today of all days?" He turned away from Abishai in exasperation. Though Shimei might also have bargained on his lenience on this particular day, David was willing to suffer his intrusive presence. He would be magnanimous for the sake of peace. *I will leave this recreant to the One who judges and recompenses wrong—for now.*

"Shimei, you will not die," David granted generously. He watched, expressionless, as Shimei bowed and smiled broadly, then moved aside with his men.

David followed Shimei's retreat with an eagle's gaze, and then turned to regard another approaching figure. His brow creased in annoyance. Mephibosheth, it seemed, had also come down to the river to meet the king. He was disheveled and dirty. His feet were unshod and his clothes had remained unwashed since the day that David had departed from Jerusalem.

The king addressed him curtly, still smarting from Ziba's claim that the man had coveted the crown during his absence.

"Why didn't you leave with me, Mephibosheth?" David's gruff question caused Mephibosheth to recoil noticeably yet he held his head aloft; he was crippled outwardly, but not in spirit. *Ever the son of a king,* David acknowledged.

"My lord, my servant Ziba deceived me. He told me that he would ready a mule because I am lame, but he never returned for me. And he has slandered my name to you, but I regard you highly. Do what you believe is right, for all my father's house were counted dead and at the mercy of my lord, yet you honored me at your own table. What right have I therefore to complain to you?"

"Let us not talk of this anymore. You and Ziba can divide the land…"

"Let him take all of it," Mephibosheth offered unexpectedly. "I am simply glad that you have returned safely." He said no more but made an imperfect bow, then signaled for aid.

As two servants came to bear Mephibosheth away, David's conscience pricked him; now he comprehended the scope of the sham through which Ziba had beguiled him and benefited. At the time, however, he had been too overwhelmed by the multiple faces of flattery and layers of deception to grasp all the threads of trickery that were woven about him. Ziba was one of an increasing number of opportunists who had chosen to take a deep draught from a poisoned cup, believing it to be a golden chalice; but its end was death.

A dishonest man will never prosper in his ruse, David reminded himself. He was comforted measurably by the knowledge of God's omnipotence and fair judgement. *What price can one pay to relieve a curse engendered through deceitfulness?*

෴ ෴ ෴

Sheba, the son of Bichri, stood with the tribe of Benjamin, preparing to herald the king as he approached Gilgal. He frowned as the king's entourage came into view.

"Aren't those men of Judah who are escorting the king?" he asked of the other men stationed in the forefront of the greeting party.

"It is Judah!" someone answered. "See? There is Ahiel." Sheba's men all recognized the figure of the large, bearded man walking in conference with the king.

"Judah," Sheba snarled in revulsion. The men of Judah had always thought overly much of themselves, but to bold-facedly elevate their tribe to the position of honor next to the king without consulting the other tribes was unconscionable! *The men of Judah will likely seek to wheedle some blessing from the king's hand, and the king will likely feel obligated to provide them some bounty, seeing they are his own. They are a duplicitous lot, these men of Judah!* Sheba surmised resentfully.

The elders of Israel stepped forward to salute David. Sheba could see that a similar current of anger was sweeping through the rest of the tribes as they similarly recognized Judah's exalted position. The backs of the elders were drawn straight and their faces were taut.

"Why have our brothers from Judah stolen you away and escorted you and your household and your men over the Jordan?" the Chief Elder accused. His tone dripped acrimony.

David stiffened at the affront.

"Because he is from our tribe," someone spoke up from behind him, the man's harsh tone indicating he was inflamed by the allegation of treachery

"Why are you so angry? Have we taken advantage of the king's favor in any way?"

The Chief Elder stepped closer, his mouth working in unveiled fury. "We are ten tribes. You are *one*. We therefore have more right to David than you do. Why then have you treated us so disrespectfully? Weren't we the first to advise that the king should return?"

The men of Judah bristled in anger. Those at the head of the tribe argued fiercely with the elders, subduing their protests.

Sheba had heard enough. He pushed forward, his arms flailing as he spoke.

"We have no share in the kingdom of David or in his inheritance!" he spat. "Every man return to his tent!"

⤸ ⤸ ⤸

The men of the ten tribes filtered away until all had withdrawn from David's presence. Their desertion was a blow to the king, who saw his hold on the reins of power suddenly begin to slip. He needed all the tribes for the promised future of his people to be realized. That one man could tip the balances so significantly!

If I dispense with Sheba, peace will likely be restored, David counseled himself. *When I reach Jerusalem, and I have dealt with my household, I will reward this son of Bichri. But for one day longer I will savor the peace.*

"To Jerusalem," David called.

There would always be time for war.

CHAPTER EIGHTEEN

Blood Revenge

Let not an evil speaker be established in the earth:
Evil shall hunt the violent man to overthrow him.

PSALM 140, EXCERPT

avid's most unwelcome task upon his return was the setting aside of his concubines who had been despoiled by Absalom's base act. The truth of the hypocrisy David still could not fathom, given Absalom's murderous condemnation of Amnon. It would be necessary to place his ten consorts in ward where they would be provided for, but forever removed from his company. Their public defilement bereft David of the option of retaining them in his household, for the king could not compound the degradation by accepting them back into his bedchamber. Therefore, to the eyes of the kingdom, they now must be widows.

On the day that David forsook his concubinage he felt twice bereaved, first of his son, and then of his wives. Now the prospect of a third loss now loomed dangerously, and David swore to protect his kingship from this latest assault. Amasa attended him in his throne room to begin his detail as the new captain of the host.

"Assemble the men of Judah within three days, and then meet me here for further instructions," David commanded. The king turned away, not allowing any discussion to ensue.

Amasa bowed, receiving his assignment with diplomacy. The task that the king had placed upon him was monumental. To David's approval, he did not balk at his first commission or attempt to adjourn the stipulated return date that David had set. *Three days.* The man would be hard-pressed to succeed. Nevertheless Amasa set out to undertake his appointed mission.

～ ～ ～

Five days after Amasa's departure, Abishai was summoned to the king's chambers.

"No more of this waiting. Come. We must move quickly." David gesticulated with clenched fists. "Sheba will do us more harm than Absalom did. Take my servants and pursue him before he escapes to a fortified city." David moved to his writing table and handed Abishai a rolled parchment.

Abishai's brow wrinkled with disquiet as he examined the scroll. It was an edict of command naming him as head of the host. *What of Amasa? Wasn't the commander due to return as planned? And what of my brother Joab? Wasn't this primarily his domain as chief?* Joab had been irate at the king's appointment of Amasa in his stead. He had ranted for hours. This latest slight by the king would infuriate him even more. Yet he could not defer the commission without insulting the king. He bowed and departed to Joab's lodging.

He found his brother in the central court.

"What did the king want?" Joab questioned gruffly.

"Sheba," Abishai said. He made his answer succinct as he sought the words to relay the king's orders to his brother, who stood stiffly. Abishai hesitated, then handed Joab the scroll.

Joab's jaw twitched as he read, but he said nothing for a moment. "When do we leave?" he said finally.

"As soon as the men can be assembled. I will inform Benaiah that his men are to accompany us also." Joab did not remark on Abishai's obvious promotion to the head of the companies, and Abishai was satisfied to leave the matter of Joab's exclusion closed, at least temporarily.

Joab raised his chin and moved inside to collect his weapons.

Abishai bit his bottom lip in thought. Joab was too quiet. He was always like that before he undertook something rash. But his brother was a man unto himself, and there was nothing that could be done to dispel Joab's distemper save leaving him be. The journey to Abel of Beth-maachah was destined to be unpleasant.

Maybe claiming Sheba's head will brighten my brother's outlook, Abishai reflected.

↶ ↶ ↶

A large company approached along the road ahead of Abishai's troop. Joab exclaimed abruptly and nudged his brother. Amasa evidently still was striving to complete the king's order.

Amasa!

Abishai watched Joab's eyes narrow in calculation.

"I shall go to greet him," Joab said evenly. He did not wait for Abishai to comment, but strode off to meet Amasa. Abishai knew his brother well enough to discern his intent. He glanced at his men, catching the eyes of two of the most trustworthy soldiers. Giving a nod of readiness, he rested a precautionary hand on his sword. Abishai kept watch on the movements of Amasa's front guard. He would support his brother in all.

Joab was wearing his battle armor with girdle and sword. He strolled leisurely toward Amasa, smiling as he went. As he neared their cousin, he unhitched his sword imperceptibly, allowing it to fall from its sheath to the ground. Joab stooped to pick it up with an air of inattentiveness and covered the last six paces to stand before Amasa.

"Are you well?" Joab asked the army commander cordially. He took Amasa by the beard with his right hand as though to offer the traditional kiss of greeting. Amasa paid no heed to the sword held lightly in Joab's left hand and drew close into the embrace of greeting. Too late, Amasa saw the shadow of hatred in the captain's hard eyes that belied the warmth of his words. Joab struck Amasa in the stomach with the sword and pushed him viciously to the ground, the severity of his blow spilling Amasa's viscera as he fell.

Immediately a captain from Amasa's troop rushed across to Joab's side. Facing toward his comrades, the man laid his hand on Joab's shoulder and thundered, "Whoever favors Joab, and is for David, let him join Joab!"

Yet the men, each accustomed to violence, stood wide-eyed as their commander's blood spilled in the way. Many gaped, trying to assimilate the suddenness of the bloodshed. The spokesman for defection to Joab's company growled in annoyance. Hefting the feet of the corpse, he dragged Amasa from the high road to an adjacent field where he threw a spread over him with callous finality. Resigned to the unexpected change in leadership, all of the men now moved off to join Joab and Abishai, though some looked askance at the shrouded body.

"Are you well?" Abishai asked Joab as they returned to the head of their expanded company.

"I am well!" Joab said. A vaguely decipherable smile quirked the corners of his lips. After a fleeting interval it was gone.

"Move out," Joab shouted to the combined army. "Move out!"

Abishai stepped back without protest, relinquishing his command to his brother's hand. *All is now as it should be,* he thought. The men were Joab's, and had been since the wars in Moab and Ammon. Abishai sighed. *This is a fact that the king should have known.*

Sheba, son of Bichri, buried himself in the life of the city, listening to the tumult outside the south wall. Abel was a bustling place with a heavy influx of traders and merchants. He had hoped by his simple ruse to evade Amasa, for the man was loyal, but not clever. However, it was whispered that it was Joab instead who was camped against the city. He was dismayed that his pursuer was not Amasa as he had anticipated. This turn of fortune meant that his plan of refuge could be in jeopardy, for Joab's reputation for war acumen was known throughout the tribes. *Still, I will be safe as long as I remain behind the fortifications. No one knows me here and it should be a simple matter to meld into a city of this size,* he comforted himself. Sheba had gained a view of the army on the first day before the gate had been barred shut against the supposed invaders. With that many men, Joab's army would be unprepared for a long siege. They would eventually need to withdraw when their supplies were eroded. He need only be patient. He would slip away from Mount Hermon when the season changed. The oak forest below, though thin, would provide adequate concealment until he reached the plain.

Sheba looked up absently, noticing the brilliance of the perpetual snow crowning the highest of the three peaks far above. Tresses of white frost cascaded from the glistening crust in an ivory mane that disappeared at the soft touch of the rising warmth of the valley. He marveled at a beauty he had never before observed. *Men of war seldom notice these things,* he realized. Theirs was a hard life from beginning to end. On the day of battle you either won or you lost, and this time, Sheba hoped that he had not cast his lot on the losing side.

≈ ≈ ≈

"Listen! Listen! Call Joab that I may speak with him!" A woman's sharp cry came repeatedly from the rampart. Abishai signaled Joab, pointing to her figure atop the battlement.

"Call Joab!" she shouted again.

Joab shrugged at Abishai's unspoken inquiry and pushed through the men on the siege mound that had been erected against the centermost rampart. The foremost men continued to batter the wall with virulence. Joab drew nearer to the woman's location. *Her garb resembles that of a wisewoman,* Joab thought. There is no harm in listening to her words. He motioned to his men, who broke off their pounding assault on the wall.

"Are you Joab?" she called down.

"I am he."

"I am one of those that are peaceable and loyal in Israel. You seek to destroy a city that is honored and is a mother in Israel. Why will you swallow up the inheritance of the Lord?"

"Far be it from me! Far be it that I should destroy the city, but there is a man within your walls who is from Mount Ephraim. His name is Sheba, son of Bichri. He has threatened King David. Deliver him alone and I will leave," Joab swore.

"His head shall be thrown to you over the wall," the woman promised. She disappeared behind the rampart.

$$\approx \quad \approx \quad \approx$$

The woman assembled all the people of the city. *We will not be slaughtered for the sake of one miscreant,* she vowed. The people were already trembling with fear. They would listen if there was any hope of salvation to be offered. Abel was not one of the cities of refuge appointed by their forefathers. In fact, this scoundrel hiding in their midst was from Ephraim, one of the chosen refuges. If he had been innocent, would he not have fled to his home city where he would have found greater favor with the elders? Why flee to Abel except to conceal himself behind its walls? Such scheming bespoke a criminal, and there could be no grace afforded here. There was too much weighing on the scales for the city to risk sheltering a reprobate amongst their number. She stood in a high window overlooking the main courtyard of the city.

"Listen!" she shouted, raising her hands for silence. The clamor eventually subsided.

"There is a man hiding amongst us—Sheba, the son of Bichri. He means harm to the king whose servants gather without the city to claim this man. Let us bring an end to this. Every man look to your neighbor. Bring two to vouch for your name. We will be here as long as it takes. No one may leave until this man Sheba is discovered. Be diligent for your own sakes and bring this man forward. If he is not here but is hiding like a coward, we shall seek him through all the stones of the city," she declared decisively.

The search continued until shortly before dusk, when a man was dragged forward. His eyes bulged in terror as he struggled in the viselike grips of his four captors.

"Have mercy…" he cried.

"We will not all of us die for a traitor," the wise woman said in finality. "His head," she instructed three men standing at her side. Sheba struggled for his life as one unsheathed his sword. The trio stepped forward and Sheba raised his eyes to the frosted mountain peaks. "So white," he sobbed incongruously. Then, the dark bulks of the brutal men eclipsed her vision of his body.

Moments later, the macabre head bounced and rolled down the siege mound as the men outside parted to allow its gruesome descent. Joab retrieved the head and nodded in satisfaction. He blew his trumpet loudly. The men retired from the wall and returned to their tents.

The woman let out a sigh. Tomorrow the soldiers would at last leave.

CHAPTER NINETEEN

The Rephaim Testing

He will not suffer thy foot to be moved:
He that keepeth thee will not slumber.

PSALM OF DAVID 121, EXCERPT

Ishbibenob tasted blood. He grunted, disconsolate at his lapse, and spat out two yellowing teeth. His molar had been broken off by the collision of the projectile with his jaw, but the eye tooth had been completely uprooted from its socket and another incisor loosened by the force of the blow. Ishbibenob probed the bleeding gap experimentally with his tongue.

"Not bad, pup!" he growled to his opponent as blood and saliva coursed over his split lip. He had been battling with this puny King of the Israelites for over an half of an hour and had acquired a newfound respect for the little man—"little" by the measure of the Anakim, brothers to the Rephaim, but of good stature amongst his own brethren. The Philistines, having subsumed many races, had made a prime enemy of these contrary Hebrews who repeatedly resisted their incusions.

Ishbibenob watched the man's muscles tense for another attack and stepped away from the anticipated lunge that sought to catch him unguarded as he reeled from the last strike. The stone that had caught him full on the cheek moments before had made him wary of the man's skill, though Ishbibenob was certain that he would prevail ultimately. He could already see the king's endurance waning.

"You will find that I am not as easy a kill as my comrade Gol-jath was, Hebrew," Ishbibenob sneered. "He was too brazen for his own good, and it earned him an early grave. I could say I mean to avenge him but it would be an untruth." Ishbibenob laughed menacingly. "I want your head for myself, pup!"

~ ~ ~

The plains of Gob rang with battle cries and clashing swords. David was undaunted by the lancing probes that his opponent feigned between scathing outbursts. This was his place. Not atop a wall, listening for the sound of runners and ruing his absence from his men's side.

The tactics of the battlefield were as familiar to David as the weight of a sword in his palm. He ignored the taunts that spewed like sour goat's milk from Ishbibenob's mouth, which continued to work at the unfamiliarity of dislodged teeth. The stream of insults was designed to unnerve him and provoke an ill-advised attack. Instead, he watched guardedly as the giant wiped the blood from his lips and grinned again. A breeze shifted the cloying air, stinging David's nostrils through the heavy odors of gore and death all around him. The man smelled of the hinder reaches of a Pharoah's stable.

"I have earned his place and armaments exceeding any in the kingdom." The giant brandished his highly polished weaponry, fresh from the smith's furnace and awaiting the cruel test against human flesh.

It seems brazenness runs in the blood of these Rephaim, David thought bitterly as he circled the formidable man searching for another opening. He could not afford to forfeit any chance presented, however small, to injure or kill his enemy. He had seized an opportunity earlier, when, as his foot had stubbed against a sizeable stone he had stooped as fast as his slowing reflexes would allow and launched the convenient missile with all the strength he could muster. It had sailed away in a brisk and smooth motion to connect with the colossal head, which jerked back in surprise and pain. However, the reward of two teeth was hardly enough to save him from the death he knew would come if this leviathan did not tire soon. And the hope of that was dimming steadily as the minutes of the battle wore interminably on. Ishbibenob outweighed David by three hundred pounds and there was no jowly fat upon the warrior whose muscles tensed threateningly against the broad war bracelets, ornamented with scenes of the carnage in war. The engravings wound their way around the bands, promising equal death to any within reach of this seasoned soldier. His threats might have been cocky, but David realized firsthand that this fighter was no trifling braggart. Others of the Rephaim were not half as skilled and depended primarily on their immense bulk to overwhelm their opponents. Not so Ishbibenob. He was not as tall as Goliath had been, but he was reputedly among the strongest of the Anakim line. David continued to evade the man's long reach as best he could. Within that grasp he would be snapped remorselessly like dry kindling. Strewn on the battlefield around them lay the broken bodies of several of his men, their limbs contorted unnaturally in death. Some Ishbibenob had maliciously clobbered, and others he had maimed irrevocably.

Red veins like the tamarisk that thrived by the River Jordan fanned out across goose egg eyeballs that followed David with calculation. The bloodshot globes bespoke a love for mixed wine, but the man's precise movements held none of the lethargy of a drunkard at that instant. David backed off a step but continued his cautious circumambulation. Ishbibenob's size belied his tremendous speed. David understood all too well that the corded muscles which now flexed dangerously could produce a sudden surge of power and Ishbibenob would be on him in an instant. David had slowed the man's initial charge with a flurry of darts. Many had been deflected harmlessly by stout armor but a few had found their mark on exposed flesh as leathery as ox-hide. Only one had penetrated to any notable depth in the soft flesh of his opponent's neck. Ishbibenob had quickly plucked it out, pronouncing a vile curse on blood-sucking pests. Nonetheless, the sharp sting of the barbs had dispelled the Philistine's initial rush and discouraged further advances.

Ishbibenob tracked the king's movements impatiently with the rock-steady tip of his sword.

"We cannot dance forever, pup!" Ishbibenob's speech had flowed freely throughout the confrontation, but David focused his unwavering attention on the large hands that clenched the leather-strapped sword hilt. David noticed the twitch of the man's thumb as his enemy incrementally tightened his grip and dove simultaneously to his right. The air where he had stood parted with an angry hum, and the heavy sword smashed into the loose gravel blanketing the battlefield. David rolled to his feet, deflecting a cut aimed at his legs. The giant had indiscriminately mutilated every contender that he had faced. Visions of Mephibosheth, crippled and facing a lifetime of derision, flashed through the king's thoughts. No! A king must be whole! Men of war would challenge any weakness and confront any flaw in one's strength with contempt. His absolute command would be undermined were he to lose even a digit to the giant.

David parried another lunging blow as Ishbibenob bulled in. His wrist was wrenched horribly by the ferocious clout and his wrist was wracked with pain from the shock of repeated blows but he held firm, clenching his fingers like a vise around his only defense, the badly battered sword. David withdrew once more from the range of his opponent's deadly weapon.

In a sudden, awkward lurch David's body twisted as his heel caught in the shin strap of a fallen soldier. He stumbled to regain his balance, willing his limbs to brace his fall, but his weary members responded sluggishly.

Ishbibenob charged forward to claim his victory as David struggled for surer footing amidst a knot of corpses, determined not to join the jumbled heap of lifeless forms. He grappled for a loose shield fallen in the thickness of the sweeping battle and raised the heavy plate above him with a desperate urgency. He coerced his racing thoughts into remedial action, dispelling the rising panic that fought to consume him from within and ensure his demise. Ishbibenob's downstroke splintered the leather-bound buckler, shearing the iron bosses from their settings. David was saved from a death blow as the over-sized sword bore down and lodged itself in the dense timber underbelly of the shield. David heaved it away with all his might, wrenching the sword from Ishbibenob's grasp. The giant yielded his grip and barged in, plunging a huge foot viciously toward David's ankle. The king scrabbled backward, evading the bone-crunching blow, and hastily retreated to a safer distance.

Ishbibenob retrieved his weapon and smashed the resistant timber from the flat of the blade, which was yet unblemished and bore testimony of the skill of its owner. The wood at last relinquished its grip and the giant roared his satisfaction. "Almost had you that time, pup," Ishbibenob howled.

Defeat closed in on David as Ishbibenob resumed his charge undeterred. *Where is there to escape to? Who can aid me?* He searched with mounting alarm. All around him, his men were beset by foes, fighting life-and-death confrontations of their own. In the blur of battle David saw his second-captain shearing across the field to gain his side. Abishai! As the commander's hand flung backward, David glimpsed the glint of a javelin extending into the sky and he threw himself to the ground. Memories of his final travails in Saul's court flooded back like unwanted flotsam. Ishbibenob was shunted back by the power of the weapon's impact. The javelin punctured the bronze breastplate below Ishbibenob's muscled midriff, but far to the left. Though Ishbibenob now grimaced in pain, the wound would not kill him. He seized the shaft and snapped it off a span shy of its armored tip.

Abishai sprinted the remaining distance to the pair, drawing his sword as he came on. He shouted for his king to withdraw even further, and David compelled his exhausted legs to bear him. His lungs clamored painfully for air. He churned backward as Ishbibenob surged forward to slash at David's retreating form. Abishai barreled between them, lashing the giant's forearm with his sword and dancing back as Ishbibenob's sword swung dangerously close. The blade clanged off of Ishbibenob's bracelet that extended halfway from his wrist to his elbow, jarring the weapon in his grip. Yet the sword did not fall. The giant's iron hold held firm.

～ ～ ～

Abishai, unsurprised by the fortitude of this entrenched man of war, immediately reevaluated his attack. The king had been fighting Ishbibenob for an inordinate spell, and though wounded in several places about his body, the gargantuan warrior had not slowed measurably. The rapidly shifting stance of each combatant made intrusion dangerous. Any act of foolhardy bravado could easily culminate in Abishai's death and ultimately the death of his belabored sovereign. *And if I fail, there is no soldier as worthy within range to assume the defense of my king. I must choose my moment—*

Rather than disengaging to reformhis attack, Abishai, his youth and agility bearing him well, sprang from his cat-like stance, his spear fully extended before him. Metal crunched against bone as Abishai's spear impaled the Rephaim giant under his broad chin. Ishbibenob sucked in a violent breath. His eyes rolled beneath lids grown slack in death. Abishai released his weapon ad stepped away as the huge body toppled to the earth.

Abishai signaled urgently to a relief contingent now arriving on the southem flank of the battle. They soon arrived, their faces etched with concern as they beheld their king, now leaning heavily on a spear for support. David waved the younger men away.

"I need a drink of water only and a moment's grace. Then I will be ready to fight again," he said confidently.

Abishai's protest rang above the others.

"You will not do battle again on the chance that your lamp, the light of Israel, is snuffed out prematurely. You are too valuable to us. There is no need to risk your life further. The captains—your men—are more than capable, and you have taught us well to follow the voice of our Lord in battle. You will not be put in jeopardy again."

Abishai's resolve was mirrored in the eyes of those surrounding him. David nodded and accepted the protection of the men's cordon as they quit the field. The heart of Israel would beat for yet another day.

⤺ ⤺ ⤺

The day's victory so encouraged the men throughout the encampment that subsequent encounters with Rephaim, who continued to fight under the Philistine banner, did not intimidate the men of Israel as in years past. Their people had recorded two significant triumphs against these descendents of the Anakim.

That year David received accounts of three further battles with the giants, whose hopes of restored supremacy continued to wane with each defeat. Of David's men, Sibbechai, Elhanan, and Jonathan, David's own nephew, entered the distinguished rank that claimed victory over these awesome foes. David uttered a prayer of gratitude to YHWH. The victories had been carved from a single stone in the hand of an eager boy, but the outpouring of glory that traveled through his people charted even greater accomplishments. *You are mighty, Lord, and in your hands the faithful flourish! We are blessed!*

CHAPTER TWENTY

Curses

I will say of the LORD, He is my refuge and my fortress;
My God, in Him will I trust.
Surely He shall deliver thee from the snare of the fowler,
And from the noisome pestilence.
He shall cover thee with His feathers,
And under His wings shalt thou trust:
His truth shall be thy shield and buckler.
Thou shall not be afraid for the terror by night,
Nor for the arrow that flieth by day,
Nor for the pestilence that walketh in darkness,
Nor for the destruction that wasteth at noonday.
A thousand shall fall at thy side,
And ten thousand at thy right hand;
But it shall not come nigh thee.
Only with thine eyes shalt thou look,
And see the reward of the wicked.

PSALM OF DAVID 91, EXCERPT

his is the third year!" Zadok moaned, clutching at his clothes in distress. He held up three bony fingers in emphasis. "Something is wrong, I tell you! We must have done something to incite this. Three years of famine is unheard of except there be a curse upon us!"

"But what could it be?" David asked through gritted teeth. He found himself pacing with comparable unease.

"If I knew, I would surely say," Zadok replied forlornly, his hand falling dejectedly to his side.

"Abiathar? Would he...?"

The other priest shook his head. "He doesn't know either, and I would hate to venture a guess lest I be wrong and provoke an even worse error. We know the Levites tend the Ark according to the Texts, and there has been no idol worship reported amongst the people. Perhaps it is a past deed. Perhaps..."

"I will inquire of the Lord," David resolved. "The wars, and now three years of famine, have depleted the city stocks to a few sacks of grain. We must know the cause or there will be no kingdom remaining within a year. We must know, and we must know soon!"

≈ ≈ ≈

David returned from his prostration before the Ark, his face grim. He dusted the earth from his robe and regarded the two priests who sat in his antechamber.

"It is because of Saul! For his bloodthirsty house!"

"Saul?" The priests voiced in unison.

"Because he slew the Gibeonites," David explained in a tone that leaked bewilderment.

"When was this?" Abiathar asked. "They are not even our people."

"Whatever Saul did, it was not favored by God. Maybe an erroneous raid...or some deed that was not sanctioned by the priests?"

"I will check the records but I know nothing of a raid," Zadok said, shrugging. "Although, early in his reign Saul was enthusiastic to rid the lands of pagans. Sometimes overly so. Still, our people have always known that the men of Gibeah are exempt from our wrath. We have always respected the covenant that our people made with them and have avoided their borders assiduously."

"That covenant was made over four hundred years ago," David recalled.

Zadok rose to his feet with a sigh. "Yes, and though secured through their trickery, a vow is sacred before a God who keeps all His promises."

"I know this all too well," Abiathar mumbled, shifting in his chair. David recognized the sadness which crept into Abiathar's voice now and again, as he recalled the curse abiding upon his own bloodline with the ever-present threat of penalty.

"Whatever the circumstances, I will do something before we all perish," David stated with finality.

∽ ∽ ∽

The men of Gibeon stood firm.

"We will have no silver or gold belonging to Saul, or his house. Nor will we ask you to kill any man in Israel on our behalf."

"Whatever you ask, I will do!" David pledged, his gaze unwavering upon the men.

"Deliver seven of Saul's sons and they will be hung by our hand in Gibeah of Saul."

"I will do it," David swore. He could not falter in this. The future of his people hung in the balance. Yet there was no easy way to condemn a man to death—to suffer his curses, his disdain, his hatred, his silence—and then to withstand a mother's anguish. Rizpah! And Merab! Yet he would do it to save his people. He would do that, and more!

∽ ∽ ∽

Rizpah spent the season of harvest in mourning for her two sons who were delivered to their deaths in Gibeah. Merab's five sons had also been sacrificed to the vengeance of the men of Gibeah, but it was Rizpah's cries that resounded in David's ears; spurred by the tears of a bereaved mother, he committed himself to the posthumous reunion of a father and his sons. He retrieved the bones of Saul and Jonathan from Jabesh-Gilead. He also collected the bones of each son who had been hanged in Gibeah. The remains of all the men of the House of Saul were then buried reverentially in Benjamin, in the sepulcher of Kish, Saul's father.

David thanked the Living God that he had been granted the leeway to spare Mephibosheth. It was the least he could do to honour the promise he had made to Jonathan. It was so long ago now, and still…

"My brother," David whispered. "I have done all in my power to keep our pact. So much has occurred since your parting, both good and bad. One day I will come to you when this is over, that we may be brothers again."

↝ ↝ ↝

The raised voices in the king's court resounded with the intensity of a thunderstorm. Joab paced around the table, unable to find the right words to persuade the king to deviate from his chosen course. "The city is vast. Why not number Jerusalem alone?"

"No! I want you to go through *all* the tribes from Dan to Beersheba. I need to know how many people there are in the kingdom," David repeated to his captains. "Why do you oppose me, Joab? What is it?"

"God has added to the nation, a hundredfold. You can see it with your own eyes. Why would you want to do this?" Joab argued.

"You need not know my reason, but it shall be done," the king insisted.

The army chief shook his head. "But for what purpose? Can we alter the number more or less? The tributes we receive are already plenteous. Why else would you this?"

"Because I command it!" David was not dissuaded even when Abishai, Benaiah, and Ithai added their voices to Joab's.

"It is unnecessary," reasoned Ithai. "The tribes are mighty and there is unity. That is all we need know."

"It is necessary!" David shouted belligerently.

"There is none other equaling our number amongst our neighbors," Abishai observed. "God is our strength. Did Adino not slay eight hundred in one day with his spear? What use have we for numbers? This count will tell us nothing!"

David pounded the table. "One must be prepared."

"Prepared for what? It is irrational. Is a count not meant for a coming season of war? What further land has our God laid out for us to conquer? Has He not promised peace?" Abishai countered.

"You will lay a charge against the Living God," Benaiah mourned, rubbing the back of his neck. "YHWH has promised to make the tribes like the sand in multitude. Will you challenge His Word?"

David simply stared at him.

"It is folly and vanity," concluded Joab.

Yet in the end they all departed Jerusalem at the king's command to commence a circuit of Israel. Joab spent nine months directing his men as they completed the census, but as the final route lay ahead, Joab became resolute and called the captains together. He stood with arms folded.

"The tally surpasses one and a half million that draw the sword. Despite the king's command we will not number the House of Levi. When our people fled from Egypt it was forbidden to number the priesthood. The king will have his census, but I refuse to compound the error by counting the priests. Neither will I continue with the count of the tribe of Benjamin. It is enough."

Faithful to their chief, the captains returned to Jerusalem, still uneasy, but satisfied that the king's anger would be stayed.

॰ ॰ ॰

As the days wore on, David's conscience burned in a fiery blaze of self-condemnation. Had it been vanity? Pride? Or an evil spirit such as he had seen afflict Saul during his days as a minstrel in the king's court? His heart writhed within him until his defense of the numeration rang hollow in his ears. Even as the count was being returned, David wished fervently that he could reverse his order. His command now seemed like the raving of the demented who were put outside the city wall for the safety of the people. He quailed when he considered the retribution which would befall him.

"I have done a great sin, Lord. Forgive my willful foolishness." Would God overlook his brash act?

His reply came the following day when the prophet Gad interrupted the breaking of his fast in his chamber.

"Choose your penalty," the prophet said directly. "Will there be a seven-year famine in the land, will you flee three months before your enemies while they pursue you, or will there be three days' pestilence in the nation? Tell me what I should say to Him that sent me."

David stood weakly from his chair and searched the room with unseeing eyes. *Penalty? What penalty could I possibly choose? Seven years famine—seven!* They had all but perished during the three years that had just passed. His people would not survive four additional years. *No!* He discarded the option. *Three months before my enemies. I lasted many years in my flight from Saul. It was difficult, but I survived. Perhaps—but no! During that time I had been suffering Saul's injustice. This time it is I who has erred. God cannot aid me in this. I have been disqualified by my own hand and, if I am killed, will Solomon be given the crown? Who will see him to the throne? With Chileab expecting to reign. Solomon…Solomon… No! I cannot desert my son. It is too risky. If I leave now there is the likelihood of another civil war, and without Solomon as king, the promised Temple may never be built…and without it, and a strong king, the people are likely to stray to other gods and condemn themselves. No! We need the Temple. It will be the heart of the people against future trials. The peace will not last forever. The greed and lust for power is too strong in the kingships. Armies will not lay dormant indefinitely. The Temple must be built and Solomon must rule. But pestilence! Our ancestors saw the devastation in Egypt and centuries later it is still spoken of with trepidation. Yet…how can I choose otherwise? Three days. We can survive three days…can't we? After that, it will be over.*

"I am in dire straits," he told Gad. "But I believe we will put ourselves in the hand of the Lord. His mercies are bountiful. I would rather his judgment than to fall into a man's hands."

❧ ❧ ❧

The plague swept over Israel. David looked from his window as the first cries of panic wound through the city where people stumbled blindly, striving to grasp the source of the sudden affliction. Some, seeing their companions smitten, ran frantically to the city gate only to fall victim to the scourge, paces from seeing escape. Women dragged the sick toward the cool shelter of doorways, and a bustle of activity erupted at the city well where pitchers of water and buckets were filled hastily to drench those inexplicably stricken by the fearsome blight.

A few of David's servants ran from his halls into the courtyard, hoping to find relief in the open air, but the heat of the day amplified the sickness and those capable of moving were driven back to the shaded recesses of the interior halls.

David retreated from the window of his house as doleful moans pervaded the walls and drowned every thought save those of death. David ran to find his wives.

"Bathsheba," he called.

She appeared from an adjacent lodging, her brow bathed in perspiration.

"Is Solomon well?" he asked, almost afraid to receive her answer.

"He is well," she replied.

David closed his eyes in prayerful thanks.

"What is this, lord? What is happening?"

"It is my doing," he answered miserably. "I cannot speak of it now. I must find the others." He turned in mid-step as he hurried toward a small house across the court. "Three days only. We need only endure three days," he reassured her. "Only three." Then he forged off.

～ ～ ～

Neither Abigail nor Ahinoam was in her quarters. The servants located them in the olive garden. Maachah, Eglah, and Abital, three of his other wives, were assisting the servants in the dining hall where they mopped the brows of the scribes, messengers, guardsmen, and a flurry of royal staff. Haggith alone lay sick in the infirmary along with Abigail's son, Chileab—the king's second born. Each suffered with a recrudescent fever. He stayed a while to comfort them, meanwhile dispatching Joab to inquire of his companies. The men of war were strong and fared well in spite of the calamity. Though several were incapacitated by the effects of the plague, few had died. Yet many more were permitted to depart to their houses to safeguard their families.

⮑ ⮑ ⮑

As the dusk encroached upon the afternoon light, David understood that thousands upon thousands would perish. Three days had appeared to be a short period to withstand the pestilence, but what he saw filled him with dread, for the evening was much worse than the morning, and he saw escalating illness as he moved through the people, seeking to instill calm amongst them. He wandered past several abandoned litters, some still enfolding their motionless occupants. The king stared a while before turning finally toward his house.

David crossed the portal with the burden of the memory of heavily weighted biers threatening to buckle his knees. He clothed himself in sackcloth and went to seek Zadok, Abiathar, and the elders of the city who had likewise donned their mourning garb. They gathered before the Ark of the Covenant. David's skin prickled with a strange heat and he cast about, expecting to find a bonfire raging within the compound, but there was no blaze to be seen. His eyes drew slowly heavenward and he gasped in awe. His body trembled violently as he beheld an angel of the Lord above Jerusalem, his Sword of scintillating brilliance extended to strike the city. David shouted in terror.

"It is I alone! Punish me alone! Let it be on me and the House of Jesse," he cried falling to the ground.

It is enough! Stay your hand! The command boomed from an unseen source.

The Sword immediately stopped its descent in acknowledgment of the will of the Lord.

From the edge of the grouping, Gad approached David, weaving through the prostrate forms of the elders surrounding David.

"It will be well, but you must erect an altar in the threshing floor of Araunah the Jebusite.

David clambered shakily to his feet. His hands still trembled from the intensity of the ordeal. He motioned for Zadok and Abiathar to accompany him and he struck a course directly for the threshingfloor.

David traveled with as much alacrity as his tremor-racked body would allow. The Sword! He could still see the flame shearing his inner vision. He willed himself to move faster still. He would no longer presume upon the mercies of the Living God. This time he would obey, and with haste!

≈   ≈   ≈

Araunah was counting his blessings. No one in his household had been struck by the plague. He had worried, for he depended on his four sons to assist him with the threshing. He had already committed himself to supplying a full quota of wheat, which had been abundant this year. The seasonal harvest had been good, and the losses he had suffered during the famine would all be erased. His sons joined him to complete the day's work. It was late, but he hoped to stay ahead of the following day's chores before supper was called. He removed a sheaf from the neatly laid stacks. As he straightened with the bundle, he froze. The sheaf slipped limply from his numbed fingers and spilled across the floor. His sons, unaccustomed to such clumsiness from a father whose deft touch had amazed them from their youth, halted their tasks, crying out that he had been stricken by the terrible plague. He staggered, and they rushed anxiously to support him from falling.

"Father! What is it?" cried the eldest, moving to offer his shoulder to his father. Only when they had approached Araunah's side did they come within view of the source their father's mortification. Their eyes bulged as the Sword flared across the sky to begin its deadly ark. Their fearful shouts jarred Araunah from his stupor. He followed on the heels of his sons as they sprinted behind the heavy wooden work tables, piled high with tools. Araunah's shielded his head waiting for the thunder of the strike; but it never came. He waited an interminable duration, quaking as he pondered the meaning of the wrathful visitation.

As a young boy, he had often dreamed of seeing a supernatural event, envying those who rendered accounts of their divine experiences. Occasionally, he would slip away from his chores to eavesdrop on the priests and prophets when they met in the square. Sometimes, he would listen to his grandfather as he sat with his friends in the gate. Oftentimes they spoke of things that were beyond his comprehension. But there were other times when he heard of the glory of God descending or the aura of the Ark of the Covenant and the mystery of the ephod. Once, a seer had mentioned the Angel of the Lord in hushed tones, but otherwise, his days had all been unremarkable and saturated with the tedium of everyday occurrences.

But today! Today his heart nearly failed him. His boyish dreams of excitement and wonder scattered like fine pebbles under the hooves of oxen. He was unable to move for fear of the angelic presence whose ineluctable Sword eclipsed the stars. Neither did his sons emerge from their hiding places.

The clamor of hurrying footsteps invaded Araunah's thoughts. He peeked tentatively over the tabletop and found his feet as his heartbeat reversed from a flutter to a rampant pounding.

"Get up! Get up!" he hissed urgently to his sons. "The king is coming."

Araunah quickly smoothed his robes and stood erect in the center of the threshingfloor.

This is a day unlike any other! He waited nervously as the king approached with his servants, who flustered behind him. He bowed before David, "Why has my lord the king come to his servant?"

"I need to purchase your threshingfloor, so that we may still the plague."

"Take it!" Araunah offered. "Do what you think is right. You can have the oxen too, for burnt offerings, and the threshing floor instruments for wood and the wheat for meat offering. I give you everything. Everything!"

At that moment, David would have given his kingdom for the threshingfloor, and he understood Araunah's eagerness to honor his request.

"No. I will pay the full price," he insisted. "I will not take what belongs to another to give to God nor offer sacrifices that I have not paid for.

David offered six hundred shekels of gold, a price that was more than fair. The construction of the altar proceeded forthwith, and the scourge ended as David's entreaty to the Lord was consummated in a supernatural gush of fire that engulfed David's peace offering.

As the ash rose into the air in a churning funnel, the Angel of the Lord ally sheathed his awesome weapon. Relief overcame David's senses, and his knees buckled from the release. He now realized how much his ploy had cost him. Accounts from his men suggested seventy thousand of his people were dead. All this time, he had been like a child testing the resolve of his father, who had so long guarded him close within his bosom that he had doubted the reality of the punishment for outright defiance.

Never again, David swore. He had endured years as a fugitive, been hunted across the wilderness, and escaped the greedy clutches of war only to endanger himself and the future of his people on a whim. He had spent decades in preparation for his dream, collecting the spoils of war, recruiting artisans and fine craftsmen who could reflect the supremacy of YHWH within the tabernacle to come. He had created great caches of iron, brass, and marble; he had hewed immense stones to lay the foundation; he had prepared with all his might and set aside his own silver and gold; and most importantly, he had devoted years to the training of Solomon in the ways of Power, providing the guidance of both father and king. He would never again put his Father to the test or jeopardize both Solomon and the hope of his people in the new Temple.

He knew what needed to be done. *My purpose will be fulfilled. I will endure to see the day of Solomon's ascension.*

CHAPTER TWENTY-ONE

Conferral of Power

How long will ye imagine mischief against a man?
You shall be slain, all of you,
As a bowing wall shall ye be, and a tottering fence.
They only consult to cast him down from his excellency:
They delight in lies;
They bless with their mouth,
But they curse inwardly.

PSALM OF DAVID 62, EXCERPT

David was an old man now and weary of deceit, but treachery was the constant companion of a king, at least, a king of power. For where there was power, there lurked shadowed eyes watching greedily, sullenly, from dark recesses and lighted halls alike. So when a knock came at the door of his bedchamber, soft, yet insistent, he was not surprised. There would always be a knock, heralding a new scheme afoot within the palace. Many were anxiously awaiting his death, he knew, but not yet. No. Not yet.

There was much to accomplish before he returned to the bosom of his fathers, and he knew that YHWH would grant him all that was needed to secure this last victory. He was one step ahead of the grasping fingers of both the living and the specter of Death, which, in these latter days, sought to snatch away all that he had won and claimed so mightily. They would be gravely disappointed, each one, for he was weak of body, yes, but far from the witless hull that they had hoped. He still possessed the cunning that had seen him through forty years as king amongst wrathful nations; these thirsted for the blood of his people since their arrival into these harsh lands. From Syria to Philistia he was revered, feared, and despised. Nevertheless he had not faltered. The fate of his people was entrusted to him, promised by God. He could not allow himself to fall short now. He would not succumb to the pull on his ailing limbs until all was complete. Even as the light waned in his eyes he would be strong.

It was regrettable that he could no longer attend regular audiences on his throne. He depended heavily on Nathan the prophet to advise him on the current affairs of the kingdom. Zadok the priest came often to his bedside; but Zadok knew little of political dealings, particularly those conducted behind locked doors and under the close cover of darkness. For this he depended on Benaiah, a shrewd and watchful warrior. His father Jehoiada had been a man of valor. They had traveled together from Kabzeel; the city was one of many that had been inherited by the men of Judah some four centuries past. The stronghold lay toward Edom in the south, its men hardened to war. Benaiah in turn was served faithfully by the Cherethites and Pelethites, and the king had entrusted his life and the protection of his son to these men; he need only endure until the set time had come.

Still, the servants fussed constantly over him, for at times he would brood on Solomon's fate to the exclusion of all else. His ruminations were without end, but speculation would avail him nothing. On occasion he would feign sleep, listening to their whispered utterances regarding his poor health. His body was outwardly declining, but within, the spirit of YHWH was infusing him with strength for the task ahead.

That year his servants, fearing for his health, had sought him a young maiden to warm his bed and minister to him. He would have fared better 'ad they carted him to the open field where he could feel the sun on his ꞁw and smell the air as crisp as the dry leaves that crackled underfoot. ꞁ he ached for the softness of a dew-misted sycamore leaf. All that was beyond him now. Sometimes his physical vulnerability assailed him like that of a newborn lamb. He needed his mind to be clear.

He had sent the woman away on occasion, unable of late to afford trivial distractions. Still she came dutifully to his bedchamber to attend his physical needs. Abishag, she was called; Abishag the Shunammite. They had brought her from the outer reaches of Shunem and she was indeed fair, but he had no need of women now to coddle his flesh; there was more at stake than a moment's pleasure.

Solomon's most discernable flaw was his susceptibility to beautiful women, just as David's had been. It was his fundamental weakness. Bathsheba bore witness to this for in her youth her face had been perfect; and David had foolishly succumbed to her loveliness. In past days he had seen a familiar glow in Solomon's eyes, and he feared the same could be his son's undoing. The grievous deeds he had committed to secure Bathsheba's embrace in the heat of his lust weighed heavily on him. Uriah had been an honorable man and a warrior of skill, fallen victim to his king's passion for his wife.

Bathsheba's father, Eliam, had covered his head in reproach toward her illegitimate conception but had stooped short of disowning her. He welcomed the marriage contract, for given Uriah's death, the stigma of widowhood would be doubly tragic for a daughter twice beset by heartbreak of losing a husband and son both to the same wretched cause.

"You will be good to Bathsheba, will you not!" It had been a statement more than a question. And David had been, though he had not needed the urging of a distressed father to propel his steps. He would marry, though it could not erase his guilt. King or not, he knew he had transgressed, and that indiscretion had cost him dearly and haunted him for years after their marriage. Furthermore, Bathsheba had come to suspect the truth of her first husband's death as over the course of the years she learned more of David's nature; his kind moments were overshadowed by a necessary harshness that he had cultivated in order to survive amongst callous men.

Kingship always required its price. During David's time, war had compassed him about on every side. His breath quickened as he remembered the spear in his hands and his sword unsheathed to champion some vital cause. The years flowed in blood: the blood of enemies, the blood of companions, of women, men, and babes by the thousands; it had stained his hands and had run in small rivulets into cracks in the baked earth across Israel. The old king sighed with a long-known grief; a grief he wished to carry with him to the grave. It was too much blood for one man to have shed.

Now his word could ultimately mean the death of one of his sons—Adonijah, most likely, for he had the spark of ambition that was constantly fanned by his companions within the court. He would spare them all if he could, but he could not allow himself sentimentalities or misgivings. The ruin of his life's purpose and the desolation of his people's spiritual hope clawed closer the longer he tarried. His aim was to avoid the civil war that loomed ominously, hinting of more bloodshed to come should he fail.

Solomon was the one. There was none other as worthy. He prayed fervently that his son would be saved the consequences of conflict. It was known that the throne had been promised to Solomon from his birth, but words could be foreswom and kingdoms wrested away by stronger hands. Lions stalked the perimeter of his sheepfold, but still he waited, sheltering his intentions close to his breast. The Temple must be built. God had made a covenant that must not be broken for any reason. Solomon was chosen by God to follow in his footsteps. *It will be so,* he swore to the emptiness of the chamber. *It will be so!*

Six of David's sons had been born in Hebron, bright rays of hope amidst the burdensome years of war. Adonijah was his fourth born and to all the obvious choice as successor to the throne. Amnon, Chileab, and Absalom had been older but each had gone the way of the earth. The sadness of this recollection made him pause as tears welled again in his rheumy eyes. Absalom he had once favored but his had been a brutal death in battle. Even when his son had made war on him, his love had still pulsed in his breast. War. Forever war! With Solomon that would all change.

Patience, he reminded himself. *It could not go on much longer.*

Patience bespoke the character of a worthy ruler. He had known for e time it would come to this, but he needed to stay his hand for the sake of diverting a bloody succession. It was his most efficacious method for discovering whether his son would surrender to his ambition for the throne. He had waded through streams of likely events and stark impossibilities to glean the most suitable course. It could mean Solomon's life if he were wrong. Though political alliances were often made in secret, he was convinced of Joab's ultimate treachery—Joab, who had taken revenge on good men under the pretense of war. *What other evils had the man perpetrated? He will surely be compensated.*

Two days ago, the first stirrings of discontent wafted in the guise of seemingly innocent palace news. Joab had commissioned the preparation of sixteen chariots with fifty runners to execute an undisclosed errand. *A procession fit for a king,* David thought, shifting his creaking limbs. Only Adonijah commanded Joab's loyalty of late. Two hundred sheep and ninety cattle were removed from the royal herds and driven to Zoheleth. *Banquet preparations, no doubt,* he concluded. Within his heart he knew. It had started.

The knock came again, firmer this time.

"Enter."

As the door drifted open, he first saw the hem of Bathsheba's robe, its blue-laced hem brushing the floor. The light silk was backlit from the hall. He had not summoned her and she would only have come to speak of Solomon, who blazed like the north star in her eyes. Bathsheba crossed the threshold tentatively. She glanced uncomfortably at Abishag then bowed her head in obeisance.

"Abishag, leave us." Sometimes he forgot that she was there but now he was alert and wary.

The young woman raised herself gracefully from the foot of his bed where she customarily sat.

"My lord," she intoned quietly. She bowed and retreated through the open doorway, drawing the door closed behind her.

He watched Abishag go then turned anxiously to Bathsheba.

"What would you have of me?" His voice raised its pitch in expectation.

Given the ear of the king and his full attention, Bathsheba came swiftly to his bedside and knelt next to his pillow.

"My lord," she breathed urgently. "You swore to me by the Lord your God that Solomon would reign after you. But even now, look! Adonijah has declared himself king and you know nothing about it! He has killed cattle and sheep in abundance for a feast, and he has called your sons and all the princes, in addition to Abiathar the priest and Joab, captain of the host. But Solomon? No! He has not called Solomon. All Israel is watching you, waiting for you to tell them who will sit on your throne after you. Otherwise, when you have passed on, my son and I will be seen as a threat."

Bathsheba's plea was interrupted by a hurried knock.

"Yes?"

Nathan bundled busily into the room. His robes were in disarray and his brow glistened with perspiration. Distress shrouded his features, evoking a sickening pallor to the normally vibrant visage. The king gestured briskly to Nathan and dismissed Bathsheba.

"I will wait in the hall." Bathsheba gave way to the seer and moved outside.

The king listened fixedly as Adonijah's treasonous exploits were confirmed by the prophet, who he discerned was the instigator of Bathsheba's panicked flight to his bedchamber.

"Call Bathsheba in."

Nathan stepped away from his bedside and whispered into the hall beyond. She came in hopefully, and he raised his hand to take hers.

He spoke earnestly. "Even as I swore by the Lord God of Israel, saying, 'Surely Solomon will reign after me and sit the throne in my stead,' even so will I certainly do today."

Bathsheba bowed with her face to the ground.

David acknowledged her gratitude with small smile, tapping the bed softly. "Call Zadok the priest, Nathan, and Benaiah," he instructed.

It is time to end this.

The three men named filed into the king's presence, eager for his command. No one needed to persuade any of them of the urgency of the day.

David laid his head back on his pillow. There would be no comfort until Solomon sat on the throne. It was good that Adonijah was feasting in En Rogel, for the peril to them all would be great should Adonijah learn of it prematurely, especially with that hoar head, Joab, as counsel. Their lives would be forfeit on the way to Gihon. Thankfully Benaiah would be with them. His prowess as a warrior would be indispensable should swords be drawn against them on the road. More importantly he was captain over an independent fighting force. The Cherethites and Pelethites who would follow Benaiah could be relied upon to complete the task using any means required. He would know they had succeeded when he heard the trumpets sound.

David gave his precise instructions, having had years to examine all the permutations influencing a challenge to Solomon's coronation.

Finally...*finally*, the day was nigh.

Solomon remembered from his youth how dangerous it was to underestimate the actions of one's brother. Amnon he had thought of as gentle and kind, and Absalom he had seen as a chivalrous adventurer. The vicious circumstances instigating both their deaths had shattered his illusion of familial brotherhood. There would be no friendly kisses of greeting, no gentle tugging of beards. *No. My brother will slay me in an instant if we are caught prematurely.*

His father had warned him often enough that this time would come. "I will make all the arrangements, but you must follow my instructions to the letter when you are sent for. It may be Zadok or Benaiah, or another whom I trust, that will come to you if the will of YHWH prevails. Nathan may not be here to aid you: he is bound by One mightier than I. He may be following the will of God elsewhere, but I am sure that you will not be left without a guide. Be strong. Prove yourself to be a man," his father would often repeat. "Whatsoever God charges you to do, then do it!"

Solomon paid close attention to his father's admonitions. Despite his short years, he had learned that within all good intentions lies the potential of failure. *I pray that I will heed his wisdom when my time of trial comes.*

The procession had wound its way toward Gihon. David himself had chosen the place for Solomon's anointing. It lay barely a half mile north of En Rogel, where Adonijah sat feasting that very hour.

Solomon dismounted gingerly from David's mule. He would have preferred the comfort of a chariot or even to have walked, but he recalled his father's words adjuring him to be faithful to his directions.

A throng was gathering at the site of the unusual procession.

"He rides the king's own mule," someone exclaimed.

"Isn't that the prophet and the priest on his right hand?" another noted.

"I thought Adonijah was the heir. He is the eldest, is he not?"

"He is, but he is full of himself. He never hails us as he passes. Even the king salutes his people."

"It seems the king has made his decision, and Solomon has the support of God."

The comments wove together in a loud buzz that drew even more spectators. Benaiah, trumpet in hand, stayed within three paces of Solomon, his keen eyes scanning the growing multitude for any signs of discontent among the watchers. His ears would be alert for any resonating disharmony. He shadowed Solomon's footsteps, until at last Zadok withdrew a horn of oil from the folds of his robe. He had collected it from the tabernacle to seal their divine mission.

Solomon knelt reverently before Zadok, who offered the oil in blessing to God then ceremoniously poured it onto Solomon's head.

The air was split by a tremendous blast of a trumpet. Benaiah removed the trumpet from his lips.

"God save King Solomon!" he shouted triumphantly. He shared a smile of accomplishment with the priest. "We did not fail our king, Zadok. We have done it."

Zadok nodded vigorously. "Indeed."

"God save King Solomon!" The cry arose like a majestic wave and ʼoke upon En Rogel with a tremendous crash. It rode upon the backs of ʼcing flutes that announced the joyous anointing of the new lord of ʼl.

∽ ∽ ∽

Adonijah halted in the middle of sampling a raisin cake; its sweet flavor degraded to the bitter taste of ash. The noise of his guests stilled abruptly, and the metamorphosis was exaggerated by the clamor of the celebrants without. Adonijah felt the pallor of a tomb invade the feasting hall. He waved to call Joab from the end of the long table, at which sat his brothers, the princes, Abiathar the priest, and several of his chosen captains.

"Why is the city in an uproar?" Joab asked the quiet room. His attention seemed focused on the sound of the trumpet. He had played the role of trumpeter at Adonijah's side for many a victory, but what was this?

"...Save King Solomon..." Adonijah finally caught the snatches of the repeated phrase, and the blood drained from his face.

He had invited the elite to his banquet, but Solomon had offered his glory to the people, and it was on them the kingship rose or fell.

"We have been countered by a common trick," Joab moaned, "and outsmarted by a decrepit old king."

Solomon's humble temperament bore a striking contrast to that of his older brothers, just as their decrepit father's had. This had made Solomon a legitimate candidate for the crown in God's eyes and those of his father the king. Adonijah pushed away the elaborate dish he had moments ago been enjoying. The wily old man had predicted his bid to usurp the crown; he'd known his elder son would flaunt the pomp, the feasting, and the celebration before the princes and selected personages. But unlike Adonijah's crowning, the people at large would not receive a secondary showing; they were instead Solomon's guests of honor. David's sons had grown up as princes, but the king was a student of the sheepcotes, of harsh nights outdoors, and simple conveniences. His people came first and so it was with Solomon under his father's watchful guidance. On days that Solomon played before him, their father's eyes would glisten unlike any other—*as though there was but one son*, Adonijah thought bitterly. Now he had been eclipsed in his father's eyes once more.

"Curse my lack of foresight!" Joab slammed his fist on the wall. "We will not be able to reverse this. David has won."

The realization that his father's prodigy had been anointed and would be crowned king in the sight of all Israel, and that he, Adonijah, would be as flotsam in the river Jordan, broken and without recourse, numbed the prince. *And those who have aided me…!* He feared to complete the thought.

Joab's revelation concerning Solomon's kingship was shortly confirmed by Jonathan, Abiathar's son who burst into the hall breathlessly.

Joab moved to Adonijah's side for the greeting.

"Come, Jonathan," Adonijah beckoned. "You are a good man. You bring good news."

Jonathan shook his head, and then his words tumbled forth in a rush. "Our lord, King David, has made Solomon king, and the king has sent with him Zadok the priest and Nathan the prophet and Benaiah and all his men, the Cherethites and Pelethites; and they have put him to ride the king's mule; and Zadok and Nathan have anointed him king in Gihon and they come from there rejoicing so that the city rang. This is the noise that you have heard. And Solomon sits on the throne of the kingdom, and moreover, the king's servants came to bless our lord, King David, saying, 'God make the name of Solomon better than your name, and make his throne greater than your throne.' And the king knelt and bowed himself on his bed. And also the king said, 'Blessed is the Lord God of Israel, who has given one to sit on the throne this day and my eyes even seeing it!'"

The hush of the room quivered with a palpable distress. There could be no doubt now. Adonijah's ascension was a lost cause. A bustle arose as guests hastened to exit the hall, having finally come to the same awful realization that Adonijah had reached moments earlier. Opponents to a king were seldom welcomed in his kingdom, and their lifespan tended to be dramatically shortened. Their loyalty was not worth their lives. The rush to the door became noisy as guests pushed pass each other, not wishing to be caught in the presence of an enemy of the new king of Power.

Adonijah quaked. He pictured his blood flowing onto the colorful ¬hions adorning the room and soaking away with no one to comfort . He might have entrusted himself to Solomon's hands alone, but his ⌐…that was another matter. He had thought the old man far enough ⌐ the grave for it to be a safe time to launch his reign. But now….

He raced from the room and burst into the brilliant sunlight. He walked quickly, hoping not to draw the attention of passersby, and made his way back to Jerusalem on the heels of the throne. Many greeted him with cheers and laughter proclaiming Solomon's supremacy. Adonijah smiled weakly and kept moving. Eventually, he entered the city gates and came to the tabernacle. It was deserted save for two priests tending the lamps.

"Are you here to worship? To give thanks?" asked the first.

Adonijah ignored the question. There was nothing to give thanks for, especially since he might be dead within the hour. He pushed passed into the inner sanctuary. The two priests bustled in after him, their voices rising an octave in protest. They watched as Adonijah caught hold of the horns of the altar to claim divine protection under the Hebrew tradition.

"Let King Solomon swear unto me today that he will not kill his servant, Adonijah, with the sword," he cried to them.

The priests regarded him with alarm. Although the noise of the celebrations carried clearly into the temple, it was obvious that the two bore no awareness of the ramifications of the political tide raging beyond the sanctuary. One priest scurried to the king's house to gain Solomon's response while the other continued to observe Adonijah with open concern, praying that no blood would be shed in this holy place.

The message came back thereafter:

"If he will show that he is a worthy man then he will not be harmed, but if wickedness is found in him, he shall die."

ᕍ ᕍ ᕍ

Solomon allowed Adonijah to go to his house after he had come to give obeisance. Time would reveal the nature of his brother's heart.

Adonijah's attempt at the throne and exclusion of those in whom King David held trust showed the depth of his deception. *If he seeks to betray me, there shall be no mercy shown again,* Solomon swore. *I will be strong against these men, otherwise my reign will be surely truncated.*

He entered quietly into his father's bedchamber. "Father, are you asleep?"

David stirred from his rest. "Solomon?"

"Yes, Father."

"Come! Come!"

Solomon knelt at his father's bedside.

"Son," he started, laying a frail hand on Solomon's shoulder. "Many things I have told you, but I want you to take heed to these last instructions."

His voice grew heated. "You know what Joab the son of Zeruiah did to me, and what he did to the two captains of the host of Israel; to Abner the son of Ner and to Amasa the son of Jethur, whom he slew and shed the blood of war, pretending peace, bloodying his girdle and the shoes of his feet. Do what you think is wise and do not let his hoar head go to the grave in peace. But be kind to the sons of Barzillai the Gileadite and welcome them to my table, for they came to my aid when I was forced to flee because of your brother Absalom. And take extra care. You have with you Shimei the son of Gera, a Benjamite from Bahurim who cursed me grievously on the day I went to Mahanaim. But he came to meet me at the Jordan on my return, and I swore I would not kill him. Do not hold him guiltless, for you are a wise man and you know what you ought to do to him; send him down to his grave with blood."

David lay back on his pillow, obviously exhausted by the release of emotions he had pent up for decades. "I am proud of you, my son. YHWH has chosen well. Keep His statutes and you will prosper. He has promised that if we continue to heed Him in truth and diligence, the throne of Israel will be established forever. Be true, Solomon."

Solomon clasped the wrinkled hand of his father, a hand that had once flashed mightily with a sword. His strength was now in his spirit alone; a spirit that would never die, but would live on in his people.

CHAPTER TWENTY-TWO

Obligations

Surely men of low degree are a vanity,
And men of high degree are a lie:
To be laid in the balance,
They are altogether lighter than vanity.
Trust not in oppression,
And become not vain in robbery.
If riches increase, set not your heart upon them.

PSALM OF DAVID 62, EXCERPT

S olomon wept at the side of his father's bier. Time had passed like an eagle's descent to its prey. After forty years on the throne, King David died. The sadness of losing a father whose love had nurtured him to maturity was tempered with some joy—that his father had achieved his goal of seeing his beloved son replace him on the throne. He had therefore passed away peacefully in his fullness of age, not plagued by regrets or recriminations that had haunted many.

His father had even insisted on a second anointing unto the Lord before the congregation of Israel. Three thousand sheep and bullocks were sacrificed for all the people. They had worshipped YHWH with their abundance, offering the materials for the Temple, because He had given them many blessings. They had offered up the materials for building the

Temple for blessing; and David had given him the pattern for the Temple that had been revealed through divine inspiration and carefully recorded for his son, to be implemented in due season. The princes and the mighty men and all the sons of the king had submitted themselves to Solomon, the new king, and he had been enthroned in royal majesty. His father had stood resolutely at his side. David's presence was a surprise to the people, who had heard of his ailing vigor and imagined him to be bedridden to his death. Strength and courage were the watchwords of the king, and by the grace of YHWH he aimed to add wisdom and understanding to these. He would be undertaking the most magnificent Temple his people had ever known. Solomon had sworn to see it complete for his father and for all Israel.

⮑ ⮑ ⮑

Bathsheba was startled to find Adonijah the son of Haggith at her threshold. The sight of the young man filled her with agitation. "Do you come in peace?" she asked cautiously.

"Yes, in peace," he assured her. "I wish to speak with you."

"Go on."

"You know the kingdom was mine and that Israel saw me as their king."

Bathsheba looked away from his hard gaze. She did not like speaking of these things. She expected that Adonijah was hoping to make her feel guilty.

"However, the kingdom is now upside down and has become my brother's since it was his from the Lord. Now I will ask one thing. Do not turn me away."

"Go on," she said, though somewhat wary of his intent.

"Speak to Solomon the king." Adonijah's emphasis of the last words eased Bathsheba's mind about his possible traitorous thoughts, yet she hesitated.

"He will not tell you no," Adonijah said in conviction. "Ask him to give me Abishag the Shunammite for my wife."

Bathsheba could see no harm in the request. Her husband was dead, and the young woman would be without comfort were she to stay unmarried.

"Well," she agreed. "I will speak to my son on your behalf."

Adonijah smiled his thanks and departed, encouraged by her willing consent. Everyone knew how important Bathsheba was to Solomon, especially since David's death. There was little he would deny his mother.

≈ ≈ ≈

Bathsheba made the request on the following day. She was always pleased to see her eldest son. He rose to greet her and bowed. He sat again on his throne and called for a seat to be set for his mother in the honored position on his right hand. After she was seated she rested her hand on the arm of his throne.

"I desire a small petition of you. Please, do not say no to me."

"Ask on, Mother, for I will not refuse you anything."

"Let Abishag the Shunammite be given to Adonijah to marry."

Solomon's back stiffened instantly. "And why do you ask Abishag for Adonijah? Why not ask for him the kingdom also." Bathsheba flushed as Solomon's words grew hot.

"He is my elder brother. Why not ask for him and for Abiathar the priest and for Joab the son of Zeruiah? God do so to me and more also if Adonijah has not spoken this word against his own life. Before God, who has put me on the throne of David, my father, Adonijah shall die today!"

Adonijah had been forewarned of the consequences of disloyalty. His subtle plot to gain a foothold in the kingdom violated their bargain and incensed Solomon thoroughly. To have given him Abishag would be to relinquish his authority as king, for the royal wives and concubines represented the power of the crown. Adonijah's ploy had sought to exploit the trust between mother and son to gain an advantage over his brother. Solomon understood that the concession of David's concubine would have been a public announcement that he had deferred his power to his elder brother, and might do so again in more significant matters. The crack would surely have widened to a chasm with the aid of Abiathar and Joab prying the lever from the shadows. Adonijah would not have proposed the scheme without the consensus of his two closest confidantes. Joab, familiar with the intricacies of war and politics, would have been the one to suggest the union with Abishag. Then Abiathar, who was sensitive to the king's disposition toward his mother, would have singled out Bathsheba, in her innocence, to be presented with the petition. Her naïveté toward the hearts of men made her the perfect scapegoat.

All in all, Solomon had decided that he would no longer pander to their games of subversion. The time for play was ended. Solomon's wrath struck as suddenly and as deadly as lightning.

᠊᠊᠊   ᠊᠊᠊   ᠊᠊᠊

Adonijah heard the commotion in his forecourt as his head servant confronted a visitor. The ring of an unsheathed sword sent him sprinting from his house in the desperate hope of escaping through the fields. Someone had come bearing weapons, and that did not bode well.

"You're a fool, Adonijah, and a coward!"

Adonijah spun at the menacing words of his accuser, just as Benaiah covered the last few strides to reach him.

"This time," Benaiah said raising his sword, "The king has granted no mercy." The sword fell in a deliberate stroke.

᠊᠊᠊   ᠊᠊᠊   ᠊᠊᠊

The curse that had dogged Abiathar's heels for years finally caught up with him. He was stung to tears as he replayed the words of the king, "Get you to Anathoth and your own fields. You are a man of death, but I will not kill you now, because you bore the Ark of the Covenant with my father and because you suffered along with him."

At the king's command, Abiathar had been thrust out of the tabernacle. He would never again be a priest of the Lord, nor experience the glory of YHWH descending in the tabernacle. For Abiathar, this exile was a sentence worse than death.

~ ~ ~

Joab knew his time was nigh. He could not escape the city. His servants had only just brought word of Adonijah and Abiathar. His only hope lay in following Adonijah's earlier course and seeking protection at the altar of God. He fled to the tabernacle and waited. He soon heard a familiar voice. It was Benaiah, as he expected.

"The king orders you to come out."

"No. I will die here," Joab shouted in reply. If I leave, I am a dead man. I might still die in the end, but there remains a chance that the king would relent. Even if I must remain here a few days, no matter! I have fasted for a much longer time.

Benaiah returned to the king to deliver Joab's reply.

"Do as he said," Solomon commanded, showing no pity. "Strike him down and bury him. The innocent blood he shed will be returned to his own head. He fell on two men more righteous and better than he. Kill him!"

God's protection at the altar did not extend to murderers, and with the king's consent to his actions, Benaiah felt no compulsion against entering the tabernacle armed. Today, Joab would be the sacrifice.

~ ~ ~

Solomon placed Zadok in Abiathar's post, while Benaiah received Joab's commission as captain of the hosts. However, the new king's wrath was not yet exhausted. One obligation to his father remained unfulfilled. He next turned his attention to Shimei, whom he summoned into his presence.

"Build a house in Jerusalem," Solomon told the man plainly. "Live there and do not go anywhere outside the city," he adjured.

Shimei clasped his hands and touched them to his lips. He had seen how ruthlessly Solomon had dispensed with those who had opposed his father, and he wished to avoid a similar fate. "What you say is agreeable," he said quickly.

Solomon raised a cautionary finger. "Know that on the day you leave and cross the brook of Kidron you will die."

"What you have said, my king, your servant will do," Shimei vowed, placing his hand to his breast.

However, after many years had passed, Shimei ventured to Gath to retrieve two of his runaway slaves. He saddled his mule and departed. His journey was reported to the king, who called him again into the court.

Solomon stood before Shimei, his height making the rough man cower. "Did I not make you swear by the Lord and warn you, saying, 'Know for certain that on the day you travel anywhere, you shall surely die?' and you said, 'The word I have heard is good?' Why then have you not kept your oath to the Lord and the command that I gave you? Moreover, you know in your heart all the wickedness you did to my father, David; therefore the Lord will return your wickedness on your head."

The king returned to sit on his throne. Today will be an end. He called to the warrior standing at the door with his sword in hand. "Benaiah...!"

⋍   ⋍   ⋍

To Solomon, there remained one final task, not on behalf of his father alone, but for all Israel. It was perhaps the most important charge of his kingship. Four years into his reign he was ready to begin his divine commission. He recruited thirty thousand men to mill cedar in Lebanon. With the aid and friendship of Hiram, king of Tyre, who had assisted in building his father's house, Solomon sourced the valuable timber. Seventy thousand men were assigned to carry loads for the Temple, and eighty thousand additional workers were delegated to quarry stones in the mountains. Solomon designated thirty-three thousand supervisors over the work. It required seven and a half years of intense labor to complete the awe-inspiring edifice.

All the walls of the Temple were carved with figures of cherubim, palm trees representing the tree of life, and open flowers. The interior of the entire Temple was gilded, even the floors. The furnishings were no less lavish. At its culmination, the Temple stood majestically on Mount Moriah, north of the city of David.

Solomon was at last ready to invite the presence of his Lord, who had

seen him through his mission; it was a dream denied a father but promised to a son.

It was now Ethanim, the seventh month of the year. Solomon assembled the elders and the heads of the tribes and the chief fathers amongst
the people. Judges, captains, governors—they all came. The priest carried
the Ark of the Covenant from the tented tabernacle that had been its house
for almost four decades while David reigned. The Ark was placed in the
inner Sanctuary of the Temple, the Most Holy Place, under the spread
wings of the two shining golden cherubim. The Ark still held the two
tablets placed within it by Moses.

As the priest left the Holy Place, a cloud filled the Temple, suffusing it
with the glory of YHWH. Solomon knelt before the entire congregation
and spread his arms toward heaven. "There is no God like You. You have
kept Your promise to my father, David."

Solomon beseeched God on behalf of his people that their supplica-
tions might be heard eternally and their penitence be met with ready forgiveness.

The congregation bowed, their faces pressed to the ground in awe as
heavenly fire scorched the offering in a fiery blaze.

Solomon looked out across the congregation and then back at the
Temple. God's house had been established, and He had accepted it from
the heart of his people. YHWH was pleased.

Solomon bowed in thanks. "We have done it, Father," he wept. "Be
at peace."

⇌ ⇌ ⇌

It was four days later when the Abdon finished recounting the chronicles
of the king whose deeds he had so painstakingly transcribed.

The House was destroyed; the Temple was no more, Abdon mourned,
but this group of men would shield the words as comfort in bosoms near
to bursting with the agony of separation and loss. The men had listened
with the attentiveness of children hearing that they were of noble birth,
though their parentage had been obscured by the passage of time. Now
someone had come to unearth a history long buried in dusty texts. The

burden of Abdon's charge lifted in the telling of the lives of his kings. He was careful to relay as accurate an account as his recollection would allow.

They were entering a shadowed place devoid of the glory of YHWH. They would journey the inexorable distance to Babylon—to the grim promise of unending captivity.

"Preserve the texts, Lord, and preserve us in the land of our enemies. May your peace be restored."

CHAPTER TWENTY-THREE

Homecoming

O God, Thou art my God;
Early will I seek Thee;
My soul thirsteth for Thee,
My flesh longeth for Thee
In a dry and thirsty land,
Where no water is;
To see Thy power and Thy glory,
So as I have seen Thee in the sanctuary.

PSALM OF DAVID 63, EXCERPT

YHWH be praised," Abdon mouthed tearfully, his hands trembling as he clasped them to his wrinkled lips. After seven decades he had all but given up hope. His eyes followed the length of the market street, its spice and linen shops thronging with boisterous traders. The stark grid of the city bore no resemblance to Jerusalem. The ache to return home had resurfaced when the king issued his edict at the day's break. Over the years there had been many rumors of impending freedom, but they had been just that—rumors. But today was different. The King of Persia had issued the brazen proclamation that very morning, in writing, where it could be denied by none nor reversed in the laws. The fall of Babylon the year before to a Persian conqueror had been the advent of change. Few had known what to expect of the new king—but this! It was more than an answer to their prayers of heartbreak these many seasons. He traced shaking finger-tips one last time over the perfect script that danced across the papyrus scroll. The official order had been pegged to a post at the King's Gate for all bridging the river to see. Abdon leaned his back against the arched portal, its stones slick with damp from the watercourse below. He sucked in a deep breath. *It is not a dream. It is not a dream!* The old man rejoiced inwardly. He clapped softly, stifling the peal of joy that sought to burst forth in wild laughter. He would dance later in the privacy of his quarters.

Abdon hastened through the cross streets toward the palace, passing the last pair of bronze gates that framed a view of the meandering Euphrates he had traversed. The way seemed much longer today. Now he willed his aging limbs to carry him swiftly to Mishael's bedside, his heart pulsing faster with the thought of the wondrous tidings he would bear. Yet as he approached the small room he suddenly slowed in indecision. *This excitement may be too much for him,* he thought in a moment of brief panic. *Nonetheless, is this not what Mishael has lived in hope of all these years. He must know. I can give him this much—he was so confident that this day would come.*

"My friend Daniel has seen it. Prepare yourself, Abdon. It shall not be long now," Mishael had whispered in encouragement. He had declared this assurance repeatedly for ten Sabbaths now. Initially Abdon could not discern whether Mishael was speaking of his own passing or the much anticipated return to their homeland, but soon he had understood. Finally the day had dawned, and they were alive to witness its unfolding and the birth of a new era for his people. And there was yet his own secret, and the perilous flight of his uncle into the deserts beyond Jerusalem. There was now a revived hope that he could complete the charge that had been placed in his hands on that fateful night at the Temple.

Abdon willed himself to enter the bedchamber. Despite its meager size it was comfortable. Mishael had done well as an official of the court and had been granted the best care available to the imperial staff. Abdon forced himself to walk calmly for the sake of his friend's fragile health. He arrived at Mishael's bedside, his exhilaration barely restrained.

"My friend," Mishael whispered, his voice weak, but warm in greeting. "What brings you here? Is this not your time for the libraries?" He regarded Abdon intently as his friend firmly clasped his own limp hand. "Is there some news?" His eyes brightened noticeably. "Tell me, *tell me!*"

Abdon could contain himself no longer, and the words contained in King Cyrus's momentous decree spilled forth in a rush.

"The king has pledged to allow the return of all Israel to their homeland to see to the reconstruction of our Temple in Jerusalem," Abdon finished breathlessly. His moist eyes took in Mishael's bone-thin frame. His friend could not last much longer like this. The physicians had said that he was simply too old to carry on. But there was now a light in his eyes that spoke of a spirit that would outlive this mortal shell. "It grieves me that you will not see the Temple rebuilt," Abdon said mournfully.

"No. Do not grieve, my friend. No weeping. It is enough that it shall come to pass, and that I have heard of it. I shall not see the Temple, but I shall see my Lord!" Mishael told him confidently. "Which of us is more blessed, eh?" He smiled. "Seek out Hannaniah and Azariah. They will surely be returning. Tell them I go with joy. We shall meet again on the other side, eh Abdon? We can celebrate together then," he said simply before closing his eyes for the final time.

As Abdon heard the words of farewell and grasped their import, he clutched at his friend's arm as if to draw him back, but immediately softened his grip. His friend had endured much, and he deserved his rest. Over the years Mishael had recounted, as the occasion warranted, his experiences and hardships faced in Babylon; his own rise to power in the king's court—the condemnation he, Hannaniah, and Azariah had endured for their defiance of the king's decree, and their subsequent supernatural deliverance from a fiery death....

Much has happened in these halls, but despite it all his face is now peaceful, Abdon thought with satisfaction. *I will never forget you and our sojourn in this harsh place, my friend.*

Abdon squeezed Mishael's hand in farewell and hurried away to find Hannaniah and Azariah. After an hour of searching he found them within the large main court. He relayed the morning's events and Mishael's parting words. Both friends wept openly as they entered Mishael's chamber. He lay as serenely as Abdon had left him, the hint of a smile curving his lips.

"It is well," Azariah said, pointing to a heavily decorated gold coin partially concealed in Mishael's half-closed fist; the ornate piece was worth a treasure. "He said he would give an offering to our Lord's House before the year had passed."

"He knew!" Hannaniah marveled.

"Indeed. His faith was strong," Azariah agreed solemnly. "Strong enough, I believe, to see him to eternity."

⌒ ⌒ ⌒

Preparations for the repatriation proceeded smoothly under the protection of the king. There were many enemies still within the kingdom who would have seen the host of his people slaughtered, but God had been with them and their jubilation rang through the streets of the cities across the newly formed Persian Empire. Nevertheless, King Cyrus's word had been clear and incontrovertible.

"The Lord God of heaven has given me all the kingdoms of the earth; and he has charged me to build a house in Jerusalem, which is in Judah. Who is there among you of all his people? His God be with him, and let him go up to Jerusalem, which is in Judah, and build the House of the Lord God of Israel, which is in Jerusalem. And whosoever remains in any place where he sojourns, let the men of his place help him with silver, and with gold, and with animals, besides the freewill offering for the House of God that is in Jerusalem."

Thank God there had been nothing ambiguous in the king's statement. They were at last free, totally free, to return home. They were also to receive aid to rebuild the desecrated Temple. The king's word was law and none could gainsay it. Not even their most powerful enemies would dare. At least not yet. The king had even demonstrated his good will by commissioning Mithredath, the imperial treasurer, to rededicate all the sacred vessels looted during the Captivity. Many had been dispersed throughout the houses of the gods of his predecessor, but they were now destined for Jerusalem under the watchful eyes of the chief fathers of Benjamin and Judah. Sheshbazzar was in charge of their transportation, and it was unlikely that a single gold plate of the fifty-four hundred precious pieces would go missing under his meticulous care.

As they journeyed away from the land of Shinar, Abdon replayed the memory of himself, huddled in the midst of a forlorn company as he recounted in despair the history of the scrolls and their valuable contents. He had seen none of those men since that day. Now the scene was contrastingly different as smiles played across the travelers' faces and songs of divine victory were sung aloud without the pall of fear cast by dominion under a severe master.

Abdon hoped that his offering would be more than the silver he had cached toward this day. He would seek to return to the Temple the life of a king and the glorious exultation of the days when the Ark was safe. All would depend on his finding the scrolls. *I pray that they have been secured as my uncle hoped.* "Hannaniah! Azariah!" Abdon said suddenly, "I must tell you of my journey and what brought me here so many seasons ago. I will need your help, I think. Mishael kept my confidence these many years, but now he is gone, and the burden is too great for an old man to carry alone. Someone else must know!"

Both Hannaniah and Azariah raised their eyebrows and exchanged quizzical looks. They had known Abdon and Mishael most of their lives and neither had gained even a hint of a mystery afoot.

Seeing their puzzlement, Abdon began to apologize, "I would have told you before but...I don't know why I didn't... I..."

Hannaniah waved him silent. "It is all right. We have all had secrets. Shinar was a place of deceit and death. Tell us. We will listen." He looked to Azariah, who nodded in agreement.

Abdon smiled in relief and started his tale for the third time. *After this,* he thought, *I pray that all will know.*

৯ ৯ ৯

"We will deliver the texts to Seraiah's son, Ezra," Abdon declared as he concluded his account at the conclusion of many days of travel. Several nights his friends had bade him go on even after the lamps had died. "He is influential at the Temple and will know what should be done."

"He is preparing writings of his own, I am told," Azariah added. "God is with his hand."

Hannaniah grew pensive. "There is much to be done. We shall start your quest after we have visited the Temple," Hannaniah proposed.

"That is well," Abdon agreed. "I know it shall be a while before I can complete this task, but I believe now that I will be granted the time and the strength to see it through."

"We will see that you do," Azariah assured. "It will be a marvelous gift."

❧ ❧ ❧

The site of the proposed Temple swarmed with craftsmen from across the nation. The remnant of the Captivity in Babylon labored diligently to stock the Temple resources, which saw an influx of additional gifts of precious vessels of gold and silver from the king of Persia. Many of the elders, priests, and Levites who had witnessed the laying of the original foundations shouted for joy when the new stones were laid. The noise of their cheers blended indistinguishably with the weeping as the children of Israel celebrated a new beginning.

"We can go now," Hannaniah said elatedly. The three men dried their cheeks and embraced one another. They stood for a long while in a huddle of kinship, savoring the renewal of a people.

❧ ❧ ❧

Their caravan departed after the Sabbath's end. For Abdon, the journey was interminable. He had waited a restless seventy-two years to complete the task that he had begun decades earlier. The caravan arrived the month of Tishri; the land was celebrating the Feast of Trumpets. Abdon disembarked eagerly.

"Come, come!" he urged his companions. He took a wavering course to a knoll overlooking the small house that lay within an olive grove. He climbed steadily, his legs trembling with both anticipation and old age. As he rounded an outcrop, he heard Hannaniah and Azariah hastening to catch up.

They would be as anxious as he to see the texts, for he had told them the legendary tales of David, their famed forefather, but to know the full history…His throat tightened at the prospect. He swallowed hard and forged upward. When he reached the top, he veered toward a tumble of boulders cloaked in prickly scrub.

"Abdon," Hannaniah shouted.

"Over here!" Abdon raised his head from the tangle of scrub. "They are here, as Uliel promised," he whispered. "Be careful of the thorns," he cautioned, holding aside a large branch to admit them to the concealed hollow. He hustled to the rear of the cave and scrambled to remove rough stones from atop an old crate that had been draped in sheepskin.

"Help me," he prompted, grunting with the exertion. They combined their efforts to drag the crate out into the open. Abdon unwrapped it with care and pried the lid open. He closed his eyes, and clasping his hands, he raised his face heavenward.

"Thank you—*thank you, God!*"

Azariah scanned the rolls for numerals and removed two scrolls from amongst the stack of papyrus. He held each gently, scanning the delicate pages in wonder.

"The Annals of Jasher…The Words of Samuel the Prophet…"

Hannaniah chose another reverentially. "The Words of Gad the Seer." He began to read, "Now it came to pass after the death of Saul, when David was returned from…" His voice trailed away in amazement though his lips continued to move silently as they followed the fine script. At the culmination of several verses, they all sat and stared into the void of a history long past. Hannaniah's eyes filled with tears as they focused on Abdon. "Today, YHWH has blessed us," he said simply.

"He has indeed, my friend. More than you know."

෩ ෩ ෩

The friends sat in the dusty cave relishing the triumph gained after a lifetime of displacement from the home of their birth. They shed their Chaldean names and spoke of the future. They would help to close a loop ripped asunder by war; a vital part of their people's past had been saved from extinction, for as memories faded, the legacies of the kings might have been erased, but the writings would stand for a long time yet. The history of Israel's greatest king would be preserved for the inspiration and guidance of their children. The cave was gloomy, but the sun shone brighter than it ever had for three men of the Captivity, now returned home.